SUPERHUMAN 1

THE MAGICIAN BOY
AND THE SAVIOR

THIERRY KOUAM

ISBN 978-1-955156-17-2 (paperback)
ISBN 978-1-955156-18-9 (digital)

Rushmore Press LLC
1 800 460 9188
www.rushmorepress.com

Printed in the United States of America

INTRODUCTION

This story is happening on a planet called Manitoba, in North America between Canada and the United States. All inhabitants of Manitoba believe in their God called Queen Mother. Queen Mother is an old woman who has all powers. She can cure people through her powers, to do miracles, to change the time and weather, and Queen Mother is able to prevent all dangers to happen on the planet and curses to fall on the planet.

The whole planet is protected and safe by their God, but the only thing that Queen Mother is not able to do is resurrect someone who is already dead. All inhabitants of the planet love Queen Mother and everyone prays in her name, and Queen Mother is living in the palace called heaven. There is a day like blessing's day where all inhabitants of the planet meet in the sacred yard of the palace to receive blessing from Queen Mother, and that day is the most important day of the planet. Sometimes, Queen Mother goes out to bless people who are sick in the hospital and the newborns.

There is a tall man, with green eyes and long black hair named Hector who is the right hand of Queen mother, the messenger of Queen Mother. He is in charge to report the news of Queen Mother over the planet, and the whole planet adores him and respects him as they do with Queen Mother, and they pray at his name as the son of Queen mother, also they believe and swear on everything Hector says.

Hector has a magic ring on his finger that was given by Queen Mother in front of the whole planet, so everyone on the planet is aware of the magic ring of Hector because it's that magic ring that makes him different from the rest of the people on the planet. That magic ring gives the powers to Hector and allows him to protect and save the planet and his inhabitants in case of danger although the fact that the planet was already protected by Queen Mother, and that magic ring helps him to save someone in case of need. But the only thing that Hector cannot do is bless people or announce a blessing meeting because only Queen Mother has that right to bless people and to announce a blessing meeting.

It was evening, the whole planet was in front of their television watching the news as usual and they suddenly saw Hector in the news who was announcing a meeting to the whole planet that was going to take place in the central church of the planet, in three weeks on the orders of Queen Mother. And that the day will be a holiday because that day will be another blessing day on the schedule of the planet, and that everyone must attend that meeting because there will be an important change that day. The whole planet was very surprised by the news of Hector, not only because they were not expecting that news, but because there were a lot of questions who were going on in their head like why the meeting of blessing is going to happen in the church not in the sacred yard as usually done? Why it is Hector who announced that meeting and not Queen Mother as usually done? Because whenever the Queen mother wants to go out for a blessing, she is the one who announces it by herself not Hector, and they know well that Hector has no right or power to announce a blessing meeting.

And they were wondering what was the important change that Hector was talking about, but none of them could find the answers to their questions, and they were curious to know that important change that was going to happen in three weeks, and they knew that if a change were going to happen, it's because there was something that was going wrong on the planet, and some of them were very afraid.

And for the first time in history, the planet of Manitoba would be attacked by one of his children named Hector, Hector would try to destroy the planet for the purpose to become the god of the planet with the help of a mysterious young wizard boy named King who was born with the powers and magic, and Hector would use the powers and magic of King to try to become the god of the planet. But during the fight, Hector would face a young magician boy named Superhuman who was born with the powers and magic, and who would try to protect the planet and his inhabitants by fighting Hector with the help of a young witch girl named Luna who was born with the powers.

And during the fight, Luna found out that she was mystically linked to Superhuman and King, and that she had the powers to control the magic of Superhuman and King. And Superhuman was surprised to find out during the fight that the energy of his magic was in Luna's body, and that without that energy, his magic was useless, and his magic would not work. And Luna was the main target of Hector, and Hector wanted to kill Luna or to destroy the energy of the magic of Superhuman that was in her body, and also to destroy the link of the magic of Superhuman that was in Luna's body to make the magic of Superhuman useless. Because Hector knew that by killing Luna or by destroying the link of Superhuman's magic that in Luna's body, the magic of Superhuman would be destroyed, and Superhuman would not be able to fight him for the purpose of protecting the planet.

And during the fight Superhuman found out that the wizarding world was in danger, and that there was a devil in the wizarding world called Deo Caeli who was destroying the wizarding world. And Superhuman mostly found out that the inhabitants of the wizarding world were the wizards who were born with magic like him. Just that his magic was a little different from the rest of the magic of the wizards. And Superhuman mostly found out that he, Luna and King were born on the planet of Manitoba for a reason, and that there was mystery around their births. Superhuman, Luna and King were completely surprised to find out that they were completely different from the rest of the children of Manitoba. Superhuman and Luna also found out that they were linked to the wizarding world, and that it was their mission and their destiny to save the wizarding world. But to save the wizarding world, they must save the planet of Manitoba first.

Because if Superhuman and Luna failed to save the planet of Manitoba, it would be impossible for them to save the wizarding world. Superhuman and Luna were also surprised to find out that Hector's goal was to prevent them from going to the wizarding world to save the wizarding world and the wizards by fighting Deo Caeli. And that Hector wanted to destroy the energy of Superhuman's magic that was inside that was inside Luna's body to make Superhuman's magic useless. Because if the energy of Superhuman's magic that was in Luna's body was destroyed, Superhuman's magic would become useless and it means that Superhuman would no longer be able to use his magic. And if Superhuman would no longer be able to use his magic, it means Superhuman would not be able to protect the planet of Manitoba and the wizarding world. And Superhuman would not be able to fight Deo Caeli to save the wizards.

And Superhuman understood that the only chance he had to protect the planet was to protect Luna first by preventing Hector to kill Luna, also by preventing Hector to destroy the link of his magic that was in Luna's body in the purpose to protect his own magic. And during the fight Superhuman found out a lot of secrets that he could not answer. But, Superhuman mostly found out during the fight that his magic and King's magic were almost similar, but with a little difference.

And during the fight Superhuman and Luna faced many obstacles to try to save the planet of Manitoba, and mostly to prevent Hector from destroying the energy of Superhuman's magic that was in Luna's body. And during the fight a mysterious dog named Berly appeared to help Luna when Luna was in danger. And a mysterious ghost appeared in Luna dream when Luna was in a coma to talk to Luna about the wizarding world and the wizards and mostly to try to prevent Luna from dying and to give the solutions to Luna how she could help Superhuman to save the planet of Manitoba. But the help of this mysterious dog called Berly and this mysterious ghost would be enough to help Superhuman and Luna to save the planet of Manitoba?

And there were some questions that were going on in the mind of Superhuman during the fight, like who he was? Why was he born with magic? Why was his magic almost similar to King's magic? Why were his magic and King's magic linked to Luna? Where did King grow up? Who was King? Why he, Luna, and King were different from the rest of the kids on the planet? He, Luna, and King were really children of the planet? Why did he, Luna, and King have the marks that no one else on the planet had? Why between all the inhabitants of the planet only He, Luna, and King were born with the powers and magic? What was the secret that was hidden behind his birth? And why did King help Hector to become the god of the planet? Who was the mysterious dog named Berly? Who was the mysterious ghost that appeared in Luna's dream? Who was Deo Caeli? Where was the wizarding world? Why was Deo Caeli destroying the wizarding world? Why was he born with a mission to save the wizarding world and the wizards? How was he linked to the wizarding world? How was he linked to the wizards? How were Hector and Deo Caeli linked?

What would be the fate of the planet and its inhabitants? Superhuman would succeed in saving the planet by preventing Hector from destroying the planet? Or Hector would succeed in destroying the planet and become the new god of the planet. Superhuman would succeed in going into the wizarding world and saving the wizarding world and the wizards? Or the wizarding world would be destroyed forever by Deo Caeli?

CHAPTER 1

❖

The Magic of Superhuman

I t was early morning, a thirteen years old boy named Superhuman woke up to get ready to go to school as usual, then he noticed that the light was shining on his right hand and he started to jump by screaming and his face was full of fear.

After a couple of minutes, he noticed that there was something written on his right palm and he looked at that palm and he read, "Stop screaming, do not be afraid." Then, he was looking at that palm with his mouth widely opened, and with the fear inside his eyes, and his whole body was shaking that a word could not get out from his mouth. He read, "Are you okay?" While he was just staring at his palm with a startled face and with his heart that was beating faster than the normal, still without saying a word. He read, "You have the magic inside you." Then, Superhuman looked at the door, and he read, "Do not run away." Suddenly, he asked, "How did you know that I wanted to run away?" He read, "I am your magic, and I am connected to your body till to your brain, so I know exactly what you think." Superhuman said, "I am very afraid." He read, "Do not worry, it's natural what is happening."

Superhuman asked, "Why am I seeing things on my right palm and why am I talking with myself?" He read, "This hand is called your magic hand, and you are talking with your magic." He said, "I am very scared because I do not understand what is happening." He read, "You will understand with the time." He asked, "What do you want from me?" He read, "You will start your mission now." He cried out, "What?" by looking at his magic palm with a surprised face. He read, "There is no time to waste because you will find your energy." Superhuman asked, "What energy are you talking about?" He read, "You need that energy for your magic." Superhuman said angrily, "Get out of my body now."

Suddenly, Superhuman saw the picture of a young girl with long blonde hair and blue eyes on the palm of his magic hand. Then, he started to stare at the picture of that young girl by smiling. And he asked, "Who is this pretty girl?" He read, "Her name is Luna." He asked, "Why do I have her picture on my palm?" He read, "She is the one who has the energy of your magic." He asked, "What do you mean?" He read, "You must find her now, before your enemy." He cried out, "Enemy?" By looking with the fear on his face. He read, "Luna is in danger." He said, "Sorry, I do not have enemies because everyone loves me like I love everybody." He read, "You were born with an enemy, and that enemy is looking for Luna now, that's why you must find her first before that enemy." He asked, "Who is that enemy?" He read, "That enemy wants to destroy the planet." He cried out, "Destroy the planet?" By looking at his magic palm with his eyes widely opened, and his mouth opened.

He read, "The planet is going to live a tragedy, the whole planet and his inhabitants are in danger." He yelled out, "Tragedy?" By looking at his palm with the terror on his face. He read, "You must save the planet and its inhabitants." He cried out "Me?" He read, "The destiny of this planet and all people living on this planet is in your hands." He asked, "How I must save this planet if I am not god?" He read, "You must find Luna first." He said, "I do not understand." He read, "Stop asking questions now, and go out and find Luna." He said, "I am going to school." He read, "You must find her first, before going to school." He said, "I cannot miss school because my parents will kill me." He read, "You have a mission and a responsibility, and you have no right to fail at it." He asked, "What is that mission?" He read, "Take off the nightdress on you and get dressed, then you will get out of the house." He said, "I need to take a shower and breakfast first." He read, "No time for shower and breakfast."

Then, Superhuman took off his dress night on him, and he wore pants and a t-shirt and he looked at the palm of his magic hand by saying, "I am ready." He read, "Go to the school of Luna, and find her." He asked, "Where is her school?" He read, "AT princess school." He cried out, "What?" And he said, "It's very far and it's to the other side of downtown." And he added, "I just heard about that school and I have never been there." He read, "You will get the bus and you ask the bus driver to drop you at princess school." He said, "Alright."

Superhuman opened his school bag, removed his bus ticket, and he left for school. After a few minutes, Superhuman was to the bus stop waiting for the bus, and by looking at his magic palm, then he saw a bus that was coming, and he started to walk through the bus, and he noticed that the light was shining on his magic hand, then he looked at his palm and he read, "Do not get this bus." He asked, "Why?" He read, "Because you will be in danger in that bus." He asked, "Which bus will I take?" He read, "You will take the next bus that will be there in six minutes." Then, after six minutes, the next bus parked, and Superhuman got inside the bus.

After half an hour, the bus started to shake, and people were feeling afraid in the bus, and they were holding the chairs that were in front of them, asking the driver to drive slowly. Then, Superhuman looked at the palm of his magic hand by asking, "What is going on?" He read, "Your enemy knows that you are looking for Luna, that's why that enemy is trying to prevent you from finding her."

And suddenly, the bus started to go faster, by shaking more and more. Everyone on the bus was screaming, even the driver, and some people were hitting their head against the bus, while other people were falling from their chairs. And Superhuman was only the one in the bus who had the balance, and he was still focused looking at his palm, and he read, "Get up and take the wheel to the driver." He asked, "What?" He read, "Stop asking questions and save those people before the accident happens." He asked, "How can I save them?" He read, "The driver lost control of the wheel, the one who is driving now it's your enemy not the driver." He said, "I do not know how to drive." He read, "Just do what you are reading on your palm." Then, Superhuman turned his head and saw people around him who were suffering, and some of them were bleeding like they were hitting their heads on the bus, the bars of the bus, and like they were falling from their chairs.

Then, Superhuman got up from his chair, and he started to run by jumping on the chairs till the place of the bus driver, and he noticed that the driver had not his hands on the wheel and that the bus was going alone, then he looked at the palm of his magic hand and read, "You have to drive till the next stop." Then, Superhuman put his both hands on the wheel and he started to drive, and the bus stopped shaking, and it was going slowly.

Everyone in the bus was looking at Superhuman with a surprised face, and they were looking at each other with the mouth opened without saying a word by wondering what was going on. For some people on the bus, it was a miracle that was happening, and Superhuman was going to save their lives, while for others it was a tragedy that was happening, and Superhuman was going to kill them. After fifteen minutes of driving, Superhuman parked the bus at the bus stop, and he got off, and people had got up from their chairs looking at him outside through the window of the bus, it was like they were dreaming, nobody in the bus was realizing what was happening, even the eyes of the bus driver were focused on Superhuman outside.

Superhuman was looking at the palm of his magic hand and a map appeared on his palm, then he asked, "What is that?" He read, "You must follow this map till school of Luna." Superhuman took a deep breath, and he started to walk by following that map on his palm. After two hours of walking, Superhuman was very tired and hungry, and he looked at his palm by saying, "I am already tired and hungry." He read, "Three minutes walk from here, there are the bicycles that are displayed outside, to the left side of the road front to a shop." He asked, "What I need to do with bicycles?" He read, "You will walk till there and you will steal a bicycle." He said, "Sorry, I am not a thief." He read, "You must gain on time because you must find Luna today." He said, "I do not even know why I am doing all those crazy things because I should be in class now." He read, "It's your destiny." He said, "I did not ask for it." He read, "No one order his destiny because everyone just finds his destiny."

Then, Superhuman started to walk by looking to his left side, and after three minutes of walking, he saw a shop and there were bicycles outside that shop, and he walked till the front of those bicycles. He looked at his palm by saying, "Those bicycles are locked with the chains." He read, "Use this magic hand and cut the chain on the bicycle you want to use." He said, "I can not cut the chain with my hand." He read, "Bend and grab the chain with this magic hand." Superhuman took a deep breath, and he looked around him, then he noticed that no one was looking at him, and he looked at the bicycles, then he walked three steps through his right side, and he bent front to a bicycle and he held the chain that was passing in the wheel of that bicycle with his magic hand.

Then, Superhuman noticed that the chain was cut, and he let the chain. And he looked at his magic palm with a surprised face, by looking at the chain that was cut on the ground. He was completely lost, he was not realizing that he cut that chain with his palm and he looked at his magic hand by asking, "How did you do it?" He read, "Take the bicycle, you want, and leave now before the security catches you." Superhuman got up, and he took a bicycle and he started to bike away.

After twenty minutes, he reached the school of Luna, and he looked at his palm by asking, "Where is Luna?"

He read, "She is in class, you have to wait here." Then, Superhuman started to bike in the yard of the school.

After nine minutes, Hector appeared in front of Superhuman. Superhuman cried out, "Hector?" By looking at him with a surprised face.

Hector said, "Stop looking for that girl?"

Superhuman asked, "Which girl?"

Hector answered, "Luna."

Superhuman looked at Hector with a surprised face, and with his mouth opened but no word was coming out. Hector said, "I am sent by Queen Mother, and she ordered you to stay away from that girl."

Superhuman said, "I am so sorry, you will talk to Queen Mother that I will never try to approach that girl again and that I will stop looking for her, and to forgive me also to bless me."

Hector said, "You are forgiven at the name of God who is Queen Mother."

Superhuman replied, "Thank you."

Then, he turned his bicycle and he started to bike away, while the light was shining on his magic hand, but he was not paying attention to that light. He biked till outside of the yard of the school and he stopped, then he looked at the palm of his magic hand and read, "Do not leave." He said, "I received the orders coming from Queen Mother." He read, "Do not obey those orders." He said, "Queen Mother is the god of this planet, and no one can dare to disobey her." He read, "You will not obey that order because you must find Luna." He asked, "Who am I to disobey to god?" And he added, "Get out of my body now and let me alone."

Then, Superhuman started to bike away, while the light was still shining on his magic hand. Superhuman reached home when his parents were looking for him with fear inside them like he had left home morning without someone seeing him and without saying to someone where he was going. And his parents had noticed that he was not at school because his school's bag was in his bedroom. Then, Superhuman's parents started to ask him questions about where he was, and where he took the bicycle, and Superhuman used his magic hand to answer all the questions of his parents and he succeeded to convince his parents without any problem. And his parents did not notice that Superhuman had got the answers to their questions through his palm, although the fact that they had noticed how he was looking at his palm when they were asking him questions.

It was evening, Superhuman was studying because he has the exams the next day, and there was the light that was shining on his magic hand and he looked at his magic palm by saying angrily, "Let me in peace now, let me study now and get out of my body." And he did not even try to read what was written on his palm. After that Superhuman had done to study, he went to bed and the light was still shining on his magic hand, then he put the blanket on his magic hand to not see that light that was shining, although the fact it was very hot.

The following day, Superhuman was in class taking an exam and the exam was very hard for him and he did not know what to write and the light started to shine on his magic hand and he looked at his palm and he saw the answers of the questions of the exam. Then, he started to smile, and he started to write the answers on his exam paper. And after ten minutes, he had finished, and he got up from his chair and he went to drop his exam paper. Everyone in the classroom was surprised to see that Superhuman had done, even his instructor, and the instructor took the exam's paper of Superhuman, and as he looked at it, he noticed that Superhuman had really finished. The rest of the day was great for Superhuman because he had done well in school, and he was very happy like after the correction of his exam, he noticed that he had got one hundred percent. And all his classmates were very surprised to see that he had got one hundred percent, even his instructor. Because Superhuman had never got more than fifty percent in class. The parents of Superhuman were very surprised when Superhuman showed them his exam's paper with one hundred percent on it.

It was evening, Superhuman was lying in his bed and he looked at his magic palm by saying, "You did an amazing work today, and from now on, you are going to be my brain because you impressed everyone even myself, and thanks to you, I am going to be the best student of my school. And everyone will respect me, and now my parents will let me play video games in peace without bothering me to go study again, also you are going to do everything for me from now." He read, "You must find Luna as soon as possible." He said, "Forget about Luna." And he added, "Do not forget that I received the orders coming from Queen Mother that I must stop looking for Luna and that I must forget about her." He read, "You must prevent Luna from getting out of her house tomorrow morning." He asked, "How?"

Then, he saw a house on his palm. He asked, "What it's?" He read, "It's the house of Luna." He asked, "Why does it appear on my palm?" He read, "You must go there now and prevent her from getting out of the house in the morning." He cried out, "What?" by looking at his magic palm with a surprised face, and he turned his head through the watch that was on his study table and he said, "It's 12:00 a.m., now, so the whole planet is asleep." And he added, "I thought that we could have an enjoyable conversation without you talking about Luna, but now I am sleepy." He read, "Luna is in danger." He said, "I am not god to protect her, or to save her." And he went on by saying, "Queen Mother who is God must protect her and save her because only she can do it." He read, "Only you can protect and save Luna." He said, "I do not want to hear that name of Luna anymore." Then, he pulled the blanket and he covered his magic hand with it, and he fell asleep.

CHAPTER 2

The Accident of Luna

The following day, Superhuman was in class, and they were doing science, and he was using his magic hand to answer all questions that the teacher was asking. Everyone in the classroom was looking at Superhuman with an amazed face, wondering what was going on with him, no one was understanding how Superhuman the most stupid student of the class had become suddenly a genius, the smarter student of the class.

It was break time, Superhuman was playing soccer with his friends, and he suddenly fainted on the pitch, and some students surrounded Superhuman and they noticed that he was unconscious, and they called for an ambulance. After fifteen minutes, Superhuman was in the emergency room of the hospital breathing by oxygen that was put on him. Then, Superhuman's eyes opened, and he was wondering where he was, and he lifted his magic hand through his face, and he read on his palm "Luna is dying right now." He said, "Do not you see that I am dying too?" He read, "Get up now and go save her." Then, the photo of Luna appeared on his magic palm.

And suddenly, his face changed like he was looking at Luna on his magic palm who was lying in the hospital's bed breathing through oxygen, with bandages around her head, and with wounds on her face. He asked, "What happened to her?" He read, "She got an accident and that's the reason you fainted on the pitch." He asked, "What do you mean by that?" He read, "You are linked to Luna, and she needs you." He said, "I am not a doctor." And he added, "She needs a good doctor and Queen Mother." Then, a map appeared on his magic palm, and he asked, "What it's that?" He read, "Follow the direction of this map, and you will find Luna."

After three minutes of hesitation, Superhuman took off the oxygen that was put on him to breathe and he got up from his hospital bed. And he started to run in the hospital with the hospital clothing on him, by following the direction of the map that was on his magic palm, and people in the hospital were looking at him with surprised faces, by wondering what was going on with him. Then, Superhuman reached a door, and he opened that door and he suddenly saw Hector inside the room close to a bed, and Luna was lying in that bed unconscious, and there was a small wind that was blowing in the room. Superhuman looked at his magic palm by asking, "What is going on?" He read, "You are receiving the energy of your magic coming from the body of Luna."

Then, Hector turned, and he looked at Superhuman by saying, "Get out of this room." Superhuman replied, "You are the one who will get out of this room." Hector said, "It's the orders coming from Queen Mother." Superhuman replied, "I will not respect those orders." Hector said, "Do not forget that Queen Mother is god." Superhuman replied, "I do not care." Hector said, "I am already taking care of Luna. She is doing fine, so do not worry about her." Superhuman started to walk through Hector by looking at him angrily, then he stopped in front of him and he looked in his eyes by saying, "I am the one who will take care of Luna, and not you." Hector said, "You are so weak to take care of her." Then, Hector handed his hand that his finger wore the magic ring through Superhuman, and Superhuman handed his magic hand through Hector too, and both started to fight with the sparks of fire that were getting out from the magic ring of Hector, and the sparks of fire that was getting out from the magic palm of Superhuman.

After twenty-one minutes of fighting with the sparks of fire, Hector disappeared and Superhuman ran beside the bed of Luna, and there was the light that was shining on his magic hand. Then, Superhuman lifted his magic hand and he read what was written on his palm, then he put his magic palm on the forehead of Luna, and there was the light that was shining between his magic palm and Luna's forehead. And after one minute and a half, Superhuman removed his magic palm on Luna's forehead, and immediately Luna opened her eyes, and she was looking at Superhuman without saying a word, while he was looking at her back by saying, "Do not worry, everything will be alright." Then, the door opened, and a nurse walked inside by looking at Luna with an amazed face, and that nurse was not realizing what was happening. She was completely surprised to see that Luna had opened her eyes, and she was focused on Luna till she was not seeing Superhuman who was in the room staring at her.

Then, that nurse opened her mouth to say something, but a word was coming out from her mouth, and she turned by running through the door. The light was shining on the magic hand of Superhuman, and Luna saw that light that was shining on the magic hand of Superhuman, and she told him about it, and Superhuman looked at his magic palm and he read, "Get out of this room now." He asked, "Why?" He read, "The nurse is coming with the doctors, and no one must see you." Then, he started to walk through the door, while Luna was staring at him without saying a word, after two minutes he reached the corner of the hospital and he looked at his magic palm and he read, "You must hide." He asked, "Why?" He read, "Because the security of the hospital is looking for you and the police too." He cried out, "The police?" with a worried face. He read, "Hector sent the police to catch you." He asked, "Where do I have to hide?"

Then, a map appeared on his palm and he read, "Follow this map by running." Then, Superhuman started to run by following that map on his magic palm, while policemen and security men were inside the hospital looking for him, and his parents were very worried in the sitting room of the hospital because they did not know where he was. Luna was out of danger, and doctors were very surprised by the way she had recovered, and all her wounds were healed. For them it was a miracle, and Luna was quiet; she was not talking even when doctors were trying to ask her some questions about how she was feeling, she was not answering them.

Superhuman was hidden under a small table that was on the second floor of the hospital. Then, Superhuman started to communicate with his magic, and he was demanding questions to his magic like why the sparks of fire got out from his magic palm, why he drove the bus a day ago, and how suddenly he became a genius student. And his magic answered him that he did all those things through his magic, and he asked where that magic came from, and his magic answered him that it's innate, that he is born with that magic because he had a mission that he would find out soon what it's. Superhuman demanded to his magic why him, and his magic answered him that no one could answer that question.

Then, Superhuman wanted to go back to his home, but his magic refused, and his magic told him that he would stay in the hospital till Luna recovers because he must protect her to prevent Hector from destroying the energy that was inside her body. Superhuman was completely lost by what he was reading on his magic palm, and when he asked his magic how he was going to live in the hospital, his magic answered him that he should use that magic palm to open the fridges that were in the stores of the hospital to steal stuff to eat, and that he should sleep under the hospital's bed of Luna because he must be there when Hector would appear to destroy that energy that was inside Luna's body.

Superhuman was already tired of his magic, and he was understanding nothing about that energy that was inside Luna's body that Hector wanted to destroy, although the fact that his magic was telling him that that energy inside Luna's body was very important. Because he needed that energy for his mission, and that if Hector succeeded to destroy that energy, it would be impossible for him to succeed in his mission, and that the planet would be in danger if he failed his mission. Superhuman started to feel hungry, and he said, "I am going to steal something to eat." He read, "No one will see you because everyone is looking for you." Then, he took a deep breath, and he saw a map appear on his magic palm, and he turned his head and looked around, then he got out of the table, and he started to walk with his head bent by following the map that was on his magic palm.

After eleven minutes, Superhuman got inside a store of the hospital, and he did everything that his magic told him, and he stole stuff to eat, then he opened the fridge with his magic's hand without putting money and he stole water and juice, and he even stole the clothes, hat, and shoes, without someone see him although the fact that the store was full of people. Then, Superhuman went to the bathroom of the hospital, he took off the hospital clothing that was on him and he wore the clothes and shoes he had stolen.

After three hours, Superhuman was very tired, and sleepy and he was trying to sleep under the table where he was hiding, and the light started to shine on his magic hand, and he read that Luna was in danger, then he got out of the table and ran till her bedroom, and he is standing up beside her bed staring at her, while she was staring at him back and there was silence between both. After a minute, Superhuman opened his mouth to talk, but before a word come out from his mouth, the light started to shine on his magic hand and he looked at his magic palm, then he got under the bed. The door opened, a doctor and a nurse got inside, then the doctor started to make a check up on Luna, and he noticed that she was recovering very well and faster than he could not imagine, then the doctor and nurse left the room.

Suddenly, Hector appeared in the room, and Superhuman saw Hector on his magic palm and immediately he got out under the bed, then Hector and Superhuman started to fight with the sparks of fire coming from the magic palm of Superhuman, and the magic ring of Hector, while Luna was just watching at them with her mouth closed. After an hour of fighting, Hector was becoming weak, then he disappeared.

During three days, Superhuman was spending his time fighting with Hector, stealing stuff in the hospital's shop to eat, hiding to avoid someone to see him, also communicating with his magic to make sure that Luna was alright, and most of his time he was under the bed of Luna. Superhuman was very tired, he had even lost weight and it was impossible for him to sleep or to get rest because Hector has become a nightmare for him. Each time, when he wanted to close his eyes or get rest, it was that time that Hector was appearing. Also, Superhuman was changing his hiding place each time because

Hector was communicating with the police by telling them where Superhuman was hiding, and that was making things harder for Superhuman.

There were pictures of Superhuman on the walls of the hospital, and the whole hospital was looking for him, and Hector had hired more people to catch Superhuman, even the police of the palace were looking for Superhuman. Hector had also ordered doctors to not release Luna because the hospital was a good place for him to destroy that energy she had inside her, but the only problem was Superhuman who was always there to prevent him from destroying that energy. Superhuman sat in the corner of the hospital very tired and weak, and he was eating the cookies that he had stolen, and there was a woman who was walking in that corner by looking at him with attention, and she started to look at the photos of him that were on the walls. Then, that woman kept walking without saying a word, but she had noticed that Superhuman was the one that the hospital was looking for days now. Then, the light started to shine on the magic hand of Superhuman, but he did not pay attention to it, and he just concentrated on eating his cookies like he was very hungry. After three minutes, Superhuman looked at his magic palm and he read, "It's too late now." He asked, "What do you mean?" But he did not get an answer, and he asked, "Hector killed Luna?" Again, he did not get an answer, then he yelled out with anger, "Luna is all right?"

Suddenly, he heard a voice who was saying Superhuman do not try to run. Suddenly, he turned his head to the left side where that voice was coming from and he saw the police who was coming through him, then he immediately got up and he turned through the right side to run, and he saw the police who was coming through him too. Then, he looked at his magic palm by asking, "What I am supposed to do now?" He read, "You are going to jail." He cried out, "What?" With a face full of fear, and his mouth stayed open, his eyes widely opened looking at his magic palm and his heart was beating with fear, then the light that was shining on his magic hand went off, and the police came and arrested him.

Luna was in her bed hospital still quiet, with her eyes opened, and she heard the noises coming from behind, then she got up from her bed and she turned her head through where she was hearing the noises, and she saw an old granddad sat at the window of her room, and they were staring at each other without saying a word. Then, that old granddad handed his hand through her, still without saying a word while she was still staring at him with silence too. After three minutes, Luna walked through him, then she pushed the chair that was inside her room beside the window, and she got on it. Then, that old granddad carried her on his lap and he jumped on the ground by outside with her, then they walked a minute and they got inside a small helicopter and they flew away. After an hour and a half of flying, they landed in the yard of a small house and they got out of the helicopter, and they walked till the front door of that house, and that granddad opened the door and they got inside, then he locked the door behind them. He showed the chair to Luna to get a sit, and she got a sit, then he walked through a corner, while Luna was staring inside the house.

CHAPTER 3

❖

The Magic Book

Luna sat in a chair. A plate of vegetable and fruit and a glass of water were put on the table in front of her, and that old granddad sat in the chair facing her. Luna was not eating. She was just looking at him without saying a word.

And that old man said, "You must eat."

Luna asked, "Where am I?"

He replied, "My name is Philip." And he added, "I want to protect you."

Luna asked, "Why protect me?"

Philip said, "You lost your parents in the car's accident."

Luna replied, "The doctors told me it."

Philip said, "I suppose that you saw the servant of Queen Mother in your bedroom of the hospital."

Luna replied, "Yeah, I saw Hector many times in my bedroom hospital."

Philip said, "The accident you did with your parents was caused by Hector, and you are the one he wanted to destroy, but unfortunately you lost your parents in that accident, but lucky he failed to destroy you." Luna said, "I do not understand."

Philip looked in her eyes by saying, "You have an energy inside your body, that Hector wants to destroy, and he will not stop till he destroys that energy that is inside you."

Luna said, "Still I do not understand."

Philip said, "Do not worry you will understand it with time."

Luna asked, "Who are you?"

Philip replied, "We do not have time to talk about me."

Luna asked, "What do you mean by we do not have time?"

Philip replied, "You are going to save Superhuman."

She asked, "Who is Superhuman?"

He replied, "Superhuman is the young boy that you saw in your bedroom of the hospital fighting with Hector." She said, "yeah, I saw a young boy of my age in my bedroom hospital fighting with Hector." Then, she asked, "Where is he?"

Philip replied, "I have no idea." And he added, "You are the one who will find him."

Luna asked, "How?"

Suddenly, Philip stayed quiet, he was not anymore talking, and he lifted his head through the ceiling with his eyes closed, while Luna was just looking at him with a surprised face, then she started to ask him if he was alright with the worries on her face. Then, Philip got up from his chair, and he looked at Luna by saying, "Follow me." And Luna got up and she started to follow Philip. Philip and Luna were walking faster towards the left corridor of the house, then they reached a door, and he opened that door, then they started to climb down the stairs, and they started to walk through a dark corner and Luna said, "I could not imagine that your house was huge like that." Philip replied, "This is the secret part of my house."

After six minutes of walking, they reached a door, and he opened that door, and they got inside a room, and he looked at her by saying, "You will stay here, and you will not get out of here, no matter what will happen, even if you hear the noises, or the screams just stay here, even if you notice that the house is shaking or burning do not get out of here." While Luna was just looking at him with fear on her face, without saying a word.

Then, he said, "Follow me." And they walked through a door, and he showed her the kitchen, the fridge that was full of food that was already made, and the juices, and fruits. Then, he showed her how to use the microwave by saying, "You just need to warm what you want to eat, so you do not need to cook." And he showed her the bathroom, also her bedroom, and there were a lot of clothes and shoes of her age in her bedroom that she should use. And Luna was very surprised and afraid of what was going on. She was not understanding what Philip wanted from her, and it was like he was waiting for her. Then, he removed a big book from a drawer of a cupboard that was in the bedroom, and he handed it to her by saying, "This book is called the magic book, and you will read it for nine days." She cried out, "What?" By looking at the book in Philip's hands with an amazed face, and her heart was beating faster than the normal, then she lifted her head and she stared at the ceiling by wondering where she was. And Philip looked in the eyes of Luna and he noticed that she was afraid, and he said, "Do not be afraid." She looked into his eyes by saying, "I do not know you." Philip said, "Trust me."

Then, Luna looked at him by breathing deeply, still with the fear in her eyes and after a minute of hesitation, she handed her both hands and she took the magic book in the hands of Philip by saying, "It's impossible to read this huge in nine days." Philip said, "I know that it seems impossible, but you must finish reading that book in nine days because it's the only solution you have to save Superhuman." Luna asked, "Why not read it by yourself and go save Superhuman?" Philip replied, "There are only two people who can read that magic book, and I am not among those two people." Luna asked, "Me and who?" Philip replied, "Not you, but instead Superhuman and someone else that I do not know who it's." Luna asked, "Why ask me to read it if I am not among those two people?" Philip replied, "Because you are linked to those two people." Luna said, "I do not understand." Philip said, "You will understand in time." And added, "Do not forget what I told you, that no matter what will happen do not get out from here." Then, Philip turned, and he started to walk through the door, while Luna was staring at him like he was going.

After a few minutes, Philip reached the living room and he sat in front of the food that he had served to Luna, and he started to eat. Suddenly, Hector appeared in front of him and Hector looked at him with terror on his face by saying, "I want Luna right now."

Philip looked at him by asking, "Who is Luna?"

Hector replied, "The one you took to the hospital."

Philip said, "I do not know what you are talking about."

Hector replied, "I know that she is here."

Philip said, "Still I don't know who you are talking about." And he added, "Except me and you nobody else is inside this house."

Hector said, "Luna has the energy of the magic of Superhuman inside her, but she does not have the magic to disappear." And he added, "Luna is an orphan because I killed her parents in a car accident, and she has no other relative, and I searched her on the whole planet, and I did not see her." Then, he said, "Superhuman is the only one who could have Luna, but I have Superhuman with me, which means that Superhuman does not have Luna, so you are only the one who knows where she is."

Philip said, "I could help you if I knew the one you are talking about."

Hector said, "I found out that you were to the hospital watching what was going on close to the bedroom of Luna, and when the police arrested Superhuman, you took Luna with you." And he added, "I was asleep when Superhuman has been arrested and it's when I woke up that I noticed that the police had arrested him. And when I reached the hospital, I noticed that the whole hospital was looking for Luna and no one knew where she was."

Then, they were looking at each other with silence, and Philip was seeing the terror on the face of Hector, then handed his hand that his finger had the magic ring through Philip, and Philip started to scream like the sparks of fire that were getting out from that magic ring were burning him.

After half an hour, Hector stopped with those sparks of fire, and he disappeared by saying that he would be back. After three days, the parents of Superhuman were very worried for him because they had found out that their little son was a prisoner in the jail of the palace, they were wondering what he did to be a prisoner in the palace, and they were banned from visiting their son. Superhuman was kept prisoner in a small cell between four walls, with no window, and he was standing up because the cell was so small that he could not lie on the floor. And when he was very tired to stand up, he sat on the floor, but he should fold both knees when he sat because he could not stretch his feet like there was no space. Since the police put Superhuman in that cell, no one had opened the door of his cell again, so he was forgotten in that cell because he was not even receiving food or water. Superhuman was suffering in his cell, he was very tired, weak, and sleepy like he was spending his nights and his days without sleeping. He was living the torture and feeling pains in his whole body, till he could not even feel hungry and thirsty although the fact that since he was in that jail, he had not put something in his mouth.

Superhuman was spending his time talking with his magic, and his magic had told him that Luna was fine, but he was still very worried about her, and he was afraid that Hector could kill her. And he was very angry with his magic because he was accusing his magic to be responsible for the torture that he was living, and mostly that his magic could not save him from where he was, and he had tried to use this magic hand to open the door of his cell, but he failed open it. And his magic told him that it was impossible for him to open his cell's door without the energy of his magic inside him because his cell's door was locked with another kind of magic.

Philip was tied in the chair in his living room with the chains by Hector, and Hector had used his magic ring to do it, and he was using that magic ring every time to torture Philip. Sometimes Hector was using that magic ring to make the house shake, and the house was shaking like there was an earthquake. And it was hard for Luna to concentrate on her reading with the screams of the cry of Philip that she was hearing till where she was, and the house that was shaking like it was going to fall. Luna was very tired and weak because since Philip left her in that basement, she had not closed her eyes, or get a rest because she was too focused on her reading. She was reading the day like the night and she didn't even have the time to take a shower or to eat.

The days were passing, and nothing had changed, Hector was still looking for Luna, and Philip was still tied in the chair although he became unconscious. Luna was still reading the magic book, and Superhuman was still living the torture in his cell. It was missing fifteen minutes for the ninth day, and Luna had done to read the magic book, and she got up from her chair and walked till the clock that was close to her bed and she put the alarm on that clock. Then, she went and lay on her bed, and she closed her eyes to sleep, and after eleven minutes she was deeply asleep, then she started to see her mom in her dream dressed like an angel who was telling her that Superhuman was in jail. She should use the magic book to open the door of the jail where Superhuman was kept prisoner, by opening that magic book to page three hundred and she should show that page face to the door of that jail.

Suddenly, Luna opened her eyes and she called mama three times, then the alarm she had put on the clock started to ring, and she turned her head through the clock, and she noticed that it was the ninth day. Then, she got up from bed, and walked to the table and she took the magic book, and she walked to the door, then opened the door and she started to walk through a dark hallway.

After three minutes of walking, she saw another door and she opened that door then she got outside, and there was darkness outside, she opened the magic book to page one hundred, and she lifted her head through the sky. Then, a light got out from that page of the magic book and went through the sky, and after a minute she saw a big hawk that was flying through her. Then, that hawk landed close to her and she got on it, and the hawk flew in space with her. After three minutes of flying, Luna saw a small bird that was flying in front of her and she led the hawk through that bird, then she started to follow that bird. After an hour, the bird landed in the yard of the palace, and Luna landed too in that yard close to the bird, and she got off the hawk with the magic book in her hands, and she saw a dog that was running through her. She was staring at the palace, and the dog came and jumped on her, and the dog started to make noises, and Luna noticed that the dog was trying to communicate with her, but she was not understanding what the dog was saying, and at the same time she was wondering where Superhuman could be.

Then, she noticed that the bird was making the noises with his wings, and she turned her head through the bird and she remarked that the bird was making signs with his head by looking at the door, and she immediately understood what the bird was saying to her. Then, she bent close to the dog and she turned her head by looking at the dog and by asking, "Where is Superhuman?" And the dog started to run to the left side of the yard, and she got up and she started to follow the dog by running. After a few minutes, the dog stopped close to a door, and Luna tried to open that door, but it was locked, and she noticed that there was not a place for the key on that door, and there was not a handle on the door too, then she was wondering how that door was locked. Then, she looked at the dog by saying, "This door is locked through inside, so we have to find another way to get inside." And the dog started to jump through the magic book she had in her hands. She did not understand why the dog was jumping through that magic book in her hands, then she bent, and she put that magic book in front of the dog, and she observed that dog was using his mouth and his paw to open that magic book.

Suddenly, she remembered the dream she had a couple of hours ago where she was seeing her mom, and she immediately took the magic book and she opened the page three hundred and got up and she walked to the front door. Then, she turned the book and she showed the page three hundred through the door, and light got out from that page and shone on the door, then the door opened, and she saw Superhuman who sat on the floor. Then, she let the book fall on the ground and she ran through Superhuman, and she started to shake him by calling his name, but Superhuman was not making any sign, and she turned her head through the dog by saying, "He is dead" with a sad voice. Then, she noticed that there was the light that was shining on his magic hand, and she looked at that hand, and she read on his palm "He is so weak, you must kiss him." Although, the fact that she was so surprised, and she was not understanding the meaning of that message on his magic palm, she kissed him.

Suddenly, Superhuman opened his eyes, and when she was trying to help him to get up, Hector appeared, and he took the magic book that was on the ground and he disappeared with it. Luna and Superhuman got out of that jail, she looked at him by saying, "We are trapped here." He asked, "Why?" She replied, "We can not get the hawk to fly back if we do not have the magic book." He asked, "Which magic book?" She replied, "It's that magic book that helped me to come here, and to save you." Then, Superhuman looked at his magic palm and he smiled at her by saying, "I have the solution." Then, he handed his magic palm through the sky, and light got out from his palm and went through the sky, and they saw a hawk that was flying through them. Then, she smiled at him by saying, "You are a magician boy." He smiled back at her by saying, "I owe you my life because without you I should not survive in the terrible jail where I could not even lay on the floor." She said, "Do not forget that you slept under my hospital bed, just to look after me to prevent Hector from killing me." Then, the hawk landed in front of them, and both got on it, and they flew in space, Superhuman was leading the hawk and he asked, "Where are we going?" Luna replied, "I have no idea." Then, he looked at his magic palm and he saw a map, and he started to lead the hawk through that map.

After an hour, they landed in the yard of the house of Philip, and they got off the hawk and they walked till the front door, then Superhuman used his magic hand to open the door, and they got inside, then they saw Philip tied in the chair with the chains in his feet, and his hands. Suddenly, Luna ran through Philip and she started to shake him by calling his name with fear in her voice, but Philip was not making any sign, and she turned her head through Superhuman by saying, "We must take him to the hospital." Then, the light started to shine on the magic hand of Superhuman, and he looked at his magic palm, then he walked close to Philip and he used his magic hand to cut the chains that were tied on Philip just by holding those chains on his magic palm. Then, he put his magic palm on the forehead of Philip, and after a minute Philip opened his eyes, and they were all looking at each other without saying a word. Then, Superhuman broke the silence by asking, "Where I am?"

Luna looked at Superhuman by answering, "Do not forget that you are the one who drove till here." Superhuman said, "It's not me, but it's my magic that showed me the direction of this house."

Philip looked at them by asking, "Where is the magic book?"

Luna replied, "We lost it."

Philip cried out, "What?" by looking at them with a surprised face.

Superhuman asked, "That magic book was important?"

Philip looked at Superhuman by saying, "That magic book is your life."

Superhuman asked, "What do you mean by that?"

Philip replied, "You will understand it with the time." And he added, "You both must go back now to find that magic book."

Superhuman said, "It's been weeks now, that I have not slept, or swallowed something even water."

Luna looked at Superhuman by saying, "We both are in the same situation because since the accident, I have not got rest, or put something in my mouth."

Philip said, "You both can not die of starving." And he added, "You must prevent Hector from reading that magic book."

Superhuman looked at Luna by saying, "You will stay to get rest. And I am going alone."

Philip said, "You both are going together."

Superhuman said, "I can confront Hector alone."

Philip looked at Superhuman by saying, "You can not fight Hector without Luna because you will need the energy of your magic that is inside the body of Luna, to fight him."

Then, the light started to shine on the magic hand of Superhuman, and he looked at his magic palm, then he showed his magic palm to Luna, and she was looking at it with an astonished face like she was seeing Hector in a darkness small room reading the magic book. Then, Superhuman said, "Let's go now, and both ran through the door, then they reached the yard of the house and Superhuman used his magic hand to call the hawk, then they flew into space. After an hour of flying, they reached a small house, and Superhuman led the hawk through the window's house, then he handed his magic hand through that window, and the sparks of fire started to get out from his palm and going through the window, and the window's glass started to break. Then, he led the hawk till close the window, and he held the hand of Luna, then both jumped from the hawk through that window, and they landed in a dark room in front of Hector who was reading the magic book.

Superhuman and Hector started to fight with the sparks of fire, and after nine minutes of fighting Hector disappeared without Superhuman succeeding to take the magic book. Luna said, "I am wondering how Hector succeeds to read in the darkness." Superhuman replied, "Hector is reading in the darkness through his magic ring." And he added, "It's that magic ring that helps him to appear and disappear." Then, he looked at his magic palm and he held the hand of Luna and both ran through the door, and they reached outside.

Then, Superhuman used his magic hand and he called the hawk, and both flew till in a forest, where Superhuman met Hector and both started to fight again.

It's been three days now, Superhuman and Luna had still not taken the magic book to Hector, they were still in the forest fighting with Hector. Each time when Superhuman was trying to get that magic book from Hector, Hector was disappearing and that was making things very hard for Superhuman, and Hector was still reading that magic book. Superhuman and Luna were very tired, hungry, and they were very worried too like they knew that Hector was still reading that book, and they were spending their nights and days running after Hector. Hector sat Inside a cave reading the magic book, then Superhuman and Luna got inside that cave and Superhuman started to send the sparks of fire on Hector, then Hector got up and he handed his hand through Superhuman, and light got out from his magic ring and turned into a big lion.

Then, Luna started to walk behind Superhuman by looking at the lion with fright on her face like the lion was walking through them, while Superhuman had handed his magic hand through the lion, and the sparks of fire were getting outside from his magic palm and going through the lion. And the lion was becoming angrier like those sparks of fire were burning him, then the lion jumped on Superhuman and threw him to the ground, and Hector ran through Luna and he grabbed Luna and he disappeared with her. Superhuman was on the ground fighting with the lion, and the lion was beating him, also the lion was tearing his skin with his claws, and superhuman was trying to prevent the lion to keep tearing his skin by using his magic palm, but unfortunately, the sparks of fire were not getting out from his magic palm.

After fifteen minutes of fighting, Superhuman was on the ground bleeding everywhere, tired, and he had also already lost his strengths. Then he noticed that the light was shining on his magic hand and he was trying to read what was written on his palm, but the lion was preventing him from reading it, and after a lot of efforts he succeeded to read, "Use your blood." But he was not understanding the meaning of those three words of "Use your blood." Because he had failed to read all that was written on his magic palm and he was still trying to read it, but the lion was still preventing him. Superhuman was so weak till he had given up the fight, and he was trying to get up to run away, but the lion was preventing him from getting up, and he was still wondering the meaning of those words he had read on his magic palm.

Then, after a couple of minutes, an idea came into his head, while he was still fighting with the lion, and he put his wound where he was bleeding in the mouth of the lion, and by accident, the lion swallowed his blood, and suddenly the lion became weak. Then, Superhuman got up and he looked around him and he did not see Luna and he screamed her name three times with fear on his face, then he looked at his magic palm and noticed that his magic was not working, and he was completely lost, and he was not understanding why his magic was not working. Then, he started to run inside the cave and the lion was following him and he got outside of the cave, then he started to run inside the forest by screaming the name of Luna, and the lion fainted on the ground because the lion was so weak to keep following him like the lion had swallowed the blood of Superhuman, and that blood was poison for the lion.

Suddenly, Superhuman heard a voice in the sky, and he lifted his head through the sky and he saw an old man with green eyes, and with baldness on his head and with a long white beard in the cloud, and that old man wore a ring in the middle finger of his right hand. Superhuman looked at that old man with a surprised face. Then, he asked, "Where is Luna?" The old man replied, "You have less than three hours to find her, and you have less than five days to get back that magic book from Hector because in three hours Hector will start to destroy the energy of your magic that is inside the body of Luna, and in five days Hector will finish reading that magic book." Superhuman asked, "Where can I find Hector?" The old man replied, "The reason why you can not find Hector it's because you are weak like you lost a lot of blood in your fight with the lion." Superhuman asked, "What can I do?" The old man replied, "You have to concentrate on yourself." Then, the old man disappeared. Superhuman closed his eyes, and a big wind started to blow on his face, and after three minutes he opened his eyes and he noticed that the light was shining on his magic hand, and he looked at his magic palm and he saw Luna lying on the ground in a jail built with the irons.

Then, Superhuman used his magic hand and he called the hawk, then he flew to the desert where he landed close to the jail where Luna was kept prisoner, and he used his magic hand to open that jail, and he walked inside, and he noticed that Luna was unconscious. Then, he put his magic hand on Luna's forehead and after a couple of minutes she opened her eyes, and he helped her to get up, then they walked outside the jail. Then, Superhuman looked at her by saying, "You must wait for me here because I am going to find Hector." Luna said, "The light is shining on your magic hand." He looked at his magic palm, and suddenly his face changed, then he showed his palm to Luna by saying, "I do not understand." She read, "You both have to kiss before you go find Hector." And she said, "Me, I do not understand the reasons why we must kiss." And she added, "It's not the first time because I kissed you the day I released you from the jail." Then, they looked at each other in silence, and Superhuman walked close to her and they started to kiss, then Superhuman used his magic hand and he called the hawk, and Luna was watching at him like he was flying in the space on the hawk.

After a few minutes, Superhuman got inside the cloud, and he saw Hector who was reading the magic book, and Hector was very surprised to see Superhuman, and he was looking at Superhuman with his face full of surprises, then he asked, "How you succeeded to find me." Superhuman answered, "You made a big mistake by getting inside the cloud because you will not be able to disappear like he used to do." Then, they started to fight and Superhuman handed his magic hand through the eyes of Hector, and Hector was trying to protect his eyes with the magic book he had in his hands, by putting that magic book through his face like the sparks of fire that were getting out from the magic palm of Superhuman were burning his eyes. And Hector was trying to disappear, but it was impossible for him to do it because he was inside the cloud and his magic was not so powerful in the cloud to help him to disappear. Then, Hector started to lose balance like he was fighting and protecting his eyes at the same time, then he gave up the fight, and the magic book fell from his hand like he was still trying to protect his eyes with that, and

Superhuman ran through the magic book, and Superhuman grabbed that book, then Superhuman used his magic hand to call the hawk and he flew till Luna, and he took her, then both Superhuman and Luna flew till Philip's house.

Philip told Superhuman and Luna that the fight had already started and that they would be ready because Hector would not give up and that both Superhuman and Luna would be always together. Then, Philip told that Superhuman would be always staying with the energy of his magic inside him and that there were two ways for Superhuman to get the energy of his magic. The first way it was that the body of Luna produces the energy of the magic of Superhuman, that when Superhuman was close to Luna, there was a small wind that blew, and that wind was getting out from the body of Luna to get inside Superhuman's body, and it was the reason why Superhuman could fight when Luna was close to him. But that energy was so weak, and it did not stay inside Superhuman's body because at once when Luna was not anymore close to him, Superhuman was not anymore able to fight. And the second way was by the saliva of Luna because her saliva contained the energy of the magic of Superhuman, that when Superhuman kissed Luna and he swallowed her saliva he was able to fight without any problem, and that that energy coming from the saliva of Luna was so strong and it could stay in his body till seventy- two hours so that when Superhuman had the saliva of Luna inside his body, he did not need her close to him to fight.

Then, Philip added that Superhuman would make sure to have the saliva of Luna in his body each time and that Superhuman would renew that saliva after each seventy- one hour to make sure that before he reached seventy-two hours that he would have already renewed that energy. And that Superhuman would always look after Luna because Hector would not stop till he destroys that energy inside her body. And Superhuman understood the reason why the sparks of fire were not getting outside from his magic palm when he was fighting against the lion, that it was because Hector had disappeared with Luna like it was the body of Luna that was giving him the energy to fight, for that the spark of fire get out from his magic palm, and that each time when the spark of fire got out from his magic hand, it was because Luna was close to him, or when he had kissed Luna.

Luna and Superhuman understood the reason why Philip demanded them to go find the magic book together, and why the magic of Superhuman asked him to kiss her when he was going inside the cloud to fight with Hector, and Luna understood why the magic of Superhuman had asked her to kiss him the day she was releasing him from the jail of the palace, and the reason why whenever she was close to Superhuman there was a small wind that blew.

Then, Luna demanded to Philip how she linked to Hector like Philip had told her that she was linked with two people who were able to read the magic book, and Superhuman was one of those people, and like she had seen Hector read that magic book she imagined that Hector was that other person. And, Philip answered her that still, he had no idea about who that other person was, but that it was not Hector and that Hector had read that magic book because he had the magic ring with him and that it was that magic ring that had helped him to read that magic book.

Then, Superhuman and Luna demanded Philip to explain to them what was going on because they did not understand how suddenly their lives changed and they became the enemies of Queen Mother who was a god of the planet because if Hector who was the messenger of Queen Mother was fighting them, it means that Queen Mother sent Hector. And Superhuman and Luna were very afraid, and they started to think that the magic that linked them was something bad and that it was the reason why Queen Mother sent Hector to destroy the energy of that magic that was inside the body of Luna. But Philip told them that he had no idea about the reasons for that magic that linked them and that he had no idea why Hector wanted to destroy the energy of that magic that was inside Luna's body. And Philip added that Superhuman must always check his magic and Superhuman would do everything that his magic asks him to do, then Philip told them that they were going to stay together, and they would keep on with their education and that Luna was going to the school of Superhuman.

CHAPTER 4

The Wizard Boy in Class

The following day, Superhuman and Luna went to school, and they were in the same classroom. Most students were very surprised to see Superhuman and they were wondering where he was, while there were a few students who had not even noticed that Superhuman was not in class during the weeks. There was a new student in class named King, a young boy of the same age, weight, and height as Superhuman. The only difference is that Superhuman has long hair and blue eyes, while King has short hair and green eyes, and King and Superhuman were looking like twins. King sat close to Luna because both were the new students, and everyone was happy to welcome King and Luna in their school. There was an assessment that the instructor gave, and the instructor talked to King and Luna to not take it because they were not in class when he was teaching the lesson about that assessment. But King and Luna decided to take that assessment, Luna told her instructor that she took the lesson about that assessment in her former school, and King said that he had never taken the lesson about that assessment but that he would like to try.

Everyone in class was focused on taking the assessment, and Superhuman was using his magic hand to do his assessment, and King was the only student in the classroom who was writing his assessment with his left hand. And the instructor demanded King if he was left-handed, and King answered the instructor that yes, he is left-handed. After five minutes, King and Superhuman got up, and they told the instructor that they had done, the whole class turned their head through them looking at them with surprised faces. And everyone was wondering how Superhuman and King finished, mostly that the assessment was very hard, and that both Superhuman and King was not in class when the instructor taught the lesson about the chapter of that assessment. Then, the instructor checked the works of King and Superhuman and he noticed that they had really done and he was very surprised, and he asked them how they succeeded to finish the work of one hour and a half in five minutes.

After an hour and a half, the rest of the class had done, and the instructor did the correction of the assessment, and only Superhuman and King had got one hundred percent. Everyone was amazed about the mark of King, and most students were not really surprised about the mark of Superhuman because they were already used to his one hundred percent. The day was going well, King and Luna were making acquaintance, and they were enjoying their time, while Superhuman was talking with his friends and his friends were asking him how he knew Luna, and how he suddenly became a genius, also where he was since more than two weeks after he fainted in the stadium. But, Superhuman was lying to them, he was not talking to them about his magic, his fight with Hector, and how he was linked to Luna.

Hector had postponed the day for the meeting for three weeks again, and the whole planet was very surprised to hear that the meeting was postponed because it was the first time in the history of the planet that a meeting like a blessing's meeting was postponed.

After a week, everything was going well, Luna and Superhuman were coming to the school every day together, and they were kissing before leaving home, and they were not kissing after seventy- one hour like Philip had told them. They were spending their time at home to kiss, and they were not kissing for the reason that Superhuman had needed the energy of his magic, but because they were in love. Luna was spending her evening studying, while Superhuman was spending his evening playing video games. Superhuman and King were both the best students in their classroom, but only Luna knew that Superhuman had the magic and that he was using that magic in class for his assessment.

There was the challenge in class, between King and Superhuman and everyone had noticed it, and they were always fighting to know who was the best between them, and there was always the right hand of Superhuman lifted, and the left hand of King lifted when there was a question. None between Superhuman and King had already given the wrong answer, their answers were always right, and they were always finishing their assessment at the same time, and they were always getting one hundred percent. Superhuman and King had started to hate each other, not only for the challenge about the best student in the classroom but also for Luna who was spending her time between both Superhuman and King. Superhuman was angry to see Luna spend her entire day close to King talking and laughing with him, while King was angry to see Luna come every morning with Superhuman and spend her break time with him. That friendship between King and Luna was causing trouble in the relationship of Superhuman and Luna because both Superhuman and Luna were always arguing when the name of King was pronounced. And Superhuman had told Luna to stop talking with King and to ask the instructor to change her place, but Luna had refused by saying that King was her best friend and that she was feeling comfortable talking with King.

It was an afternoon, Students were in class and they had just returned to their break, and the instructor gave an assessment to do in a team, then the instructor separated students, and he demanded Luna to go work in the group of Superhuman. While King was working with other students, and King was not concentrated on the assessment, his eyes were always staring at Luna, and there was anger inside him when he was seeing Superhuman smiling at Luna by touching her long hair with his fingers. Then, King looked at the watch on the wall and he said in his head we still have an hour of work, and I will not stay here watching at Superhuman making his ugly smile at Luna, then he got up and he asked permission to the instructor by saying that he was going to the toilet, then he left the classroom.

Suddenly, the classroom started to shake, like there was an earthquake, and students started to scream by falling on the floor, other students were falling on others, it was impossible to hold the table. Except for Superhuman who had no problem, it was obvious that what was happening had no effect on Superhuman, and he was looking around him with a surprised face like he was seeing students on the floor who were screaming. Then, Superhuman noticed that the light was shining on his magic hand, and he looked at his magic palm and he read, "You must concentrate to stop the disaster that is happening." Then, Superhuman closed his eyes, and he crossed his hands like he was praying, and the wind started to blow in the classroom, then after a minute everything became calm, and some students got up, while other students were on the floor unconscious. Students who had got up were looking with fear on their faces, and they were breathing deeply with their heart beating with fear, and they were very surprised about what had happened, and no one was understanding what had caused it. Then, King walked inside the classroom and Superhuman was looking at him with a surprised face, while other people were trying to help those who were still on the floor.

Then, Superhuman started to use his magic hand to help students who were unconscious on the floor, and he was putting his magic palm on their forehead and they were getting up, but no one could imagine that those students who were unconscious were getting up because Superhuman was putting his magic palm on their foreheads. King was close to Luna who was unconscious on the floor, and he was trying to help her, and Superhuman ran through where Luna was, and he pushed King angrily, then he put his magic palm on Luna's forehead, and she opened her eyes and he helped her to get up. It was a terrible day for those students, and they finished their day with fear inside them. It was evening, Superhuman, Philip, and Luna were talking about what had happened to the school, and Superhuman was accusing King to be responsible for the disaster that had happened in the classroom. And Luna started to defend King by saying that it was impossible that it was King because when that disaster happened King was not in the classroom, and that King was a normal human being who had no magic or power. Superhuman told Luna that his magic fought with the magic of King when he was trying to stop that disaster, then Luna and Superhuman started to argue about that, and for the first time, they went to bed without kissing.

The following day, it was lunchtime some students were in the lunchroom warming their food in the microwaves, Superhuman and Luna were there too, with their food in their hands waiting their turn to use the microwaves. King was in the corridor alone, watching Superhuman and Luna, and he lifted his left palm through his mouth, and he said a word through his palm. Suddenly, the microwaves stopped working, and people were wondering what was going on, everyone was surprised to see that all microwaves had stopped at the same time, and they noticed that there was still the light. And there were people who were trying to make the microwaves work, but it was impossible and those who had their food inside could not even remove it because the microwaves were not opening.

Then, Luna looked at Superhuman and she demanded him to use his magic to find out what was going on with the microwaves, then Superhuman talked with his magic, and he walked till close to the microwaves. Then, Superhuman put his magic palm on the microwave that was close to him and it started to work, and everyone was looking at him with a startled face, except Luna who had a smile on her face, and Superhuman was walking through the microwaves by making those microwaves work, just by touching it with his magic palm. Most students were looking at Superhuman with the eyes widely opened, and the mouth opened like they were watching for something unreal, they were not believing what Superhuman was doing with his palm, and they were wondering how he was doing it, while the rest of students in the lunchroom had the eyes focus on Superhuman and with the smile on their faces, and they were enjoying what Superhuman was doing with his palm. Then, Luna started to clap her hands, then the rest of the people followed her by clapping their hands, and by screaming the magician boy because it was a miracle for them what Superhuman was doing, while King was looking at them with a face full of anger. The following day, King was the first student to reach school, he had not taken the school's bus like usual and he was hidden behind a tree where the buses of the school park for students to get off.

After a half-hour, the first bus of school parked with students inside, and King handed his left hand called his magic hand through the bus by behind and the sparks of fire got outside from his palm and went through the bus. People were on the bus trying to open the bus's door, but the door was not opening even the driver was trying to open his door without succeeding. Then, the second bus parked, and King used his magic hand again to lock the doors of that bus, while people were trying inside to open the door without succeeding. People were very afraid inside those two buses, and no one was understanding what was going on, and after six minutes the third bus parked, again King did the same thing, and in that third bus there were Superhuman and Luna.

People were still trying to open the door without success and the driver tried to make a phone call to call for help but unfortunately, his phone was not working, and he was not understanding the reasons why his phone was not working because everything in his phone was looking alright. Luna saw the light that was shining on the magic hand of Superhuman and she told him about it, then Superhuman looked at his magic palm and he got up from his chair and he started to walk through the bus, while people were looking at him and some of them were calling him the magician boy. Then, Superhuman put his magic palm on the door's bus, and the door opened, and students inside the bus started to scream of joy by screaming the magician boy, and they started to get off the bus. Then, Superhuman walked through other buses and he used his magic hand to open the doors of those buses, and all students were clapping their hands by calling Superhuman the magician boy, although the fact that some of them were very surprised by what Superhuman did, and they were wondering how he did it. While King was looking at them with a folded face full of rage, and his eyes full of anger, by breathing deeply and by trying to control himself to not cause a disaster, and King turned his head through Superhuman looking at him with hatred by saying in his head I would get rid of you, and he was repeating the same thing in his head.

Then, King, unable to keep enduring the love that students were giving to Superhuman, bent his head and he looked on his magic palm and he was thinking about what disaster to cause, to get his revenge on Superhuman and all students who were screaming the name of Superhuman like the magician boy. Then, King opened his mouth to talk to his magic and suddenly the wind started to blow, then King lifted his head through the sky and the wind was blowing on his face, and he started to walk through his classroom still with anger inside him.

CHAPTER 5

$$\diamond$$

Superhuman Prisoner

The whole school was very worried about the mystery that was going on in school, and most of the students and instructors were very afraid, while there were few students who were finding it funny, and they were spending their time trying to imitate Superhuman by touching things with their palm. Superhuman and Luna were spending their time arguing more and more, and those discussions had definitely ended their relationship.

After five days, all students were in class and suddenly the light started to shine on the magic hand of Superhuman, and he looked at his magic palm and there was a surprise on his face like he was reading what was written on his palm. Then, he immediately tore a sheet of paper and wrote a note on it, and he folded it then he handed it to his neighbor to give it to Luna. After three seconds, Luna received that sheet of paper, and she opened it and she read, "I am in danger, I need the energy of my magic." Then, she turned her head through Superhuman looking at him with fear on her face, while he was looking at her back. Then, she grabbed the pen that was in front of her and she wrote on that same sheet of paper, and she folded it then she handed it to the one who was in front of her, to give it to Superhuman.

Then, Luna got up and started to walk through the outside door, and the instructor asked her where she was going, and she replied to the instructor that she was not feeling good, that she wanted to get air outside. King was looking at his magic palm, and he knew what was going on because he was following the conversation between Luna and Superhuman through his magic palm. Superhuman got that sheet of paper that Luna had sent him, and he opened it and he read, "Let's meet outside in the corridor, I am going there right now, so I am waiting for you there." Then, Superhuman got up, and suddenly the classroom started to shake. And people started to scream by falling on the floor, and Superhuman was trying to stop the disaster that was going on, it was hard for him to stop it because he did not have the energy of his magic inside him, and like Luna was not in the classroom for that her body gives him the energy of his magic.

After fifteen seconds, Superhuman succeeded to stop that disaster that was happening, and he started to help students who were on the floor to get up. Suddenly, the school director walked inside the classroom with Hector and two policemen, and the director stayed in front of the students and he said, "Superhuman is under arrest, and he is banned from coming to this school forever." And Hector said, "Superhuman is not only banned from education in this school, but he is banned from education on this planet." Everyone was surprised in the classroom, and Superhuman was looking at the school director with an amazed face, and Superhuman had the mouth opened but no word was coming out. The instructor of the classroom looked at the school director by asking him why Superhuman was banned from education? And the director answered that Superhuman was a wizard boy, that Superhuman was responsible for all curses that happened to the school, and in the classroom.

Suddenly, the whole classroom turned their head through Superhuman by looking at him with a surprised face, and some students had their mouth opened but no word was coming out, while others had their eyes widely opened, and except King who was smiling. Except for King, no one in the classroom was realizing what was going on, it was like they were dreaming, some of them were turning their heads looking at each other without knowing what to think or to say. Then, Superhuman got up and he said, "That's not true because I am not a wizard boy, but instead a magician boy." Hector looked at Superhuman by saying, "Of course that you are a wizard boy, and its Queen Mother who found it out, and that you are here to destroy the planet." Superhuman looked at Hector by saying, "There is a wizard boy on this planet, but that wizard boy is not me and you know it well." Hector looked at Superhuman by saying, "Queen Mother is god and she can not make a mistake." And he added, "You are not the magician boy of this planet because Queen Mother found out who is the magician boy of the planet."

Then, Hector ordered policemen to arrest Superhuman. Policemen started to walk through Superhuman, and Superhuman looked at his magic palm by saying, "Help me." and he read, "You do not have the energy of your magic to defend yourself, so there is nothing you can do." Then, he handed his magic hand through policemen who were already close to him, but the sparks of fire did not get out from his palm. Then, Superhuman looked around him and he did not see Luna, and he understood that everything was over for him, that there was not Luna to give him the energy of his magic by kissing him or through her body. Then, Superhuman was arrested and Luna was still in the corner of the school, worried and waiting for him like she was not yet aware of what had happened.

Philip was in the kitchen making food, and he heard the noise of footsteps, and he started to walk towards the front door with the knife that he was cutting the onion to the kitchen with it in his hand. Then, Philip met Luna who was staring at him with a sad face wet with tears, and he remarked the red marks on her cheeks, and that her blue eyes had become red like she had spent the years to cry, and that her whole body was trembling of fear that she could not even make a move, and he could hear her heart who was pounding than the normal and that her hair that was tied when she was leaving the house morning was untied, and he understood that something bad had happened.

And Philip asked, "What is going wrong? And why are you not in school?"

Luna replied with a sad voice by saying, "Superhuman."

Philip said, "I do not understand."

Luna said, "Superhuman has been arrested."

Philip asked, "By who?"

Luna replied, "By Hector."

Philip cried out, "What?" And the knife that was in his hand fell on the floor, and he was looking at her with an amazed face. After a few minutes of silence, Philip demanded why Superhuman did not use his magic to defend himself? And Luna answered that Superhuman could not defend himself because he did not have the energy of his magic inside him, and that she was not in the classroom when Superhuman has been arrested for that her body gives the energy to his magic. Then, Luna talked about her last conversation with Superhuman before he had been arrested and she added that she was outside in the corner of school waiting for him to give him the energy of his magic. And that she did not see when Hector and his men came to arrest Superhuman because if she had seen them, she should run back in the classroom to give him the energy of his magic by kissing him, or for that her body gives him the energy of his magic.

Philip asked why Superhuman did not have the energy of his magic inside him? And Luna answered him that it had been more than a week that her relationship with Superhuman was not going well and that they were always arguing for no reason. Because Superhuman was accusing King to be the wizard boy of the classroom and being responsible for all curses and disasters that were happening to the school, and he did not want her to stay close to King again, or to talk with King again. But she refused to listen to what he was saying or do what he was asking her to do because it was the jealousy that was making him think that King was the wizard boy of the school.

Philip asked her when she last kissed Superhuman? And Luna answered that it was been four days, as the last time that Superhuman and her kissed. Philip told her that four days was more than seventy-two hours and that Hector knew that Superhuman did not have the energy of his magic inside him, and that was the reason why Hector came to school to arrest Superhuman today, then Philip looked in the eyes of Luna by saying, "Everything is over."

Luna said, "Tonight when the whole planet will be asleep, I will go to save Superhuman by using the magic book." And she added, "I can not go now because I can not now fly with the hawk with the daylight." Philip took a deep breath, and he looked in the eyes of Luna by saying, "I do not know if you will succeed to save

Superhuman this time. Because Hector has already read one part of that magic book, and Hector knows the content of the part of the magic book he read, and he will use it against Superhuman."

Luna said, "I do not understand."

Philip said, "The magic book is talking about the magic of the magician boy who is Superhuman, and inside that book, there are the weaknesses of the magic of the magician boy who is the weakness of the magic of Superhuman."

Luna said, "I read that magic book, and there are only some pages that I understood in that huge book. Then she asked, "Why did I not understand the rest of that book?"

Philip answered, "I have no idea."

Luna asked, "Where did you get that book?"

Philip replied, "Sorry, I am not allowed to talk about that book."

Luna asked, "Where will Hector keep Superhuman?"

Philip replied, "I have no idea." And he added, "You are the one who is in danger now because Hector will try to destroy that energy inside you, despite the fact that he has Superhuman." Then, Philip told Luna that she should stop going to school and that she was going to live in the basement of the house now. And Luna was very surprised, and she was not understanding the reasons why Philip was demanding her to live in the basement of the house.

News of the arrest of Superhuman was spread over the school, all students and teachers had spent the day talking about it. All classmates of Superhuman like most of the students of the school believed that Superhuman was the wizard boy of the school because he suddenly became a genius, and he was doing things that no one could understand like what he had done on the microwaves and the bus's door. A lot of people were aware of the story of Superhuman because students of his school had talked about it to their parents, brothers, sisters, and friends. That's how the news was spreading over the planet.

Superhuman was kept prisoner in a small dark house built with stones, and there was no hole in that house, even the ceiling of that house was built with the stones, and the air was not getting inside that house. Superhuman was lying in a small bed, wondering how he was not yet dead in that jail where he could not even breathe, and there was a lamp that was shining inside. Superhuman was surprised to see that his jail was built with stones because there was no house built with stones on the planet, and it was the first time to see something built with stones. He was very worried because his magic was not working, he could not even communicate with his magic, even the light was not shining on his magic hand, and he was not understanding what was going on, for that his magic was not working. And he was more worried for Luna that Hector could kill her like he was not there to protect her, and he was worried about her friendship with King too because he knew that King was a wizard boy and that King was in love with her.

There were the red fruits that were looking like apples, but that were not apples, and those red fruits were served to Superhuman like food. But he was not eating although he was hungry because he was focused on his magic and he was trying to talk to his magic, but his magic was not responding to him. Luna sat in her bed and she had crossed her feet, and she had the magic book in front of her, she was thinking and worried about Superhuman, by wondering where he could be, and she was trying to find in the magic book how she could save Superhuman. But it was hard because despite the fact that she had read that magic book she could not understand more than half of that book, and there were only some pages in that book that she could understand.

Then, she looked at the watch that was on her table and she noticed that it was midnight and she got up from her bed with the magic book, and she wore her shoes, then ran through the door. After a few minutes, she reached outside, and she opened that book to page one hundred and she lifted it through the sky, and she saw the hawk that was flying through her, then the hawk landed front at her and she got on it, and the hawk flew through space. Luna was looking around her in the space, she was looking for the bird that should show her the direction, then she saw the bird that was flying through her and she started to smile, then the bird came and stopped in front to hawk. She was not understanding why the bird had stopped, and she was wondering what was going on, and she was thinking what to do because it was that bird who should help her to lead the hawk through where Superhuman was. After three hours, the bird did not move, and she started to remember the conversation she had had with Philip when she announced to him that Superhuman had been arrested, then she returned to the house.

It was morning the whole planet woke up with the news about a Superhuman named the wizard boy of the planet. A journalist named Liza had published the news talking about the wizard boy of the planet, with the photo of Superhuman in the front of newspapers. Liza had written everything that had happened to the school of Superhuman, and all things that Superhuman had done, and how stupid Superhuman was before, and one day he became a genius. People were fighting to get the newspapers about Superhuman, everyone was curious to read the newspapers about the wizard boy. Hector had postponed the meeting for three weeks again, but no one was paying attention to the news of Hector and about the meeting that was postponed, the name of Superhuman was in the mouth of the whole planet. Philip woke up and he walked into the living room and he saw a sheet of paper on the table and he took it and he read, "I decided to keep going to school because I must find out how to save Superhuman." Signed by Luna.

The entire day was very hard for Luna, everyone at school was talking about Superhuman like a wizard boy, and most people had tried to avoid her at school because they were saying that she was a relative of Superhuman. Except for King who had talked to her, and he even brought her his support by saying that he was sure that Superhuman was not a wizard boy like people think. That he was sure that there was someone else who was responsible for all disasters that they lived in at school, and Luna was very happy to hear those words coming from King. Luna told Philip about what had happened when she tried to go find Superhuman at midnight. And Philip told her that she had succeeded to save Superhuman last time by using the magic book because the magic of Superhuman was communicating with the magic book. And that now like Hector had read one part of the magic book, it meant that Hector found out some weakness of the magic of Superhuman, and that meant that Hector put Superhuman someplace where the magic of Superhuman could not communicate with the magic book, and that was the reason why she did not succeed to find the way to go where was Superhuman.

After three days, Luna was in class quiet and she was looking sad, and King was concentrating, staring at her, and he was not paying attention to what the instructor was talking about. Then, the instructor noticed that King was not focused on what he was saying, but that King was instead focused on Luna, and he asked King to change the place with another student named John. King got up and he gave a fake smile to the instructor, but there was anger inside him, and he got a seat at his new place, where he spent the rest of the day. The following day, Luna and her classmates started the class in the computer room because they were going to work on computers and King sat close to Luna.

Then, the instructor walked inside the classroom and he saw King close to Luna, then he demanded King to change his place, by saying that he did not want to see him sit close to Luna again. King got up and walked to an empty place where he got a sit, and he looked at the instructor angrily and he said in his head I am not here for school, but I am here for two missions. And you will not prevent me from succeeding in those missions. Then, King lifted his magic hand through his mouth, and he talked to his magic to cut the light. Suddenly, the light went off, and a student said, "We are not lucky today because the light does not want us to work on computers."

After three hours in the computer room, there was still no light, and they went to lunch. King had lost Luna when they were getting outside of the class for lunch, and he was outside looking for her, then he walked inside the lunchroom and he did not see her. And he lifted his magic hand through his mouth, and he asked his magic to find Luna, then the picture of Luna appeared on his magic palm and she was standing up close to a balcony. Then, King ran to where Luna was, and she was surprised to see him, and she asked him how he found her. And King lied to her by saying that he followed her when she left the classroom. Then, they started to talk, and King looked at Luna by saying, "It's been days now you are looking sad, and you are not eating at lunchtime."

Luna replied, "It's because I am not doing well."

King said, "I imagine that it's about Superhuman."

Luna replied, "I miss Superhuman a lot. And I am very worried for him mostly that I do not know where he is now."

King said, "I imagine." And he added, "I know that it's hard but for your health, you must forget about Superhuman."

Luna said, "I can not forget Superhuman."

King said, "You know well that you will never see him again."

Luna asked, "Why will I never see him again?"

King replied, "Do not forget that Superhuman is accused to be the wizard boy of the planet, who means that everyone considers him like a dangerous enemy and like a poison for the planet. And Queen mother will never accept that a wizard boy lives on her planet because a wizard person is just there to destroy this planet."

Luna said, "Superhuman is a magician boy, not a wizard boy."

King said, "I trust you, but you have to prove it."

Luna said, "That's why I am here."

King asked, "What do you mean?"

Luna replied, "To prove that Superhuman is a magician boy, not a wizard boy like everyone thinks."

King asked, "How are you going to prove it?"

Luna replied, "I do not know yet, but I am going to prove it."

King said, "You have my support, I am ready to help you in case you need it."

Luna looked into his eyes and she said, "Thank you for your support." And she added, "We have to go back to class now."

King said, "I am not going back to class."

Luna asked, "Why?"

King replied, "Because the instructor banned me from sitting close to you and I am not comfortable in my new place."

Luna said, "You can talk to the instructor that you are not comfortable with your new place, and there he will give you another place."

King said, "The only place where I can feel comfortable it's close to you. And the instructor will never give me that place."

Luna asked, "Why close to me?"

King answered, "Because you are the only reason why I am here at this school."

Suddenly, they started to look at each other in the eyes without saying a word.

Suddenly, John joined King and Luna and John looked at Luna by saying, "I was looking for you because the class has already started." Luna looked at King by saying, "Please, I want you to come to class with us." Then, she looked at John by saying, "Let's go." Then, she turned, and she started to walk through her classroom with John, while King was following them by looking at John angrily, then he lifted his magic hand through his mouth, and he demanded his magic to show him what the instructor was doing. Then, the instructor appeared on his magic palm, and he saw the instructor who was explaining the lesson in front to students by making gestures with his hands, and there was a book opened on the desk of the instructor behind him, and King demanded his magic to make that book disappear.

After fifty seconds, King, Luna, and John got inside the classroom, and they saw the instructor who was looking for his book. Most students in the classroom were very surprised, and they were not understanding what was going on because they had seen that book on the desk of the instructor because it was that book that the instructor was using to teach the course. While there were few students who had not seen that book that the instructor was looking for because they were not concentrating on what the instructor was teaching. And they thought that the instructor had forgotten his book somewhere. Then, a student said, "If Superhuman was here, we should accuse him of being responsible for it." Another student said, "Maybe Superhuman is getting his revenge now." King said, "Or maybe we accused Superhuman wrongly, and that he was not responsible for all tragedies that happened to this school, and that the responsible is still hiding among us." Everyone turned their head through King and looking at him with a surprised face, even Luna.

Then, they continued with their course, and they forgot about the book of the instructor till at less an hour for the end of the school, when suddenly a student named Mark interrupted the class with screams, and everyone in the class turned the head through Mark, by looking at him and by wondering why he was screaming. And they had all noticed that Mark had his right hand handed through the desk of the instructor, and a student asked, "Mark, why are you screaming?" Mark opened his mouth to talk but his mouth was shaking that a word could not get out, and some students had observed that Mark was sweating, and that he was breathing deeply, and that there was fear in the eyes of Mark, and they were still asking Mark what was going on, but Mark was not saying a word, and Mark had still his hand handed through the desk of the instructor.

Then, a student got up from his chair, and he was looking at Mark, and he remarked that the right hand of Mark was handed through the desk of the instructor, and that student looked through the direction of the hand of Mark who was handed, and suddenly the face of that student changed, and he screamed by saying, "The book of the instructor has appeared." And the whole class turned their head through that student, and another student said, "Stop joking when we are worried about what is going on with Mark." And the whole class heard a voice that said, "It's true."

Then, everyone turned the head through the desk of the instructor, and most students were looking at the desk of the instructor with the mouth opened, and other students were looking at the desk of the instructor with the eyes widely opened, and there were few students who had got up from their chairs still by looking at the desk of the instructor, even the instructor himself had turned his head through his desk. They were all looking at the book of the instructor that was opened on his desk and it was the same book that had disappeared on the desk of the instructor that had appeared again. Everyone was very surprised except King.

No one was realizing what was going on, even the few students who had not seen the book of the instructor before were not understanding what was happening because those few students had seen that the desk of the instructor was empty when the instructor was looking for his book, and now they were seeing a book opened on the same desk that was empty coming from nowhere. And there was silence in the room, they were all afraid and scared, and King was looking at how his classmates were afraid and he was laughing because he was the one who made that book appear again. Then, King got up and he broke the silence by saying that the classroom was cursed and that he was so afraid to stay in that classroom again, then he grabbed his bag and ran through the door, and all the rest of the students followed him outside with their bags.

The instructor called his colleagues and the school's director and he explained to them what happened with the book, and everyone was afraid to touch the book, and no one could explain what was happening, and the manager gave them a new classroom, and they locked that classroom with that book inside. Luna arrived home and she told Philip what happened to school with the book of the instructor, and Philip was not really surprised, and he told her that there was a wizard boy who existed. Also, other students told their parents what happened to the school, and parents were very worried for their kids, and most of the parents told their kids to stop going to that school, that their kids must change school. Except for King, Luna, and Philip, the rest of the students and parents were sure that it was Superhuman who did what happened to the school with the book of instructor.

Superhuman was still in jail suffering, and his magic was still not working, also he was becoming tired and weak and he was very sick. The only food that Superhuman was eating was those red fruits that were served to him every day without water, but he was not feeling so thirsty because those fruits he was eating contained a lot of water, and he was sometimes eating those fruits not because he was hungry but because he was thirsty.

The following day, the classroom of Luna was almost empty, most of the students were not in a class, and King came to school at break time and he used his magic hand to find where Luna was. Then, King and Luna were spending their break time together, and when Luna asked King why he did not come to school in the morning, King answered her that he was afraid to come to that school again, with what had happened yesterday with the book of the instructor. King invited Luna to go eat together but she refused by saying that she did not have an appetite, and he insisted by saying that she must try to eat something, not for herself, but just to make him that pleasure. And Luna promised King to go eat with him the next day if he comes to school in the morning, and he agreed. Then, King told Luna about his feelings through her, and she was very surprised to hear King said that he was in love with her, and she even did not know what to say to him, except that she was in love with Superhuman.

It was evening, Philip and Luna was at the table eating supper, and Luna was not eating like usual, and she was just thinking. Then, Philip tried to persuade her to eat something because she was losing weight, and she was looking tired and weak. And he told her that she had not put something in her mouth since Superhuman has been arrested, and to try to forget about Superhuman, and to take care of herself. Also, to focus on her school because she was not studying anymore, even her homework she was not doing. And the instructor had told Luna about her marks who were going worse and worse, and her homework that she was not doing.

Then, Philip told Luna too, to stop spending her time trying to understand what was written inside the magic book because no matter how many times she would read that book, she must not understand what she was not supposed to know. Because there was only one small part in that book that she could understand and when she read it for the first time, she understood it. And that there was a big chance that she should never see Superhuman again. Because if Hector had not tried to destroy that energy inside her, since that Superhuman had been arrested, it means that Superhuman should never be released from where he was. That Superhuman was not anymore a threaten for the project of the planet, that no one would see Superhuman again, and that the energy of the magic of Superhuman who was inside her body was useless now because except Superhuman no one could use it, and that it was the only reason why Hector let her live with that energy inside her body.

The words of Philip scared Luna, and she left the table before Philip finished talking, and she was very afraid to never see Superhuman again. Luna did not close her eyes during the whole night like usual since Superhuman has been arrested, but she did not spend her night trying to understand the writings of the magic book as usual. She spent her whole night with fear inside her, thinking about what Philip told her about Superhuman when they were taking supper, she was very afraid to never see Superhuman again like Philip was talking to her. And she had decided to go to the palace in two days to find Superhuman by herself.

It was 8:00 a.m., Luna was in the classroom, and King was in the classroom too, but the classroom was almost empty because most students were still not coming to class, since the mystery that had happened about the book of the instructor. King sat alone, and he was bored, and he was not paying attention to what the instructor was saying, and he was in class because he wanted to go with Luna for lunch as she obliged him yesterday. King had his both hands put on the table that was in front of him, and he bent his head through his magic hand, and he asked time to his magic, and 9:00 a.m., appeared on his magic palm. Then, he said in his head that he would not stay in that class till 12:00 p.m., the hour of the lunch, and he asked his magic to change the time, and make 12:00 p.m., appears in a couple of minutes, and to change the weather outside too by making it dark.

Suddenly, the sun that was outside disappeared and the weather started to become dark, and after eleven minutes King said, "It's lunchtime now, and I am very hungry." Everyone turned the head through King by laughing. And a student said, "We just got inside the classroom, so you have to wait again for lunch." Another student asked King if he did not take his breakfast when he was coming to school. King said, "It's 12:00 p.m., now, and it's time for lunch." Then, the instructor asked King to stop bothering the class. King asked the instructor to look at his watch.

Then, some students turned their head through the clock that was on the wall, and they noticed that King was right, that it was 12:00 p.m., Everyone was surprised about the time, no one was understanding or could explain how the time went faster, no one noticed what was happening, and when they looked outside, they noticed that the sun was gone and that there was a little darker. Then, they went to lunch and most students in the school were not hungry like they had taken breakfast two hours ago when they were leaving home. King and Luna were together walking through the lunchroom, and Luna had told him that she was not hungry because Philip had obliged her to eat breakfast in the morning, and she ate.

But King told Luna that she promised him yesterday that they should eat lunch together and that she should try to eat even if it's a little bit. They got inside the lunchroom, and they noticed that the lunchroom was not full like usual, and that most people who were inside the lunchroom were not eating lunch, that they were just talking to spend their lunchtime. Then, they walked to where the food was served in the lunchroom, and they stayed in line, and King demanded to Luna what she wanted to eat, and she answered him that she wanted to eat pizza. After four minutes, it was the turn of Luna and King and they asked for pizza, and the server told them that the pizza was over, that they must wait or come back in fifteen minutes. And the server explained to them that the time went faster till they did not have enough time to make food and the only thing they made was pizza and it's finished because all students ate pizza.

Then, King saw people who were in front of him, and other servers were serving pizza to those people, and he asked that server why his colleagues were serving the pizza to those students in front of him. The server answered King that those students in front of King were the first people who ordered the pizza, and now the tickets for pizza were finished which meant that all pizza was already reserved. Suddenly, the face of King changed and there was anger on his face, and he told the server that he needed the pizza right now, that he did not care if people had already reserved pizza, that he wanted to eat pizza right now. Luna turned her face through King, and she told him to calm down, that they came late and that it was not the fault of the server if the pizza was finished, then she grabbed his right hand by saying, "Let's go and come back in a couple of minutes for our pizza."

Then, they walked away, but King was still angry, and he said in his head that nobody would eat pizza, then he lifted his left hand through his mouth, and he talked to his magic without Luna noticed it. Suddenly, the lunchroom started to shake, and people started to scream by falling on the floor, the tables and the chairs were shaking and falling, there was food on the floor. Luna was on the floor too, and there were people on her.

There were people outside the door of the lunchroom who was screaming and crying like they were seeing other students on the floor inside the lunchroom, and those who had tried to get inside the lunchroom to rescue people who were on the floor had fallen once they had put their feet inside the room. King was the only person inside the lunchroom, who was not on the floor, and he was trying to help Luna, but it was hard because there were people on her, then he demanded his magic to stop the disaster that was happening.

Suddenly, the lunchroom stopped to shake, and some students got up and most of them were bleeding from their foreheads, their mouths, and their noses like they had fallen on the tables, chairs, and on other people. And like the tables and chairs had fallen on them too, most of them were feeling pains on their bodies, and they were some people who were unconscious on the floor, and some people had called ambulances for those people who were on the floor. Luna sat in the chair, and she was bleeding a little bit from her forehead, and King was close to her taking care of her. There was the journalist Liza, and some of her colleagues who were there with their cameras, and no one was understanding what was going on or could explain what had happened for that the lunchroom started to shake, or what had caused it. Most people were breathing deeply, and their heart was beating faster like they were going to have a heart attack, and the rest of the people were breathing with the fear on their faces.

Then, King saw Liza with her mike in her hand trying to interview students, but no student wanted to talk to her, and he walked till Liza and he asked her what she wanted to know. Liza asked King what he thought about what happened at school? King answered that it was very scary what they were living in that school and that it was not the first time that it happened. Liza asked him if he was afraid? King answered that he was a brave boy who never feels fear. Liza asked him what caused that disaster? King answered that it was the magic of the wizard boy. Liza said that the wizard boy who was Superhuman had been already arrested for weeks now. And King told her that the wizard boy was still alive, and that the wizard boy had not yet died, and that the planet should be in peace only the day that the wizard boy would die. Then, King turned and walked away. Liza ran after him, trying to ask him some questions again but he refused to talk to her again.

After an hour, the news of what had happened to school had already spread over the planet through the newspapers of Liza, people were buying the newspapers of Liza like they were buying bread for breakfast. Liza had put the photo of Superhuman in front of her newspapers with the headline like "The magic of the wizard boy named Superhuman is still torturing his classmates. Superhuman called again the wizard boy is still acting through his magic since where he is." Liza had also put a small picture of King in front of her newspapers and she had written a small headline like "The only brave boy of the planet" close to the picture of King. The whole planet was very afraid about what was happening, and they were wondering why Queen Mother did not kill Superhuman to prevent him from destroying the planet, and all students of that school, even the instructors had decided not to return to that school. It was evening, Hector made a speech to the national television of the planet at the name of Queen Mother to calm the whole planet, and he promised to the whole planet that Superhuman was under the control of Queen Mother. That Queen Mother had destroyed the magic of Superhuman after what happened to the school, and that all students and instructors must return to school without any fear because no one would hear the talk again about Superhuman, or see him again.

After the speech of Hector, the whole planet was now calm, except Luna who was very afraid, and she was worried about Superhuman. She could not stop thinking that maybe Superhuman was dead, like Hector said in his speech that "No one would hear talk about Superhuman again or see him again." Philip had made a tea for Luna to make her asleep, and after an hour that Luna drank that tea she started to sleep. Luna was lying in her bed dreaming, she was seeing her mom who appeared in her dream and she called, "Mom." Her mom replied, "Do not worry my daughter." Luna asked, "It's really you?" her mom replied, "Yeah, it's me." Luna said, "I am happy to see you again." Her mom said, "My daughter you will not give up, you must save Superhuman because he is dying, and if he dies it will be a tragedy for the planet and its inhabitants. Because the planet and its inhabitants are in danger now, and only Superhuman is able to protect and save the planet and its inhabitants." Luna asked, "Where is Superhuman?" Her mom replied, "You must find him." Luna asked, "How?" Her mom said, "You will have a visit this morning, and your visitor will bring you a gift that you will recognize." Luna asked, "Who is that visitor?" Her mom replied, "That visitor is your key to find Superhuman."

Then, her mom disappeared. Luna called mom, mom and no one replied then she opened her eyes, and she handed her hand and she turned on the light, then she got up and she looked at the watch on the table and she read 3:00 a.m., Then, Luna started to walk into her bedroom, thinking about her dream, and she remembered the last dream she did where she saw her mom, who was telling her to open the magic book to the page three hundred to save Superhuman when he was a prisoner to the palace and it was exactly what she had done that day to save Superhuman. Then, she started to think about the visitor who was coming, and she was wondering who that visitor could be, and she decided to return to bed and sleep again if she could dream about that visitor again.

Luna woke up at 7:00 a.m., and she was angry because she had not made the dream like she was thinking, then she got up and she went to take her shower to wait for that visitor, that her mom told her in her dreamlike she should not go to school because it was the weekend. After a half-hour, Luna had done with her shower, and she was walking through the door, then when she opened the door, and she suddenly saw Philip at her door who was ready to knock at the door. Philip looked in her eyes by saying, "There is a visitor for you." Luna looked at Philip with a surprised face and she said, "It means that my dream was true." Philip asked, "What do you mean?" Luna replied, "We will talk about my dream later." And she asked, "Who is that stranger?" Philip replied, "I did not ask his name."

Then, Luna asked Philip to let her alone with that stranger because they have a lot to talk about, and she walked to the corner of the living room. And Luna started to walk inside the living room, and suddenly her face changed, and the expression that was on her face was like she had seen a phantom, then she stopped walking, and she was staring at King who sat in the chair with an amazed face like she was seeing a monster, with her mouth opened, then she kept walking slowly through King with a silence. But King was not seeing her because he was focused on looking at his magic palm, then Luna standing upfront at him looking at him with a lot of questions that were going on in her head. She was wondering if King was the stranger that her mom talked to her in her dream, or that that stranger had not yet come, then she broke the silence by saying, "Morning."

King lifted his head and he smiled at her, then he got up from his chair and he walked two steps in front of her, and he looked in her eyes by asking, "How was your night?"

Luna looked at him and she hesitated for a couple of seconds, then she answered, "It was good. And she asked how about yours?"

King replied, "I dreamed about you."

Luna said, "I hope it was a nice dream." And she added, "Let's get a seat."

King walked through the table who was close to them and he took a box of pizza that was on that table, then he handed it to her saying, "We did not have the chance yesterday to eat pizza, but today we are going to eat pizza without any accident."

Luna took the pizza by saying, "Thank you so much." And she added, "There is no class today, that means that we have the full day for us, so we can eat the pizza later."

Then, Luna walked close to the table and she put the pizza on the table. King turned, and he walked to the chair where he was sat, and he took his bag and he opened it then he removed a small box from that bag, then he walked till face to Luna, and he handed her that box by saying, "It's a gift for you." Luna looked into his eyes, and she started to think about the dream she did, and she took the gift by saying, "Thank you." Then she opened that box and she removed a little butterfly toy that was put on the hair. And she started to look at that toy with a surprised face, and she started to remember the day that she had the accident in which she lost her parents. She was seeing everything in her head like how her mom was helping her to get a dress that morning of the accident, while her father was combing her hair, then how her father put a butterfly on her hair that day, and the butterfly that was in her hand was looking like the same butterfly that her dad had put in her hair that day. And now Luna had no doubt that the visitor that her mom told her in her dream was King, and the evidence was the gift that she recognized as her mom told her. Luna lifted her head and she looked at King who was smiling at her, and she asked, "Where did you get this butterfly?"

King asked, "Do not you like it?"

Luna said, "I grew up with the butterflies flying in the garden of my house, and I was spending my time running after the butterflies trying to catch them."

King said, "I am glad that you love the butterflies, and that you love my gift."

Luna said, "You knew well that I love butterflies."

King asked, "what do you mean?"

Luna asked, "Why among all gifts that exist you chose a butterfly like my gift."

King said, "As for me, I can not tell you why I chose a butterfly to keep you." And he added, "I guess it's just a chance."

Luna said, "It's so perfect to be a coincidence because even the color it's my favorite color. Then she asked, how did you know that I live here?"

King answered, "I followed you one day after school when you were going home."

Luna said, "I imagine that you followed me through your magic because we do not get the same bus to go or to back to school."

King looked at her with a surprised face and he asked, "What do you mean?"

Luna asked, "Where is Superhuman?"

King replied, "I am completely lost on what you are talking about."

Luna said, "I know who you are, and I know that you are the one who caused all the disasters that Superhuman is accused of."

King said, "Still I do not know what you are talking about."

Luna said, "Where Superhuman is now, he can not use his magic so it's impossible that it's him who made the book of the instructor disappear in the classroom or caused the disaster that happened in the lunchroom yesterday."

King said, "If it's not Superhuman who caused it, know that it's someone else because I do not have the magic."

Luna said, "Superhuman was always getting one hundred percent in class because he was using his magic. Then she asked, "how you are always getting your one hundred percent if you do not have the magic?" King answered, "Because I am smart."

Luna said, "Nobody is perfect."

King asked, "What do you mean?"

Luna replied, "It's impossible that you have never got less than one hundred percent in class, or give a wrong answer to a question, or even make a mistake if you are a normal human being."

King said, "I better go now."

Luna showed him that butterfly he gave to her, by saying, "This butterfly it's the butterfly that I had on my hair the day I did the accident in which I lost my parents, and it's that day that I lost this butterfly because when I woke up in the bed hospital, I did not see it till today you brought me it." King looked at her without saying any word, and he started to walk through the front door, and Luna was looking at him as he was walking away. Then, King put his hand on the door to open. And Luna said, "Please tell me where Superhuman is before leaving."

King turned through her and he said, "Superhuman is dead."

Luna cried out, "Dead?" by looking at him with fear in her eyes.

King said, "You must forget about Superhuman because you will never see him again."

Luna said, "I know that Superhuman is a special human being who is different from the rest of human beings and that to kill him it's very different from the way we kill other human beings."

King said, "I know you found it out in the magic book." And he added, do not forget that you did not understand the whole magic book."

Luna asked, "What do you mean?"

King answered, "There is only one way to kill a magician human being, and Superhuman is dying by that way."

Luna said, "Still I do not understand."

King said, "There are red fruits that look like apples but that are not apples, and those fruits are the poison for Superhuman, and since Superhuman has been arrested he is eating only those fruits everyday, without knowing that he is eating the poison who is going to kill him."

Luna asked, "Are you telling me it because you want me to forget Superhuman, or are you telling me the truth?"

King said, "Superhuman is going to die tomorrow at 3:00 a.m.,"

Luna cried out, "What? and she asked how?"

King said, "That poison kills someone after 216 hours that that person ate, and it's been 200 hours now that Superhuman is eating that poison, so it lacks 16 hours more before his death."

Luna turned her head through the watch that was the wall and she said, "There is 11:00 a.m., now."

King said, "Exactly, that means that in 16 hours the planet will bury Superhuman."

Then, they were looking each other in the eyes without saying a word, and Luna was breathing deeply, with her heart who was beating with fear, and after a minute, Luna broke the silence by saying, "I want to see Superhuman."

King said, "That's impossible."

Luna said, "I want the evidence that Superhuman is dying."

King said, "His dead body will be shown to the whole planet in 16 hours and you will see it."

Luna said, "I do not trust you, that Superhuman is dying because you are telling me it because you want me to forget about him."

King lifted his magic hand through his mouth, and he talked with his magic, then he showed his magic palm to Luna. Suddenly, there were tears flowing down the cheeks of Luna, like she was seeing Superhuman dying in his bed through the magic palm of King. Suddenly, the light started to get from the magic palm of King and going through the face of Luna, and that light was shining on her whole body, and Luna started to feel unwell, and it was like she had the dizziness, then she turned and she was trying to walk away by holding the chairs that were close to her like she was losing the balance. Then, she fell on the carpet, and King stared at her lying on the carpet like a dead person, then he opened the door and he left.

After an hour, Philip got into the living room, and he was surprised to see Luna deeply asleep on the carpet, and he tried to wake her up, but she did not open her eyes, and he carried her to her bedroom, by wondering what was going on with her. After twelve hours, Luna started to dream, and she was seeing her mom in her dream, who was telling her to wake up now and to go save Superhuman. Then, Luna opened her eyes, and she handed her hand and she turned on the light, and she got up from the bed, and she was looking lost, she was looking like she did not know where she was. She turned her head through the watch on the table, and noticed that it was midnight and she was trying to remember what had happened, and suddenly she cried out, "Superhuman?"

Then, she rushed through the table and she grabbed the magic book and ran till outside, there was the moon who was shining outside then she used that magic book and she called the hawk with. Luna was on the hawk, and the hawk was flying with her, and there were the images of the shape of a map that was coming in her head, and she was leading the hawk through the images that were coming in her head. Although the fact that she was a little bit afraid because she was not understanding the meaning of those images, mostly that it was the first time that she was seeing the images in her head, and she was just following those images without knowing exactly where she was going, but she was just hoping that those images were taking her to where Superhuman was.

After more than two hours of flying, Luna got into the space of a forest, and she was wondering why those images were taking her to the forest, and she kept leading the hawk till where she saw a small house built with stones in the middle of the trees. And, the last image that was coming in her head was the yard of that house built with the stones, and she landed front to that house and she got off the hawk, and she rushed through the door of that house, then she started to knock at that door by screaming the name of Superhuman, and there was not the handle or the place of a key on that door. After a couple of minutes, she remembered how she had used the magic book to open the door of the cell of Superhuman when he was kept prisoner to the palace, and she opened the magic book on page three hundred and she showed that page through the door and the light did not get out from that page to shine on the door like she was thinking.

Suddenly, she heard a voice behind her coming from the sky, and she turned, and she lifted her head through the sky, and she saw the same old man with the long white beard that Superhuman had seen in the forest when he was trying to get the magic book to Hector. Old man said, "You can not open that door with the magic book because the magic of Superhuman is not connected to that book now like his magic is not working." Luna asked, "How can I open this door?" Old man said, "Put your left palm on the door, and concentrate." And he added, "You must be fast because in less than three minutes, it will be 3 am and Superhuman will die."

Then, he disappeared. Luna turned through the door, and she put her left palm on the door, and there was the light that was shining between that palm and the door, she was shaking of fear that Superhuman will die. Then, after two minutes and thirty seconds the door opened, and Luna ran inside the house, and the wind was getting outside of Luna's body and going through Superhuman, and there was a lamp on the floor that was shining. Superhuman was lying on the bed, and it was like he was already dead, and Luna knelt on that bed, and she started to shake him by calling his name, but he was not making any move. Then, Luna checked the magic hand of Superhuman, and she noticed that the light was not shining on it, and the tears started to flow down her cheeks, and she opened her mouth by saying, "He is gone." And she added, "Please, Superhuman do not let me alone." Then, an idea came in her head, and she bent her head through the mouth of Superhuman and she started to kiss him.

And suddenly, Superhuman started to react, and he started to cough, and the light started to shine on his magic hand, and Luna was looking at him with the joy that he was still alive on her face. Then, Luna looked at his magic palm and she read, "You are in danger get out of this house before that door closes, and if that door closes your magic will stop working because your magic is working through the natural air that is outside and that is getting inside this house through that door". Then, Luna helped Superhuman to sit on the bed, and she stood behind him then she grabbed him through his shoulders and she helped him to get up, and she passed his hand through her shoulder, by holding him and helping him to walk. Superhuman was unwell, and he was very weak, then they reached outside, and Superhuman started to vomit the fruits that he had eaten during all the nine days he spent in that house.

Suddenly, a hawk landed in front of them and King got off that hawk with his face full of anger, then he handed his magic hand through Superhuman before Luna and Superhuman opened their mouths to say a word. Superhuman and King were fighting with the sparks of fire, while Luna was screaming by asking them to stop fighting, then King opened his mouth to talk and one of the sparks of fire that were getting outside from the palm of Superhuman got inside the mouth of King, and by accident, King swallowed it, then he fainted on the ground. Luna ran through King and she bent close to him, and she started to shake him by calling his name and King was not making any reaction, and she turned her head through Superhuman by saying, "He is dead." Superhuman said, "He is just weak because he swallowed a spark of fire that got out from my palm." And he added, "Let's go." Then, he used his magic hand and he called the hawk and they flew through space.

After an hour of flying, they saw another hawk that was flying through them and it was King who was on that hawk, and Superhuman asked Luna to hold him very well because King was coming for a fight. Superhuman started to avoid King by flying on another side, while King was still trying to fly through Superhuman, then after a half-hour, King succeeded to be face to Superhuman. Then, they started to fight, and both hawks were shaking like they were losing balance because they were leading their hawk just with one hand like they were using their magic hands to fight. Luna was screaming, and she was losing the balance, and it was not easy for her to hold Superhuman like the hawk was shaking by going in all directions, then the hawk turned to the left side and Luna completely lost balance and she fell from the hawk. And suddenly, King screamed by calling the name of Luna, with his face full of fear like he was seeing her falling. And Superhuman screamed with his face full of anger like he was watching Luna who was falling, then he jumped from his hawk by flying through Luna, and King jumped from his hawk by flying through Luna too.

Then, Superhuman grabbed Luna in the space before she falls on the ground, and they landed on the ground without a problem. Luna looked at him and she said, "Again you saved my life." Superhuman replied, "Do not forget that you are in this situation because you came to save me." Luna lifted her head through space, and she saw King who was flying through them, and she demanded Superhuman to help King because if King fell on the ground he would die or get hurt. Superhuman replied to her that King is a special human being with magic inside him, that he could not get hurt or die if he falls on the ground. Then, Superhuman handed his magic hand through the space and the sparks of fire started to get outside from his magic palm going through King.

Luna noticed that those sparks of fire that Superhuman was sending into space were preventing King to fly, then she asked Superhuman to stop sending those sparks of fire that King was losing the balance with those sparks of fire. And Superhuman told her that he was trying to prevent King to land close to them because King was coming for a fight. King wanted to fight in space where he was, but he did not have enough balance to use his magic hand for fighting, and he could not land on the ground. Because the sparks of fire that Superhuman was sending through him was preventing him from flying through the ground, then King chose to call the hawk, and the hawk came, and he got on it, then he flew away. Luna watched at King how he was flying away, and she said, "I hope he will not come again." Superhuman replied, "I hope too." Luna asked, "What time is it now?" Superhuman looked at the palm of his magic hand he read 5:00 a.m., and he showed it to Luna. Then, Luna asked, "What to do now?" And she added, "Some people are already waking up, and we can not use the hawk to fly in space with daylight because people will die of scaring mostly that everyone thinks that you are a wizard boy." Superhuman looked at his magic palm, and he looked at Luna by saying, "I have the solution."

Then, he grabbed her hand and they started to walk. After an hour of walking, both were very tired, then they saw a car parked close to the street, with nobody inside and around it, then Superhuman used his magic hand to open the door of that car, and they got inside, and they drove till home. Philip was in the living room, sat in the chair taking his breakfast, and he saw the front door opened and he looked with an amazed face like was seeing Superhuman and Luna walking inside.

Then, Luna explained to Philip and Superhuman her conversation with King of yesterday morning, and what happened when King showed her his magic palm, and how she saw Superhuman who was dying through the magic palm of King. She also talked about the fruits that were the poison that Superhuman was eating in that jail, and the images of the map she was seeing in her head when she was going to find Superhuman, but she did not talk about her mom she saw in her dream. And Philip told Luna that if when she saw the magic palm of King, she lost control and she fainted on the floor, it was because she was getting contact with the magic of King, which meant that King was the second person to whom she was linked.

And that the images of the map that were coming in her head were coming from the connection she had with the magic of King. And that she opened the door of where Superhuman was kept prisoner by putting her left palm on the door, it was because that door was locked through the magic of King, and the magic hand of King was his left hand, and that she was connected to that left hand of King, and that it was the reason she succeeded to save Superhuman. Luna and Superhuman were very surprised with what Philip told them, then Luna asked Philip how she was connected to King, and why? Philip answered her that he had no idea how she was linked with King and that he had no idea why she was connected to King. Philip added that things would be harder because Hector knew already how to kill the magician boy who was Superhuman, which meant that Hector had read the most important part of the magic book. And that was the reason why Hector did not come to try to get the magic book when Superhuman was a prisoner because he already knew the most important who was how to kill the magician boy who was Superhuman.

Then, Philip talked to superhuman that Hector found out a lot of his weakness in the magic book and that the house built with stones was one of his weaknesses because his magic did not work with the stones, also that Superhuman would never eat those fruits he ate those last days when he was a prisoner. Because those fruits were a dangerous poison for his magic and his body that would kill him in less than ten days, in exactly 216 hours after that he ate it. Superhuman asked Philip why he did not talk to Luna and him about it before Hector caught him? And Philip answered that he had never read the magic book, and he had no idea about what was written inside that magic book, and that he had no power to read that book, that he just there to analyze what was happening, that everything he told them was based on what they lived, and what Luna said.

That he did not know that the wizard boy was King till Luna explained what happened with King like he did not know that King was the second person to whom Luna was connected, till she told how she succeeded to save superhuman like he did not know that the stones were a weakness for the magic of the magician boy, till Superhuman told that his magic was not working in the house built with the stones. Luna asked Philip if Queen Mother and Hector knew that the wizard boy of the planet was King. Philip answered that they will find out the answer to that question soon. Superhuman, Luna, and Philip spent their entire day talking about King.

CHAPTER 6

✦

The Agreement Between Superhuman, Luna and Hector

It was 5:00 a.m., the whole planet was still on their bed asleep like it was the weekend. Suddenly, there were screams coming from each house on the planet, some people were lying on their bed shaking, and they were trying to hold something, while other people were on the floor of their bedroom with pieces of stuff that were falling on them. The houses of the planet were shaking like if there was an earthquake, and everyone was screaming with faces full of fear, except Superhuman who was not feeling what was going on.

Superhuman was lying in his bed deeply asleep, and he was not aware of what was happening because his room was not shaking. Then, Superhuman turned on the bed and he noticed that the light was shining on his magic hand and he looked at his magic palm, and he immediately jumped from his bed and he ran to the bedroom of Luna. And he saw Luna who was shaking on her bed, holding the edge of the bed to not fall, then he jumped on the bed and he held her, and she told him to stop the disaster that was happening. Superhuman tried to concentrate to stop the disaster but it was hard, and he asked his magic how to stop it, and his magic answered him through his magic palm to go outside to stop it. Then, he let Luna and he rushed through the door, and he ran to the front door and he opened the door, then suddenly his face changed, and he was looking with a surprised face like he was seeing the storm outside. He started to wonder what it was because it was his first time seeing the storm. After all, the storm was not the weather of their planet.

Then, he looked at his magic palm and he walked outside, and he got inside the storm, and he lifted his magic hand through the sky and the sparks of fire were not getting out from his palm. Then, he looked at his magic hand and he noticed that his magic was not working, and he tried to communicate with his magic but still, his magic was not working, and he was not understanding what was going on. Then, he returned inside the house, and his magic started to work, and he read what was written on his magic palm, and he ran through the window and he opened the window. Then, he handed his magic hand through the window, but his hand was inside the house, and the sparks of fire were getting outside from his palm and going outside.

After a couple of minutes, the houses stopped shaking and he walked till close to the window and he started to look outside, he was looking at the storm outside wondering what it was and what caused it. Then, he heard the footsteps behind him, and he turned, and he saw Luna and Philip who had worn the jacket on them shaking and he asked them why they were shaking? Luna told him that the cold was getting inside the house and that he must stop it. Superhuman tried to stop the cold without success and he told Luna that the cold was coming from the storm that was outside and that he was unable to stop that storm. Philip and Luna looked through the window and they were surprised to see the storm, and Philip told them that the storm was sent through the magic of King and that Hector knew that the storm was one of the weaknesses of Superhuman that the magic of Superhuman could not stop.

Luna told Superhuman and Philip that they must do something so that people would die of cold and that the whole planet would be scared now by seeing that storm outside because no one knew what it was, and no one had ever seen it before. Superhuman looked at his magic palm and he was surprised to see Hector and King in the palace who were talking, and he showed his palm to Luna and she was surprised to see Hector and King sitting around a small table drinking coffee by talking together. Luna and Superhuman turned through Philip by asking him what King was doing to the palace talking with Hector. Philip answered them that they would find out by themselves.

Superhuman decided to go to the palace despite the fact that it was dangerous for him to go there to confront Hector and King, but it was the only solution he had like he could not stop the storm. And Luna decided to go with him, and he refused to go with her by saying that it was dangerous, that Hector and King could kill her there. But Luna insisted to go with him, and Philip convinced Superhuman to go with Luna, by saying that she was the only one who could help him in case of need, mostly that she was the one who had the energy of his magic inside her body. And Luna told Philip that she kept the magic book secretly and that there was a letter on the table of her bedroom, that she wrote last night and that if she did not come back, he would take that letter and read it.

Then, Superhuman and Luna walked outside and Superhuman tried to call the hawk, but his magic was not working, and he returned inside the house, and he stayed inside then he handed his magic hand through the door and he called the hawk without his magic hand be in contact with the storm, then they flew through the palace. The whole planet was inside their house like the prisoners feeling cold, no one could go out not only because it was cold, but because they were afraid to go out, and they were scared by the weather they were seeing through the windows of their house, and they were wondering what it was. Most people were lying in their bed with blankets on them, they were all scared, they were breathing with fear, no one could explain what had happened early morning like the houses were shaking, and they were scared about the storm they were seeing outside through the windows because they did not know what it was like, it was their first time to see it.

Everyone on the planet was thinking that it was Superhuman who was responsible for all disasters that were happening on the planet, even that storm outside. The whole planet was wondering why Queen mother could not make that storm disappear and kill Superhuman. Superhuman and Luna landed in the garden of the palace, and they got off the hawk, then they walked to the entrance of the palace and the light started to shine on the magic hand of

Superhuman like he was not anymore on the storm. Superhuman looked at his magic palm and he read "You are in danger" and he showed his palm to Luna, and she read what was written on it, and she asked him to not fight. Because they were in the palace to convince King to stop the storm, and that the fight would only make things worse, only King could stop that storm outside, and that they would obey King if necessary, for that he stops the storm. Then, they kept walking through the hall of the palace, and security men came and arrested them, then the chief of the security went and talked to Hector that they arrested Superhuman and Luna, and Hector ordered to put Superhuman in the prison that was built yesterday with the stones and to put Luna in a comfortable jail inside the palace.

Hector and King were together, and King was looking at the magic book through his magic palm, and he was not seeing it. Then, King told Hector that he was not seeing the magic book, and they were surprised to see that King's magic was unable to see the magic book. King told Hector that a day ago when he went to Philip's house to visit Luna, he tried to find her bedroom through his magic and he did not see her and that he did not understand why he could not find her because he was seeing the whole house of Philip with all rooms on his magic palm, but he did not see Luna. Hector told King that probably Luna should be outside when he was looking for her that day inside the house, and he did not look for her outside because his magic is able to see the whole planet. Then, King and Hector decided to keep Superhuman in jail for 216 hours and to feed him with the fruits that would kill him, and they decided that they were going to start to work on their project.

Superhuman was in his jail, and he could not communicate with his magic because his magic was not working like his jail was built with the stones, and he was on a small mattress that was put on the floor and there was the plate of fruits in front of him. And he noticed that the fruits that were in front of him were the same fruits he had eaten a couple of days ago, when he was a prisoner in the forest, and he understood that Hector wanted to kill him.

Then, he started to worry about Luna, afraid that King and Hector could kill her, and he was angry with himself because if Luna was in danger, he could not protect her or save her like he was kept prisoner and his magic was not working. And he was wondering what King was doing to the palace talking with Hector, and if Hector and Queen Mother knew that King was a wizard boy. Also, he was wondering the reasons why Hector wanted to kill him, and not King if he was the magician boy and king the wizard boy, and he was trying to understand the reason why he and King had the same magic with the only difference that he was a magician and King was a wizard. Luna was kept prisoner in a comfortable jail with the bed inside and she could get out of her jail to go to the washroom, and there was food that was served in front of her with juice and water, but she had not touched it since that it was served, despite the fact that she was hungry.

Luna was walking inside her jail, looking through the window of her jail with a worried face, and she was watching the storm outside through the window of her jail, and she was very worried for the whole planet. She knew that all inhabitants of the planet had not put their feet outside since morning because they were inside their house scared by the storm like they did not know what it was because they had never seen it before. She was also worried for Superhuman, she had no doubt that he was kept prisoner in a prison built with the stones to make him weak, and to prevent the communication between him and his magic. She was hoping that Superhuman remembered that the fruits had the poison in them and that he must not eat them because she knew that Hector would try to kill Superhuman.

And she was afraid that maybe there was another way to kill the magician boy who was Superhuman that Hector found out in the magic book, and that she and Superhuman did not know. Then, she said to herself that except her, there was no one else who could save Superhuman, and she started to think about how to save Superhuman although the fact she was in jail. She was afraid too that Hector would destroy the energy of the magic of superhuman who was inside her body, as she was in that jail alone without Superhuman close to her to protect her, mostly that that energy inside her was very important and that it had been awhile that Hector was trying to destroy it.

Then, Luna walked to the door of her jail, and she started to knock on the door, by screaming and after a few minutes two security men came to look at what was happening to her, and Luna told them that she wanted to talk with King. After an hour, Luna had not seen King, but King had received her message, just that he was thinking if he should go to see her or not. While, Luna was still in her jail watching the storm outside through her window jail, worried for people of the planet and she was saying that King and Hector had kept people in their houses like prisoners. Then, she walked to the door, and she started to knock at the door by making noises, but no one was coming, and King was lying in his bed watching what Luna was doing through his magic palm. It was evening and there was still the storm outside, and the whole planet was lying in their bed, with a blanket on them feeling cold, and there were people who had not got up from their bed since morning, and who had not put something in their mouth.

The whole planet was hating Superhuman and everyone was saying that he was a curse for the planet, and they were still wondering why Queen mother had not stopped that storm outside, and why she was watching Superhuman destroy the planet without doing anything. Philip was lying in his bed worried about Superhuman and Luna, and he knew that they were in danger and he was very afraid that Hector destroyed the energy of the magic of Superhuman who was inside Luna. He was worried for the planet too because he knew already the wizard boy, and that the whole planet was in danger with that wizard boy, and that there was only Superhuman who could protect the planet and if the energy of the magic of Superhuman was destroyed it would be impossible for Superhuman to protect the planet.

It was morning, there was still the storm outside, and people had started to pray Queen Mother on their beds to protect them, the fear had increased inside people, and they were wondering if that cursed storm would disappear or if they were going to spend the rest of their life like the prisoners inside their house. Superhuman, Luna, and King had not closed their eyes during the whole night. Superhuman had spent his whole night walking in his jail thinking about Luna and the whole planet that he had abandoned, unable to protect them in case of danger, and he was hoping that King stopped the storm outside because he did not know that there was still the storm outside like his jail was covered everywhere and there was not the window to see outside. While, Luna had spent her whole night at the window of her jail watching the storm outside, worried for the planet and wondering why King and Hector decided to punish all the inhabitants of the planet. And King had spent his whole night lying in his bed watching Luna through his magic palm.

The breakfast was served to Luna and she had refused to eat till she talked with King, and the same fruits were still served to Superhuman, but he had not still touched it. King had found out through his magic palm, that Superhuman was not eating since yesterday, that he had not touched those fruits that were served to him, and King talked to Hector about it. Hector was very angry when King told him that Superhuman was not eating, and he demanded King to oblige Superhuman to eat those fruits. Superhuman was lying on his mattress thinking, and he heard the footsteps inside his jail, then he turned his head and he saw King who was walking through him. Then, he got up from his mattress, and he walked two steps through King, and they were looking each other in the eyes angrily without saying a word.

After three minutes, Superhuman broke the silence by asking, "Where is Luna?" King answered, "Forget about Luna because you will never see her again." And he added, "I am here because I want you to eat those fruits that have been served to you since yesterday." Superhuman answered, "Those fruits will get inside my mouth only when I will be dead." Then, King handed his magic hand through Superhuman, and the sparks of fire started to get outside from his palm and Superhuman started to scream like the sparks of fire that were getting outside from the magic palm of King were burning him. King was still torturing Superhuman, and Superhuman was screaming pains and Superhuman could not protect himself like his magic was not working.

After eleven minutes, King left the room and Superhuman took off his t-shirt and his whole body became red, and there was sweat that was flowing down on his whole body like water and he was feeling pains on his whole body. Luna was still at the window of her prison, watching the storm outside when King walked inside her jail, and she told him that he must stop the storm because he was keeping people prisoners inside their house. And Luna added by saying that if she and Superhuman came to the palace, it was because they wanted him to stop that storm outside and that it was the reason why Superhuman did not fight when security men arrested them. King told her that the storm was a punishment like she betrayed him by going to save Superhuman in less than a couple of seconds of his death. And he added by saying that when he showed his magic palm to her, he did not know that she could save Superhuman, and he could not even imagine that she could think to go save Superhuman.

Then, King told Luna that it was the big mistake of his life, by showing her his magic palm and that he regretted it because Superhuman should be dead now if he had not shown her his magic palm. And Luna told King that his enemies were she and Superhuman, not the whole planet and that it was unfair to punish the whole planet for her fault. And King told her that he did not care about the planet, that the one who is born to protect the planet was Superhuman not him, that he was born for a mission that was very different from the mission of Superhuman, then he left. Luna walked beside her bed, and she knelt then she started to pray by asking her parents to help her, and by asking her mom to come tell her about what to do and how to protect the planet. Hector and King were worried about how they could force Superhuman to eat, and Hector told King that they must find the magic book because inside that magic book they could find another way to kill the magician boy who was Superhuman. Then, King started to find the magic book on his magic palm, after an hour the magic of king had not found the magic book.

Then, Hector asked King to find Philip because Philip could give them that magic book like it was him who had that book. Then, King spent three hours looking for Philip over the planet on his magic palm without success, then King and Hector were wondering where Philip could be. Because they were surprised to not see Philip, like the magic of King was able to see each house on the planet, and all rooms of each house with all people living in the houses. Then, Hector told King that the only reason why king's magic was unable to find the magic book and Philip it was that Philip ran away from the planet with the magic book. King told Hector that there was another reason else because it was impossible that Philip ran outside of the planet with that storm outside in less than 48 hours.

Hector said that probably Superhuman and Luna helped Philip to run away before they came to the palace because they knew what should happen and they wanted to protect the magic book. And King said that he would find out if Superhuman and Luna took Philip outside the planet before they came to the palace, then he lifted his magic hand through his mouth and he talked to his magic and he looked at his magic palm. Suddenly, the magic of King became weak and his magic was unable to find what King had asked to search, and King looked at Hector with a surprised face by crying out, "Luna?" Then, they got up and they ran to the jail of Luna and they saw her lying on the floor unconscious. Immediately, Luna was taken to the hospital of the palace. Luna was lying in the bed's hospital unconscious, and she was seeing the shadow of her mom in her mind who was telling her to not say anything about Philip, the magic book, the house of Philip, and about the chocolate that the dog gave to her when she was coming back from the toilet.

After two days, the situation of the planet had not changed, there was still a storm outside and the whole planet was still a prisoner in their house, and Luna was still unconscious on the hospital's bed. People had started to lack stuff at home like food because it has been four days now that no one went outside for errands, most people were saying that it was the end of the planet, that Superhuman was killing the planet with all its inhabitants.

Everyone on the planet had lost hope, even in their god Queen Mother. Even inside the palace, people were thinking that it was Superhuman who was killing people with that storm outside, and they were all wondering why Hector was letting Superhuman alive. Hector wanted to drink coffee, but the coffee was finished in the palace, and he asked King to stop the storm to allow people to go outside for errands, but unfortunately King could not stop the storm because his magic was still weak like Luna was still unconscious in the bed hospital.

King and Hector was spending their time yelling at the doctors who were taking care of Luna because they were not understanding why Luna was still unconscious after three days. And King told

Hector that there was something going wrong, that the sickness of Luna was not natural, that Luna could not become unconscious just because she spent 35 hours without eating. And that Luna was a witch girl who was connected with two magics, one good magic who was the magic of the magician boy who was Superhuman, and another bad magic who was the magic of the wizard boy who was himself. That even if Luna spends a century without eating nothing would happen to her, that she would just feel hungry like everyone, but she would be fine.

King and Hector spent the day thinking about what had happened to Luna, wondering why Luna was unconscious, and both Hector and King started to be worried not only because they had lost control of the situation on the planet. But, also because with Luna unconscious it would be impossible for them to realize their project, and they could not keep working on their project like the magic of King was not working because they needed that magic to work. The following day, it was 9:00 a.m., there was nothing in the palace for breakfast, and there were a lot of people who were sick on the planet, and in each house of the planet, people were suffering. King and Hector had spent their night in their office thinking, and the day of the meeting was approaching, and they were not ready, and there was still the storm outside, and King could not stop that storm like his magic was not working, and no one could get inside that storm.

Then, King told Hector that the only solution they had, was Superhuman. And Hector asked King how Superhuman could help? Because if Superhuman came to the palace himself it was because Superhuman could not stop the storm. King answered to Hector that Superhuman could heal Luna, and after that Luna would be healed, he would be able to use his magic because his magic was not working like Luna was unconscious like she linked to his magic, and that if Luna stayed unconscious his magic would never work, and he would never be able to stop that storm outside or use his magic for something else even to work on their project.

And Hector understood that he did not have the choice that if he wanted to realize his project, Superhuman was his only solution because with Luna unconscious it was impossible for King to use his magic. Hector and King agreed that they were going to use

Superhuman to heal Luna for that King used his magic, and after they would find how to kill Superhuman. Superhuman was lying on the mattress in his jail, tired, feeling hungry, and thinking about Luna and the planet, without knowing what was happening out of his jail. Then, the door of his jail opened, and he turned his head, and he saw two security men who were walking inside, then he got up from his bed, and those two security men asked him to follow them, and Superhuman started to follow them without asking a question. King and Hector were in the hospital room of Luna, watching her lying in the bed's hospital unconscious, then the door opened and Superhuman was behind two security men. Superhuman had turned his head through the sky looking at the storm that was still outside with a sad face, thinking about the inhabitants of the planet who would be suffering from that storm.

Then, he started to feel the wind that was blowing on him, and he cried out, "Luna?" Then he turned his head through the door, and he saw Luna who was lying in the hospital's bed, then he pushed security men who were in front of him, and he ran till close to Luna's bed. Superhuman started to shake Luna by calling her name, with fear on his face and the light was shining on his magic hand, and he was not even paying attention to that light that was shining because he was just focused on shaking Luna. King looked at Superhuman by saying, "You have a message on your magic hand." Then, Superhuman looked at his magic palm, then he put that magic palm on the forehead of Luna, and there was the light that was shining between his magic palm and Luna's forehead. Everyone in the room was looking at Superhuman, but King was looking at Superhuman with the rage on his face like Superhuman had his magic hand on Luna's forehead.

After seven minutes, Luna opened her eyes and she looked at Superhuman with a surprised face first, then she smiled at him and she said, "Please take me with you, I do not let me alone again." Everyone in the room was watching Superhuman and Luna with a surprised face, except Hector and King. For doctors and security men who were in the room, it was a miracle what Superhuman did to Luna with his magic hand. King looked at his magic hand and he noticed that his magic was working, then he turned his head through security men, and he ordered them to take Superhuman to his jail.

Suddenly, Superhuman turned and he handed his magic hand through those security men by saying, "Do not even dare to walk through me." Then, King handed his magic hand through Superhuman too. And everyone was looking at them with panic on their face except Hector, then Luna got up from her bed and she stood up behind Superhuman by holding his clothing. Hector looked at Luna by saying, "Get out of this room." Luna looked back at Hector by saying, "Do not waste your time because I will not let Superhuman alone." King looked at Luna by saying, "You have no choice but to obey because there is still the storm outside and I am only the one who can stop it, so I still have control over both of you." Superhuman looked into the eyes of King by saying, "Luna and I came here and we accepted to become your prisoners because we wanted you to stop the storm outside, but you did not do it, despite the fact that you had us like prisoners." Luna looked at King by saying, "You are just a devil without a heart, who is torturing a planet without any reason." King said, "If I am on this planet it's because there is a reason." Luna said, "I am wondering why Queen Mother and Hector allow you to live on this planet, mostly in this palace with them knowing that you are a wizard boy, that you are responsible for all the disasters that are happening on this planet like that storm outside."

Suddenly, a doctor cried out, "It means the wizard boy is King, not Superhuman." Suddenly, King turned through that doctor with his magic hand handed to this doctor, and the sparks of fire got out from his palm and went through that doctor and that doctor fell on the floor. And suddenly, Luna started to scream, while the rest of the people in the room were looking at that doctor on the floor with their faces full of fear, and their mouths opened but unable to say a word, except Hector who was not surprised with what King did. There were tears flowing down on the cheeks of Luna and the colleague of that doctor who was on the floor.

Then, Superhuman and Luna walked till close to that doctor who was on the floor, and Luna looked at Superhuman by saying, "Please, save that doctor." Superhuman said, "I will need the energy of my magic inside me to save him because I can not save him just with the energy coming from your body because the energy coming from your body is very weak to save someone who is dying." King looked at Luna by saying, "Do not even dare to kiss Superhuman." Luna looked at King by saying, "Of course that I will kiss Superhuman, not only because I am the one who has the energy of his magic, but also because he is my sweetheart."

Then, King handed his magic hand through another doctor, and he turned his head through Luna by saying, "I am the one who is your sweetheart, so if you dare to kiss Superhuman, I will kill this doctor that you are seeing my magic hand handed on him." Superhuman and Luna were looking at King with worried faces, while the rest of the people in the room were shaking with fear. Superhuman said, "There is no time to waste because If I do not save this doctor who is lying on the floor he will die." King replied, "I know it well, but he is going to die." Luna looked in the eyes of King by saying, "Please, let Superhuman save this doctor." King said, "I decided that this doctor will die." Luna said, "I beg your pardon, to let us save this doctor." King said, "I do not want you to kiss Superhuman again, so it's impossible to save that doctor." Then, Superhuman handed his magic hand through King. And King smiled at Superhuman by saying, "It's useless because you can not fight and save that doctor at the same time because the time you are going to use to fight me that doctor will be already dead." And he added, "If you start the fight here now know that other people will die again because the sparks of fire that will get out from my magic palm will kill other people."

Then, the light started to shine on the magic hand of Superhuman, and he looked at his magic palm, then he looked at that doctor on the floor with a sad face, and he said with a sad voice, "He is gone." Then, the tears started to flow down the cheeks of everyone in the room except Hector and King. Hector ordered security men to carry the dead body of that doctor and to leave the room, and he also ordered another doctor to leave the room and he told them that no one would be aware of what happened in that room. Then, they left the room and there were only Superhuman, Luna, King, and Hector in the room.

Then, King looked at Superhuman by saying, "Now, you have to go back to your jail."

Superhuman said, "Only my dead body who will return to that jail."

King said, "If you do not return to your jail, I will never stop that storm outside."

Luna looked at King by saying, "It's been almost a week that there is a storm outside, and Superhuman was in jail and you did not stop the storm. And you just killed an innocent doctor in front of us for no reason, so there is nothing that guarantees that if Superhuman returns to his jail, you will stop that storm."

Hector said, "We need the magic book to stop that storm."

Luna looked at Hector by saying, "We will not give you the magic book, we will not tell you where Philip is, and we will not answer any of your questions."

Then, King and Hector looked at each other with surprised faces, and Hector asked, "How does she know that we were looking for Philip?"

King replied, "I have no idea."

After a half-hour of thinking, and talking without any agreement. King looked at Luna by saying, "You will stay with me, and I will stop the storm outside."

Superhuman said, "It will never happen because she is my beloved." And he added, "I am going with her now."

King said, "She is my beloved too, and she is going to stay with me."

Luna looked at King by saying, "I am agreed to stay with you if you stop the storm and if you let Superhuman go."

Hector said, "No because Superhuman will never leave this palace alive."

King looked at Luna by saying, "I agree."

Luna said, "I will respect my word, and I want you to respect your own too."

Superhuman looked at Luna by saying, "I hope that you are joking."

Luna looked back at Superhuman by answering, "No, I am not kidding."

Superhuman asked, "How about us?"

Luna said, "Our love is important, but the protection of the planet is more important."

Superhuman said, "I can not accept that you stay with King."

Luna looked in the eyes of Superhuman by saying, "I am sorry if I am hurting you by that decision, but we have to think about the planet first before thinking about our love, that's why we are born. And it will be selfish to abandon this planet with all his inhabitants, just for our love."

Superhuman said, "We do not even know the reasons for this fight, we do not know what is happening on this planet, and I do not know why I woke up a morning and I found this magic inside me, like yourself you do not know why you have the energy of my magic inside you."

Luna looked at Superhuman by saying, "Both of us are born to protect this planet."

Superhuman asked, "To protect against who?"

Luna replied, "It's obvious that King was born to destroy this planet because if he was on this planet for a good reason, he should not be torturing people with that storm outside, or he should not kill that doctor that we watched him kill." And she added, "We must prevent King from destroying this planet."

Superhuman said, "If King was here to destroy the planet he should not be living in the same palace with Hector and Queen Mother who is god."

King looked at Superhuman by saying, "It's time to leave now."

Superhuman replied, "Of course that I will leave, but with Luna."

Luna looked at Superhuman with tears that were flowing down her cheeks and she said, "Please, leave this palace."

Superhuman said, "I refuse to let you alone with that devil of King."

Luna said, "Do not worry, I am not alone."

Superhuman asked, "With who you are?"

Luna replied, "With some people and with your heart too."

Superhuman asked, "Which people are you talking about?"

Luna replied, "I am with people that you do not know." And she added, "I will talk about them to you another day."

King looked at Luna by saying, "Here is the last time you see Superhuman because you are not going to see him again."

Superhuman looked at Luna with a sad face by saying, "I am very afraid to lose you."

King looked at Superhuman by saying, "You already lost her." And he added, "leave now."

Luna looked at King by saying, "You have to stop the storm first." And she added, "I will kiss Superhuman for the last time."

King cried out, "Kiss him?" by looking at Luna with a surprised face. Then he said, "I will stop the storm, but you will not kiss Superhuman because now you are my fiancé."

Luna said, "Superhuman does not have the energy of his magic inside him, and now he is able to use his magic to fight because the energy he is getting, is coming from my body like I am close to him. And if he leaves this room alone, my body will not be able to give him the energy of his magic, and he will not be able to fight in case of danger."

King said, "There will be no danger."

Luna said, "I do not trust you." And she added, "Nothing is telling me that when Superhuman will get outside of this room, you will not send your security men to arrest him."

Then, King agreed that Luna kissed Superhuman, and he stopped the storm outside. Superhuman and Luna kissed with tears on their faces, then Superhuman left the palace with a sad face full of tears. Hector told King that he was afraid that they did not make a good agreement by leaving Superhuman go. King answered to Hector that they did a great deal because after 72 hours Superhuman would not be a threat for their project anymore because the magic of Superhuman would be useless like there would be not Luna to give him the energy of his magic again. And that like they had Luna with them it was already a victory. The whole planet was at their window looking outside through the window's glass, everyone was seeing how outside was shining with the sun, and that the storm was over, but there was still the fear on their face and inside them.

No one had opened his door, they were afraid that the storm would start again, and they were very afraid for their lives. Superhuman had reached home, and he used his magic to find where Philip was, then he explained to Philip what happened to the palace. Then, Philip gave him the letter that Luna had left the day they were going to the palace. Superhuman read the letter of Luna with tears flowing down his cheeks, he was very sad, and he understood in that letter the reasons why Luna had chosen to stay at the palace with King. Superhuman wanted to return to the palace to take Luna with him because he did not want her to stay there, but Philip convinced Superhuman that it was very a bad idea to do that, that he was putting the whole planet in danger by doing that, and that he was born to protect the planet not to destroy the planet. And that even if he was in love with Luna, and that he was jealous to know that she was with King in the palace, he must think about the planet first before thinking about his love like Luna did, that the decision of Luna was to protect the planet by allowing him to fight King.

CHAPTER 7

The Planet Living the Tragedy

T he following day, everyone woke up and the first thing they did was to look through the window, but despite the fact that there was not a storm outside, most people did not get out of their house, and there were just a few people outside. Only the journalist Liza who had written about what had happened on the planet for almost a week, and in front of her newspapers there were the pictures of Superhuman and the storm, with the headline like "The wizard magic". Luna was in the palace sad thinking about Superhuman and the planet, and there were a lot of questions in her head, like what King wanted? Why did King, Hector, and Queen Mother work together? Why did King and Superhuman have the same magic with the only difference that one magic it was to protect and another magic it was to destroy? Why was she connected to both magics? How she was connected to the magic of King? Why did her mom tell her in the dream that she should not talk about the chocolate that the dog gave to her? But Luna could not find any answer to her questions.

The days were passing, and people were getting outside from their houses, and the fear was disappearing inside them, and they were trying to forget the hell they lived with the smile on their face. The activities had restarted on the planet, students had found their way of school, while workers had found their way of work. Superhuman was spending his days at home, he had not returned to school, and he was using his magic hand to watch what was happening on the planet, and he was watching inside the palace, he was watching Luna, King, and Hector, and he was aware of everything that Hector and King were planning to do.

Luna had started to recover the smile although the fact that she was still thinking about Superhuman, and she had two good friends were Maria a housekeeper who works in the palace, and the dog named Berly the one that had given her the chocolate, and it was the same dog who had showed her where Superhuman was the day she came to release him when he was to jail. Berly was a big dark dog of Queen Mother. When Luna was not talking with Maria, she was in the yard of the palace playing with Berly, and she had told King that she wanted to return to school, and King told her that she should wait. King and Hector were spending their time inside the office working, and when Luna asked King what he was doing in the office every day with Hector? King answered her that it was a secret that she did not need to know. It was the eve of the meeting day, and Hector had made a speech to the television to remember about that meeting to the whole planet, by saying that that meeting was very important because they were going to protect the planet and all its inhabitants, to avoid all the curses that happened on the planet during those last months to happen again.

The whole planet was happy about the speech of Hector, they were eager for the next day, there was hope inside them that they should not live a sad moment again, and that Superhuman would not be able to destroy the planet again. Hector and King sat in the living room, happy and drinking wine by celebrating their victory with the smile on their faces, and with their eyes focused on the watch on the wall by counting time, eager for the following day. Luna was lying in her bed worried about what was going to happen the following day, wondering what King and Hector were going to do the following day knowing that nothing coming from King could be good, and she was hoping that superhuman would prevent King and Hector from destroying the planet.

It was early morning, all streets of the planet were full of people walking through the church, and parents had held the hands of their kids, and kids who could not walk were in their strollers. There was no car in the streets because it was impossible to drive with all people who were in the streets, and the day was declared like a day off by Hector, and no office or shop was opened. King, Luna, and Hector were inside the church and the church was already full, and most people were still outside unable to get inside. There was a huge table in front of Hector with the rosaries on that table, and there were photos of Hector on those rosaries. Superhuman was lying in his bed still asleep, and he turned on his bed to change the side and he noticed that the light was shining on his magic hand, and he looked at his magic palm, then he suddenly jumped from his bed, and he ran through the kitchen and he opened the refrigerator and he removed a thermos, and he opened that thermos and he started to drink the contents of that thermos.

Then, he put the thermos back in the refrigerator, and he ran through the outside door, while Hector was in the church making a speech talking about the important change that was going to happen on the planet, how they should protect themselves from the wizard boy who was Superhuman. That those last months were horrible for everyone on the planet, mostly the five days of the storm. And that Queen Mother saw how her people were suffering and she decided to end with that pain. Then, that Queen Mother, and the new angel of the planet named King who was the magician boy of the planet, worked to make sure that such a curse like a storm would never happen on the planet again. That Superhuman would not be in any more danger for them, that they made the rosaries for all inhabitants of the planet, and that everyone would wear that rosary in his neck during twenty-one days without removing it. That, everyone, would take a shower, would sleep, would go everywhere with that rosary in his neck without removing it, even kids and newborns because it was those rosaries who would protect them.

Then, Hector introduced King to people like the magician boy of the planet, who was going to protect them and to protect the planet that everyone was safe with King on the planet, and people started to clap their hands by screaming the name of King like the magician boy with the joy on their face. Except for Luna who was not clapping her hands, she was looking at people who were screaming the name of King with a worried face, while King was smiling at them, and there were the journalists and cameramen in the church who were taking the pictures of King. Then, Hector asked people to make a line, that each person would walk till where he was to get his rosary, and after that, someone got his rosary, he would walk through the outside door to allow people who were behind him to get for them the rosaries. Luna was looking at how people were fighting to stay in line with the fear on her face, and she was wondering where Superhuman was, and why he was not coming to protect those people by preventing them from wearing those rosaries. People were outside in the yard of the church, waiting their turn to get inside the church. Suddenly, they heard a voice who was screaming the name of Superhuman, and people started to turn around by looking everywhere, then some of them saw Superhuman in the space who was flying on the hawk.

And suddenly, there was a huge crowd and people started to run in all directions by screaming with fear on their faces, and there were people on the ground, and some people were falling on others, and kids were crying. Superhuman was in the space and he was trying to land at the door of the church, but it was impossible with the crowd who was there, then he looked at his magic palm and he saw a window. Then, he flew till to that window and he handed his magic hand through that window, and the sparks of fire started to get outside from his magic palm and went through the window and broke the window's glass. Everyone in the church had their head turned through the window where they were hearing the noises, and they saw Superhuman who was jumping from his hawk through the window.

Suddenly, everyone in the church started to scream by saying, "The wizard boy," and by running through the door, even the first person who was close to Hector to take his rosary ran away without taking it, except Luna who was running through Superhuman, there was the crowd inside the church people were screaming, crying and falling on the floor. King started to run through Superhuman with anger on his face, and Superhuman had held the hand of Luna, then Luna saw King who was running through them and she turned her head through Superhuman and she kissed him, then she asked him to not fight with King close to people. Because the sparks of fire that get outside from the magic palm of King was dangerous for people, then she ran away and Superhuman started to run through the corner where there were not people.

Hector was running through people with the rosaries in his hands, and he was trying to hand the rosaries to people who were running through outside, and suddenly he fainted on the floor and it was Luna who had knocked him by behind with the chair. People bent close to Hector trying to get those rosaries, and Luna screamed at them by telling them to not touch those rosaries to get outside and go back to their home, and no one touched those rosaries and they kept running through outside.

Luna stayed there to make sure that no one should touch those rosaries, while King and Superhuman were in the corridor fighting with the spark of fire, all journalists had run away, except the Journalist Liza who was still in the church by filming what was going on. After eleven minutes, the church was empty, and there were only Superhuman, Luna, and King in the church, also Hector who was still unconscious on the floor of the church.

Then, Superhuman ran through the table where there were the rosaries and he handed his magic hand through those rosaries, and the sparks of fire started to get outside from his magic palm and going through those rosaries. While King was behind Superhuman sending the sparks of fire through his back. Then, Superhuman ran till where Hector was lying on the floor and he handed his magic hand through those rosaries that were on the floor close to Hector, and the sparks of fire were getting outside from his magic palm going through those rosaries, and King was still behind Superhuman burning his body with the sparks of fire that were getting outside from his palm. And Superhuman was feeling pains on his back like he was focused on the rosaries and he was not defending himself from the sparks of fire that were getting outside from the palm of King. Then, Luna saw how Superhuman was suffering like King was sending the sparks of fire on his back, and she carried a chair and she ran behind King with that, then she knocked King with that chair, and King fainted on the floor.

Then, Superhuman turned through Luna and he held her hand by saying, "Let's go." And she looked into his eyes by saying, "Sorry, I can not go with you." And she added, "I have a deal with King and if I go with you, things will be worse because he will not hesitate to get his revenge on the whole planet." Then, she said, "Do not forget that King still has an advantage over us, who is in control of the storm and I can not take that risk to go with you and abandon the planet and all his inhabitants in the hands of King." Superhuman looked into her eyes without saying a word, and there was silence between both Superhuman and Luna, and they were just at looking each other eyes to eyes, then Luna walked two steps through him and she put her right hand on his cheek by still looking in his eyes, and she said, "Thank you for the wonderful job you just did." And she added, "Please, make sure to still have your eyes on the planet because King and Hector will not stop till they succeed to get what they want." Then, she kissed Superhuman and she said, "You must go now before King gets up." Superhuman turned and left. Then, Luna went, and she bent close to King and she started to shake him.

After a few minutes King got up, but Hector was still on the floor unconscious and they called an ambulance which took Hector to the hospital part of the palace. All people were in their house, they had locked their doors and windows with fear inside them, afraid that Superhuman would get inside their house with his hawk, they hated Superhuman and they were angry with Queen Mother like she was unable to kill Superhuman or to prevent him from destroying the planet. Hector had got up from his hospital's bed angrily with Luna like she had kissed Superhuman in the church, and he demanded King to kill Luna, but King refused by saying that he could not kill her not only because he loved her, but also because he was linked to her. And that the death of Luna would only make things worse because they needed her to realize their project, and King gave an example to Hector by saying that Hector could just see how things were worst and his magic was not working when Luna was unconscious.

Hector wanted to send policemen to the house of Philip to arrest Superhuman, but King told him that it would be useless that no one could arrest Superhuman now like Superhuman had the energy of his magic inside him as Luna kissed him in the church. That Superhuman could be arrested only after 72 hours when that energy inside him would be over or expired, and King told Hector that they had better start to work for the next meeting. Because Superhuman had destroyed all the rosaries that they had made with the sparks of fire coming from his magic hand, those rosaries were useless now, so those rosaries could not have affected people anymore. Because Superhuman had destroyed the energies that were on those rosaries, with the sparks of fire of his magic palm.

Luna was sent to jail by Hector because she had betrayed them by kissing Superhuman to the church, and she was sleeping on a wet floor. Superhuman and Philip were together, and Superhuman was watching Luna lying on the floor of her jail, through the palm of his magic hand, with anger on his face and he wanted to go to the palace. But Philip was trying to calm him by saying that it was not a solution to go to the palace, that things would be worse if he goes there.

The following day, there were a lot of people outside, although the fact that they were still afraid, and people were walking in the streets with their head lifted through the sky, to make sure that Superhuman was not flying above them on his hawk. Only Liza who had published what had happened yesterday to the church, there were the photos of Superhuman and King in front of newspapers fighting in the church with the sparks of fire, and with the headline like "The fight between the wizard boy and the magician boy." And there was another photo of Superhuman on the hawk in newspapers, and people were buying those newspapers to read what had happened in the church like everyone had run away after that they had seen Superhuman. The days were passing, and the name of Superhuman was still in the mouth of people, and they were still afraid.

After 72 hours, Hector sent the police to Philip's house to arrest Superhuman and Philip, but the police did not see them, despite the fact that the police had searched the whole house. Hector demanded King find Superhuman and Philip through his magic palm and to also check if they had left the planet, and King spent an entire day looking for Superhuman and Philip without succeess. And the magic of King told him that Superhuman and Philip were still living on the planet, then King and Hector were surprised, wondering where Superhuman and Philip were hiding inside the planet, for that the magic of king was unable to find them.

King told Hector that the only solution to find out where Superhuman and Philip were hiding it was to find the magic book because only the magic book had that secret, but still King was unable to find the magic book through his magic. Then, they went to the jail and they asked Luna to tell them where the magic book was, also where Philip and Superhuman were hiding in exchange for her freedom, but Luna just looked at them without saying a word. And before Hector and King left the jail of Luna, Hector talked to Luna that she would be released only when she would tell them where Superhuman, Philip, and the magic book were. Hector and King were in their office thinking, then Hector demanded King to send the storm outside to make the pressure on Superhuman and Luna, that with the storm Superhuman would show up, or Luna would tell them where the magic book was. And King wanted to send the storm as Hector asked but his magic told him that the storm outside now would be not the solution, then King and Philip decided to destroy the energy of the magic of Superhuman who was inside the body of Luna to make the magic of Superhuman useless, and for that, they released Luna from the jail because they could not destroy that energy when she was jail.

It was evening, Luna was in her bedroom sat on her bed, reading a book called Power of Kids by Thierry Kouam, that Maria gave her when she was released from jail, with Berly close to her, and she was wondering why King and Hector had released her from the jail, mostly that she did not say a word about the magic book, Superhuman, and Philip. And she was wondering too why King did not send the storm outside, to make pressure on Superhuman and her, and she was very afraid that King and Hector had another worst plan because she knew that King and Hector could not release her from jail for no reason.

Then, the door of her bedroom opened, and King walked inside and sat on the bed face to her and he looked into her eyes with a sad face, then he started to apologize for the bad way he treated her, and that if he sent her to jail it was because he was jealous like she had kissed Superhuman at the church. While Berly was looking at King with an angry face like King was talking to Luna, then Luna accepted the forgiveness of King, and she told him that she would always be the side of the planet, and she would never betray the planet. And that she would be against whoever would want to destroy the planet, even if it was Superhuman. Then she told King that she would help him if he was going to protect the planet, and she would not hesitate to betray Superhuman if Superhuman was going to destroy the planet.

Then, Luna showed to King the book that she was reading by telling him about the story of the book, how a young girl of her age fought against a monster and a lord who wanted to destroy a Kingdom, and that she would not hesitate to behave like that young girl, and that she was ready to fight even against Queen Mother to protect the planet. Then, King told her that they have to forget what happened during those last months, and focus on their love, then he moved his mouth through the mouth of Luna to kiss her, and suddenly Berly Jumped on King and prevented him from kissing Luna.

Then, Berly started to bark by looking at King angrily, and Luna was very surprised with the behavior of Berly through King, and she was trying to calm Berly, and it was when King left the room that Berly stayed quiet. The following day, Luna wanted to go to school, but King refused by saying that she could not go to school alone when he had not yet found out where Superhuman was hiding because he did not want her to see Superhuman and give him the energy of his magic.

The days were passing, and Luna was feeling lonely in the palace, she was spending her days with Berly that was always in her feet like her shadow, and she was sometimes talking with Maria, and their conversation was based on Queen Mother, Hector, and King. Luna was very surprised when Maria told her that it has been a while that nobody has seen Queen mother and that no one had an idea where Queen Mother was. Maria also told Luna that no one knew where King was coming from, that it was Hector who brought King to the palace after that Queen Mother had disappeared, and that since she born in that palace, it was the first time that Queen Mother disappeared, and that it was also the first time that the planet was living that curse that causes the disasters on the planet. But Luna did not say anything about herself and Superhuman to Maria, although the fact that Maria said that it was Superhuman who was responsible for those disasters on the planet. It has been the days now that Luna had not put her eyes on King because he was spending his whole days and nights in the office working with Hector. Luna was very worried about what King and Hector were doing in the office, mostly that Hector had announced another meeting that was going to take place in three weeks, and she was hoping that Superhuman was watching King and Hector be aware of what they intended to do.

Everything was going well on the planet like the days were passing, although the fact that people had still the fear inside them, and Superhuman was spending his time watching King and Hector through his magic palm, and he was also watching Luna make sure that she was doing well. Luna was still spending her time with Berly by thinking about what Maria had told her about Queen Mother, King, and Hector, and she was wondering where Queen Mother could be, and where King was coming from, and why Hector was working with King knowing that King was a wizard boy, but she was unable to answer one of her questions. It was the eve of the meeting day, Hector and King were in the office talking about the plan of the following day, about how they will control Luna to avoid her to approach Superhuman if Superhuman comes to that meeting, and they decided to not let Luna to the palace. Because Superhuman would be probably watching them through his magic hand, and Superhuman could come to the palace to get the energy of his magic to her and come to the meeting place to destroy their meeting. Then, they decided to use Luna to that meeting like a trap to catch Superhuman if Superhuman came, just that they should make sure that even the body of Luna would not be able to give the energy to the magic of Superhuman.

It was midnight, Superhuman was lying in his bed watching Hector and King through his magic palm, and he was aware of their plan to catch him, but at the same time, he was very afraid that Hector and King could find out the secret of Luna. Then, he got up from his bed and he took the small bag that was on his bed that he had put his clothes inside, and he carried that bag on his back, and he rushed through the kitchen. Then, he opened the fridge and he removed the thermos and he started to drink the content of that thermos, and he put back that thermos in that fridge. Then, he ran till outside and he used his magic hand to call the hawk, then he flew on his hawk till behind the former palace of the planet, and he started to fly at low altitude behind the walls of that palace, by looking at his magic palm, and he was seeing policemen in front of the place, and he was seeing people inside that palace too.

Then, he lifted his magic hand through his mouth and he asked his magic how he could get inside that palace, and a map appeared on his magic palm, and he followed that map, and he turned to the left side of the palace and saw a small window, and he handed his magic hand through that window and the sparks of fire started to get out from his palm and going through the window, and broken the window's glass. Then, Superhuman flew close to the window, and he jumped from his hawk and he held the window and the parts of glass that were on the window hurt him, then he jumped inside a washroom. Then, he tore his t-shirt and he made a bandage for his wound as he was bleeding to avoid his blood on the floor and that someone saw it and noticed that there was a stranger inside the palace.

Then, he looked at his magic palm and he saw the position of everyone who was inside the palace, and he got out of the washroom, and he started to walk through a corner by looking at his magic palm to make sure that nobody was coming through him. Then, he saw a door and he asked his magic if he could open that door to get inside the room, then the inside that room appeared on his magic palm, and he noticed that it was an empty bedroom, then he used his magic hand and he opened that door. And he got inside that room and he closed the door behind him, and he went under the bed, and he started to watch everything that was happening in that palace.

It was early morning, the streets were full, with parents and their kids walking through the former palace of the planet, where Hector had called for the meeting, everyone had the fear to see Superhuman to that meeting. They were all hoping that Superhuman would not come to destroy that meeting and that Hector, Queen Mother, and King would succeed in protecting them and protecting the planet. Luna was inside the huge room of the palace where the meeting was taking place, surrounded by policemen who were looking after her, to make sure that if Superhuman gets inside that room she would not approach him. And Hector had told those policemen that if Superhuman gets inside that room, they must carry Luna and get out with her, and Luna was looking tired because she had not closed her eyes during the whole night because she was thinking about that meeting.

The eyes of Luna were focuseded on the rosaries that were on the table front to Hector and King, and she was afraid people were getting inside the palace for the meeting. And Luna was afraid that she would be not able to protect Superhuman like she did last time by kissing him or by staying close to him, to make King and Hector believe that she was still the one who give the energy to the magic of Superhuman. Luna was very afraid that things could go wrong, and that King and Hector would find out that Superhuman had another way to get the energy of his magic who was still coming from her, but by another way that only her had the secret.

The meeting had started, and Hector was making the traditional speech, and the eyes of everyone were focuseded on Hector, even the policemen who were watching Luna. Except for Luna who was not paying attention to what Hector was saying. Luna had her eyes focused on the windows and the doors of the palace, to see if Superhuman was coming, and she had started to worry like she was not seeing Superhuman, and she was afraid that people would wear those rosaries that Hector and King had made. Suddenly, Luna started to feel the wind that was getting outside from her body, then she opened her mouth and cried out, "Superhuman?" But, no one heard her like they were all focused on Hector.

Then, Luna started to look around her, but she was not seeing Superhuman, but she was feeling that he was in the room because she was feeling the energy of his magic that came from outside of her body. Luna still had her eyes looking everywhere in the room, but still, she was not seeing Superhuman. And she said in her mind that she must move away to prevent policemen who were watching at her not to catch her when Superhuman would start to fight. And there King and Hector would not find out her secret, who was how she does to give the energy to the magic of Superhuman. And there, Hector and King would think that Superhuman was still getting that energy directly from her body.

Then, Luna lifted her head and she looked at those policemen who were there to watch at her, and she noticed that those policemen were not watching at her, but that they were watching at Hector. Then, Luna turned through her right side and she started to walk away, and she was walking among people without someone paying attention to her because everyone was concentrating to listen to Hector. After a couple of minutes, Hector had done with his speech, and people started to walk through him to get the rosaries, and the first person who was walking through Hector was a young boy who had worn black clothes and a cap, and he was bending his head like he was walking through Hector. And, that boy was a little bit far from the table that was in front of Hector, then he handed his right hand, and the sparks of fire started to get out from his palm going through the rosaries that were on the table. Suddenly, People started to scream in the room, by running through the outside door, and there were people on the floor, and other people were falling on them, while Superhuman and King were fighting with the sparks of fire.

Then, Superhuman noticed that the sparks of fire that were getting outside from the palm of King were going through people, and he started to run through a door where there were no people, and King started to run after him. While Hector was in the room looking for Luna among the crowd. And Luna was in the room looking for Superhuman, she had noticed that Superhuman and King were not in the room anymore, and she was wondering where they could be like she did not see them when they were running through a door. Then, Luna saw King who was coming from the door where he had followed Superhuman, but she did not see Superhuman with him, and she said in her mind that Superhuman would be out because if he was still inside the room, she should feel it through the energy of his magic getting outside from her body.

Then, Luna ran among the crowd till outside, and she was in the yard of the palace looking for Superhuman, and suddenly she saw Berly who was running through her with a pack of biscuits in his mouth. Then, Berly jumped on Luna, and she bent close to Berly and she took him in her arms, and she looked at Berly by asking, "Berly, what are you doing here?" Berly had put that pack of biscuits in the hand of Luna, and he had one of his front paws on that pack of biscuits that were in the hand of Luna, and he was looking at her.

And Luna was understanding that Berly was asking her to eat that pack of biscuits, and she started to remember the chocolate that Berly had given her to eat, and that after that she had eaten that chocolate, she got sick and she fainted in her jail. Luna asked Berly why she should eat that biscuit, but Berly was just making a sign to her to eat that biscuit, then Luna looked into his eyes by saying, "Berly, if only you could talk." And she started to look at that pack of the biscuit, and she noticed that she had never seen that biscuit, then she tore the packing of that biscuit, and she looked at the biscuit with a surprised face, then she looked at Berly by asking, "Where did you get this biscuit because I have never seen it." And she added, "I will eat this biscuit just to please you because you are my friend, and we do not refuse a gift coming from a good friend like you. Then, she said, "I hope that this biscuit will not make me sick, like chocolate you had given me." And she put the biscuit in her mouth, then she broke it with her teeth, and she started to chew.

Inside the meeting room was already empty, there were only a couple of people who were still on the floor, and King saw Hector who was front at the table looking at those rosaries that Superhuman had destroyed with a face full of anger and despair. Then, King walked to where Hector was, and he looked at Hector by saying, "We failed again." Hector replied, "Luna betrayed us again." And he added, "We must destroy that energy of the magic of Superhuman that is inside her. King said, "I have been busy those last weeks working on those rosaries, that I did not have time to destroy that energy that is inside her." And he added, "I will destroy that energy before tonight." Hector asked, "Where is she?" King replied, "I have no idea." Then, King asked his magic where Luna was, and he saw her on his magic palm outside playing with Berly, and he showed his magic palm to Hector and Hector was very surprised to see Luna and Berly outside, and they walked till outside where Luna was.

Then, Hector and King took Luna with them in the car, without saying a word to her and Luna wanted to get inside the car with Berly, but King refused, and Berly was running behind the car that they were inside. Luna sat in the seat behind in the middle of

King and Hector feeling sorry for Berly, and she was turning her head through Hector and King looking at them with silence and she could see the anger on their faces. Luna knew that Hector and King were angry because Superhuman had succeeded in preventing the meeting from happening. And she was afraid about what was going to happen not to her but to the whole planet.

Suddenly, Luna started to feel unwell, she was sweating and at the same time she was feeling cold till she was shaking, no one was understanding what was happening, and Hector ordered the driver to drive to the hospital that was close to where they were. Hector took off his jacket and he wore it on Luna, then King took her in his arms and his eyes were focused on her eyes, and he was asking her with a sad voice to not die now, and to not let him alone, that he really loved her, that he needed her, that they had a mission, to wake up for that they realize their mission and live their love. While Luna was looking back at King with a disappointment in her eyes, and she said to him with a sad voice, "Please, do not destroy the planet." And her eyes closed. Then, King started to shake her, by screaming her name with tears who were following down his cheeks, and Hector put his palm on the heart of Luna then he stared at King with a sad face, and there was silence. Then, after three seconds Hector opened his mouth and said with a sad voice "She is gone."

Suddenly, King screamed, and he laid the head of Luna on his knees, and he lifted his magic hand through his eyes, and he started to stare at his magic palm with his mouth opened, by breathing deeply, and with tears that were still flowing down his cheeks. Superhuman got inside the palace where the meeting had taken place, and the palace was empty, security men and people who work in that palace had run away. But there were three people who were lying on the floor, that the sparks of fire that had got outside of the magic hand of King had touched them, and Superhuman was there for those people, then Superhuman lifted his magic hand through his eyes and he read, "On time".

Then, Superhuman walked through them, and he put his magic palm on the forehead of those three people who were on the floor, and they got up and ran away once they saw Superhuman without even knowing that it was him who had just saved their life. Then,

Superhuman started to walk into the room by staring at the pictures that were on the wall, and those pictures were based on the history of the planet, then he saw a camera that was on the floor, and he looked at that camera and he noticed that the camera was on. Luna was lying in the hospital's bed breathing by oxygen, and King and Hector were in the room staring at her. Hector wanted to destroy the energy of the magic of Superhuman that was inside Luna, but King refused by saying that it was a risk to destroy that energy inside her now in her health's condition.

Because by destroying that energy of the magic of Superhuman inside her, an accident could happen, and that accident could affect his own magic to him, like himself he was connected to Luna. So, Hector could not anymore destroy that energy inside Luna because since the day where King made a mistake by showing his magic palm to Luna in the house of Philip things changed, and that day Luna got in contact with the magic of King like she was already naturally linked to him. And from that day, Hector lost his power to destroy that energy of the magic of Superhuman inside her because it was a big risk for the magic of King if Hector tried to destroy that energy inside Luna because by destroying that energy he could unknowingly destroy the link that connects Luna with the magic of King and if that link was destroyed it should have a big impact on the magic of King. So, there was only King now who was able to destroy that energy of the magic of Superhuman who was inside Luna, but it was completely impossible for King to destroy that energy when Luna was in the coma lying in the hospital's bed.

The following day, most people on the planet woke up with red eyes and headaches. No one had closed the eyes during the whole night because they had spent their night thinking about what had happened to the former palace. And Everyone had started to ask where Queen Mother was because no one had seen her since the months now, and for some people, she had run away by abandoning the planet to Hector and King. The parents of Superhuman were arrested on the order of Hector, and they were kept prisoners in the jail of the palace, and King had spent his entire day looking for Superhuman through his magic palm without success. Hector had made a speech in the news, where he told the whole planet to search for Superhuman, and that whoever who would see Superhuman must call the police, that Superhuman was still a danger for the planet and its inhabitants, and for that everyone must protect the planet by catching Superhuman. There were photos of Superhuman everywhere on the planet like a dangerous enemy.

The days were passing and no one on the planet had seen Superhuman, and King was still looking for Superhuman through his magic palm without success, and the house of Philip was appearing on the magic palm of King when he was looking for Superhuman, but all the rooms of Philip's house were empty, and King was not seeing Superhuman in Philip's house. King and Hector were completely lost, they were not understanding what was going on with the house of Philip because the magic of King was telling them that Superhuman was hiding in Philip's house, but when they were searching that house through the magic of King, they were not seeing Superhuman or Philip in that house.

They had even sent the police to Philip's house, but the police did not see someone. Hector and King knew that the magic of King could not lie or make a mistake, but they were not understanding why Superhuman was not appearing on the magic palm of King. Luna was still in the coma, while Superhuman was spending his days like his nights watching Luna lying in the hospital's bed and his parents in jail with a sad face. Superhuman wanted to go to the palace to help Luna, but Philip disagreed with that idea by saying to let Luna in the coma. That it was a good thing if she was in the coma. King and Hector had announced to the whole planet a new day of the blessing meeting that was going to happen in three weeks, and no one on the planet had reacted well about that new meeting.

Everyone was already tired about the blessing meeting, and they were saying that Queen Mother should arrest Superhuman first or kill him before trying to organize the meeting. Hector and King were sure that the new meeting that they were going to organize will not fail like the two last meetings because Luna was in a coma and there was no chance for Superhuman to destroy that new meeting as he did before like he did not have the energy of his magic inside him, and Luna should be unable to give him the energy of his magic like she was in the coma. After twenty- one days in a coma, Luna woke up, and she was doing well but she had pimples on her body as if she was suffering from chickenpox.

Everyone was happy to see that Luna had come out of the coma, but they were all surprised to see the pimples on her body, but the doctors just said that Luna was suffering from an allergy. Except for King who knew of what Luna was suffering for, and King told Hector that things were going worse for them, that he was unable to destroy the energy of the magic of Superhuman that was inside the body of Luna for the moment. Because his magic was an allergy to those pimples who were on Luna, and that it was dangerous for him to be in contact with the body of Luna, that for the moment there was nothing they could do except to wait till those pimples on the body of Luna disappear. But there was one thing that King was not understanding and it was what had caused those pimples of the body of Luna.

Then, King told Hector that those pimples on Luna's body isn't a sickness that they had another enemy who was in touch with Luna, and who was not Superhuman because Superhuman had no idea about the King's magic. And it was that unknown enemy who had caused those pimples on Luna's body to prevent him from destroying the energy of the magic of Superhuman that was inside the body of Luna. Then, King used his magic to find out how those pimples appeared on Luna's body, but unfortunately, he did not find it and he asked his magic who's the person closest to Luna, and the magic answered him that it was Maria. And King told Hector that it could not be Maria who was responsible for those pimples on Luna because Maria was a normal human being and that the one who made those pimples appear on Luna's body was not a normal human being but instead a ghost.

Then, King and Hector were spending their time trying to find that mysterious person who was close to Luna, and who had made those pimples appear on her body. Hector wanted to ask Luna the mysterious person who was close to her, but King disagreed with that idea of Hector, by saying that Luna would never tell them that mysterious person even if they threaten her to send the storm outside, that Luna would never betray people with who she was fighting for the same cause who was to protect the planet and his inhabitants. The situation was going harder for King and Hector, now that they had two enemies who were Superhuman and the mysterious ghost who was close to Luna, that they did not know. Then, King and Hector decided to postpone the meeting that was going to take place in two days for an unknown date because they were afraid that things could go wrong to that meeting, with the mysterious ghost that they could not control. Because they had no idea about who that ghost was, and it should not be good for them that the meeting fails again because the whole planet had started to lose confidence in them, and they did not want to take a risk.

King and Hector had planned to catch the mysterious ghost, and Superhuman and for that, they decided to follow Luna through the magic of King, then King allowed Luna to return to school when she would feel well. Superhuman had watched everything that had happened to the palace, and he was happy to see that Luna had woken up from the coma, but he was surprised to see those pimples on Luna's body. Then, Superhuman started to think about the mysterious ghost that he heard King and Hector talk about, and he checked through his magic to know who that mysterious ghost was, but his magic did not tell him who was that mysterious ghost. And Superhuman asked Philip about that mysterious ghost, but Philip answered him that he had no idea about that mysterious ghost.

It's been a week now, that Luna was going to school, and she was always wearing pants and shirts with long sleeves that covered her body because she still had those pimples on her body. But Luna was not welcomed in class by most of the students, except her old friend John, no one was talking with her and nobody wanted to work with her, even when the teacher was giving the workgroup, there was only John who agreed to work with her. Students were saying that she was the sweetheart of the wizard boy who was Superhuman, that she also had the wizard magic inside her.

After school, Luna was spending her time studying in her bedroom with Berly close to her, and she was thinking about Superhuman a lot, and she missed him a lot too, and when she was not studying, she was with Maria and Berly who was still in her feet. Luna had explained everything to Maria about Superhuman, King, and herself. Maria was very surprised about what she heard from

Luna, and Maria was not understanding the reasons why Hector and King wanted to destroy the planet. King and Superhuman were spending their time following Luna through their magic hands, and both wanted to know the mysterious ghost who had caused the pimples on the body of Luna. And King wanted also to catch Superhuman by following Luna through his magic palm, it was why he allowed Luna to go to school because he wanted Superhuman to approach Luna, and there he should see where Superhuman was hiding.

And since Luna had started school, King and Luna had not seen each other because Luna was busy with her studies, and King could not approach her because those pimples on her body were dangerous for his magic. Even though she was missing King a lot, and Luna was missing Superhuman too, then both King and Superhuman wanted to see her. And King decided to take a risk and to approach Luna even for a second despite the fact that there were still those pimples on her body because he was no longer supporting to stay without seeing her.

It was lunchtime at school, Luna and John were in the yard of school talking, then John saw King who was coming through them, and he smiled at Luna by saying, "King is coming." Luna turned her head and she saw King who was walking through them, and she looked at John by saying, "I wonder what he is doing here." John said, "It's obvious that he is here for you." Luna said, "I am very surprised because since I got out of the coma, we have not seen each other, and we are living in the same house, so why did he come here to see me, while he can see me at home if he wants." John smiled at her by saying, "I am pretty sure that you missed him, and he decided to make you a surprise." Luna said, "It's obvious that we will not spend our break time together." John said, "I am a little bit jealous because I like to have you every moment." Luna smiled at him by saying, "Do not be jealous."

Then, she turned her head and she saw King who was close to her, then she opened her arms through John by smiling at him, then John walked two steps through her, and they hugged. King was close to Luna and John and he was looking at them angrily how they had taken each other in their arms by smiling, and John had given his back to King. And King lost control of his anger and the jealousy to see Luna in the arms of John made him crazy.

Then, King without thinking handed his magic hand through the back of John, and the sparks of fire got out from his palm and went through the back of John. Suddenly, Luna started to scream like she was seeing the sparks of fire getting outside from the palm of King, and suddenly John fell on the ground like a dead body with his eyes closed. And Luna bent close to the body of John and she started to shake him by calling his name with tears who were flowing down her cheeks. John was surrounded by students who were looking at him with tears flowing down their cheeks, while other students were looking at King with a surprised face, and they were not understanding that it was King who had made John fainted.

Then, some students bent, and they put their hand on John's heart and they noticed that John's heart was not beating anymore. And one of the students looked at Luna by saying, "He is gone" with a sad voice. Luna looked at the dead body of John on the ground with her mouth opened, unable to say something, and with her face wet with tears, then she lifted her head and she looked at King by asking, "Why did you kill John?" King looked at her without saying a word, then he turned and left. Luna was crying on the dead body of John, and there were students and instructors who were coming to see what happened to John. Then, a student saw Superhuman who was coming through them, and that student stared at Superhuman with a surprised face, and there was fear on the face of that student, then that student started to walk away without saying a word. Then, other students saw Superhuman too, and they started to run away, and one of them screamed by saying, "Superhuman is coming."

Everyone turned their head and they saw Superhuman, and a voice said, "Let's run away and call the police that the wizard boy is here." Then, Luna lifted her head and she saw Superhuman who was coming, and she noticed that people were running away, and she said, "You do not need to run away because Superhuman is not the wizard boy but instead the magician boy, so he can not hurt us or do something bad to us." Everyone was walking by behind with a heart that was beating faster than normal as Superhuman was approaching them, and they were all ready to run away, and they had made a huge space because they did not want to be close to Superhuman.

After a couple of seconds, Superhuman was close to the dead body of John, and Luna lifted her head looking at him with tears in her eyes, and she said with a sad voice, "Please, save John." Everyone was looking at the magic hand of Superhuman like the light was shining on that hand, then Superhuman lifted his magic hand and he looked at his magic palm and he read, "You have nine seconds."

Then immediately, Superhuman bent close to the dead body of John, and he put his magic palm on the forehead of John without saying a word. The eyes of everyone were focused on the magic hand of Superhuman who was on John's forehead, and they were all seeing the light that was shining between the palm of Superhuman and John's forehead. After nine minutes, John opened his eyes and he started to breathe deeply like if he was running, and everyone was looking at John with an amazed face and most of them had the mouth opened but no word was coming out, it was a miracle for all of them, and some of them turned their eyes on Superhuman looking at him with a surprised face without really understand what was going on, they were not realizing that it was Superhuman who had just saved John.

Then, Superhuman grabbed the hands of John and he helped John to get up, and he looked at John by asking, "How do you feel?" John looked around him and he was amazed to see that everyone was staring at him with a surprised face, and he asked, "What is going on here?" No one answers the question of John, then Luna walked two steps through John, and she handed her both hands to John, and she held both his hands, by looking into his eyes, then she asked, "Are you doing well?" John was staring at Luna with a surprised face, and he asked, "Why are you crying?" Luna said, "Please, just tell me how you are doing."

John turned his head and he looked at people around him, and he noticed that most of them had cried and that their eyes were still wet, and he turned his head looking at Luna and by asking, "Can you tell me what is going on here?" Luna was just looking at him without saying a word, everyone was quiet even the instructors. After three minutes, Superhuman broke the silence by asking,

"John, did you remember what happened?" John replied, "It's the question that I am asking here in the past ten minutes, and no one is answering me." Superhuman looked into John's eyes by saying, "You were unconscious, and everyone thought that you were dead." John cried out, "dead?" With a surprised face, then he asked, "How unconscious?" Superhuman looked at John by answering, "You were talking with Luna, and you suddenly fainted on the ground, that's the reason why we are all here with tears in our eyes because we were afraid that you'll die."

Most of them took a deep breath, and an instructor looked at John by saying, "It's exactly what happened." John said, "I do not remember that I fainted." And he added, "What I remember it's that I was here talking with Luna, and we saw King who was coming to see her, then Luna and I hugged by saying that we will see each other later in class because she was going to spend her break time with King." Luna looked at John by saying, "It's exactly what happened." And she added, "You fainted when you were in my arms." John said, "Still I do not remember when I fainted. And he asked, "Where is King?" Luna answered, "King left a couple of minutes ago." John looked at Superhuman by asking, "What are you doing here?" Superhuman answered, "I was hanging outside, and I decided to come visit here." John said, "You are taking a risk by hanging outside like that because everyone is looking for you like they all think that you are the wizard boy." Superhuman asked, "And do you think that I am a wizard boy?" John took a deep breath and he looked at Superhuman by saying, "It's true that we are not best friends, but we have known each other since kindergarten where we played and cried together."

Then, John paused, and everyone was looking at him, and he went on by saying, "It's true that you changed a lot, you ran away from your house without even saying a word to your parents." And he added, "Since the months now you are doing incredible things, that no one can understand or explain it, but I know that you are unable to hurt someone, and I have no doubt that you are not the wizard boy, but instead the magician boy." Superhuman looked at John by saying, "Thank you so much." And he added, "You are only the person who trusts me on this planet." Then he handed his hand to John, and John shook his hand, and both smiled. Then, John said,

"I am not only the person who trusts in you because even Luna has no doubt that you are the magician boy who is fighting to protect our planet."

Then, a student looked at Superhuman by saying, "Me too, I trust in you now." Another student said, "I have no doubt now that Superhuman is a magician boy, not a wizard boy." Then, a student named Alex walked till face to Superhuman, and he looked at him by saying, "Couple months ago, you released us from the buses in this school when we were locked inside those buses, and now you just saved John's life, without forgetting what you had done a few months ago in the lunchroom with the microwaves." And he added, "It's true that everyone is wondering why you destroyed the blessing's meeting of Queen Mother who is our god, that she organized to bless us and to protect the planet, but only you know the reasons why you prevented those blessing's meeting to happen. But now I am sure that if you destroyed those blessing's meeting it's because you have a good reason, and now for me, you are the magician boy, not the wizard boy." Superhuman smiled at Alex by saying, "I thank you all for your support, and I am very grateful." Then, he took Alex in his arms.

Suddenly, almost all students started to scream by saying that we trust in Superhuman too, and he is a magician boy, not a wizard boy, but there were few students who were quiet and those few students still had doubts about Superhuman. Then, an instructor demanded students to return to their classrooms because the break time was over, and a former classmate of Superhuman said that Superhuman was coming into the classroom with them. The instructors said that Superhuman could not get inside the classroom because he was banned from education on the planet by Queen Mother. And the students like Alex and John decided that they were not going to class if Superhuman was not coming with them, and most of the students joined the idea of Alex and John, although the fact that Superhuman was trying to convince them to return to class without him, some students refused by saying that they were all a family and that they must support Superhuman who was their brother.

The instructors were very surprised by the support that students were giving to Superhuman, and they did not know what to do because even Superhuman was unable to convince the students to go to class without him. Then, the manager of the school, unable to control the situation, demanded that the students go home and come back the next day. And Alex told the manager that even the next day if Superhuman was not in a class, they would not get inside the classrooms because they could not be studying while Superhuman is at home. Luna was quiet with a beautiful smile on her face, happy and very surprised at the same time by seeing how suddenly people started to love Superhuman.

Superhuman thanked students and instructors, and he told them that he was very busy now and that he had no time for education at the moment, and he turned to go, but Alex grabbed his hand by saying, "If you go, we will go with you." Most of the students started to clap their hands by supporting the idea of Alex, and the manager of the school agreed that Superhuman would come to school the following day, but that it would be their secret because if someone was aware of that they would be all in trouble, and Queen Mother would not hesitate to close the school.

Almost all students were happy with the decision of the manager, and they decided to return to the classrooms to finish their courses, although the fact that they were hungry like King had spoiled their break time by preventing them from eating with what he did to John. And there were also some students who were not happy at all with the decision of the school manager because they were afraid of Superhuman, and for them, Superhuman was still the wizard boy, even if he had saved the life of John. Superhuman was very happy to go into the classroom with his former classmates, even like it was just for a couple of hours. Because he knew that he should not come to class the following day not only because he did not want to take a risk to put the lives of students and instructors in danger, but also because he was busy following King.

Superhuman was in the classroom and sat close to Alex, and they were talking like old friends till they were not paying attention to what the teacher was saying in front of the class, and Superhuman was always checking his magic hand to make sure that King was not aware of what was going on at school. After school, Superhuman and Luna went to talk together, and both were so happy to see each other again, and Luna asked Superhuman how he succeeded to arrive on time to save John. Superhuman answered to Luna that he was already at school when King tried to kill John, that he was hidden behind the wall of school watching everything through his magic hand. And that he was at home watching television and the light started to shine on his magic hand, and he tried to know the reasons why the light was shining, then he talked with his magic and his magic asked him to follow King.

Then, he followed King and he noticed that King was coming to school, then he picked the car and he drove as fast as he could to make sure to arrive at school before King, to be able to prevent King from causing a disaster. Then, Superhuman asked Luna about the pimples that were on her body, and the mysterious ghost. And Luna answered him that she had no idea about how those pimples appeared on her body and that doctors said that it was an allergy. Luna was very surprised when Superhuman told her about the mysterious ghost, and she said that she had no idea about the mysterious ghost, and Superhuman told her that he heard about the mysterious ghost in the mouth of King. Then, he told everything to Luna, how King and Hector organized a plan to catch himself and the mysterious ghost by using her.

Superhuman did not want Luna to return to the palace, but Luna told him that she could not run away from King because the only way to save the planet and to prevent King from destroying the planet, was her presence close to him to have eyes on everything he intended to do. Also, to keep their secret she should stay close to King because if he finds out that secret, he would not hesitate to kill all inhabitants of the planet, then Superhuman agreed that she returns to the palace, despite the fact that it was hard for both to live separately.

King had told Hector what had happened to the school, that he killed an old classmate named John when he saw Luna in his arms. Hector was very mad, and he told King that King should control his jealousy and that he should ban Luna from returning to school. Hector was very worried about what people should think when they would hear that the one who was supposed to protect the planet, the one he named the angel of the planet, the magician boy of the planet killed someone for no reason. Luna was in her bedroom with Maria, and she had told Maria what had happened to the school, and Maria was very surprised to hear what King had done, but she was happy to know that Superhuman had arrived on time to save John. And Luna slept without seeing King.

Superhuman had told Philip what had happened to school too, and Philip was not really surprised about what King did. All students of that school had told their parents, siblings, and friends what had happened to the school, and everyone was surprised to hear that King who was the magician boy of the planet killed someone and that it was Superhuman who was the wizard boy of the planet who saved that person that King killed. And no one believed it, and everyone said that it was a joke, by saying that everyone could kill someone except King because King was born for the good things and to save people and that everyone could save someone except Superhuman because Superhuman was born for the dreadful things and to destroy people.

The following day, it was early morning all people were running through where Liza was working to get a newspaper. Liza was the only journalist who had written about what had happened to the school about Superhuman and King, and other journalists were aware of that story, but they did not believe that King killed someone and that Superhuman resurrected that person who was killed by King, and they refused to write about that story by saying that it was jokes. Liza had put the pictures of King and Superhuman in front of her newspapers, with the headline like "Who is the magician boy and who is the wizard boy?" People were completely lost when they were reading newspapers, they did not understand how King who lived in the palace with Queen Mother, who was their god, killed someone, and that it was Superhuman who was trying to destroy the planet who resurrected that person that King killed.

That story in the newspapers was unbelievable for everyone, and they were saying that it was not true because first, no one could resurrect someone, and that even Queen Mother who was god had never resurrected a dead person, and that it was impossible for Superhuman the wizard boy who had the bad magic that could only destroy to resurrect a dead person. Only students and instructors who were at school and who had seen with their both eyes what had happened, knew that that story in newspapers was true, and themselves they were wondering how King, who lived in the palace, like the son of Queen Mother, tried to kill John.

And they were wondering the reasons why King wanted to kill John, and most of the classmates of john and Luna knew that it had been a while that King was in love with Luna, even their instructor knew that. And they started to think that King tried to kill John because he was jealous because it was obvious to everyone that John was in love with Luna too. And they started to think that it could be the same reasons why King and Superhuman were fighting because Superhuman and Luna were in a relationship before, and now Luna lived in the palace and she would be probably in a relationship with King too. King was in his bedroom deeply asleep, and the door opened, then King opened his eyes and he saw Hector who was walking inside with an angry face with a newspaper in his hand. Then, Hector threw that newspaper he had in his hand on King without saying a word, and King got up and he sat on the bed with the blanket on his feet, and he took that newspaper and he started to read with a surprised face.

Then King looked at Hector by saying, "It can not be possible." Hector replied, "You have the evidence in your hands." King said, "Superhuman can not resurrect someone, he can only save someone when that person is not yet dead." And he added, "When I left school yesterday John was already dead." Hector said, "You can check by yourself through your magic." Then, King lifted his magic hand through his mouth, and he asked his magic to show him John his former classmate, and he looked at his magic palm with an amazed face like he was seeing John who was getting ready to go to school.

Then, he jumped from his bed angrily, trying to get outside and Hector prevented him from getting out by asking, "Where are you going?" And King answered that Luna betrayed them for the third time and that it was the time to act. Hector told King that they had a more important problem to solve now, that the whole planet would be doubting about them now with that news in newspapers, then he demanded King to check what people think about that story in newspapers.

King checked through his magic the opinion of people about that story in newspapers, and his magic told him that except students of school and instructors who had seen what had happened, no one else believed that story. King and Hector were very happy that most people did not believe that story in newspapers, and King asked Hector to close that school and punish the students and instructors of that school. But Hector refused by saying that if they close that school, it would catch the attention of people and they would start to think that it may be true that story in the newspapers.

And Hector told King that Luna was only responsible for what had happened to school and that she was only the one who should be punished. Because she was still giving the energy to Superhuman, and that if Superhuman had succeeded to save John it means that Luna had kissed him. Because for that Superhuman saves someone who was dying, he needed to have the energy inside his body because only the energy that was coming from the body of Luna could not help him to save someone who was dying.

Suddenly, King ran through the door angrily, and he went to ask the security men to put Luna in jail, and Luna was arrested when she was kissing Maria to go to school, and she was kept prisoner in a dark jail. After three days, the whole planet had already forgotten what had happened to the school, and Luna was still in her dark jail, and she was sleeping on the floor because there was not the bed or the mattress in that jail, and she was receiving food from a housekeeper. Superhuman was spending his time watching Luna in her jail, through his magic hand with the tears in his eyes, he was suffering by watching Luna in that jail, and he wanted to go to that jail to release Luna, but Philip prevented him from doing it.

Maria was very sad, and she was spending her time crying, feeling useless and weak, unable to save Luna who was in jail, while Berly was spending his time barking in front of the jail door of Luna. John had gone to the palace to see Luna, but security men kicked him out violently, and he was very worried for Luna like she was not coming to class. And John knew that something was going wrong in the palace, and that probably Luna was in danger and he started to think about how to save Luna. King and Hector were spending their time thinking about what to do, King was still looking for

Superhuman, and he was watching Luna from her jail through his magic palm to know if the mysterious ghost was visiting her.

King told Hector that they should release Luna from the jail and send the storm outside so that it was the only solution to trap Superhuman or to know the mysterious ghost. But Hector refused by saying that they could not send the storm outside now. Because with what had happened to school four days ago it would increase the doubt of people. Mostly that all students and instructors of that school, already knew that it was not Superhuman who was responsible for all disasters that were happening on the planet like he had saved the life of John.

It was evening, Liza sat in her living room, drinking tea by watching the news, and she heard the doorbell rang, and she looked at the clock on the wall and she noticed that it was 11:00 p.m., and she got up from her chair by wondering who was ringing at her door at that time. Then, Liza walked the door, and she opened the door and she saw a young boy in front of her who was staring at her with silence. Liza looked at him with a surprised face for three minutes without saying a word, then Liza broke the silence by asking, "Are you, John?"

The young boy answered, "Yes, I am John."

Liza asked, "What are you doing here?"

John replied, "I know that you wanted to talk to me four days ago about what happened to the school."

Liza said, "Yes, but your parents refused me to interview you, and they forbade me to approach you." John looked Liza in her eyes by saying, "I am here to talk with you."

Liza asked, "Do your parents know that you are here?"

John replied, "Nobody knows that I am here."

Liza said, "It's too late to be out at this time mostly for a kid of your age, so I will drive you to your home." John said, "I am not anymore a kid."

Liza said, "You are a teenager who it's not different from a kid."

John said, "You have to listen to me first."

Liza said, "You are underage, and I can not listen to you or take your statement without the authorization of your parents."

John said, "You must listen to me."

Liza said, "Sorry, I can not because it's against the law like you are just a teenager." And she added, "Let me grab my key's car, then I will drive you to your home."

Then, Liza turned, and she walked inside the living room and John followed her inside. It was early morning, people were full front of the press's house of Liza buying newspapers, Liza had written a short story about Superhuman, Luna, and King. And Liza had put the pictures of three of them in front of the newspapers with Luna in the middle of Superhuman and King, with the headline like "The war of love between the magician boy and the Wizard boy." People were reading newspapers, and they were very surprised, and they were wondering if all the disasters and the tragedies that were happening on the planet since the months now, and the torture that they were all living every day, also the fear that they were living with every second, it was just because Superhuman and King wanted to win the heart of Luna.

People were wondering if Superhuman and King were destroying the planet just for the love that they had for Luna, and everyone was completely lost mostly when they read that Luna was in danger in the palace, that King had kidnapped Luna and that it had been four days now that no one had seen her. People were wondering how Luna could be in danger in the palace close to King who loved her, and that story in the newspapers was not making any sense for people. Luna sat on the floor inside her jail, very tired thinking about the planet and very worried for all people living on the planet, then she heard the footsteps and she turned her head through her left side, and he saw a security man who was walking through her.

The security man walked till face to her and he told her that she was free and that King and Hector wanted to see her, then Luna got up and she walked to the living room where she met King and Hector, and both King and Hector had newspapers in their hands. Luna was face to Hector and King staring at them with silence, while they were staring back at her without saying a word too. After a minute, King handed the newspaper he had in his hand to Luna without saying a word, and Luna took that newspaper in the hand of King without saying a word too. Then, Luna looked at the front of the newspaper and suddenly her face changed like she saw her picture in the middle of pictures of King and Superhuman, then she started to read. After a few minutes, Luna lifted her head and she looked at King by asking, "Who did it?"

King answered, "Of course that it's your lover."

Luna said, "It's impossible that it's Superhuman because he can not take this kind of risk."

King replied, "It's your other sweetheart."

Luna cried out, "You?" by looking at King with a surprised face.

King replied, "Not me, but your foolish lover named John."

Luna cried out, "John? And she asked, "Why did John do it?"

King replied, "Of course that he was worried for you like you were not coming to school, and he even came here to see you, but I ordered security men to kick him out, then he chose to go see the journalist."

Luna said, "There is no place in the newspaper who mentioned that it's John who is responsible for it." King said, "Do not forget that I am a wizard boy." And he added, "I found out that it's John through my magic hand."

Hector looked at Luna by saying, "John saved you and he released you from the jail." And he added, "I hope that you are going to save him too."

Luna asked, "What do you mean?"

King replied, "Last time John was lucky that Superhuman arrived on time to save him, but this time he will not have that chance anymore."

Luna looked in the eyes of King by saying, "John did not say anything bad about you, he even did not mention the fact that you tried to kill him. And the newspaper talked about you and Superhuman in the same way, with the same question wondering the magician boy and the wizard boy between both of you."

King said, "The bigger sin of John was to put his eyes on you, he should never fall in love with you."

Luna asked, "It's the reason why you tried to kill him a couple of days ago?"

King replied, "I did what any man who loves his fiancé should do." And he added, "I came to school that day to spend lunchtime with you like it was the weeks that we had not seen each other since you had come out of the coma. And I wanted to show you my love, but when I arrived at school, I saw you in the arms of John and I did not control my jealousy."

Luna said, "That's interesting, your way to show me your love, like by destroying the planet, killing people like the doctor you killed in front of me in my bedroom hospital, and by sending me to jail."

King said, "The only responsible for those things you just quoted is you." And he added, "I know that I had promised you to not send you to jail again, but I felt betrayed when I found out that you kissed Superhuman, and in my anger, I sent you to jail."

Luna cried out, "Kissed Superhuman?"

King said, "Superhuman can not save someone who is dying without the energy of his magic inside him, even if you are close to him because the energy that is coming from your body is not strong enough for that Superhuman saves someone who is dying, so you kissed Superhuman for that he saves John."

Luna looked at King with a surprised face, and she said in her head, I am wondering if it's the magic of King who told him that I kissed Superhuman for that Superhuman saves John because I did not kiss Superhuman that day he saved John. But, it's better than King thinks that I kissed Superhuman than to think that there was another way for Superhuman to get the energy of his magic because if King finds out that secret I have, everything will be over not only for me but even for the planet. Then, she opened her mouth and asked, "It's your magic who told you that I kissed Superhuman?"

King replied, "I did not need to ask my magic because it's written in the magic book that the magician boy can only save someone who is dying with the energy of his magic inside him." And Luna said in her head that if King knew it from the magic book, it meant that he could know my secret too, then she opened her mouth and she asked, "Have you ever read that magic book?"

King answered, "No." And he added, "But Hector read one part of that magic book."

Luna asked, "Would you know the contents of that magic book through your magic?"

King replied, "No." And he added, "The only way to know the contain of that magic book it's to read it." Luna said in her head I understand now, why they have no idea about that secret.

Hector looked at Luna by saying, "The journalists are waiting."

Luna asked, "Which journalists?"

Then, King told Luna that they released her from jail because they wanted her to talk to journalists, and Luna refused by saying that she prefers to return to jail than to lie to the whole planet by telling the good things about King. But King told her that he would kill John if she refused to talk to journalists, then Luna agreed to talk to journalists because she did not want the worst to happen. It was evening, the whole planet was at home in front of their television watching Luna in the news, who was talking about her relationship with King, and she said that she was not at school for four days because she was sick, and that King and she are fiancés and that everything was going well. Liza was in her living room, sat in front of the television with a book on the table that was in front of her, and with a pencil in her hand, watching Luna in the news by taking notes. Then, Liza heard the doorbell rang, and she got up from her chair and she walked to the door, and she opened the door, and she was face to a young boy who had short hair and blue eyes. Liza was looking at that young boy with a surprised face without saying a word, then that young boy handed his right hand to her by saying, "My name is Jack."

Liza shook his hand by saying, "I am Liza."

Jack said, "I am here because I want to talk with you."

Liza asked, "About what?"

Jack answered, "About Superhuman."

Suddenly, the face of Liza changed, and she was looking at Jack with a startled face, and after a minute without talking she broke the silence by asking, "Do you know Superhuman?"

Jack answered, "Not really."

Liza asked, "What do you mean by that?"

Jack replied, "I met Superhuman a couple of times."

Liza asked, "Where Superhuman hides?"

Jack replied, "I have no idea."

Liza asked, "How and where did you meet Superhuman?"

Jack asked, "Are we going to talk here?"

Liza said, "Sorry, I forgot to invite you inside."

Then, Liza moved at the door, and Jack walked inside, and she followed him behind. Liza showed Jack a place where he got a sit and she served him an orange juice, then she moved a chair and she sat face to him. And Jack told Liza that he came to see her because he noticed that she was the only journalist who was interested in what was happening on the planet, and who was interested in the story of Superhuman and King, to know the magician boy and the wizard boy between both. Then, Jack told Liza that he had no doubt that Superhuman was the magician boy. And Liza looked at him very surprised with her mouth opened, and she demanded Jack why he was saying that Superhuman was the magician boy? And Jack answered her that a couple of months ago, it was a Tuesday at 8:00 a.m., he was on the bus going to school and the bus started to shake, by going faster and everyone on the bus was screaming. And there were people in the bus who were falling, while other people were holding the chairs, or the irons of the bus to not fall, and other people were hitting themselves against the bus, and the driver had already lost control of the bus.

Jack went on by saying that everyone was already dead in that bus, and no one could imagine getting out of that bus alive, then he saw a young boy got up from the chair who was in front of him, and that young boy ran without a problem till the seat of the driver although the fact that the bus was shaking. Then, that young boy held the wheel with his hands, and suddenly the bus stopped to shake, and the bus stopped to go faster, then all people who were on the floor in the bus got up, and everyone in the bus was looking at that young boy with a surprised face, even the driver who was close to him. It was like a miracle that was happening, then that young boy controlled the bus till the next stop, where he parked the bus, and he got off the bus without saying a word, and it was the first time that I was seeing that young boy.

Liza asked, "Who was that young boy?"

Jack answered, "It was Superhuman."

Liza looked at Jack without an expression on her face, and without saying any word, then there was silence between both. After two minutes, Jack broke the silence by saying, "It seems that you are not surprised by what I just told you."

Liza took a deep breath, and she replied, "Not really." And she added, "I received a childhood friend of Superhuman here yesterday, who told me the good things about Superhuman too, and that childhood friend of Superhuman believes too that Superhuman is a magician boy."

Jack asked, "Why did you not publish it in the newspapers that Superhuman is the magician boy?"

Liza replied, "That boy of yesterday is a young boy like you, and probably the same age as you, who is underage, so without the pieces of evidence, I can not publish something like that mostly coming from an underage person."

Jack asked, "You mean that you are not going to publish what I just told you?"

Liza answered, "I can not without the evidence." And she added, "Do not forget that if Superhuman is really the magician boy, it means that King is the wizard boy."

Jack said, "It's been weeks now that I am thinking about the identity of King, about who he is, and I tried to make the investigations and I found out that no one knows King on this planet."

Liza said, "It's been months now that I am trying to know where King comes from, but I found no result on him, and no one knows his parents or his ancestors on this planet. And I found out that the only school that King went to on this planet it's that school where he tried to kill John, and Superhuman was going to that school too."

Jack looked in the eyes of Liza by saying, "It can not be a coincidence that in all schools of this planet King who is coming from nowhere chose to go to the same school where Superhuman was going."

Liza asked, "What do you mean?"

Jack replied, "If King went to that school it's because there was a reason."

Liza looked at Jack with a surprised face and she said, "I understand everything now."

Jack asked, "What do you mean?"

Liza said, "According to John, that childhood friend of Superhuman, and who is the classmate of King and superhuman, all disasters started to happen in class when King arrived. And once when superhuman had been arrested those disasters stopped only for three days, but after there were still the disasters that were happening in school, and those disasters stopped only when King stopped to come to school."

Jack said, "It means that King caused those disasters for that Superhuman to be arrested."

Liza said, "Exactly." And she added, "King lied to the whole planet even to our god Queen Mother because she thinks that King is a magician boy who is here to help the planet, and to fight against Superhuman that we all think that he is the wizard boy." And she added, "I still remember the attitude of King the day he talked to my mike when the tragedy had happened in the lunchroom of his school."

Jack asked, "How was his attitude?"

Liza answered, "King was the only student who was not afraid that day, and he was confident enough till he told me that he was a brave boy, and when I asked him what he thought about that tragedy that had happened, he answered me that it was the wizard magic that had provoked that tragedy."

Jack said, "It's obvious that King is the wizard boy." And he added. "We must help Superhuman to fight King."

Liza asked, "How?" And she added, "No one knows where Superhuman hides."

Jack said, "We have to let everyone know that King is the wizard boy."

Liza said, "We need evidence to convince people because no one believes what I write in my newspapers."

Jack said, "The last meeting that happened in the former palace, Superhuman saved my life and the life of other people too, so you can use that like evidence."

Liza asked, "How?"

Jack replied, "There was the crowd in the room that day, and people were running in all senses, and I do not know what happened. I found myself unconscious on the floor, then when I opened my eyes, I saw Superhuman who was bent close to me looking in my eyes. And I suddenly got up and ran away, but when I was getting out, I turned my head and I saw Superhuman who was putting his right palm on the forehead of the rest of the two people who were unconscious on the floor, and that's how those two-people got up and ran away." Suddenly, Liza cried out, "My camera."

Then, Liza got up from her chair and she ran through the door that was face to her, and after half a minute, she came back with the car's key in her hand. And she told Jack that she lost one of her cameras and that she was filming the blessing meeting that day in the former palace with that camera. Then both went to that former palace to search that camera. The whole planet was disappointed with the speech of Luna on the television, everyone was expecting Luna to talk about Superhuman in her speech, to tell them the reasons why Superhuman was trying to destroy the planet, and to talk about where he hides.

People were wondering who was really Luna? And how did she know both Superhuman and King? Superhuman was very angry with Luna like she told in her speech that she was the fiancée of King, despite the fact that he knew that she did that speech to avoid that King to kill John. And King was very angry with Luna too, like in her speech she did not talk that Superhuman was the wizard boy of the planet, and the one who was trying to destroy the planet.

It was 7:00 a.m., There was a crowd in front of the house of newspapers of Liza, people were fighting to get a newspaper. Liza had published the whole story that Jack had told her last night, how Superhuman had saved people in the bus, and how Superhuman had saved people in the former palace of the last meeting. Liza had found her camera that she had lost in the former palace, the housekeepers who work inside that palace had found that camera, and they kept it without watching the content of the camera, and when Liza got that camera, she watched the content, and like the camera was turned on that day, the camera had filmed everything. Liza and Jack had found the evidence that they were looking for. And there were the pictures of Superhuman in front of newspapers with the headline like "The magician boy of the planet." And there were also some photos of Superhuman in the newspapers who were showing how he was saving people who were unconscious on the floor in the former palace. Liza had also put the pictures of King in the newspapers with the questions above his photos like "Who is king? Where does the King come from? What does he want?"

The doubt had started to settle inside everyone who was reading those newspapers. Everyone who was reading the newspaper was very surprised by what they were reading about Superhuman, and they were wondering if it was true. King was in his bed deeply asleep, then the door opened, and Hector walked inside, and he saw King deeply asleep in the bed, then he screamed the name of King three times, and King opened his eyes and King turned on the bed, then King saw Hector who was staring at him.

King looked at Hector by asking, "What is going on?"

Hector replied, "I have no idea."

King asked, "Why did you wake me up?"

Hector replied, "That journalist named Liza will not let us work in peace."

King asked, "What did she do?"

Hector replied, "I heard that there is a large crowd in front of her newspaper house fighting to buy the newspapers."

King asked, "What did she write this time?"

Hector replied, "I am here because I want you to find out what she published."

King lifted his magic hand through his mouth, and he talked to his magic, then he looked at his magic palm and he started to read all the content of the newspapers that Liza had published through his magic palm. Suddenly, the face of King changed, and he opened his mouth and he talked to his magic, while Hector was just looking at him with a surprised face, and Hector turned his head through the window and he noticed that there was a storm outside.

Hector said, "You sent the storm outside."

King lifted his head and looked at Hector by saying, "It's the only solution to prevent people to keep reading those newspapers that Liza published." And he added, "All people who have already read the content of those newspapers will forget about that because they will be focused on thinking about that storm outside, and how to return to their house."

Hector asked, "What Liza wrote this time."

King said, "We have another enemy who is Liza, and she is more dangerous than Superhuman and the mysterious ghost that we still do not know who it's. Because Superhuman and the mysterious ghost are just acting without talking, but that cursed journalist called Liza talks too much, and she will make us lose the confidence of inhabitants of the planet."

Then, the door opened, and Luna walked inside angrily, and she looked at King by saying, "We have an agreement."

King looked at Luna by saying, "I know it."

Luna said, "It seems that you forgot it because there is a storm outside."

King got up from his bed and he walked three steps in front of Luna, and he looked at her by saying, "The only one who's responsible for that storm outside it's Liza because she spent her whole night writing things against me."

Luna asked, "Can I see what she wrote against you?"

King replied, "I do not have a newspaper with me."

Luna asked, "How did you know that what she wrote is against you if you have not read the content of newspapers?"

King replied, "I read the content of those newspapers through my magic palm."

Luna looked in the eyes of King by saying, "Do not forget that you are the one who told me that you can not read the content of the magic book through your magic, so I do not understand how now you read the content of the newspapers through your magic."

King said, "The magic book is a special book, that is different from the rest of the books, that's the reason why there are only two people who are born to read that magic book."

Luna said, "I do not understand."

King said, "It's true that I can not read the content of the magic book through my magic, but I can read all the books that exist through my magic, except that magic book."

Luna said, "The storm outside will not solve the problem, or will not erase what Liza wrote."

King said, "The storm outside will prevent people from getting outside of their houses, or offices to go get those newspapers."

Then, Luna stared at King with a sad face for a couple of minutes, then she turned and left without saying a word. All the streets of the planet were empty, there were empty cars on the roads because when the storm started people who were driving got out of their cars running through a shelter. People who were walking in the streets when the storm started, ran through the houses that were close to them, and they knocked on the doors of those houses to get inside because they were running away from the storm. People were very afraid about the storm that was outside, and those who had read the newspapers had already forgotten about what they had read because they were focused on the storm that was outside.

It was early morning, there was still the storm outside, and Maria was inside the palace looking for Luna, no one had seen Luna, she was not in her bedroom. Maria went to the door of the bedroom of King, and she started to knock at the door, but King did not open the door, then Maria removed a sheet of paper that she had folded from her pocket and she slid it under the door of King. Superhuman was walking in the house like a crazy boy, angrily by watching Luna who was walking in the storm alone through his magic palm, and he wanted to go outside to rescue her. But Philip prevented him from doing it, by saying that if Luna decided to go outside in the storm it was a way to make the pressure on King to stop that storm outside and that if he went to see Luna in the storm things would be worse because King would find it out.

After an hour, King woke up and he saw a sheet of paper that was folded close to his door, and he got up from his bed and he walked till to that sheet of paper and he bent, and he picked up it, then he opened it and he read "Luna is missing". Suddenly, his face changed, and he opened the door and he ran to the kitchen, where he met Maria and he demanded where Luna was. And Maria answered him that she saw Luna last night at 11:00 p.m., and Luna was worried about the storm that was outside, and that since this morning she was looking for Luna without success.

King talked to his magic, and he looked at his magic palm and he saw Luna who was walking in the storm alone, then he rushed till outside, and he used his magic hand and he called the hawk, then he flew through the direction of Luna. Luna was walking in the storm tired, feeling cold and hungry, then she lifted her head through the sky and she saw King who was on the hawk flying through her. Then, King landed in front of Luna, and he got off the hawk and he walked to face her, then they were looking each other in the eyes without saying a word. Then, King broke the silence by saying, "We have to return to the palace."

Luna said, "I am linked to Superhuman and you, and I am wondering why me?"

King replied, "I have no idea."

Luna said, "I know how I am linked to Superhuman, but I have no idea how I am linked to you." Then she looked into King's eyes by asking "How am I linked to you?"

King answered, "That's a secret."

Luna said, "I want to know that secret."

King said, "Sorry, you can not."

Luna asked, "Where is Queen mother."

King answered, "I have no idea."

Luna said, "It's been the months now, that no one knows where she is." King looked in her eyes without saying a word. Then, Luna asked, "Why do you want to destroy the planet?"

King replied, "I have another plan for this planet."

Luna asked, "What is that plan?"

King answered, "It's a secret." And he added, "We have to return to the palace now."

Luna said, "You have to stop the storm, to allow people who are outside since yesterday to return to their house and allow those that you kept prisoners in their houses to go outside for their needs."

Then, King told his magic and the house of the newspaper of Liza appeared on his magic palm, and there was a violent wind that was blowing only in that place where people were reading the newspapers, and that wind was so violent till people were losing balance, and everyone was trying to hold something to not fall on the floor. Suddenly, all the newspapers that were inside that house started to fly away, even those people who had held newspapers in their hands, those newspapers were getting outside from their hands and flying away.

And Luna was watching at the magic palm of King with a surprised face, how newspapers were flying away by disappearing, and how everyone was looking surprised and scared. And she asked King what he was doing. And King answered her that he did not want people to keep reading those newspapers, and Luna told him that he should do it since yesterday than to send the storm outside. Then, King stopped the storm and both King and Luna got on the hawk and they flew to the palace. King and Luna walked inside the palace, and they noticed that there were people around the radio, and Maria ran and took Luna in her arms with joy tears flowing down her cheeks.

Luna looked at Maria by asking why they were all around the radio. Maria answered Luna that there was a woman who was crying on the radio, that her two kids who were twins had disappeared yesterday in the storm that was outside, and suddenly the face of Luna changed and there was worry on her face. Luna looked around and she did not see King, then she ran to the door of the bedroom of King, and she opened the door, then she walked inside, and she looked at King who was lying in his bed, and she told him about twins that Maria told her who had disappeared in the storm. And, King answered her that he did not care, and Luna begged him to use his magic and to find those kids, but King told her that he was not working in the police to find missing people, that the police would find them.

Luna told him that the police could take a lot of time to find those kids, but that with his magic hand he could find those kids in a couple of seconds. But King refused to use his magic to find those kids, despite the fact that Luna begged him and told him that she was ready to do whatever he wanted, that he just needed to ask her, even to betray Superhuman if he finds those kids. But King refused by saying that he was the wizard boy, not the magician boy to save people. And Luna told him that if he really loved her like he says he must save those kids to show her his love, but King still refused although the fact that he told her that he really loved her.

Alex was in the living room of his house playing video games, and he heard the doorbell rang, then he got up and he walked to the door, then he opened the door and he saw Superhuman front at him.

Superhuman looked at Alex by saying, "I can see that you are surprised to see me." Alex asked, "How did you find my house?" Superhuman asked, "Do you still trust me?" Alex replied, "Of course, I do." Then, he moved at the door by saying, "Get inside." Superhuman looked in the eyes of Alex and said, "If I am here it's because I need your help." Alex said, "You know well that you can count on me on whatever you want." Superhuman said, "I want you to come with me." Then, Alex wore his shoes and he left with Superhuman.

After fifteen minutes, Superhuman and Alex reached a small farm and there was a big tall tree, then they walked behind that tall tree and they saw two kids who were standing up. And suddenly, Alex cried out, "Who are those kids?" Superhuman answered, "They are kids who disappeared since yesterday in the storm." Alex asked, "The missing twins that the radio was talking about an hour ago?" Superhuman answered, "Yeah, they are." Then, they walked till near to those kids, and Alex started to scream by moving from behind like he was seeing a big long dark snake that had lifted his head staring at those kids. Superhuman walked in front of those kids, and he was face to face with that snake, and he was staring at the snake while the snake was staring back at him, and there was a ball close to the snake.

Then, the snake started to move by going through Superhuman, and Alex started to scream the name of Superhuman with fear on his face, by saying that the snake will bite him. Then, Superhuman handed his magic hand through the snake, and the sparks of fire started to get outside from his magic palm going through the snake, and Alex was watching what Superhuman was doing with a surprised face and his mouth opened. After a couple of seconds, the snake was dead, and Alex looked at Superhuman by asking, "What was coming outside from your palm?" Superhuman replied, "Let's help those kids first, and after we will talk about me." Then, he walked two steps through the ball, and he bent, and he picked up that ball, while Alex was walking through those kids.

Superhuman walked through those kids and he bent face to them by looking in their eyes, and he asked, "Are you both alright?" Those kids were just looking at him by shaking without saying a word. Alex asked, "Are they deaf?" Superhuman replied, "No, they are just tired, weak, hungry and they are feeling cold that's why they are shaking." Alex said, "They are wet too, and we must call the ambulance because they have been here since yesterday in the same position." Superhuman said, "We must take them to their home." Alex asked, "How will they walk if they are even unable to open their mouth to say something?" Superhuman replied, "We will carry them on our backs. And I will find their house through my magic palm." Alex asked, "How will you find their house through your palm? Superhuman replied, "Let's take them to their home now, and you will see how I will find their home." Then, they carried those kids on their backs and Superhuman took the ball in his hand, and they left. While the family of those twins, the friends, and the police were outside looking for those kids since the storm had stopped.

After fifteen minutes of walking, Superhuman and Alex were in front of the house of those kids, and Superhuman rang the doorbell twice. And after a couple of seconds, the door opened, and they saw a young girl with green eyes and long hair who was looking at them with an amazed face, with the mouth opened but no word was coming out. Alex said, "We found those kids on the farm." That girl said, "Those kids are my little brothers."

Then, she moved at the door by saying, "Get inside." Then, Superhuman and Alex walked inside, and they put those kids on the sofa. Then, Alex walked to face that girl and he handed his hand by saying, "My name is Alex." The girl shook his hand by saying, "My name is Cynthia." But Cynthia was focused on looking at Superhuman, and suddenly she started to shake, then Alex and Superhuman noticed how she was shaking with fear on her face. Alex walked a step-through Cynthia by asking, "Are you okay?" Cynthia handed her finger through Superhuman by trembling more and more, and with her mouth opened, but she was shaking till a word could not come out. Alex walked two steps through Cynthia again and he put his hand on her shoulder by looking in her eyes, then he asked, "Are you alright?" While Cynthia was walking by behind still with her hand handed through Superhuman, but Superhuman was understanding why Cynthia was behaving like that.

Suddenly, they heard a noise, and Cynthia started to scream, then Superhuman turned and he noticed that one of the twins had fainted on the floor. Then, all of them rushed through that kid who was on the floor, and Alex had taken Cynthia who was still shaking with fear in his arms, and they were looking at what Superhuman was doing. Superhuman had put his magic palm on the forehead of that twin who was on the floor, and there was the light that was shining between his magic palm, and the forehead of that twin. After a few minutes, that kid opened his eyes, and Superhuman carried him and laid him on the sofa.

The eyes of Cynthia were focuseded on Superhuman, and she was not understanding what he had just done, and Alex said that they must call a doctor. But, Superhuman said that it was not necessary to call a doctor, and he demanded Cynthia to change the clothes of those kids, give them a warm shower, feed them and let them sleep well because they were very tired and weak like since yesterday, they had not closed their eyes, and that it was the reason why one of them fainted. Cynthia was just looking at Superhuman without saying a word, and Alex turned his face through Cynthia and he looked in her eyes by saying, "Please, tell me what is going on." Superhuman said, "Cynthia is like that because she thinks that I am the wizard boy."

Alex smiled at Cynthia by saying, "Do not be afraid, my friend is not the wizard boy, but instead the magician boy."

Cynthia said, "There are his photos everywhere on the planet, who says that he is the wizard boy, and who is responsible for all curses that are happening on this planet."

Alex looked in the eyes of Cynthia by asking, "Do you trust me?"

Cynthia looked back in the eyes of Alex, with hesitation without saying a word and after a few minutes she broke the silence by saying, "Yes, I trust you."

Alex said, "If you trust me, you must trust my friend too."

Cynthia took a deep breath and she said, "I trust him too."

Superhuman looked at Cynthia by saying, "Thank you for trusting me." And he added, "We have to go." Cynthia said, "Thank you for bringing me, my little brothers." And she added, "I am so sorry by the way I welcomed you."

Superhuman smiled at her by saying, "I do not worry your behavior was normal, and everyone should behave in the same way."

Cynthia said, "Please, get a sitter and I will serve you something to drink."

Superhuman said, "We can not get a seat because we have to let you take care of your little brothers, and we have something to do now."

Cynthia asked, "Where did you find my little brothers?"

Alex said, "We found them in a small farm not far from here, and they were standing in front of a big snake that was looking at them."

Cynthia cried out, "What?" with the fear on her face.

Alex said, "Do not worry because Superhuman killed that snake with his magic."

Cynthia looked at Superhuman by saying, "I do not understand."

Superhuman said, "Your little brothers were playing their ball, and the ball went outside, and they got out too to pick up their ball, then when they reached outside, they noticed that the torrent of water was carrying their ball away. And they started to follow their ball in the storm and in the rain, till that farm where the ball stopped, and when they wanted to take their ball, a big snake got out from the brush and scared them. Then, they felt afraid of that snake to take their ball, like the snake was close to their ball, and the snake was staring at them, also they were afraid to run away or to scream, and they stayed there till we found them."

Cynthia said, "Those kids were playing the ball inside here, and the front door was opened, and I was to the kitchen with my parents making food, and we were talking about the storm that was outside and the wizard boy. Then, when we came into the living room, and we noticed that they had disappeared. Then, we called the police and radio to tell them about the missing of my little brothers, but no one was picking up the phone like there was the storm outside, and it seemed that no one was working, till today when the storm stopped we succeeded to join the police and the radio."

Alex looked at Superhuman by asking, "How did you know what happened?"

Superhuman looked back at Alex by saying, "You know well who I am." And he added, "Let's go now." Cynthia said, "Please, wait for my parents, I will call them now because I am sure that they will be happy to thank you both for what you did."

Superhuman said, "Sorry, we must go because I am taking a risk to be outside, and I am putting Alex in danger too." Then, he looked in the eyes of Cynthia by saying, "Please, no one will know that I am the one who saved your little brothers."

Cynthia said, "Do not worry the secret is kept."

Alex turned face through Cynthia and he held her both hands by looking in her eyes, and he said, "It was a pleasure to meet you." And he added, "I hope we will see each other again."

Cynthia smiled at him by saying, "You know the way of my house, and you are welcome in my house." Then Superhuman and Alex left.

After ten minutes, the house of Cynthia was full of people and journalists who were coming to meet those twins who had disappeared in the storm, everyone was surprised to see them alive, and at the same time, they were very proud that nothing bad had happened to those twins. And when people demanded to Cynthia how she found those twins, she lied to them by answering that she was going out, and when she opened the front door, she saw her little brothers in the veranda of the house, and that she had no idea if they came alone, or if it was someone who had taken them there. Everyone was very surprised by the answer of Cynthia, and they were wondering who brought those kids, and where were those kids, but no one could answer their questions because those twins were deeply asleep. Luna was in her bedroom, sat in her bed, with her feet crossed and with a sad face, then the door opened, and Maria walked inside, and she smiled at Luna by saying that those twins who were lost, have been found and that they were doing well. Immediately, Luna jumped from her bed with a huge smile on her face, asking Maria how did she know that? And Maria answered her that the news was talking about it, and that those kids were doing well, but that no one knew where they were and who took them to their house.

Suddenly, Luna stayed quiet for a couple of seconds, staring at Maria then Luna opened her mouth by saying, "Superhuman." Then, Maria started to stare at Luna with an amazed face, and Luna walked through Maria and she held Maria both hands by looking into her eyes, and she told Maria that she had no doubt that she was sure that it was Superhuman who had saved those twins. King and Hector were in their offices, and they were aware of those twins who have been found, and they knew that it was Superhuman who had saved those kids, and they were angry knowing that Superhuman was still a threat for them and that Superhuman was still working to earn the confidence of people. But, at the same time, they were glad to know that no one was aware on the planet that it was Superhuman who had saved those kids, and now they were determined to catch Superhuman and they were thinking about a strategy.

The whole planet was happy to hear on the radio that those kids had been found and that they were alright, but most people on the planet were afraid, people had started to live with fear and wondering when that curse that was going on will end. And now the main question that everyone was asking in his head was where was Queen Mother? Why since that Superhuman and King appeared on the planet no one had seen Queen Mother again? and some people started to think that Queen Mother had abandoned them.

It was 9:00 p.m., Liza was in her living room reading the book that was talking about the history of the planet, and she was trying to understand the reasons for the fight between King and Superhuman. Then Liza heard the doorbell that was ringing, and she got up and walked to the door and she opened the door, then she saw jack who was staring at her. Liza welcomed Jack with a nice smile, and they walked inside, then they sat. Then, Jack told Liza that he found the answer about their doubt of the day, that he had pieces of evidence that it was Superhuman who had saved those twins. Jack went on by saying that Cynthia who was the big sister of those twins was her best friend and that he was with Cynthia and she told him that it was Superhuman who had saved her little brothers. Just that Superhuman had asked her to keep it as a secret that no one should be aware of that. Liza was not surprised about what Jack said and she was very glad to hear that she had the evidence of what she was thinking because she knew that it was Superhuman who had found those kids, but she did not have the proof. Then, Liza grabbed her handbag and her car's key and she asked Jack to take her to Cynthia's house, then both ran through the door.

It was early morning, people woke up by looking through the windows to see if there was a storm outside, and although the fact that there was not the storm outside, they were afraid to go outside because they were afraid that the storm could start once they were outside. Most people were at home, even some students had refused to go to school, while there were other people who had surrounded the house of newspapers of Liza, with the newspapers in their hands reading with a surprised face what Liza had written. Liza had succeeded to convince Cynthia last night to tell her what had happened with her little brothers and how Superhuman had saved them, and Cynthia had told everything to Liza. And Liza had written what Cynthia had told her in the newspapers.

People were coming more and more to get newspapers, and everyone who was reading the newspaper was surprised and they had started to have doubts in King, and trust in Superhuman. Suddenly, those newspapers started to get out of their hands and flew away, all of them were looking at what was happening with a surprised face as newspapers were flying away and disappearing. Then, some of them started to remember that it was the same thing that had happened yesterday when they were reading the newspapers, just that yesterday they thought that it was the violent wind that was blowing that was making the newspapers flying away. Then, they started to feel afraid, and some of them started to say that it was the cursed magic of the wizard boy who was doing it, then they started to run away.

Superhuman and Philip were at home, and Superhuman was very worried for the inhabitants of the planet, and he had watched what had happened with the newspapers, and he was very worried knowing what King was able to do with his magic. Superhuman was thinking about how to end that war between King and him, although the fact that he did not know the reasons for that war between King and him. And Superhuman demanded Philip how to stop that war that was destroying the planet, and Philip answered him that he had no idea, then Superhuman tried to communicate with his magic to know how to end that war that was torturing the inhabitants of the planet. And his magic answered him that he had a mission, and that he had not yet succeeded his mission, and that only when he would succeed his mission that the fight would end. And Superhuman was completely lost because he did not know exactly what his mission was, and his magic did not tell him what exactly was that mission.

King and Hector were in their office thinking about how to get rid of Liza who was becoming more and more dangerous, and Hector said he would send policemen to kill her or arrest her and put her in jail. But King refused that idea of Hector, by saying that it was better for them to let Liza alive for the moment and watch her each second to know what she was doing. Because Liza already knew that he was the wizard boy and that Superhuman was the magician boy, and that Superhuman could try to get in touch with Liza because with what happened today with the newspapers, Superhuman would try to protect her, and that could help them to know where Superhuman hides.

Then, King told Hector that they were winning the war against Superhuman because everything would be over in less than thirty hours because he was going to destroy the energy of the magic of Superhuman that was inside the body of Luna in less than thirty hours. And King went on by saying that, he made the researches through his magic and he found out that those pimples on the body of Luna had a duration, two hundred sixteen-four hours (264 hours), and since Luna woke up from her coma with those pimples on her body, two hundred thirty- six hours have already elapsed now (236 hours). And Hector asked King what would happen if, after twenty-eight hours, those pimples appeared on the body of Luna again? And King answered Hector that those pimples could not appear again on Luna's body because it appears only once. And that the mysterious ghost could not take the risk to make those pimples appear on Luna's body again because if those pimples appear again on Luna's body, she would die.

Because it was those pimples who had sent Luna in the coma for twenty-one days, and if it appears again on Luna's body, Luna will get in the coma for the second times, for the same reason and this time she will have no chance to get out of that coma alive because her body would be unable to support the charge of those pimples on her again for the second times. And King added that if those pimples do not disappear on Luna's body in less than twenty-eight hours, the body of Luna would be unable to keep supporting the charge of those pimples and she would get into a coma and die.

Because those pimples were not a sickness but a dangerous poison, and that if Luna had supported the charge of those poisons on her body, it was because she was a witch because a normal human being should die the first second that those pimples appeared on his body or her body. Hector asked King if he found out who was that mysterious ghost, who prevented them from destroying the energy of the magic of Superhuman who was inside Luna, by making those pimples appear on Luna's body. And King answered that not yet, that he was still looking for that mysterious ghost. Hector was very glad to know that in less than twenty-eight hours, those pimples that had prevented King to destroy the energy of the magic of Superhuman who was inside Luna's body would disappear and that King should be able to destroy that energy. And after that energy in Luna would be destroyed the fight would be over, and they would be the winners and Superhuman will not anymore be able to prevent them to realize their project, like without that energy inside Luna, the magic of Superhuman was useless.

CHAPTER 8

❖

The Death of Jack

The following day, it was 8:00 p.m., Jack was in the living room of his house doing his homework and he heard the doorbell rang, he got up from his chair and walked to the door, and he opened the door and he saw Liza face to him. Liza looked at Jack by asking, "Are you surprised to see me?" Jack answered, "Yes, and he asked, how did you find my house?" Liza said, "I spent more than 29 hours to find your house." Jack said, "You mean it's since yesterday that you are looking for my house." Liza replied, "Since yesterday morning." Jack smiled by saying, "It was hard for you to find my house because I am not famous like you, no one knows me on this planet." And he added, "I took just an hour to find your house because you are a famous journalist, and everyone knows you." Then, Jack moved at the door by saying, "Get in." But Liza refused to get inside the house by saying to Jack that if she was there at that time it was because she needed his help, then Jack asked her how he could help her. Liza answered him to follow her and they would talk when she would be driving because they must gain on time.

Then, Jack wore his shoes and he went with Liza without saying a word to his parents who were already asleep. Jack and Liza were in the car driving on the way to Cynthia's house, and Liza had explained to Jack what had happened with newspapers, and she said that she had no doubt that it was King who had made those newspapers disappear to prevent people from reading them. But she was determined to take off the mask of King, for that the whole planet knew who he was, that King was the wizard boy who wanted to destroy the planet. Then, after a couple of minutes, they reached Cynthia's house, and Liza stayed in the car, and Jack went to knock at Cynthia's house. After a few minutes, Jack came with Cynthia, then Liza got out of the car, and she explained to Cynthia what had happened with the newspapers, and she told Cynthia that if King had destroyed those newspapers it was because the information that was in those newspapers were true.

Then, Liza demanded Cynthia to make a video recording where she would talk the whole story about how Superhuman had saved her little brothers. And Cynthia refused by saying that it was too dangerous because she had made a promise to Superhuman to keep it secret and that she could not put Superhuman in danger. But Jack convinced Cynthia by saying that what they were doing was for the planet, that they were trying to protect the planet, to prevent King from destroying the planet, and that at the same time they were helping Superhuman who was fighting alone against King, and who did not have the support of the planet. Then Cynthia finally accepted to do that video recording, and they found a place to do it, then Liza held the camera and Cynthia started to tell the story about how Superhuman had saved her little brothers while Liza was recording what Cynthia was saying. After ten minutes, they have finished, and Cynthia got inside her house, while Liza and Jack took the road and they were going to give that video recording to a television channel so that the whole planet watches it.

After eleven minutes of driving, Liza and Jack reached a crossroad and they were close to the house of that television channel, and suddenly Liza started to lose control of the car, the wheel of the car was not turning anymore, and she screamed at Jack by saying open the car's door and jump out. Jack tried to open the car's door, but he noticed that the car's door was locked, and the car was going more and more faster and they were screaming inside the car, by showing their hands through the window's glass to ask for help.

Suddenly, there were other drivers who were screaming in their cars too because they were losing control of their cars, and people who were in the street were running in all directions by screaming, while other people had their head lifted through the direction of the sky, watching Superhuman and King who were in the space flying on their hawks by fighting, with the sparks of fire that were getting out from their magic palms. Superhuman was trying to prevent King to keep sending the sparks of fire through the cars because when the sparks of fire that were getting outside from the magic palm of King were touching the cars, those cars were losing direction and the drivers of those cars were losing control of their cars.

Then, Superhuman noticed that the cars were hitting each other in the street, and he jumped from his hawk and he landed on a car, then he started to use his magic hand to stop the cars, and he was running by jumping on the cars and by touching those cars with his magic palm to stop them. Then, King flew through the direction of the car of Liza, and he handed his magic hand through Liza's car and the sparks of fire got out from his magic palm and went on the car of Liza, and suddenly the car of Liza got out of the road and went and hit a tall big tree that was on roadside. Then, King flew away, and people on the street were screaming with tears flowing down their cheeks, the journalists and ambulances were already there.

And Superhuman was helping people that their cars had crashed to get outside of their cars, and there was the light that was shining on his magic hand, but he was not paying attention to that light that was shining on his magic hand because he was so busy helping people. There were camera men who were filming Superhuman, and journalists were making the reportage live, and all television channels were showing what was happening, and people were at the home front to their television watching breaking news, with fear inside them and with tears flowing down their cheeks. Superhuman was helping people who had fainted to get up by putting his magic palm on their foreheads, and those people were getting up, while people who were injured were taken to the hospital in the ambulances.

People were watching what Superhuman was doing with the surprised faces, and there were people who had joined Superhuman, and together they were helping people to get outside the cars. But only Superhuman could open the doors of cars that the sparks of fire coming from the magic palm of King had touched because the sparks of fire that contain the magic of King had blocked those car's doors.

And a policeman saw the light that was shining on the magic hand of Superhuman, and he told Superhuman about it, then Superhuman looked at his magic palm, and he saw Liza and Jack in the chairs of the car bleeding with their eyes closed.

Suddenly, Superhuman started to run through the car of Liza, and there were journalists, policemen and people who were running behind him, then Superhuman reached Liza's car and he saw people who were trying to open the door of the car without succeeding, and he used his magic hand to open the car's door. Then, Superhuman and other people removed Liza and Jack from the car, and Superhuman asked people to lie Liza and Jack on the ground before taking them to the hospital, then Liza and Jack were lying on the ground with their eyes closed bleeding from their mouths, their noses, and there were the wounds on their foreheads. And Superhuman bent close to Liza and he put his magic palm on Liza's forehead, and after a couple of seconds Liza opened her eyes, and she was trying to open her mouth, and Superhuman looked into her eyes by telling her to not talk that she was so weak.

People were happy to see that Liza was alive because they all thought that she died, and Superhuman asked to take Liza to the hospital, then he got up and walked through where Jack was lying, while Liza was taken to the ambulance. Superhuman bent close to Jack and he put his magic palm on Jack's forehead, and after a minute Jack had not opened his eyes, and people started to look with worry on their faces, even Superhuman started to feel afraid. Then, a red light started to shine between the magic palm of Superhuman and Jack's forehead, and Superhuman looked at that red light with fear on his face, and with his mouth opened but unable to say a word, then he lifted his head and he looked at people with tears that were flowing down his cheeks. While People were staring at Superhuman with fear on their faces, wondering why he was crying, and the heart of everyone was beating faster than normal, and other people were feeling fear till they were shaking.

Then, Superhuman removed his magic palm on Jack's forehead, and he looked at his magic palm, and he read "You arrived too late." Then, Superhuman started to scream at his magic palm by saying, "Save Jack, save Jack" by crying, and the tears started to flow down the cheeks of everyone around him like they had understood by the cries of Superhuman that Jack was gone. Then, Superhuman knelt close to the dead body of Jack, and he started to shake the dead body of Jack by crying, and by calling the name of Jack to wake up, then he sat on the ground and he lifted the head of Jack and he put it on his laps by crying. And people were in front of their television watching Superhuman with a sad face and tears in their eyes. After fifteen minutes, Superhuman was still crying on the dead body of Jack, and people came, and they lifted Superhuman, and other people covered the dead body of Jack with a blanket.

Then, a journalist walked close to where Superhuman was and that journalist handed the mike through the mouth of Superhuman, and Superhuman said, "Jack was a hero who loved his planet, and he died for the love of his planet because he was fighting to protect his planet". Luna and Maria were in the bedroom in front of the television watching what was happening, and Maria had taken Luna who was crying in her arms, then the door opened, and King and Hector walked inside with anger on their faces. Then, King handed his magic hand through Luna by looking at her angrily, while Luna and Maria were looking back at King with fear on their faces.

King said, "I will kill you right now and none between Superhuman and me will have this planet."

Luna and Maria started to shake, and Maria walked two steps in front of the magic hand of King and she looked in the eyes of King by saying, "You will kill me first, before killing my daughter."

King looked in the eyes of Maria angrily by saying "I hope you know well who I am."

Maria replied, "I just watched what you did a half-hour ago, how you killed that young boy named Jack, and how you sent a lot of people to the hospital."

Hector looked at Maria by saying, "Leave this room."

Maria replied, "I will not let my daughter alone."

Luna walked through King and she looked into his eyes by saying, "Please, do not hurt Maria." And she added, "I am ready to do everything you want."

King looked back at Luna by saying, "It's too late now."

Luna said, "I beg your pardon to let Maria alive."

King said, "You should think about it first before betraying me."

Luna cried out, "Betray you?" by looking at him with a surprised face.

King said, "You kissed Superhuman again."

Luna cried out, "kissed Superhuman?"

King replied, "I just fought with Superhuman, and Superhuman had the energy of his magic, and we both know well that only your body content that energy of the magic of Superhuman, that means that you are the one who gave that energy to him for that he uses his magic to fight me."

Luna looked at King without saying a word, and she said in her head I have not seen Superhuman it's been weeks now, and I do not even remember the last time I kissed Superhuman. But if I deny that I had not given that energy to Superhuman, King could find out the secret who is between Superhuman and me. Then, King shouted at Luna by saying, "I want you to tell me now where Superhuman is."

Maria looked at King by saying, "Luna has no idea about where Superhuman is."

Suddenly, Luna walked to Maria and she stayed in front of the magic hand of King who was handed to Maria, to prevent King from killing Maria. And King looked at Luna by saying, "You can not protect Maria because I will kill her."

Luna said, "I am ready to do whatever you want, but you have to let Maria alive." Then, Luna turned her head through Maria by asking Maria to leave the room, but Maria refused to let her alone, and King said that Maria would not leave the room because if Luna did not answer his questions, he would kill Maria. Hector looked at Luna by asking, "Where and when you gave that energy to Superhuman?"

King looked at Hector by saying, "She gave that energy to Superhuman in the storm."

Luna said, "Do not forget that the magic of Superhuman does not work in the storm."

King looked at Luna by saying, "It's true that the magic of Superhuman does not work in the storm, but Superhuman can receive the energy of his magic in the storm and keep it inside his body, just that he can not use it in the storm."

Luna said in her head I must invite something to prevent King not only to kill Maria but also to prevent him from finding out the secret of how Superhuman gets the energy of his magic. There was silence between all of them.

Then, Hector broke the silence by saying, "The energy that Superhuman used a couple of hours ago to fight, Luna did not give him that energy in the storm. Because it's been more than three days that there was the storm outside, and the energy of the magic of Superhuman expires after 72 hours, and three days it's 72 hours. So, if Luna had given that energy to Superhuman in the storm, he could not use that energy to fight three hours ago because that energy should already have expired."

Luna said, "It's true that by looking at the time now it's been more than three days that there was the storm outside, but not yet 72 hours that Superhuman received that energy."

Hector looked at Luna by asking, "What do you mean?"

Luna replied, "It's been 64 hours now that Superhuman received that energy."

King asked, "What do you mean by that?"

Luna replied, "Four days ago when there was the storm outside, I left this palace at 8 am and Superhuman met me in the storm at 9:00 a.m., so if we calculate well from that hour till now and it's 64 hours that are already elapsed."

King said, "I do not understand."

Luna replied, "The first day it's not 24 hours but instead 15 hours because we start to count from the hour that Superhuman received that energy, and the second day it's 24 hours, the third day it's 24 hours, and the fourth day which is today, it's just an hour because it's 1:00 am, now, so the total of hours it's 64 hours." Hector and King looked at each other without saying a word.

And Hector said, "It means that Superhuman still has the energy of his magic inside him for 8 hours."

King looked at Luna by saying, "It means when I met you in the storm that day at 11:00 a.m., you had already met with Superhuman, and you did not tell me." And he added, "You are going to regret your betraying because it's your fault if people are hating me now and if people found out who I am. Because when I went to kill Liza and Jack to prevent them from giving their video recording to the television channel, I did not know that Superhuman had the energy of his magic to fight because If I knew it, I should use another method to get rid of Jack and Liza."

Luna said, "I am ready to go to jail to pay for my betraying."

King replied, "I will not send you to jail, but I will find a way to earn back the confidence of the whole planet, by making Superhuman responsible for all curses that are happening on this planet." Then, King turned and walked through the door and Hector followed him.

It was 6:00 a.m., people were still awake on the planet, and most people had not closed their eyes during the whole night, except kids who had slept, people had spent their whole night talking about the fight that they had watched between Superhuman and King. Except, Luna, Maria, Cynthia, and all students and instructors of the school of Superhuman were not surprised to see Superhuman saved people who were hurt in the accident like they had watched how Superhuman had saved the life of John. But, the rest of the people who had watched that fight was very surprised to see what Superhuman was doing. People were very surprised to see how Superhuman was crying on the dead body of Jack, and everyone was wondering who Jack was for Superhuman. Superhuman had earned the confidence of more than eighty percent (80%) of the population of the planet, just less than twenty percent (20%) who had still the doubt about Superhuman.

For most of the inhabitants of the planet, Superhuman was the magician boy, mostly that they had seen people working with Superhuman by touching him and by talking with him, and Superhuman did not kill them. Even people who were working with Superhuman to help people who were hurt had just realized after that they were working with him, and they were very surprised that they had touched and talked with Superhuman, and they were very proud that they worked with the magician boy of the planet. There was a question that everyone on the planet was asking, and that question was why King was living in the palace of the planet, with Queen mother the god of the planet if he was the wizard boy of the planet? But, no one could answer that question. And that question was making the doubt in the mind of everyone, and that question was the reason why there was still those less than twenty percent of people who still had doubts in Superhuman like the magician boy. Because for them if King was the wizard boy he could not live in the palace with their god.

King and Hector were spending their time thinking about how to gain back the confidence of the whole planet, that King had lost last night in the fight with Superhuman, and they were regretting their decision because they had not killed Liza the first day, she started to publish news against King. King and Hector knew well that they needed the confidence of the whole planet to realize their project, and they were busy thinking about how to gain the confidence of people that they forgot the pimples that were on Luna's body. Like, King should destroy the energy of the magic of Superhuman who was inside the body of Luna after that those pimples should disappear.

Hector and King had organized a plan on how to catch Superhuman to make him responsible for all curses that were happening on the planet, and in their plan, they knew that Superhuman could not defend himself. Because Superhuman should not have the energy of his magic to fight like more than 72 hours had already elapsed like Superhuman had received the energy of his magic. Luna was in her bedroom in front of the mirror looking at her body, and she was in front of that mirror since 3:00 am, when she had noticed that the pimples that were on her body had disappeared. Luna was completely lost, and she did not understand what was going on, why those pimples had disappeared on her body once alone, without letting any scar, and why those pimples did not disappear like a wound that heals with a process small by small. Mostly that she had not taken any medicine for those pimples, and she was thinking about the mysterious ghost that Superhuman had told her, that he heard King and Hector talked about.

Then, the door of her bedroom opened, and Maria walked inside with a tray of breakfast in her hands, then Maria put that tray on the table, and she walked to Luna. Then, Maria took Luna in her arms, and she tried to calm Luna like Maria already knew about those pimples because she was with Luna when Luna noticed that those pimples had disappeared on her body. Luna told Maria that she was not going to school because she had the feeling that a tragedy was going to happen, and that she wanted to be there to prevent King and Hector from destroying the Planet. And Maria told Luna that she was very worried too, that since 1:00 a.m., that Hector and King left this bedroom, they were in their office and they had not got out even for breakfast, and they had not asked for breakfast too, that she had no doubt that the worst tragedy was going to happen.

And Luna told Maria that she had thought that King should send the storm outside to prevent people to think about the fight he has had with Superhuman last night because King used the storm for two reasons one was to try to catch Superhuman, and another reason it was to prevent people to think about him like a wizard boy. Because when people started to have doubts about King, he sent the storm outside to scare people, for that people started to feel afraid and think about the storm, and he also used the storm when a journalist writes something against him, and he used the storm to prevent people to get out to get the newspapers or to read the newspapers. And Luna added that if King had not sent the storm outside till now, it meant that the worst was going to happen.

Then Maria demanded Luna to run away and go to hide where Superhuman was hiding like she knew the hiding of Superhuman, and like till now, King had not succeeded to find out that hiding place. But Luna completely refused by saying that she could not abandon the whole planet in the hands of Hector and King, that things would be worse if she ran away because she was the guarantee that King had. And that King thought that with her close to him he had the control and the advantage on Superhuman.

Maria tried to convince Luna to run away by saying that she was lucky this morning at 1:00 a.m., that King did not find out that she had not met in the storm with Superhuman, that if Superhuman showed up again by fighting, King would know that there was a secret that Luna had hidden from him. And King would find out that Luna had lied to him during all this time, by saying that Superhuman was getting the energy of his magic directly from her and that King would not hesitate to kill her even if he really loved her. Because for King his project that he was fighting for it for months now, was more important than the love he had for her.

Luna answered Maria that she knew well that although the fact that King really loved her, even if he tortured her sometimes, King would not hesitate to kill her if he discovered the secret of how Superhuman gets the energy of his magic. Because King was born for a mission that was more important than everything, even more important than the life of inhabitants of the planet, but that she would not run away because she was not afraid to die. Because she was born for a mission to protect the planet as Superhuman and she would not run away from her mission and abandon the whole planet just because she was afraid to die. Then, Maria started to cry in the arms of Luna by saying that she would die if Luna dies, that Luna was only the family she had, the kid she had never had, and Luna was trying to calm Maria by saying that nothing bad would happen, that everything would be fine.

Superhuman was at home still sad about the tragedy that had happened yesterday, mostly about the death the Jack, and he was feeling responsible for the death of Jack. Because he was saying that if he had arrived on time, he should prevent that tragedy to happen because when he arrived King had already started to provoke the accidents, and he started to fight with King, and at that same moment he could not control all the sparks of fire that were getting out from the magic palm of King by going through people and the cars. Superhuman was regretting too why he had not gone to talk to Liza and Jack, to stop searching the pieces of evidence against King, like he was aware of what Liza and Jack were doing.

Superhuman was now more focused on King, and he was aware of what King and Hector had intended to do, but he did not know what to do, how to prevent that plan of King and Hector to happen without putting the life of people in danger. Superhuman knew too that this time things would be worst because he had watched through his magic palm the conversation of 1:00 a.m., between King, Luna, Hector, and Maria, he was afraid that when he would use his magic to prevent the plan of King, at that moment King would find out that there was a secret of how he was getting the energy of his magic, and at that time the life Luna and all inhabitants of the planet would be in danger.

Then, Superhuman wanted to go to the palace to take Luna with him, but he knew that Luna should not accept to run away from the palace like he had watched the conversation between Luna and Maria, where Maria was asking Luna to run away but Luna refused. And he knew that Luna was right when she said that they were born for a mission and that that mission was to protect the planet, even if they did not know exactly the reasons for that fight, but he loved Luna so much that he was afraid that King would kill her. And Superhuman knew that he was the worst enemy of King and that King could kill Luna just to hurt him like King knew that he loved Luna too.

Superhuman was thinking about a plan how to remove Luna to the palace, without herself knows, but at the same time he was afraid that the missing of Luna in the palace would make things worst, and that King would not hesitate to kill his parents who were in jail in the palace, and the whole planet would be in danger too. Then, Superhuman did not know what to do, and he started to ask himself how to end that fight if there was a way to end it, and there were questions in his head like where was Queen mother? Why could not King find where he is hiding through his magic? Because Superhuman knew that it had been months now that King was looking for him through his magic palm. How was Luna linked to King? Who was the mysterious ghost that King and Hector are talking about everyday? Why did those pimples disappear from the body of Luna? Why the sparks of fire that come out from his magic palm could not kill people, and the sparks of fire that come out from the magic palm of King kill people? How was his magic different from the magic of King? Why did King live in the palace knowing that he was a danger to the planet? And what was the reason for that war between King and him?

But, Superhuman could not answer any of those questions, and when he demanded the answers of those questions to his magic, his magic refused to give him those answers by saying that he would find those answers by himself. King and Hector were still in their office since 1:00 a.m., when they had left the bedroom of Luna, and they were watching downtown through the magic palm of King, they were seeing how downtown was full of people going in all directions, and with the traffic of cars. King smiled at Hector by saying, "Now, I am going to be the superhero of this planet." And Hector smiled back at King by saying, "Everyone on this planet will love you, and no one would doubt you again because no one will forget this historic day that they are going to live."

Suddenly, they saw Superhuman in the space who was flying on his hawk, and they turned their heads looking at each other with surprised faces, with their mouths opened but no word was coming out. After six seconds, King broke the silence by saying, "I do not understand." Hector replied, "Myself, I do not know what is going on. And he asked, "What to do now?" King replied, "I will send the storm outside to catch Superhuman." Hector replied, "You know well that our plan cannot work with the storm, and it's the reason why we did not send the storm outside this morning." King got up from his chair by saying, "I am going to confront Superhuman." Hector looked at him by saying, "It's too late now because what we have planned is going to start in less than a minute, and it's impossible to change our plan now." And he added, "We are still not sure that Superhuman has not the energy of his magic inside him." King asked, "What if Superhuman has the energy of his magic?" Hector answered, "It will mean that Luna lied to us." King said, "I am going to kill Luna." Hector said, "Get a sit first and let's watch if Superhuman has the energy of his magic. And you would kill Luna later if she betrayed us again."

Then, King sat, and they kept watching what was going on downtown through the magic palm of King. Most people who were downtown had lifted their heads through the sky watching Superhuman, who was flying on the hawk, while other people were running away by screaming the wizard boy. And the police and journalists had already received the phone call that Superhuman was in downtown flying in the space on his hawk and they were coming. There was a big white truck among the cars that were in the street, and Superhuman was flying through that truck. Suddenly, the back door of that truck opened, and a big elephant jumped out and that elephant hit the first car that was close to him with his trunk, and that car went and crashed into another car with people inside.

Then, the elephant started to run through people, while people were running away by screaming, and there were a lot of people who were falling on the ground, people had thrown everything that they had in their hands away to run faster as they could. There was a huge traffic, and people were getting outside of their cars to run, people were scattered in the street running in all directions without even looking around them, and other people were lying on the ground bleeding. The elephant was using his trunk to hit the cars that were close to him, to find his way to reach people, but fortunately those cars that the elephant was hitting were empty because people were already out of those cars. There was a small kid of five years old who was trying to run as fast as he could, and the elephant was running right behind that kid, then the elephant handed his trunk through that kid to hit him.

Suddenly, Superhuman jumped from his hawk and threw himself on that kid, and they fell on the ground together. Then, the elephant started to run through them, and Superhuman handed his magic hand through the elephant, and the sparks of fire started to get outside from his magic palm going through the elephant. Then, the elephant stopped and started to shake his head, like the sparks of fire were burning his head, and Superhuman got up from the ground still with his magic hand handed through the elephant, and he used his other hand to help that kid who was on the ground to get up. Then, the elephant turned and started to run through another side of the street, and Superhuman ran and jumped on the elephant and he grabbed the trunk of the elephant with his both hands, and the elephant started to shake his body.

Then, the elephant ran and hit his body through the cars, and Superhuman lost the balance on the elephant, and he fell on the ground, and he suddenly handed his magic hand through the elephant who was close to him looking at him. Then, the elephant turned and changed direction and started to run on another way, and Superhuman got up from the ground and climbed on the car that was close to him. Superhuman started to run by jumping on the cars, by taking another direction that was opposite to the direction that the elephant was running through, then after a few seconds, Superhuman landed face to the elephant, with his magic hand handed through the elephant. Then, the sparks of fire started to get outside from his magic palm by going through the elephant, while the elephant was looking at Superhuman angrily, and the elephant was not trying to shake his head or to move away although the fact that the sparks of fire were burning his head.

There were people around who were watching Superhuman and the elephant, and there were journalists who were making the reportage and the camera men were filming, and the whole planet was already aware of what was happening downtown. And people who were to work or school had returned to their home, and almost the whole planet was front to their television, with the fear on their face watching what was going on downtown. Luna was in her bedroom and sitting in her bed, with a worried face thinking about how to protect the planet by stopping King to keep killing people and torturing people, but she was not aware of what was going on downtown.

Then, the door of her bedroom opened, and Maria walked inside, and Maria noticed that Luna had not touched the tray of breakfast that she had put on the table since the morning. Luna got up from her bed and looked at Maria by saying, "You look sad." Maria said, "I was worried about you." And she added, "My daughter you must run away from this palace now and go where Superhuman hides, King has not yet found that hiding place." Luna said, "You know well that it's impossible, that I will never abandon this planet." Maria looked in the eyes of Luna with tears flowing down her cheeks and she said, "My daughter, I do not want King to kill you." Luna looked at Maria with an amazed face, asking "Why are you crying?" Maria replied, "King found out that you lied to him, and that Superhuman has still the energy of his magic inside him." Luna asked, "How did he find out?" Maria replied, "Superhuman is in downtown now fighting against a big elephant." Luna cried out, "What?" by looking at Maria with a worried face. And she asked, "How did you know that?" Maria replied, "The radio is talking about it, and the television is showing it."

Then, Luna rushed through the television that was in her bedroom, and she turned it on, and Maria walked close to her. Luna started to shake with her mouth opened, and with her face full of fear like she was watching Superhuman face the elephant, and Maria took Luna in her arms. Superhuman had still his magic hand handed through the elephant, who was staring at him with his eyes full of anger like the sparks of fire were burning his head, and there were the small wounds on the head of the elephant that the sparks of fire had made. Then, the elephant started to walk through Superhuman angrily, and Superhuman was walking by behind still with his magic hand as the elephant was walking through him.

Then, Superhuman found himself blocked between the cars that were there that the drivers had abandoned, and Superhuman was trapped among those cars like he was walking from behind without watching. Then, Superhuman was leaned against a car, face to the elephant and it was impossible for him to move or to escape, then the elephant ran through Superhuman angrily although the fact that he still had his magic hand handed on the elephant. Then, the elephant used his trunk and started to hit Superhuman, and Superhuman went and fell away. Suddenly, there were screams of fear over the planet, all people who were watching had the fear on their face, even the voice of journalists who were making the reportage had changed, there was the worry in their voice, people were shaking with fear in front of their television. Everyone was worried about Superhuman mostly people like Luna, Maria, Alex, Cynthia, John, Philip, and students of the school of Superhuman, they were all watching how the elephant was hitting Superhuman with his trunk.

Luna, like a lot of people, had tears who were flowing down their cheeks, and Alex had run away from the house without saying a word to his parents, and his parents did not notice that he had left. Except Hector and King who were in their office enjoying the fight, through the magic palm of King, like the elephant was hitting Superhuman. Superhuman was on the ground, and he had grabbed the trunk of the elephant with both hands and with all his strengths, and the elephant was trying to throw him away. Then, the elephant started to drag Superhuman on the ground by walking with him, and Superhuman was still holding the trunk of the elephant, despite the fact that he was dragging on the ground. Suddenly, there were the stones that were hitting on the elephant, and people turned their heads to see where the stones were coming from, and they saw Alex on the top of a car who was throwing the stones on the elephant. The elephant started to lose concentration like the stones were hitting him, then the elephant stopped to fight and stopped to drag Superhuman on the ground too, and the elephant was trying to turn through the direction of where the stones were coming from.

Then, Superhuman took that advantage that the elephant had lost the concentration on him, and he got up and he walked three steps away from the elephant, while Alex was still throwing the stones on the elephant. Then, Superhuman lifted his head through where the stones were coming from, and he saw Alex who was throwing the stones on the elephant, and he started to scream at Alex by asking Alex to leave, to go back home, but Alex was not paying attention about what Superhuman was saying. The elephant started to run through where Alex was, and Superhuman noticed it, and he started to run through the left side of the elephant by handing his magic hand, and the sparks of fire were getting out from his magic palm and going to the left side of the head of the elephant. Then, the elephant turned and looked at Superhuman angrily, with a tired face full of blood, while Superhuman was still burning the face of the elephant, with the sparks of fire and the elephant was bleeding. Then, the elephant started to run through Superhuman faster, and angrily although the fact that he was losing a lot of blood, and Superhuman was running away, and the elephant was running after Superhuman. Then, Superhuman lost control of the fight like he was prosecuted by the elephant because he could not turn to fight the elephant with his sparks of fire, and it was hard for Superhuman to run because there were cars that were parked everywhere.

Suddenly, the elephant used his trunk to carry Superhuman from behind and threw him away, and Superhuman went and hit himself against a small truck that was parked, then he fell on the ground, and he saw the elephant who was running through him angrily. And Superhuman started to turn under that truck that the elephant had thrown him on it, and the elephant was beside that truck unable to go under the truck to find Superhuman. And Superhuman got up on another side, and he was looking very tired and bleeding, and there were the wounds on his face and his forehead, and everyone was looking at him with a sad face.

Then, Superhuman ran through a small car that was not far from where the elephant was, and he climbed on that car, then he jumped face to the elephant, and he was looking at the elephant angrily, while the elephant was looking at him with a tired face. Then, Superhuman handed his magic hand through the elephant, and the sparks of fire started to get out from his magic palm and went through the elephant, and the elephant was just staring at Superhuman without making any move. Because the elephant was very tired and weak to keep fighting or defending himself, also the elephant had already lost a lot of blood with all the wounds that were on his head and his body.

Then, after a couple of minutes, the elephant fell on the ground with his eyes opened, and after a couple of seconds the elephant closed his eyes and the elephant died. Superhuman took a deep breath, and he lifted his head through the sky, while the eyes of everyone were focused on him, and the fear on the face of everyone was gone, and the smile had taken the place of that fear because everyone had the smile on their face. Some people started to clap their hands by screaming Superhero, and the rest of the people followed by clapping their hands and by singing Superhero, even in the houses everyone was singing Superhero. Then, Superhuman noticed that the light was shining on his magic hand, and he looked at his magic palm and he read "You are in danger." Then, he lifted his magic hand through the sky, and the hawk started to fly through him.

Suddenly, a violent wind started to blow, and the rain was falling, and there were storm and darkness, and People started to run through the huge mall that was close to them. Luna and Maria were still in front of the television, and Luna was worried, and she had a sad face because she was understanding the meaning of the storm that was outside. Luna knew that King had sent the storm outside to follow Superhuman and to see where Superhuman hides, like in the storm the magic of Superhuman could not work and Superhuman could not run away from King in the storm.

Then, Luna looked around her and she stared at the tray of the breakfast that Maria had come with since morning, then she looked at Maria. And Maria looked back at her by saying, "You have not opened your mouth since the fight finished." And she added, "I thought that you should be happy like Superhuman succeeded to survive in that fight against the elephant because you were crying when the elephant was dragging him on the ground." Luna said, "Please, I need your help." Maria replied, "My daughter, you know well that I am ready to give my life for you." Luna walked close to the television and she turned it off, then she went and took the knife that was on the tray of breakfast, and Maria walked to face Luna, looking at her with a surprised face.

Then, Maria asked, "What are you going to do with that knife?" Luna said, "I will hurt myself." And she added, "You will go knock on the office's door of Hector and King and tell them that when you got inside my bedroom, you found me lying in my bed bleeding. And no one will know that we were together and that I watched the fight between Superhuman and the elephant." Maria cried out, "What?" by looking at Luna with the fear on her face. Luna said, "I want to attract the attention of King to prevent him from catching Superhuman because King is following Superhuman right now through his magic palm, and Superhuman can not escape from King in the storm. And I do not want King to see where Superhuman hides." Maria said, "I do not understand." Luna said, "Superhuman is flying through home without knowing that King is following him because Superhuman's magic is not working in the storm to see that King is following him." Maria looked in the eyes of Luna by saying, "It's obvious that you really love that boy of Superhuman." Luna replied, "yeah, I really love him." And she added, "But, I am not doing it only for the love of Superhuman, but for the love of the whole planet because if King finds out where Superhuman hides it will be the end of this planet."

Maria said, "Still there are a lot of questions that I do not understand." Luna replied, "There is no time for the questions now." And she added, "Everyone on this planet has the questions that no one can answer like where is Queen Mother? What does King want? What is the reason for the fight that is happening on the planet? and a lot of other questions." Then, Luna cut her right hand and her left hand, with the knife she had in her hand. Suddenly, Maria screamed, and she put her both hands on her mouth by looking at how Luna was bleeding. Luna looked at Maria by saying, "Please, go now."

Then, Maria turned, and she ran through the door. Hector and King were in their office, watching Superhuman who was flying in the space on his hawk, through the magic palm of King, then they heard the noises on the door, and Hector got up and went and opened the door. Hector saw Maria who was shaking by crying, and he asked, "Why are you crying?" Maria replied, "Luna is dead." King cried out, "What?" and he turned his head through the door by looking at Maria. Hector asked, "What happened?" Maria said, "I have no idea of what happened." And she added, "I got in her bedroom and I just found her lying in her bed bleeding." King said, "She can not be dead because if she was dead my magic would not be working." And he got up from his chair and all of them rushed through the bedroom of Luna. After a few minutes, they reached the door of Luna's bedroom, and King opened that door and they got inside, and they saw Luna who was lying in the bed with her eyes closed, bleeding from her both hands. And King ran through the bed and he climbed on the bed, and he bent close to Luna and he started to shake her by calling her name. Then, King looked at Maria who was crying and he screamed at her to go call a doctor, and Maria turned and left the room. Then, King looked at the hands of Luna and he looked at Hector by saying, "She cut herself."

Hector said, "I do not know if the better solution it's to let her die."

King looked into Hector's eyes by saying, "Do not forget that I am linked to her and that without her alive it will be impossible to realize our project, so she can not die now because we need her alive to realize our project."

Hector said, "Do not forget that she betrayed us."

King said, "That's the reason why we need her alive because she must tell us where Superhuman got the energy of his magic, and where he hides."

Hector said, "There's only one way for Superhuman to get energy of his magic and we both know well that the only way is by Luna." And he added, "I even read in the magic book that the only way for the magician boy to get the energy of his magic it's through the witch girl, and we know that the magician boy is Superhuman, and the witch girl is Luna."

King said, "There is one thing that I do not understand."

Hector asked, "What do you mean?"

King replied, "If it's been more than 72 hours that Superhuman got the last energy of his magic, so where did he get the energy that he fought against the elephant with? Because we both know that he could not use that energy that Luna gave him in the storm four days ago to fight against the elephant because that energy expired since 9:00 a.m.,"

Hector answered, "The only answer to your question, it's that it's less than 72 hours that Superhuman got the energy of his magic."

King said, "It means that Luna lied to us that she last met Superhuman in the storm."

Hector replied, "Exactly, that the last time that Superhuman received the energy of his magic from Luna it was not in the storm. Because it's obvious that if Superhuman used the energy of his magic an hour ago to fight against the elephant, it means that it's been less than 72 hours that he met with Luna."

King said, "I am wondering where they met, for that Superhuman receive that energy."

Hector replied, "School." And King looked at Hector with a surprised face, without saying any word.

Hector said, "Luna and Superhuman met at school because it's the only place where they could meet." King said, "Superhuman is banned of education on this planet."

Hector said, "Do not forget that since the day that Superhuman saved the life of John, he got the support of all students and instructors of that school, so nobody will betray him if he comes to school." And he added, "Luna went to school the following day of the storm and it's that day she gave that energy to Superhuman, and it's made sense that Superhuman had the energy of his magic to fight today. And it's true that from that day till today it's been three days, but those three days is less than 72 hours, and mostly that we do not know the time that Luna gave that energy to Superhuman, so probably Superhuman has still the energy of his magic inside him that he can use for some hours again."

King said, "We allowed Luna to go to school because we wanted to use her to catch Superhuman, but she is the one who used that advantage of school to betray us." Then, he looked at Luna on the bed angrily by saying, "You will never get out of this palace again."

Hector asked, "What are we going to do like Luna is in the coma again."

King asked, "What do you mean?"

Hector replied, "The first time that we found Luna in her jail unconscious, you were unable to work with your magic or to search for something through your magic. And the second time that Luna was in the coma you were unable to destroy the energy of the magic of Superhuman that is inside her, and when she came out of the coma, she had pimples on her body and your magic is allergic to those pimples. Because those pimples were the poison for your magic, and it was impossible for you to approach her to destroy that energy inside her."

King looked at Hector by saying, "Nothing will happen to my magic this time because what Luna has now it's a natural sickness, and the mysterious ghost is not responsible for this sickness." And he added, "The first time that we found Luna unconscious in her jail it was the mysterious ghost who was responsible for that, like the second she got into the coma and came out with the pimples on her body."

Hector said, "The pimples that were on her body have already disappeared, so you must destroy the energy of the magic of Superhuman who is inside her body right now."

King looked at Hector by saying, "I swear that Superhuman will never have the chance to meet Luna again." And he added, "I can not destroy that energy inside Luna in those conditions that she is now, so I will destroy that energy when she will be able to open her mouth and her eyes. Because to destroy that energy her mouth or her eyes must be opened"

Hector asked, "Why not keep following Superhuman to find where he hides."

King said, "That's a clever idea."

Then, King looked at his magic palm and he noticed that Superhuman was already gone, and he said to Hector that it was too late that they lost Superhuman. Then, they started to wonder where was the doctor that Maria went to call, and King told Hector that they had more important things to do than to stay close to Luna, and they walked through the door. There was Maria who was hidden in the corner with a small bag of pharmacy in her hand, and she saw Hector and King who were getting outside of the room of Luna, then she ran till inside Luna's room and she locked the door behind her. Then, Maria opened that bag's pharmacy she had, and she removed the medicines and she started to make the bandages on the wounds of Luna. Then, Luna opened her eyes and she smiled at Maria, and Maria smiled at her back by saying that if she had put in enough time, it was because she wanted to gain on time, she wanted King to focus on her. Luna told Maria that she had heard the whole conversation between King and Hector, that Superhuman was safe.

Then, Luna explained everything that she had heard from King and Hector, and both Maria and Luna were wondering about the mysterious ghost who was in touch with Luna, and that Luna did not know. Luna told Maria that she was very worried and afraid, that King was going to destroy the energy of the magic of Superhuman that was inside her and that she had no idea how to prevent it from happening. Because King and Hector did not talk in their conversation about how King should destroy that energy, and that if she knew how King should destroy that energy, she should prevent it from happening. And Maria told Luna that there was nothing they could do to prevent King from destroying that energy inside her, that the only thing to do was to hope that the mysterious ghost who was in touch with her would prevent King from destroying that energy. And Luna replied to Maria that the energy of the magic of Superhuman inside her was the protection of the planet because if that energy was destroyed, the magic of Superhuman would stop working.

That, if Superhuman was using his magic now to fight, it was because she had the energy of his magic inside her that was communicating with the magic of Superhuman, despite the fact that she was not close to him. And for that, they could not put all their hope on the mysterious ghost, that they did not even know who it was, that they must prevent King from destroying that energy inside her. Maria told Luna that if they could not put their hope on the mysterious ghost, the only solution now was that Luna run away from the palace and go to the place where Superhuman hides. Luna replied to Maria to forget about the idea to run away from the palace because she would never do it. And Luna added that she heard in the conversation of King and Hector that she must have the eyes and mouth opened for that King destroys that energy inside her.

Then, Luna looked in the eyes of Maria by saying that they would do everything to avoid that King approach her, and for that, everyone would think that she is in a coma, and that she could not receive the visits. And Maria agreed with the idea of Luna by saying that she would ask for help from Doctor Thomas who was a good friend of her, but they were afraid that King could use his magic to find out their plan. Superhuman was lying on the sofa very tired and weak, and Philip had made the bandages on his wounds, and he was worried about the storm that was outside, and people were outside in the shelters that the storm was preventing them to get back to their house.

But, Superhuman was happy to know that King did not succeed to see where he hides because when he got inside the house, he asked his magic if King followed him till home, and his magic answered him that no, then he looked at his magic palm and he saw King and Hector who were in the bedroom of Luna. The whole planet was scared about what they had watched, everyone was afraid, and Superhuman became their Superhero and everyone trusted in him and loved him. Alex was named the hero of the planet, everyone was surprised to see how he had helped Superhuman by throwing the stones on the elephant, and for a lot of people without Alex, the elephant should kill Superhuman, and the courage of Alex was admired by the whole planet mostly by Cynthia, except King and Hector who had not appreciated seeing Alex helped Superhuman.

After that fight with the elephant, no one on the planet had the doubts again about Superhuman, but the doubts were now on King, and everyone was wondering why it was King who was living in the palace and not Superhuman. The whole planet had accepted Superhuman like their magician boy, but everyone was wondering who was responsible for the storm, and all the curses that were happening on the planet everyday. There were a lot of people outside in the mall, and in the shelters waiting for the storm to end, for that they return to their home, and people who were at home were very afraid about the storm that was outside. King and Hector were in their office, very tired and completely lost, they had lost control of the situation of the planet, King had checked through his magic to know the percentage of people who had still the doubt on Superhuman, and he found out none, and that the doubt was based on him now, that the whole planet had already accepted Superhuman like the magician boy. King and Hector did not know what to do, mostly that the only person who could help them to catch Superhuman and change things was Luna, and she was in a coma.

Doctor Thomas had told Hector and King that Luna was in the coma and that she would not receive any visitors. And doctor Thomas wanted to send Luna to a hospital outside of the palace, but King and Hector refused by saying that Luna could not get outside of the palace. King and Hector were watching the storm through the window of their office, without knowing what to do, to stop that storm or not to stop it, and they were hating Superhuman with all their strengths, by regretting the disaster that they had caused by using the elephant. Because the plan of King and Hector was to use that elephant to gain the confidence of all people, that King had lost in his fight last night against Superhuman where Jack lost his life.

King had released that elephant from the sacred forest, to go downtown to scare people, destroy things and kill people, and after he should go downtown and kill that elephant himself. And there the whole planet should see him like the Superhero, the magician boy and there he should earn back the confidence of the whole planet that he had lost, but Superhuman made his plan fail. It was midnight. King and Hector was deeply asleep in their beds, while there were still people outside waiting for the storm to stop for that they return to their house.

Most people on the planet were not asleep, people who were at home were worried for their relatives who were outside, and people were wondering why Superhuman could not stop the storm, to allow people who were outside to return to their home. People who were outside in the malls and the shelters were very tired, and they were all sat on the floor, and kids who were with them were crying, and they were wondering why Superhuman had not yet stopped the storm. Superhuman was lying on the sofa, watching people who were outside through his magic palm, feeling weak and useless like he was unable to help those people who had hope in him to stop the storm. Superhuman was watching his best friend Alex who had saved his life, with the sadness on his face, like Alex was asleep on the floor in the mall. Luna was in her hospital bedroom, with Maria worried about people who were outside, and Luna was thinking about what to do without finding a solution.

It was 10:00 a.m., King woke up and he went to the dining room for his breakfast, and he met Hector who was waiting for him, then both started to talk about the situation of the planet, and Hector told King that they had already lost the confidence of all inhabitant of the planet. Hector added that even the police who were supposed to arrest Superhuman did not arrest him when he was helping people to get outside of their car's accident, and yesterday in his fight against the elephant the police were supporting him.

Then, King and Hector started to think about a new plan to arrest Superhuman, and they were now only focused on the arrest of Superhuman. And they had decided that after the arrest of Superhuman, they should win back the confidence of the whole planet by making Superhuman responsible for all curses that happened on the planet. The plan of King and Hector was to arrest Superhuman and keep him prisoner in his special jail built with the stones, where his magic could not work, and he was going to stay in that jail forever. King and Hector were regretting the agreement that had been made with Superhuman, by releasing him in exchange to keep Luna, for them it was their worst mistake because they should never release Superhuman from his jail. Even if they did not have a choice that day, like Luna was unconscious in the coma and the magic of King was so weak that it was not working, and there was the storm outside that King could not stop, and they needed Superhuman that day to help Luna to get out of the coma, and for that, the magic of King works, and for that King stop the storm that was outside, as the magic of King was not working because Luna was in the coma.

It was 3:00 pm, after hours of thinking King decided to stop the storm because it was important for him to stop that storm because he had a new plan for the following day, and that plan could not happen in the storm. All people who were outside had run through the direction of their home after that the storm was over, and Superhuman was happy to see people return to their home, even Luna was very proud to hear that King had stopped the storm. The following day, the streets of the planet were empty, there was no one outside, all inhabitants of the planet had decided to stay at home, they were all afraid to go outside and that the storm could start when they were outside.

All schools, offices, and shops were closed. Hector and King were in the palace very angry like everyone had decided to stay at home because they needed people outside for their new plan, and with everyone at home, it was impossible that their plan to work. Hector wanted to make a speech to order people to get outside of their house and go to their jobs, but King told Hector that no one would obey him because everyone on the planet was living with fear, that people were not feeling safe anymore, mostly with the storm.

CHAPTER 9

The Torture of Alex

The next day, the situation on the planet had not changed, nobody was outside, everyone had decided to stay at home again, Hector and King were furious by the behavior of all inhabitants of the planet, then Hector made a speech where he ordered everyone to get outside of their house and go outside for their jobs. That he did not want to see someone at home again the following day, and that the one who would stay at home would be in trouble. The whole planet listened to the speech of Hector, and nobody paid attention to that, and it was the first time that they did not pay attention to the speech coming from Hector because the speech of Hector was like the speech of their god Queen Mother.

People were afraid to go outside because they were not feeling safe outside anymore, and Superhuman was spending his time watching Luna, Liza, and Alex to make sure that they were fine because he knew that King could kill them just to get his revenge. King and Hector were so busy, focused on Superhuman till they had forgotten Luna, and they had not even asked Doctor Thomas who was taking care of Luna how she was doing, or even Maria that they knew that she was close to Luna. Luna was in her bedroom hospital with artificial respiration on her that was not working, Doctor Thomas had put it in case if King or Hector got inside the room, and there was Berly under the bed of Luna the day like the night. Maria was spending her time in the bedroom of Luna, except for doctor Thomas, nobody was aware of their plan, Maria was taking food and water to Luna everyday, and she was telling Luna what was happening on the planet, and about the behavior of King and Hector.

The following day, there were just a couple of people outside, most of the inhabitants of the planet were still at home, the schools were empty because all the students were still at home. King and Hector were a little bit sad, like there were just some people outside, mostly that people they needed for their plan were not outside, and Hector made another speech by saying that he would ban education on the planet if students keep staying at home, because for him, students are made for school not at home. The whole planet had received the speech of Hector with surprise and disappointment because for parents it was unfair that Hector threatened them to ban education to their kids if they did not allow their kids to go to school.

Everyone was expecting Hector to talk about the situation of the planet, to talk about the insecurity of the planet, to talk about all curses that were happening on the planet for almost a year now. People were expecting Hector to answer some of their questions like Where was Queen mother? Who was King? Why was King living in the palace and not Superhuman? Why were King and Superhuman fighting? Why was it Superhuman who was protecting them, not Queen mother who was their god, or King that he had named the angel of the planet and the magician boy of the planet? After that speech of Hector, people had a hard evening, and they went to bed angrily.

It was 8:00 a.m., the streets were full of people, there were cars of the school full of students in the streets, all offices and shops were opened and the houses were almost empty because people were out for their jobs. King and Hector were in their office, watching people outside through the magic palm of King, with a smile on their faces. The day spent without a problem, although the fact that the day was hard for everyone because people were outside with the heart beating of fear that something could happen, that the storm could start, and parents were to their work worried about the security of their kids who were at school. No one was quiet on the planet during the entire day, everyone was expecting the worst to happen, but everyone went to bed with a smile on their face, hoping that the following days will be the same.

It was 5:00 am, Liza was lying in her bed hospital with her eyes opened, and with the bandages around her head, and other parts of her body like her hands and feet. Then, the door of her bedroom opened, and Liza turned her head through the door, and she saw Superhuman who was walking inside by looking at her with a sad face, while Liza was looking back at him with a surprised face. Superhuman walked close to the bed, and he looked in the eyes of Liza with tears who were flowing down his cheeks, and he said, "I am so sorry."

Liza looked back into his eyes with tears in her eyes by saying, "I am sorry too."

Superhuman said, "You do not have to be sorry."

Liza said, "I treated you like a wizard boy who wanted to destroy the planet, and for that, I have to be sorry because I was wrong."

Superhuman said, "You did not know who I was, so it was your right to treat me like a wizard boy."

Liza said, "I am aware of your fight against the elephant and I thank you for everything you are doing for this planet."

Superhuman said, "I am sorry for Jack."

Liza said, "You tried your best to save us, but unfortunately Jack did not have the chance." And she added, "Thank you for having saved my life."

Then, the light started to shine on the magic hand of Superhuman, and he looked at his magic palm, then he looked at Liza by saying "We have to go."

Liza asked, "Where are we going?"

Superhuman replied, "I came to take you with me."

Liza asked, "Why?"

Superhuman replied, "I will explain to you later." And he added, "There is no time to waste."

Liza said, "The doctors will not let you take me with you."

Superhuman replied, "No one knows that I am here, and no one will see us when we will leave."

Then, Superhuman turned and he walked to the table that was in the room, and he took the box of the drugs that were on that table, and he put it in the pocket of the jacket that he had worn on him. Then, Superhuman walked back till close to the bed of Liza, and he helped her to get up from her bed, and Liza told him that she must change her clothes because it was a risk to get out with hospital clothes on her. And Superhuman replied to her that there was no time to change the clothes and not to worry because no one will catch them. Then, Superhuman held the right hand of Liza, with his left hand, and she was behind him, and they were walking through outside, and Superhuman was looking at his magic palm to see the position of security men of the hospital, and to make sure that no one was coming through where they were walking.

The eyes of Liza were focuseded on the magic palm of Superhuman, and she was wondering how he was doing to see people on his palm, and Superhuman was using his magic hand to open the doors that were locked. After a few minutes, Superhuman and Liza reached the parking of the hospital, and they walked to a nice car, and Superhuman used his magic hand and he opened the doors of that car, and they got inside. And Liza looked at Superhuman by saying, "You have a nice car." Superhuman smiled at her by saying, "It's not my car." Liza asked, "Who this car belong to?" Superhuman replied, "I have no idea." And he added, "We are just stealing it." Liza smiled by saying, "I did not know that the magician boy was a thief." And she added, "I thought that you were with your hawk and that we should fly on your hawk." Superhuman smiled at her by saying, "I can see that you are not afraid." And he added, "The hawk will be for another time."

Then, Superhuman started the engine of the car, by using his magic hand, and he started to drive with his left hand, and his eyes focused on his magic palm, watching Hector and King who were talking in their office. Liza was scared by listening to the conversation between Hector and King through the magic palm of Superhuman. Then, Liza was asking questions to Superhuman like where King come from? Who was King's family? What were the reasons for King to destroy the planet? Why did King live in the palace? Why did Hector allow King to destroy the planet knowing that he was a wizard boy? And where was Queen mother? Superhuman answered to Liza that it was the same questions that he was asking himself everyday since the months now and that he had not yet succeeded to answer even one of those questions, that even his own magic refused to answer him those questions. And Superhuman added that the most important question that he really wanted to find the answer to, was how to stop all the tragedies that were happening on the planet every day, and how to end that cursed war between King and him so that people of the planet could live in peace. And Liza looked at Superhuman by saying, "I found the answer to your most important question."

Superhuman looked back at her by asking, "What is that answer."

Liza replied, "The only answer it's to kill the wizard boy who is King."

Superhuman said, "King is not a natural human being."

Liza asked, "What do you mean?"

Superhuman replied, "Nobody can kill King, even myself."

Liza asked, "Even with the bullets, and the poison?"

Superhuman replied, "It will not work."

Liza asked, "You mean that King is undying?"

Superhuman replied, "King can only die from a natural death."

Liza said, "It means that we will keep living this hell, that King wants us to live till the day he will die." Superhuman replied, "It's what I am afraid of."

Liza said, "Just fear will kill a lot of people on this planet." And she asked "how about you?"

Superhuman replied, "Myself, I can only die of a natural death."

Liza said, "It means that the one who will die first between King and you will be the loser of the war, and it means too that if you die first King will be free to do whatever he wants on this planet. King will be the owner of this planet because there will be no one who will be able to fight him, or prevent him from doing whatever he wants. Then Liza asked, what is the difference between King and you?"

Superhuman replied, "The only difference I know that exists between King and me it's that the sparks of fire that get out from my magic palm can not kill a human being." And he added, "I just use those sparks of fire to prevent people from arresting me, to destroy all terrible things, to destroy all negative energies too, also to kill bad animals, and to fight King. While the sparks of fire that get out from the magic palm of King kills a human being."

Then, Superhuman parked the car in front of the house of Alex, and he demanded Liza to wait for him in the car, then he got out of the car and walked to the front door of the house. Alex and his parents were still in bed asleep, and they heard the doorbell that was ringing, and the noises coming from the front door, then Alex's dad got up from his bed and walked till to the front door, then he opened the door and he saw Superhuman face to him. And Superhuman told Alex's dad that he came to take Alex with him, that Alex was in danger, and the dad of Alex was surprised about what Superhuman was saying, and he was asking Superhuman to explain to him why Alex was in danger.

Suddenly, Alex joined them with his clothes night on him, and Superhuman asked Alex to follow him, and Alex wanted to go change the clothes night that was on him, and to wear the shoes, but Superhuman said that there was no time to waste that they must go like that. Then, Alex followed Superhuman with his dress night on him, without shoes, and they got inside the car, and Superhuman introduced Alex to Liza. Then, Superhuman started to drive, and he noticed that the light was shining on his magic hand, and he looked at his magic palm and he read, "You are in danger."

Suddenly, Superhuman put his foot on the accelerator and he pressed it, then the car started to go faster, Liza and Alex were wondering what was going on, and they were screaming at Superhuman to drive slowly, but Superhuman was not paying attention to what they were saying. After three minutes, Superhuman was being chased by the police's cars for speeding, but he was still driving faster by doubling the cars that were on the streets without paying attention, and the cars were leaving the streets to let the place to the police cars that had put the sirens.

Everyone in the street was looking at the car that Superhuman was driving by wondering who the crazy driver was who was on the wheel of that car. Even the police did not know that it was Superhuman that they were pursuing, like Superhuman had hidden his face with a hat. Liza was in the car shaking and she was screaming at Superhuman to stop the car, that there were the sirens of the police cars that were screaming around them, and that the police were asking them to stop the car, but Superhuman was not paying attention to Liza's words.

Suddenly, Superhuman noticed that the police cars surrounded him, and he stopped the car, then he looked through the window's glass, and he noticed that policemen were getting outside of their cars with the guns in their hands handed through his car. Alex said, "It's over for us." Liza looked at Superhuman by asking, "What to do now?" And she added, "Policemen are coming with the guns in their hands." Then they started to hear the voice of policemen who were asking them to get outside of their car, and Superhuman looked at his magic palm, then the car started to get up from the ground, and everyone outside, even policemen had the head lifted through the sky, by looking with the surprised eyes how Superhuman was driving in the space.

Then, some policemen started to shoot in the space, through the car of Superhuman, but it was a waste of time because Superhuman was already gone, it was like they were watching a miracle, they even did not know what to think, they were just wondering who it was in that car. Philip was walking inside the house, with his eyes focused on the watch on the wall, worried about Superhuman, and he was wondering why Superhuman had not yet reached home, afraid that maybe something worse happened. Then, Philip started to hear the noises coming from the back door, and he walked through the back door, and he saw Superhuman, Liza, and Alex who were walking inside. Superhuman introduced Philip to Alex and Liza.

Alex and Liza were looking at the house with surprised faces, and after a couple of minutes, Liza looked at Superhuman by asking, "Where we are?" Superhuman answered, "We are in a safe place." Liza asked, "Why is it a little bit cold inside the house? And why are the lights on in the morning?" Superhuman replied, "We are in the basement, that's the reason why it's a little cold, and there will be darkness if we turn off the lights like we are in the basement." Alex said, "It's my first time to see a house with a basement." Superhuman replied, "Me too, this house it's the first house I saw with a basement." Liza said, "I did not know that there was a house on this planet built with a basement." Then, Philip said, "We will not spend our time talking about the house." And he added, "Let's go to the kitchen for breakfast."

Then, all of them walked through the kitchen. People were getting out of their houses going to their jobs, and students going to school. Maria was in the hospital bedroom of Luna, she had told Luna that Hector and King had spent their whole night in their office and that till now they were still in their office. And Luna was worried, she knew that King and Hector had a plan, but she did not know what plan it was. Then, she was wondering what that plan could be, and she was hoping that Superhuman was aware of what King intended to do and that Superhuman must intervene on time. The day was going without a problem, King and Hector had not got out of their office, and they had not asked for something to drink or to eat.

It was 3:00 p.m., the streets had started to be full, there were people who were coming back from work, and students who were coming back from school. Suddenly, a bus stopped in the middle of the road, and that bus was a school bus, and inside that bus, there were pupils who were coming back from school and going home. The driver of that bus was trying to restart the engine without success, and the driver tried to open the bus's door, but the door was not opening, then the driver started to look inside the bus by wondering what was going on.

There was the traffic that had started on the road, like that bus had stopped in the middle of the road, after seven minutes there was a huge traffic, and it was impossible to drive. Then, People went, and they tried to open the doors of that bus without success, and they even tried to push the bus outside the road, but the bus was not moving. No one was understanding what was going on, and kids who were inside that bus had started to cry, and people had already called for help. After ten minutes, there were the tow truck and the lift truck that was trying to carry that bus, or move the bus did not succeed, the bus was not moving on the ground although people were using a tow truck to move it, and lift truck to lift it, no one could explain what was happening. Kids were feeling hot inside the bus, till they were sweating, and other kids were crying of starving and thirsty.

People were coming more and more to see what was going on, there were journalists who were making the reportage, while the camera men were filming, and other people were at the home front of their television watching what was going on. Everyone was worried for those kids inside the bus, and most people had started to feel afraid, and people were saying that it was another day of the curse, that it was the wizard boy who was responsible for what was going on. Then, some people had started to run through their house, even people who were still at work had started to run through their house, after that they had heard what was going on with kids in the bus. Shops and offices were closing their doors, and most people were afraid that the storm was going to start and prevent them from returning to their houses. Although the fact that the streets of the planet had started to be empty, there were still people around that school bus that kids were inside, and people were still trying to move that bus on the road without success. People had even tried to break the bus's door, and the glass windows without succeeding. People were in front of their televisions with tears in their eyes, wondering where Superhuman was, why Superhuman was not coming to save those kids on the bus.

Maria had told Luna what was happening on the planet, and Luna had left her hospital bed and she was in her bedroom with Maria in front of the television watching what was going on with the tears that were following down her cheeks. Luna was wondering why Superhuman was not coming to help those kids, and at the same time she was afraid that maybe something bad had happened to him, that's why he was not there to help those kids. King and Hector were in their office looking tired, by watching what was going on through the magic palm of King. King and Hector had started to think that Superhuman had not the energy of his magic inside him because it had been a while now that those kids were inside that bus, and Superhuman had not yet come, but they were sure that Superhuman was watching what was going on.

At the same moment, King and Hector were not surprised that Superhuman did not have the energy of his magic inside him because it had been more than 72 hours now that Superhuman had not seen Luna. And they were expecting Superhuman with the smile on their faces, they knew that Superhuman could not open the doors of that bus without the energy of his magic inside him. King and Hector were waiting for Superhuman to come himself in the palace to exchange his own life against the life of those kids in the bus, and they were very happy because, for them, they had already caught Superhuman because they knew that sooner or later Superhuman would show up in the palace, he would come to exchange his own life for the freedom of those kids in the bus because he would not support that those kids die. People who were trying to move the bus on the road, or to break the bus's doors were already tired, they had tried everything they could without success, and kids were still crying inside the bus, and those kids were tired, hungry, and starving. Suddenly, people started to scream around the bus, like they saw a kid who had fainted inside the bus, camera men had handed their cameras through the window's glass of the bus, and people were front to their televisions crying by seeing that kid who had fainted inside the bus.

Luna was crying in the arms of Maria who was trying to calm her, and Luna wanted to go confront King, but Maria prevented her from doing it and that she would only make things worse because King would find out that she was not in the coma. Then, Luna looked at Maria by saying that they must make another plan to distract King, that she was sure that if Superhuman had not yet come to save those kids, it was because he knew that King was using those kids to catch him. Superhuman was walking inside the house like a crazy boy, and Liza was trying to calm him. He wanted to go outside to save those kids in the bus, even if it should be his last mission, and the end of his life, he was tired of watching those kids suffering in the bus.

Superhuman knew what was the plan of King and Hector, he had watched King and Hector talked about that plan three days ago, he knew that King and Hector thought that he did not have the energy of his magic inside him, but in their plan, King and Hector had decided that in case that he had the energy of his magic inside him, King should set off the storm. Superhuman knew that once when he should go outside, and when he should be close to that bus that kids were inside, King should trigger a storm to prevent him from opening that bus of school that kids were inside, like his magic did not work in the storm, and there King should arrest him. Superhuman wanted to go to the palace to exchange his own life against the life of those kids because it was the only way to save those kids like he knew that he could not open that school's bus that kids were inside because once he should approach that bus, King should send the storm to prevent him to open the doors of that bus to release kids. Superhuman had tried to use his magic to open the doors of that bus from home, but he did not succeed.

Philip, Alex, and Liza were preventing Superhuman from going out because they knew that he could not save those kids inside the bus, at least to exchange his own life against the life of those kids. Philip sat at the door to prevent Superhuman from getting outside because Philip knew that if Superhuman was going out it would be the end of everything. King and Hector were still in their office, wondering if Superhuman was dead, they were surprised to see that he had not shown up, even after that a kid had fainted in the bus.

Then, King and Hector heard the noises coming from the door of their office, someone was knocking at the door, and they looked at each other with a surprised face because they were not expecting someone, and everyone in the palace knew that when they were in their office no one had the right to come knocking at the door, no matter what was happening. And Hector smiled at King by saying that he had no doubt that Superhuman came, then he got up from his chair and he walked till the door, and he opened the door, and he saw a housekeeper with a tray in her hands, and there were two cups of coffee in that tray. Hector looked at that housekeeper with a surprised face, without knowing what to say, and that housekeeper handed the tray of coffee to Hector without saying a word, then he took those both cups of coffee that were on the tray, despite the fact that he had not demanded those coffees. Then, Hector walked to his chair with those two cups of coffee, and he put one cup of coffee in front of King, saying, "Those cups of coffee will help us to get rid of tiredness, and it will make us feel better and awake." And they started to drink their coffee, even like they had not asked for it.

After fifteen minutes, the situation was still the same, people were still in front of their televisions with their hearts beating with fear, that those kids inside the bus were going to die. All the people who were around that bus were looking through the window's glass of that bus with tears flowing down their cheeks, they were feeling sorry and pity for those kids inside the bus, unable to help them. They had tried everything they could without success, and they were all expecting only for a miracle to save those kids inside the bus. Then, a kid that his dad had carried him on his shoulder started to knock the head of his dad by saying, "Superhuman." And that kid had lifted his other hand through the sky, with his finger handed through Superhuman who was flying on his hawk. Then, people who were close to that kid, heard how that kid was calling the name of Superhuman, and they turned their head looking at that kid, and they noticed that that kid had one his hand handed through the sky, and they lifted their heads through the sky in the same direction of the hand of that kid, then they saw Superhuman who was coming on his hawk.

Then, they all started to scream the name of Superhuman with joy on their face, and the rest people lifted their heads through the sky, and they saw Superhuman, and everyone started to clap hands by screaming the name of Superhuman. All cameras were handed through the sky on Superhuman, and the police were asking people to move on one side to make the space for Superhuman. While, other people were moving the trucks that were close to that bus away, and people were at the home front to their televisions by jumping with joy like they were seeing Superhuman on their television. Then, Superhuman landed on the ground not far from that bus, and he got off on his hawk, and he started to walk through that bus, and the eyes of everyone were focused on him, everyone was quiet with their heart who was beating faster than the normal, some people had the mouths opened but no word was coming out, other people were breathing deeply, and they were all wondering if Superhuman would succeed to open the doors of that bus.

Then, Superhuman reached the bus, and he handed his magic hand through the bus's door, and he grabbed the door and he opened it. And suddenly there were the screams of joy over the planet, the screams of happiness were coming everywhere. Policemen got inside the bus to help those kids to get out, and there were the ambulances for the kids who had fainted, and kids who were not doing well, and there was a smile on the face of everyone like they were watching those kids getting outside of the bus. After eleven minutes, all those kids were outside in the arms of their families, and two ambulance attendants had carried the kid who had fainted on the stretcher getting out of the bus with that kid.

Everyone was staring at that kid lying on the stretcher of the ambulance, like a dead kid breathing by artificial respiration, with a sad face and the tears flowing down their cheeks, the smile of joy who was on their face was gone, to give place to the sadness. Even people who were in front of their television had tears who were flowing down their cheeks when they saw that kid getting outside the bus lying on the stretcher. Luna was watching that kid on the stretcher with tears in her eyes, hoping that Superhuman would save that kid. Superhuman was outside, and he was staring at that kid lying on the stretcher with a sad face, like ambulance's attendants were taking that kid to the ambulance car, then the light started to shine on his magic hand, and he lifted that magic hand through his face and he looked and his magic palm.

Then, Superhuman started to walk through that kid, and a policeman saw Superhuman who was walking through the direction of that kid, and that policeman demanded the ambulance's attendant who had carried that kid to wait. Then, Superhuman reached that kid who was lying on the stretcher and he put his magic palm on the forehead of that kid for a couple of seconds, then he removed his magic palm on the forehead of that kid. Then, that kid opened his eyes and got up off the stretcher, and suddenly everyone had the eyes widely opened and the mouth opened but no word was coming out, by looking at that kid with an amazed face, and by looking at them it was like they were all dreaming. Then, Superhuman handed his magic hand through the sky, and his hawk started to fly through him, and the eyes of everyone were lifted through the sky focused on Superhuman who was flying on his hawk, and they were all wondering how he was doing all those incredible things.

Luna had returned to her hospital bedroom, and Doctor Thomas had put back that artificial respiration on her again, and Maria was close to her. Luna and Maria were so proud that their plan worked, and that their plan allowed Superhuman to save those kids who were inside the bus, but Luna was very worried about what would happen after King and Hector would find out about the plan, she had made with Maria to allow Superhuman to save those kids who were in the bus. And Luna asked Maria to run away, and she wanted to show Maria where Superhuman was hiding, and although the fact that she begged Maria to go join Superhuman and Philip, Maria refused by saying that she would never let her alone. Then, Luna was wondering why King could not find through his magic palm where Superhuman was hiding, and how the magic of King and the magic of Superhuman were different.

Luna knew that Superhuman had an advantage over King because Superhuman was watching King from where he was through his magic palm, and King could not watch Superhuman through his magic palm. And she did not know the reason why King's magic could not find the place where Superhuman was hiding, and it was another question like a lot of other questions that she could not answer. All inhabitants of the planet were inside their house, with the name of Superhuman in their mouth, they were all swearing at the name of Superhuman now, that they had forgotten their god Queen mother.

Everyone on the planet had decided to not go out again, till they were sure that they were safe, and everyone had the reserve of food inside the house because since that the curses like the storm had started on the planet, they had all bought a lot of stuff and food to keep home to use it in case of danger. Superhuman, Liza, Alex, and Philip were all sat around a small table, all quiet but we could see on the face of Superhuman and Philip that they were anxious. Then, Alex broke the silence by asking, "Someone can tell me what is going on here because I do not understand the meaning of this silence."

Philip took a deep breath and turned his head through Superhuman by saying, "I imagine that you are worried for Luna."

Superhuman said, "I am afraid about what will happen if King and Hector find out that Luna is not in the coma, and the plan she made with Maria for that I save those kids who were inside the bus."

Philip said, "The time has come."

Liza looked at Philip by asking, "What do you mean?"

Philip answered, "We have to expect the worst."

Alex asked, "What do you mean by that?"

Philip answered, "King has been careless, and he made a big mistake. Because he was obsessed by the fact that Luna has the energy of the magic of Superhuman, and he loves Luna for making him a little bit blind." Superhuman said, "Still we do not understand."

Philip said, "King is going to find out all the lies of Luna."

Superhuman asked, "How King is going to find out the lies of Luna?"

Philip looked at Superhuman by saying, "Since this war started, I found out that King has two weaknesses, and I found out that you have three weaknesses."

Superhuman asked, "What are the weaknesses of King?"

Philip answered, "The magic of King can not reach underground, that's the reason why since the months that King is looking for us through his magic, he can not find us."

Liza looked at Philip by saying, "I do not understand."

Philip said, "We are living here in a basement, that's the reason why King can not see us through his magic palm." And he added, "This is the only house of this planet that has the basement, even the palace does not have the basement, and except us here and Luna nobody else is aware that this house has the basement, it's a big secret that even Hector who is the right hand of Queen mother does not know." Superhuman said, "It means that this basement is our protection." And he looked at Philip by asking, "What is another weakness of King?

Philip replied, "The magic of King has a delay on the time, that's the reason why King can not see what is going to happen."

Alex asked, "What are the weaknesses of the magic of Superhuman?"

Philip replied, "The magic of Superhuman can not work in a house built with the stones and in the storm too, and the body of

Superhuman does not produce the energy of his magic. Because he gets the energy of his magic from Luna and that energy expires after 72 hours, and Superhuman has a poison who can kill him." Then, Philip added, by saying, "The only advantage that Superhuman has on King, it's that the magic of Superhuman has an advance on the time, while the magic of King has a delay on the time. That's the reason why Superhuman is always aware of what King intends to do, and when danger is going to happen the magic of Superhuman lets Superhuman know by the light that shines on his magic hand."

And Philip went on by saying, "King has two advantages on Superhuman, the first it's that, the magic of King can work remotely, so King can stay in his office, or in his bedroom and order to his magic to provoke a disaster like he was doing in classroom as he did with the elephant, and like he did today to block kids in the bus. While the magic of Superhuman can not really do it because the magic of Superhuman can not work in distance. Then the second that the magic of King works without the energy, so King can fight during the years without stopping, also King knows that to make the magic of Superhuman useless he must destroy the energy of the magic of Superhuman that is inside the body of Luna, and Superhuman has been so lucky that till now King has not yet succeeded to destroy that energy inside Luna."

Liza took a deep breath by saying, "King has a lot of advantages on Superhuman, and it means that the whole planet is really in danger."

Alex looked at Philip by asking, "How do you know that?"

Philip replied, "I just try to analyze what is happening, and to find the answers to some questions that I have in my mind."

Liza asked, "How to end this war that is destroying the planet?"

Philip looked at Liza by saying, "That's the most important question that we all have in our mind, but none of us has the answer to that question." Then, Superhuman, Philip, Liza, and Alex spent their whole night talking about the situation of the planet.

It was early morning, King and Hector were in their office, they had just opened their eyes, they had spent their whole night in their office. King and Hector were looking tired, and they were crying from the headaches like they had slept in the chairs with their heads bent on the desk, and they were wondering what they were doing in the office early morning, and there were two empty cups of coffee on their desk. Then, King noticed that there was a photo of a bus on his magic palm, and he looked at his magic palm with an amazed face without understanding what was going on, then he showed his magic palm to Hector who was not understanding what was happening too.

And after a few minutes of thinking, King and Hector started to remember what was going on, and why they were in the office. Then, suddenly, King cried out, "Superhuman?" By looking at Hector with a surprised face. And Hector cried out, "Luna?" By looking at King, and both rushed through the door, and they ran till the hospital part of the palace. King and Hector opened the door of Luna's room, and they looked inside, and they saw Luna who was lying in her hospital bedroom with artificial respiration on her, and Maria who was asleep in the chair with the blanket on her, then they closed the door.

King and Hector were walking in the corner of the hospital, angrily without understanding what was going on, then King stopped, and he looked at Hector by saying, "I do not understand how Superhuman succeeded to open that school's bus without the energy of his magic inside him." Hector looked back at King by saying, "The only explanation it's that Superhuman came here and he got the energy of his magic by kissing Luna, then he went, and he released kids who were inside the bus." King said, "If Superhuman was here security should let us know." Hector said, "Do not forget that the whole planet is behind Superhuman now, even people who work in this palace." Then, they walked to the room with a hidden camera, and they asked the security man who was inside that room they wanted to watch all the videos of yesterday. After ten minutes, they had finished watching all the videos, and they had even watched the video three days ago, but they did not see Superhuman get inside the palace, then they left that room. King and Hector started to walk inside the palace like crazy people, without even knowing where they were going, and the employees of the palace were looking at them with surprised faces by wondering what was going on with King and Hector.

After fifteen minutes, walking inside the palace, King stopped, and he looked at Hector by saying, "It's true that Superhuman is a magician boy, but he is not invisible, so how he succeeded to get inside this palace without a hidden camera film him." Hector said, "Nobody can answer that question except your magic." Then, King started to check everything that had happened in the palace those last weeks through his magic palm, and after three minutes the face of King had started to change, and he was looking at his magic palm with a surprised face, and Hector looked at King how King was looking at his magic palm, then Hector asked, "What is going on." But King did not respond to Hector, he was just focused on his magic palm, and after a couple of minutes King lifted his head and he showed his magic palm to Hector. And Hector was watching at the magic palm of King with a surprised face like he was seeing how Luna had organized a plan with Maria, and Maria had made two cups of coffee and Maria put a sleeping pill inside that coffee, and she gave it to a housekeeper who came knocked at the door of their office and served them those two cups of coffee. Hector looked at King by saying, "It means that Luna is not in the coma." King replied, "Since Luna got inside this palace, we are living in the lies, no word coming out from the mouth of Luna was true.

Then King looked in the eyes of Hector with his face full of anger by saying, "The time has come to end with this war." And they turned, and they started to walk through the hospital side. Luna was still in her hospital bed with artificial respiration on her, and Maria sat in the chair still asleep, then the door opened, King and Hector walked inside, then King handed his magic hand through Luna by saying, "Get up of that bed and tell me the secret that is between superhuman and you." Maria opened her eyes, and she saw King and Hector inside the room, and she looked at King with a face full of fear, like he had handed his magic hand through Luna, and Luna was still in her bed with her eyes closed.

King screamed at Luna by saying, "Get up now or I am the one who will kill you in that bed."

Maria asked, "What is going on?"

Hector looked at Maria by saying, "You know well what is going on because you are the one who had put a sleeping pill in the coffee that the housekeeper had served to us."

Then, Luna opened her eyes, and King looked at her by saying, "Remove that artificial respiration on you." Then, Maria got up from her chair, and she walked close to the bed of Luna, and she removed the artificial respiration that was on Luna, and Luna got up and she sat on the bed by staring at King, then Maria sat on the bed too close to Luna. The King's eyes still focused on Luna and he said, "Your lies are over now because I found out through my magic that everything you told me were lies. And I know that you are not the one who gives the energy to the magic of Superhuman because you did not kiss Superhuman the day where he saved the life of John, you have never met Superhuman in the storm, you hurt yourself with the knife to attract my attention to distract me for that Superhuman runs away in the storm without a problem." And King added, "You told Maria to make two cups of coffee and put the sleeping pill inside and serve those two cups of coffee to Hector and me for that Superhuman released the kids who were inside the bus." Then, King went on by saying, "I found out too that since you got inside this palace, you have never kissed Superhuman, so I want to know where Superhuman got the energy of his magic."

Luna answered, "I have no idea."

King looked at his magic palm, and he showed that magic palm to Luna. And Luna read "lie" in the magic palm of King, and she understood that King was checking what she was saying through his magic.

Hector looked at Luna by saying, "You are only the witch girl of this planet, and it's written in the magic book that only the witch girl has the magic of the magician boy." And he added, "We all know that the magic book can not lie, or make a mistake, so you are the only person who has the energy of the magic of Superhuman, and you know well how Superhuman gets that energy from you."

King looked at Luna angrily and he said, "My love for you made me blind, and I trusted you blindly, without checking the words you were saying to me, then you took an advantage of that and you lied to me by looking in my eyes."

Luna looked in the eyes of King by saying, "We do not torture a woman that we love, and we do everything to make sure that the one we love is always smiling with happiness, and shining like sunshine, that she lives in the light, not in the darkness like the prisons you sent me."

King said, "You know well that it's your fault if I tortured you."

Luna said, "I am just doing what I was born to do."

King replied, "I am doing what I was born to do too."

Luna asked, "What were you born to do?"

King answered, "The same thing that you."

Luna said, "I am born to help Superhuman to protect this planet."

King said, "Do not forget that you are linked to me too."

Luna asked, "What do you mean?"

King replied, "It means that you were born to help me to destroy this planet too."

Luna said, "I chose to protect the planet, not to destroy the planet."

King said, "It means you chose the side of Superhuman, and like you chose the side of Superhuman, it means that you are my enemy." Then, he handed his magic hand to her by saying, "Tell me now where Superhuman is, and how he gets the energy of his magic." Luna and Maria were looking at King with fear in their eyes, without saying a word.

After twenty minutes of silence, Hector looked at King by saying, "The better solution is to kill Luna, there is none between Superhuman and you will be the winner of this war. Because even by destroying the energy of the magic of Superhuman that Luna has inside her, we are not sure that it will work or it will be the solution because Superhuman has another way to get that energy."

King looked at Hector by saying, "You are right, the death of Luna is the only better solution because no one between Superhuman and me will win this war, and no one between both of us will have her." Then, King turned his head through Luna by looking in her eyes, and with his magic hand still handed on her. Hector noticed that the magic hand of King was shaking, and asked, "Why is your magic hand shaking?"

King answered, "I am not succeeding to kill her."

Hector asked, "Why?"

King answered, "I love her too much, that I do not have enough of strength to kill her, or to see her dead." Hector said, "If you do not kill her now, you will lose everything, you will lose the war against Superhuman, and you will lose her too because she loves Superhuman and she will go with him."

King turned his head through Hector by looking at him angrily and by saying, "It will never happen because the fight is already over, and this is the time of the revenge that we are going to live."

Hector asked, "What do you mean?"

King answered, "Just watch what is going to happen." Then, King left the room, and Hector followed him.

After four minutes, Luna, Maria, and Doctor Thomas were arrested and put in the separate jails of the palace. Luna was locked in the jail built with the stones, in the jail that was built for Superhuman, and where Superhuman was kept when he was a prisoner to the palace. Luna was walking inside her jail with fear on her face, worried for Maria and Doctor Thomas who were kept prisoners in other jails too. And Luna was thinking about the words that King said to Hector like "The fight is already over, and this is the time of revenge that we are going to live." And she was very afraid about what King was going to do. Superhuman was very nervous, and Alex was trying to calm him, they had watched what had happened in the palace, and Superhuman wanted to go to the palace, but Philip prevented him to do it, by saying that it would be a big mistake and that he was putting the whole planet in danger by doing that. The torture for Superhuman was that he did not know if Luna was doing well or not because his magic could not reach the jail where Luna was like she was kept prisoner in the jail built with the stones.

It was already 10:00 a.m., the planet was like a desert, there was nobody outside, the streets were empty, and everything was closed, people were in their homes looking through the windows to see if there was a storm outside. King and Hector were in their office, thinking about what could make Superhuman get out from where he was hiding, and show up, then they got an idea to use the journalist Liza who was in the hospital. Then, King checked through his magic to know in which hospital Liza was, and the house of Philip appeared on his magic palm, and he looked at his magic palm with a surprised face. King showed his magic palm to Hector, and they understood that Superhuman had taken Liza with him, and King asked his magic to know how many people were hiding with Superhuman, and his magic answered him that there were three people with Superhuman, and he was wondering who the third person was.

Because Hector and King knew that Philip and Liza were with Superhuman, but they had no idea about the third person, and King did not ask his magic the name of that third person. Hector and King spent their full day thinking how to catch Superhuman, and they were determined to catch him, but they were still wondering why the house of Philip was empty, and when they were looking for where Superhuman and Philip were hiding it was that Philp's house that was appearing on the magic palm of King. And King had searched all the rooms of Philip's house through his magic palm and he noticed that all the rooms of Philip's house were empty. Hector and King were wondering where Superhuman and other people were sleeping in that house if the rooms of that house were empty.

It has been three weeks now, and nothing has changed on the planet, all inhabitants of the planet were still in their house, nobody was getting out, but the situation of the planet was not going well. Because most people were already tired to spend their complete day at home despite the fact that they still had the stuff like the food at home, but the situation was going worse in the hospitals. Because there were people who were working, and staying in the hospitals, for almost a month now because they were afraid to return to their house and they were already very tired. King and Hector were already very tired, they were not even paying attention to the situation of the planet like everyone had decided to stay at home.

King and Hector were spending their time looking for Superhuman without success, and they had watched all the houses of the planet through the magic palm of King, and they did not see Superhuman. And the house of Philip was still empty although the fact that the magic of King was telling them that Superhuman was inside that house, they were completely lost. King and Hector were not understanding what was going on, why they were not seeing Superhuman in that house through the magic palm of King like they were seeing all inhabitants of the planet in their house through the magic palm of King and they knew that the magic of King could not lie or make a mistake.

King had visited Luna in her jail many times to try to get information about where Superhuman was hiding, and how Superhuman gets the energy of his magic, but Luna did not say a word to him about Superhuman, although the fact that he threatened her by saying that he was going to send the storm outside and to destroy the planet. And Hector had visited Maria at her jail to try to convince her to tell him everything she knew about Superhuman, but no word had come out from the mouth of Maria, although the fact that Hector threatened her to kill Luna because he knew that Maria loved Luna like her daughter. Superhuman, Alex, Liza, and Philip were still in the basement worried about the situation of the planet, they were spending their time watching what was happening on the planet through the magic palm of Superhuman, and they were all wondering how to end that fight because people should not stay in their house forever. And they were watching how King and Hector were spending their time to find where they were hiding, also they were wondering how Luna was doing like the magic Superhuman could not see Luna in her jail. Superhuman was very sad, and he was spending the bad moments like he could see Luna, and he did not know if she was well treated or not, and mostly that if she was in danger he could not know, and he could not protect her because his magic could not see her.

The following day, Philip, Liza, and Alex woke up and they went to the living room, and they saw Superhuman sat on the sofa with an anxious face, and they all stared at him with surprised faces, and they asked him what was going on. Then, Superhuman asked them to get a sit, and they all sit on the sofa with their eyes focused on him, then Superhuman took two deep breath, and he told them that last night he was watching King and Hector in their office through his magic palm till 11:00 pm, when King and Hector decided to go to bed. And after an hour King and Hector were in their beds deeply asleep, and himself he went to bed and he started to sleep. Then, after a couple of hours, he started to make nightmares, and he opened his eyes and he felt that he had headaches, and suddenly the light started to shine on his magic hand. Then, he looked at his magic palm and he saw King and Hector who were in their office organizing a plan for tomorrow morning, and he looked at the watch that was on the table close to his bed and he noticed that it was 3:00 a.m.,

Then, Superhuman told them the whole conversation he had heard between King and Hector, and all of them started to feel afraid about the plan of Hector and King. Philip looked at each of them by telling them that they must do everything possible to prevent that plan that Hector and King had organized to happen and that they had less than 17 hours to do it. Because if that plan of King and Hector worked it would be the end of the fight, and the victory of King, and the end of the planet because Superhuman would be caught. Then, they all started to think about how to prevent that plan of Hector and King to happen. Maria was in her jail, and she was crying about Luna, like did not know how Luna was doing, and if Luna was still alive because she knew that King was able to kill her, even if he loved her and even if he was linked to her.

Luna was in her jail, tired and weak, it had been weeks now that she had not slept, and she was worried about Maria and Doctor Thomas that she did not know how they were doing, and if they were still alive. Luna was very worried about the inhabitants of the planet like she had no idea about what was happening outside, she did not know if King had sent the storm outside or not like she was in a jail built with stones, even the ceiling of that jail was built with the stones and there was no window or roof to feel or see if there was the storm outside or not. Luna was wondering how she was still alive and how she was breathing in that jail, where the air was not entering inside, and she was spending her time wondering how Superhuman was doing, and she had the feeling that a tragedy was going to happen.

It was evening, Superhuman, Alex, Liza, and Philip were very tired, they had spent their full day thinking how to prevent the plan of King and Hector without finding a solution, and none of them had put something in the mouth, even water, and Liza had not even taken her medicines. Superhuman had even asked his magic to help them to find a solution to prevent that plan to happen, and his magic answered him that there was no solution, that there was nothing who could prevent that plan of King and Hector to happen, and that there was nobody who was able to cancel that plan. Then, Superhuman demanded Philip, Alex, and Liza to run away, and let him alone, and there he would be caught alone, but they all refused his proposition, and they said that they were fighting together and that it was not his fight alone. Philip said that it was impossible to run away from King because no matter where they would go, King would find them through his magic palm because the house where they were was the only place on the planet where King could not find them through his magic.

Then, Superhuman told them that the only solution was that he goes to the palace, and there King would send him to jail forever, and he would stay in that jail till he's dead. And that there maybe he would prevent them from dying because he had no doubt that when King would catch them together, King would not hesitate to kill them, knowing that they were people who supported him in his fight. But Liza and Alex refused the preposition of Superhuman by saying that he could not give up the fight like that and that they were not afraid to die, that they did not care about what King would do to them when he would arrest them. And Liza proposed to Superhuman, Alex, and Philip that they must find a way to let the whole planet know about what was going on, about who was really King because if King caught them, it was very important that all inhabitants of the planet know that King was a wizard boy.

Superhuman found the proposition of Liza very good, but he said that if they did that, they would make things worse because they would provoke the anger of King. And that King could do something really terrible that they would regret their choice to have talked to the whole planet that King was a wizard boy, that they had to remember that the magic of King works in distance, that King could stay in his office and hurt people inside their house. Philip told them that if they were in touch with Luna, and that if Luna knew how she was linked to King, Luna could prevent that plan of King and Hector to happen, and she could even stop the fight. But nobody had an idea how Luna was linked to the magic of King, except King who knew himself how he was connected to Luna. Then, they looked at each other with a sad face, without saying a word, and there were tears who were flowing down the cheeks of Superhuman, and he was feeling sorry for the whole planet that he was unable to protect. Then, Alex got up from his chair, and he walked through his bedroom without saying a word.

It was early morning, King and Hector were at the dining table taking their breakfast, by talking about their plan that was going to happen, after their breakfast. Then, the chief of the security of the palace came and told Hector and King that there was a young boy outside who said that he had an appointment with them. Hector and King looked at each other with an amazed face, and Hector asked, "Are you expecting someone?" King answered, "I know nobody on this planet, and you know it well." Hector asked, "Who it can be?" King looked at the chief of security and he asked, "It's Superhuman?" The chief of the security answered, "No, it's not Superhuman." Hector said, "It will be a kid who lost his way, or who is crazy." And he looked at that chief of security by saying, "Go talk to that boy to go away."

Then, King looked at his magic palm, and he turned his head and he called the chief of the security who was going to come back, then King looked at his magic palm with a surprised face for a couple of seconds, and he showed his magic palm to Hector. Hector was looking at the magic palm of King with a surprised face like he was seeing a young boy on that magic palm, and he was wondering who that young boy was. Then, Hector looked at King by asking, "Who is that young boy?" King answered, "It's the boy who wants to see us." Hector asked, "Do you know him?" King answered, "I found through my magic that his name is Alex, but I have no idea about who is." Hector said, "Use your magic to find out who is." Then, King bent his head and he started to look at his magic palm, and after a minute King got up from his chair and he looked at Hector by saying, "Let's go outside, that boy of Alex is a friend of Superhuman." Then, King, Hector, and that chief of security walked outside, where they met Alex. And King looked at Alex by asking, "Where is Superhuman?" Alex replied, "It's the reason why I am here." Hector said, "We want to know where Superhuman hides." Alex replied, "I am ready to take you where Superhuman hides."

Then, Hector called the police of the palace, and a driver, then they took the road, King was driving a car with Alex and Hector inside, and Alex was showing the direction to King, and there was another car behind who was following them with the police inside. After an hour of driving, they reached an old house not so far from a bush, and they parked the cars in front of that house, and they got outside from their cars, and they walked to the front of the door of that house. Alex pushed the door of that house, and they all walked inside, and everyone looked inside the house with a surprised face, and King asked, "Where is Superhuman?" Alex replied, "If Superhuman is not in this house, he will be in the forest that is behind the house because it's the only place he goes."

Then, they searched all the rooms of those houses, and they saw the clothes that belonged to Superhuman, and they saw the pots in the kitchen and some stuff like food too. But they did not see Superhuman in the house, and there was nobody in the house too, then they went into the yard of the house, and King looked at Alex by saying, "Now I want you to tell me where Superhuman is." Alex turned face through the house, and he handed his finger through the bush that was behind the house, by saying, "Superhuman is in that forest." While King was just looking at his magic palm each time when Alex was talking. Hector said, "We will call more men to search that forest." and King looked at Hector by saying, "It will be a waste of time to search that forest." And he added, "We have to return to the palace." Then, they got inside the cars, and they started to drive through the palace.

Superhuman, Liza, and Philip were still in the living room asleep on the sofa, they had spent the whole night in the living room thinking how to prevent the plan of King and Hector to happen, then they all fell asleep without realizing. Then, Liza opened her eyes by yawning, and she looked around her with a tired face, and she saw Superhuman and Philip who were asleep, then she woke them up. Superhuman opened his eyes, and he looked at Liza by saying, "I have a headache." Philip said, "We all have a headache." Liza said, "It's normal to have headaches, with the situation that we are living in now. Then she asked, "Alex is still asleep?" Philip answered, "Alex will probably still be asleep in the bed." And he added, "Alex was very tired last night when he went to bed." Liza turned her head and she looked at the clock on the wall, then she looked at Superhuman by saying, "There is something that is happening on the planet right now." Superhuman asked, "What do you mean?" Liza replied, "It's not normal that at this time, we have not yet any reaction to the plan of King and Hector." Philip looked at Superhuman by saying, "Liza is right." And he added, "We should not be in this house at this time."

Then, Superhuman looked at his magic palm, and suddenly he cried out, "Alex?" With fear on his face, then he got up from his chair, and he rushed through the door without saying a word, then Liza got up from her chair and she ran through the door, then she grabbed Superhuman by asking, "What is going on?" And Philip joined them. Superhuman replied, "There is no time to waste now." Philip asked, "Where are you going?" Superhuman answered, "To the palace." Philip asked, "King is killing Luna?" Superhuman replied, "Not Luna, but instead Alex." Liza and Philip cried out, "Alex?" at the same time, and Philip asked, "How Alex?" Superhuman said, "I have to go save Alex right now before King finishes killing him." Liza said, "Alex can not be at the palace because he is in his bed asleep."

Superhuman looked at his magic palm, then he showed it to Liza and Philip, and both Liza and Philip were looking at the magic palm of Superhuman with their hands on their mouths unable to say something, like they were seeing Alex in a dark room, sat in a chair face to King and Hector who was standing up by staring at him. Liza asked, "What time King came here?" Philip replied, "I do not think that king was here because if he was here it's not Alex that he should catch, but instead Superhuman." Liza said, "If King was not here, how can we explain that Alex is in the palace right now?" Philip looked at Superhuman by saying, "check what happened, with Alex."

Then, Superhuman started to check in his magic palm, and they were all watching at the magic palm of Superhuman with surprised faces like they were seeing Alex who was getting out of the house with a bag on his back, that he had put clothes of Superhuman inside, and some stuff like food too, and with a pot that he had put on his head. They kept watching Alex who was walking the outside in the night, alone in the street with a torch that was on in his hand that he was seeing the road with, till an old house not far from a bush, and Alex got inside that old house and put the stuff he had, and he got outside of the house and walked till the palace.

Then, they watched how Alex took King and Hector to that old house by saying that Superhuman was in that old house. Then, they looked at each other with surprised faces, unable to say something, after a couple of seconds, Liza broke the silence by asking, "Why Alex did that?" Superhuman replied, "Only Alex has the answer to that question." Then, he turned by saying, "I am at the palace to prevent King from killing Alex." Philip put his hand on the shoulder of Superhuman, by saying, "Turn and look at me." Superhuman turned and looked at Philip, and Philip said, "Alex done what he did for you and for the Planet." Superhuman asked, "What do you mean?" Philip replied, "Alex knew what the plan of King and Hector was. And he knew well that there was no solution to prevent that plan to happen, and he knew that if that plan had happened it should be the end of everything, and King should keep you prisoner till your dead." Liza looked at Philip by asking, "You mean Alex went to the palace to prevent King and Hector from applying their plan this morning?" Philip replied, "Yeah, Alex went to the palace to distract King and Hector, he wants King and Hector to pay attention to him and forget about their plan." Liza said, "I understand now." And she added, "That's the reason why till now King and Hector had not exerted their plan."

Superhuman said, "I have to go now." Liza looked at Superhuman by saying, "You can not go to the palace because Alex's already sacrificed for the planet." Superhuman said, "I can not let King kill my friend." Philip looked at Superhuman by saying, "You know well that Alex is a very brave man, with a lot of courage and you know well that Alex is not afraid to give his life for you and for this planet. And Alex already chose to die for the planet, to give you another chance to beat King and save the planet if possible." Superhuman said, "I am the one who should give my life for the planet, not Alex because I was born for that, and it's my responsibility not the responsibility of Alex." Liza held both hands of Superhuman by looking in his eyes, and by saying, "It's too late to save Alex because even if you go to the palace King will still kill Alex. And he will keep you like a prisoner, then he will be the winner." Then, Philip and Liza succeeded to convince Superhuman to give up the idea to go to the palace, and they all went and sat on the sofa watching what was going on through the magic palm of Superhuman. King and Hector were standing in front of Alex who sat in the chair.

King looked in the eyes of Alex angrily, and he asked, "Where is Superhuman?"

Alex replied, "Superhuman is in the forest."

King was staring at Alex with his face full of anger, without saying a word. After three minutes of silence, King walked close to Alex, and he showed his magic palm to Alex, and Alex read what was written on the magic palm of King, then Alex understood that King was aware that he was lying. King looked at Alex by saying, "I know well that you are the best friend of Superhuman." And he added, "I found out through my magic that you are the one who had thrown the stones on the elephant when Superhuman was fighting against the elephant, and that you were living in the same house with Superhuman till this morning that you left that house."

Hector looked at King by saying, "It means that this boy of Alex was the third person, who was with Superhuman, like we had found out through your magic that there was Liza, Philip and someone else in the same house with Superhuman."

King looked at Hector by saying, "Yeah, Alex is that third person who was with Superhuman." Then, King looked at Alex by saying, "Now tell me where is that house you were living with Superhuman."

Alex said, "That house is the house where I took you this morning, close to the forest."

King said, "Superhuman has never been in that house where we went this morning."

Alex said, "The clothes that were inside that house were the clothes of Superhuman, and you can check it through your magic."

King said, "I know well, that those clothes were for Superhuman, but you are the one who had put it in that house." Then, King asked, "Why did you decide to talk about Superhuman?"

Alex replied, "I decided to betray Superhuman because I found out that he is a wizard boy, that he is the one who is destroying the planet, and who is responsible for all curses that are happening on the planet." King looked at Hector by saying, "It's obvious that this boy of Alex is laughing at us."

Then, King and Hector kept asking the questions to Alex to find out where Superhuman was. After an hour, King and Hector had not succeeded to get the information that they wanted from Alex, and King handed his magic hand through Alex who still sat in the chair, when suddenly Hector screamed by saying, "Do not kill him."

King looked at Hector by saying, "He does not want to talk, and the only solution now it's to kill him." And King still had his magic hand handed to Alex, while Alex was looking at the magic hand of King who was handed on him, with fear on his face, and his heart beating faster than normal, knowing that he was going to die.

Hector said, "Do not worry we will oblige Alex to tell us, where is Superhuman." And Hector walked two steps face to Alex, then he handed his hand that his finger wears the magic ring through Alex, by showing that magic ring on Alex. Then, the light got out from that magic ring and went through Alex, and those lights turned into the chains and tied Alex on the chair, then Alex started to scream by crying pains like the sparks of fire were getting outside from the magic ring of Hector and burning his body. After seven minutes, Hector stopped to torture Alex with the sparks of fire, and Hector had tried to make Alex talk where Superhuman was hiding, but Alex had decided to keep the silence although the threats that he did to Alex.

King looked at Alex by saying, "You had better tell us where Superhuman is if you want to get out of this room alive. Because no one will save you in this room, even Superhuman will not come here to save you. Then he asked where is Superhuman?"

Alex answered, "Superhuman is in the forest."

Hector looked at Alex by saying, "You know well that it's impossible to lie to us because everything you say, King checks it through his magic, and the magic of King is saying that Superhuman is not in the forest. Then he asked, where is Superhuman?"

Alex answered, "Superhuman is in the forest."

Suddenly, the face of Hector changed, and he became angry, then he handed his magic ring through Alex and Alex started to scream like the sparks of fire were burning his body. Superhuman, Liza, and Philip were watching how Hector was torturing Alex, through the magic palm of Superhuman with tears flowing down their cheeks, and Superhuman wanted to go to the palace but Liza and Philip prevented him from doing it. Luna was lying on the mattress in her jail, and she was shaking, she was feeling cold because she had a fever, then she heard the door of her jail opened, and she turned her head through the door, and she saw two security men who were dragging Alex on the ground by getting inside the jail with him, and she cried out, "Alex?" With a surprised face.

Suddenly, Luna got up from her mattress, and she rushed through the door, and she bent close to Alex who was lying on the floor, and those two security men left the room, but the door was still open. King and Hector were outside watching Alex and Luna through the magic palm of King, to hear the conversation between both Luna and Alex to know if they would talk about where Superhuman was hiding. Luna lifted the head of Alex and she looked into his eyes, and she noticed that he had fainted, and she started to scream his name by shaking him, with tears who were flowing down her cheeks.

After a few minutes, Alex opened his eyes, and he looked at Luna with a tired face, and Luna looked back at him by asking, "What happened?" Alex opened his mouth to talk, but he was barely talking that Luna could not understand what he was saying. Then Luna sat on the floor, and she put the head of Alex on her lap, and she bent her head by looking at him with tears flowing down her cheeks. Alex said, "Do not say any word, it's a trap." Luna asked, "What do you mean?" Alex replied, "I am sure that King is watching us, through his magic to know if we will talk about where Superhuman hides."

Luna looked at the body of Alex, and she noticed that his body was all red, then she remembered that the day where she and Superhuman had found Philip tied in the chair with the chains, and they had noticed that the body of Philip was all red because he had been tortured by Hector, and she understood that Alex has been tortured by the same way that Philip had been tortured. Then, King and Hector walked inside, and King looked at Alex and Luna with a face full of anger, then King demanded Luna to get up and come where he was. Alex looked in the eyes of Luna by saying, "I chose to die for the planet, and I am already dead so no matter what will happen do not say a word." While Luna was looking at Alex without saying a word just by crying, then she got up and walked to where King was. Hector walked through Alex, and he looked at him by asking, "Where is Superhuman?" Alex replied, "Superhuman is in the forest."

Then, Hector started to torture Alex with the sparks of fire that were getting outside from his magic ring, and Alex was screaming in pain. And Luna was screaming by saying, "Please stop it, please stop it." King looked at Luna by asking, "Are you going to tell us where Superhuman is?" Luna looked in the eyes of King with tears who were flowing down her cheeks by saying, "Please release Alex." King said, "I will release Alex, only when you will decide to tell me where Superhuman hides." Luna said, "Alex has no idea about where Superhuman is." King looked at his magic palm, then he showed it to Luna, and she read "Alex knows where Superhuman is" on the magic palm of King. Then, Luna understood that it was impossible to lie to King. Then, Luna turned her head through Alex, and she saw how he was suffering, and she looked at King by saying, "I am ready to tell you where Superhuman is."

King said, "I listen to you."

Luna said, "You must demand Hector first to stop torturing Alex."

King said, "I am the one who gives the other here."

Luna said, "I am not giving you the orders, just that I want to talk with Alex first."

Then, King asked Hector to stop torturing Alex, then Luna ran through Alex and she bent close to him, and she looked at Alex with her face wet of tears, how Alex was weak and tired. Then Luna said, "Alex, I am so sorry, I can not keep watching King and Hector torture you like that." And she added, "I will tell King where Superhuman hides, and there you will be released." Alex opened his mouth to talk, but he was so weak that he could not pronounce a word, then he made the signs with his head, by looking at Luna, and she understood that he was refusing that she talks to King where Superhuman is hiding. Luna turned her head through King, and she looked at him by saying, "Alex is so weak, so I want you to give us some hours, the time for Alex to recover a little bit, there I will try to convince him to let me tell you where Superhuman hides."

King said, "You do not need the authorization of Alex, to tell me where Superhuman hides, and if you want to save the life of Alex, you must tell me now where Superhuman hides."

Luna said, "I can not tell you where Superhuman is without authorization of Alex because I am doing it for Alex, so need his authorization, also I want a guarantee that you will not kill Alex, after that, I told you where Superhuman hides."

Hector looked at King by saying, "We must give them some time."

King said, "Alex can not stay in this jail because the air does not enter here."

Hector asked, "How did Luna breath in this jail if the air does not enter here?"

King answered, "Luna is a witch, and she has some natural energies inside her, who help her to breath inside this jail."

Hector said, "We can let the door open, and there the air will get inside the jail, and Alex will breathe."

King said, "That's a good idea." And King turned and left with Hector.

The following day, King and Hector had still not succeeded in getting information to Luna and Alex about where Superhuman was hiding, although the fact that they had spent the whole night torturing Alex in front of Luna, and Alex had begged Luna to not talk where Superhuman was hiding. King and Hector had taken Alex in the forest where Alex was kept prisoner, and Alex's jail was built with the irons, and outside of his jail, there was a big lion that was looking at him, and the lion was walking around Alex's jail, trying to get inside. Alex was lying on the mattress in his jail, suffering, weak, tired, and he was feeling cold with the wind that was blowing inside his jail, and he was scared by the lion that was walking around his jail, by making noise and trying to get inside his jail. King and Hector had decided to keep Alex prisoner in the forest in those conditions to trap Superhuman, they had decided to put pressure on Superhuman, they knew that Superhuman would not support for a long time to see Alex suffer in that jail, and it was the reason why they did not kill Alex, so they wanted to use Alex to arrest Superhuman.

Superhuman, Liza, and Philip were watching Alex since his jail in the forest, through the magic palm of Superhuman, and Liza and Superhuman had tears in their eyes like they were watching Alex who was suffering. Superhuman, Liza, and Philip knew the reasons why King and Hector had decided to keep Alex in the forest like a prisoner, and they were thinking how to save Alex in that forest, but at the same time they knew that King and Hector were watching Alex since his jail through the magic palm of King. Superhuman knew that once he should go to save Alex, King should trigger the storm to arrest him.

It was evening, Luna was in her jail, sitting on the mattress, tired and very weak, she had not put something in her mouth since King and Hector removed Alex from her jail, she had spent the complete day crying by wondering if Alex was still alive, and where he could be if he was still alive. Luna was wondering too how Alex knew where Superhuman was hiding, and she was wondering why Superhuman had not prevented King from arresting Alex like she did not know that it was Alex who had come himself to the palace to see King.

Luna was very afraid about the situation of the planet, mostly that she was not there anymore to control King by allowing Superhuman to prevent the disaster that King wanted to cause to happen, and she was very afraid for all inhabitants of the planet, that maybe they were dying. Then, there was a question in the head of Luna, since the months now and that question was preventing her to sleep, she was spending her days like her nights to search the answer of that question, she knew that the answer of that question was the end of the tragedy that the planet was living and the peace of the planet. Luna tried to get up and she was very weak that she suddenly fainted on the mattress, then her eyes closed, and she was unconscious, and she started to see her mom who was talking to her, and her mom was telling her that the answer of her question was inside the magic book and that only Superhuman who could find that's the answer. Then, the eyes of Luna opened, and she cried out, "Mom, mom, mom?" Then, she got up and she sat on the bed, and she started to think about what her mom told her, and she started to remember about the magic book by wondering where the answer to her question could be in that magic book.

Cynthia was in the living room with her parents, talking about the situation of the planet, and they were very worried by wondering till when they would stay at home like the prisoners, then they heard the doorbell that was ringing, and they looked at each other with surprised faces. They were wondering who it could be, and they were wondering if people had started to get out of their houses, and Cynthia turned her through the watch that was on the wall and she read 11:00 p.m., and she told her parents that it was 11:00 p.m., and Cynthia's dad said that they should not open the door and that they had to turn off the light and go to the bed.

Then, they got up from their chairs, to go to their bedroom, and they suddenly heard the footsteps and they looked at each other with fear on their faces, then Cynthia's dad started to walk through the door, where the footsteps were coming, and he met with Superhuman, and he cried out, "The magician boy?" By looking at Superhuman with an amazed face. Superhuman looked at Cynthia's dad and he said to him to not feel any fear, that he used his magic hand to open the door, and that he was there because he wanted to talk with Cynthia, then Cynthia and her mom joined them, and they were very proud to see Superhuman. Then, they invited Superhuman to sit at the table, and Cynthia's parents thanked Superhuman like he had saved their twins, and they started to talk about the situation of the planet, Cynthia's parents wanted to know what was happening on the planet, while Cynthia was just asking to Superhuman about Alex, and that she wanted to see Alex.

After a couple of minutes, Superhuman said that he wanted to go out with Cynthia and that he should come back with her, and Cynthia's parents accepted without a problem although the fact that it was almost midnight. Then, Superhuman and Cynthia walked outside, and they got inside the car, then Superhuman drove away. Liza and Philip were at home with fear inside them, they were afraid that King could see Superhuman outside and trigger the storm to follow Superhuman, or to catch him because they knew that King and Hector were not asleep, that they were in their office watching Alex in the forest through the magic palm of King, to know if Superhuman was coming to save Alex. Liza and Philip were also worried about Cynthia that they were going to be involved in that war, and they had told Superhuman that it was a big risk to involve Cynthia in that fight, and they all knew that Cynthia could die.

Even if Cynthia was the only solution that they had found like they had spent their whole day thinking about how to save Alex without finding the solution. And Superhuman could not go into the forest to save Alex because King had not stopped to watch Alex through his magic palm, since that he kept Alex prisoner in that forest. Then, the door opened, Superhuman and Cynthia walked inside, and Liza took a breath when she saw Superhuman like she was afraid that King could see Superhuman outside, and Superhuman introduced Philip to Cynthia like Cynthia and Liza already knew each other.

Then, Superhuman explained to Cynthia what was going on with Alex, and he showed Alex to Cynthia through his magic palm, and Cynthia started to cry when she saw Alex prisoner in the forest in the magic palm of Superhuman. Then, Superhuman explained his plan to all of them, Philip and Liza found that plan very dangerous, but Cynthia agreed to participate in that plan, although the risk she knew that she was taking. Philip told Cynthia to think very well before taking any decision because she would not survive if things were going wrong, but Cynthia answered that she did not need to think, that if it was to save Alex, she was ready to give her own life.

Then, Superhuman told Cynthia exactly what she should do, the words, questions, and answers she would use when the moment would come, then he drove Cynthia back to her home, while Philip and Liza started to make some change in the basement. The basement was very huge, and it had a door that was showing outside, Philip and Liza were moving some stuff to another side of the basement, then Superhuman joined them. And they spent the whole night building a divider wall with plywood to separate the basement into two, also they made another door that was showing outside to the left side of the basement. But Cynthia did not know that they should divide the basement and Superhuman did not tell her about that because he did not want to put her in more danger.

It was early morning, King and Hector were in their office very tired, they had spent the whole night watching Alex in the forest through the magic palm of King. And they were very surprised to see that Superhuman had let his friend Alex sleep in the forest, and they were wondering if Superhuman would let Alex die in that forest. King and Hector knew that if Superhuman had not come to save Alex, it was because Superhuman was watching them through his magic. King told Hector that he was going to trigger the storm in the forest, to put pressure on Superhuman because when Superhuman would see Alex suffer in the storm, he would not resist, and he would try to save Alex. Suddenly, they heard noises that were coming from the door, and they noticed that it was someone who was knocking at the door, then Hector got up from his chair, and he walked to the door. Hector opened the door and he saw his chief of security who told him that there was a young girl who wanted to talk about Superhuman and Alex.

Then, King and Hector ran to the living room, where they met Cynthia and they looked at Cynthia with surprised faces, while Cynthia was looking at them with fear in her eyes. King looked in the eyes of Cynthia by saying, "This face is familiar to me." And he asked, "Where is Superhuman?" Cynthia opened her mouth to talk, but her mouth was shaking that a word was not coming out. And Hector looked at Cynthia by asking, "Are you going to talk or not?"

Cynthia took a deep breath and she said, "I want Alex first."

King said, "I am the one who gives the orders here not you."

Cynthia said, "If I am going to betray Superhuman, I want a guarantee that Alex is still alive."

King looked in the eyes of Cynthia angrily, saying, "I hope you know who I am."

Cynthia said, "I know that you are the wizard boy, who wants to destroy the planet, who is responsible for all curses that are happening on the planet, and who killed my best friend Jack."

King asked, "How do you know Superhuman?"

Cynthia answered, "I first met Superhuman the day he came to my house with my little brothers, so it's Superhuman who had saved my little brothers."

King looked at his magic palm, and he looked at Hector who was looking at him by saying, "She is telling the truth." And he added, "I remember now that she is the girl that Liza was interviewing." Then he turned his head through Cynthia by asking, "How do you know Alex?"

Cynthia answered, "Alex is a friend of Superhuman, and I met Alex the same day that I met Superhuman, they were together when Superhuman brought my little brothers at home."

King asked, "Why is Alex so important for you?"

Cynthia answered, "I love him."

King looked at his magic palm, and he looked at Hector by saying, "She is telling the truth." And he looked in the eyes of Cynthia by asking, "Where is Superhuman?"

Cynthia replied, "I want to make sure that Alex is still alive."

King said, "Do not give me the orders."

Cynthia said, "I am not giving you the orders, I am just making a deal."

King looked at her angrily by saying, "You know well that I can kill you."

Cynthia said, "If you kill me, you will never catch Superhuman, so I am your only solution to catch Superhuman."

Hector looked at King by saying, "I hope this girl is not playing with us."

Cynthia looked at Hector by saying, "I was with Superhuman, Liza, and Philip last night."

King looked at his magic palm and he looked at Hector by saying, "She is telling the truth." And he looked at Cynthia by saying, "I will not release Alex, till I have Superhuman."

Cynthia said, "I will take you where Superhuman hides and you will release Alex. But first I want to make sure that Alex is still alive."

King asked, "Where does the Superhuman hide?"

Cynthia replied, "First, I need to be sure that Alex is still alive."

Hector looked at King by saying, "We do not have the choice."

King looked at his magic palm, then he showed it to Cynthia, and the tears started to flow down her cheeks like she was watching Alex in his jail, through the magic palm of King. Then, Hector and King were very surprised when Cynthia told them that Superhuman was hiding in the basement of Philip's house. Hector did not believe Cynthia, by saying that there was no house on the planet that had the basement, that he had all the plans of the houses of the planet, and no house had the basement even the house of Philip.

And that Queen mother had banned building the houses on the planet with the basement. But, when King checked through his magic, he noticed that Cynthia was telling the truth, and King understood why he was unable to see where Superhuman hid through his magic, and they were wondering how Philip built that house with a basement. Then, King told Hector that there was a mysterious secret that they must discover because there was another mysterious person who was involved in the fight. And that mysterious person knew about his magic, also that mysterious person knew about the weakness of his magic because only that mysterious person knew that his magic could not reach the basement. Hector replied to King that that mysterious person could be only Philip because it was also Philip who had saved Luna to the hospital after that Superhuman had been arrested by the police, and it was still Philip who had the magic book. And King said to Hector that this mysterious person could not be Philip because Philip was a normal human being without any power or magic. Hector replied to King that there were a lot of mysteries that they did not know like the mysterious ghost, the mysterious secret, and the mysterious person.

Then, King told Hector that they must go to the basement of Philip's house now, and Cynthia told them that Superhuman would be not at home for the moment, that she had an appointment with Superhuman in three hours, so that they could go in three hours. And King said that they were going to wait in that basement, that even if his magic would not work in that basement the important thing for him was to see the mysterious basement where Superhuman was hiding. Then, Hector called the police of the palace, and they took the road to the house of Philip with Cynthia. Superhuman, Liza, and Philip were in the basement and they had watched the conversation between King, Cynthia, and Hector through the magic palm of Superhuman and they were very happy about how that conversation had happened, even if it did not happen as they had planned, but the most important was still to prevent that King kills Cynthia. Superhuman, Liza, and Philip were watching King, Cynthia, Hector, and the police who were coming, through the magic palm of Superhuman, then they moved to the other side of the basement like they had divided the basement in two.

After half an hour, King, Cynthia, Hector, and the police reached the house of Philip, and Cynthia took them behind the house, and King used his magic hand and he opened the door, and they all got inside the house. Cynthia looked in the house with a surprised face, she had remarked that the house was different from what she had seen last night, that the basement had become small, and she was wondering what had happened, but she did not notice that the basement was divided. Superhuman watched King and Hector inside the basement through his magic palm, and he got out from the side of the basement where he was, and he reached outside then he used his magic to call the hawk, and he flew in the space on his hawk. Philip and Liza were still inside the basement, with fear inside them, and their hearts were beating faster than normal because they were afraid that King could leave the basement, and they knew that if King was going outside his magic would work and he would see Superhuman outside.

Philip and Liza were watching King and Hector who were at the other side of the basement through the small holes they had put on the plywood. Superhuman was in the space of the forest where Alex was kept prisoner, flying through the jail of Alex, then he landed not far from the jail where Alex was kept prisoner, then he got off on his hawk, and he started to run through the jail of Alex, and he saw a big lion that was running through him too. Then, Superhuman noticed that the lion wanted to jump on him, and he suddenly handed his magic hand through that lion, and the sparks of fire got outside from his magic palm and going through the lion. The lion stopped and started to look at Superhuman angrily, by shaking his head, and by making noises while Superhuman kept burning him with the sparks of fire that were getting outside from his magic palm. After a few seconds, the Lion jumped on Superhuman and threw him on the ground, then they started to fight, Superhuman was trying to kill the lion by sending sparks of fire in the lion's mouth, while the lion was trying to kill Superhuman by tearing his skin. The fight was very hard for both, but the lion was stronger than Superhuman, and

Superhuman was losing a lot of blood like a lion was tearing his skin with his claws.

Then after a few minutes, the lion was becoming weak like Superhuman was sending the sparks of fire inside the lion's mouth. After fifteen minutes, the lion lay dead on the ground, and Superhuman got up with blood on his whole body, and he ran to the jail where Alex was kept imprisoned. Superhuman used his magic hand to open the jail's door, and he ran close to Alex who was lying on the ground like a dead person, then he bent close to Alex and he put his magic palm on the forehead of Alex, and Alex opened his eyes.

Alex was so weak and very tired, that he could not even talk, and he was looking at Superhuman like a stranger, he did not recognize Superhuman, then Superhuman helped Alex to get up and to walk outside. And Superhuman used his magic hand to call the hawk, and he helped Alex to get on the hawk, then they flew through space. King, Cynthia, Hector, and the police were still in the basement waiting for Superhuman. King had decided to stay in the basement till Superhuman come, despite the fact that his magic was not working in that basement, and although Hector told him that they should go because it could be dangerous for them if Superhuman found them there like King's magic was not working in the basement. And King replied to Hector that even if his magic was not working, Superhuman could not kill him and that there was nothing to worry about because the magic of Superhuman could not kill a human being. Philip and Liza were still watching King and Hector through the holes that were on the plywood, with fears inside them, and by wondering why Superhuman had not yet come, then they heard footsteps coming through the corner, and they turned their head through that corner and they saw Superhuman who was walking by holding Alex. Then, Liza and Philip ran through Superhuman and Alex, and they helped Alex to walk to the living room, and they lay Alex on the sofa. Liza looked at Alex with tears that were flowing down her cheeks. Philip looked at Superhuman by saying, "We need a doctor for Alex."

Superhuman replied, "Alex is so weak, but he will recover."

Liza said, "Alex spent two days without putting something in his mouth, even water he has not drunk." And she added, "I have to make food for him."

Superhuman looked at Liza by saying, "Alex is unconscious, he can not eat something now."

Philip and Liza looked at Superhuman with surprised faces, and Philip asked, "How Alex is unconscious?"

Superhuman replied, "The torture that Alex lived affected him."

Liza looked at Alex on the sofa, then she turned her head through Superhuman, by saying, "Alex has the eyes opened and he is breathing normally, so I do not understand how he is unconscious."

Superhuman said, "Alex lived a traumatize those last days, and it's normal that he reacts like that."

Liza asked, "You mean that Alex is not hearing us like we are talking in front of him right now?"

Superhuman replied, "No, Alex is not listening to us, and he does not even know where he is."

Philip looked at Superhuman by saying, "The important is that Alex is still alive, and we will take care of him." And he added, "Now, we must release Cynthia to prevent King from killing her because she is in danger in the hands of King."

Superhuman said, "I am going to the palace first because I must release Luna and other prisoners."

Liza said, "It's too dangerous to go to the palace because King can catch you."

Superhuman said, "I will be fast." And he added, "When King will find out that we used Cynthia to release Alex, he can kill all prisoners who are in the palace, to get his revenge if we do not release them."

Philip said, "Do not forget that Cynthia is also in danger."

Superhuman replied, "Everyone is in danger, but we can use this advantage to save everyone."

Liza asked, "How you will take all of them."

Superhuman replied, "I will go to the palace with the hawk, and there I will steal one of the cars that are in the parking of the palace, then I will take them with that car." And he turned and left.

Liza looked at Philip by asking, "What happened with Superhuman?"

Philip asked, "What do you mean?"

Liza replied, "You did not notice that Superhuman was bleeding?"

Philip replied, "I have no idea." And he added, "Only Superhuman knows what happened."

Liza said, "We were busy talking about Alex, that we did not find a second to ask Superhuman what happened for that he is bleeding." And she added, "it seems that Superhuman was attacked by an animal because the wounds that are on his body are coming from the claws of an animal."

Philip said, "It's obvious that Superhuman was attacked by the lion that was running, around the jail of Alex, by trying to get inside the jail."

Liza said, "It's exactly what happened." And she added, "Let's watch what is happening to the other side of the basement."

Then, they walked to the plywood and they kept watching King and Hector to the other side of the basement. There were people in the yard of the palace, who had lifted their heads through the sky, watching Superhuman who was flying in the space, through the jail of Luna, and most people had the smile on their faces like they were watching Superhuman flying on his hawk. Then, Superhuman landed not far from the jail of Luna, and he got off on his hawk, then he ran to the door of the Jail of Luna, and he used his magic hand and he opened the door jail, and he ran inside till close to Luna. Superhuman was staring at Luna who was lying on the mattress that was on the floor, with her eyes closed like a dead person, with tears who were flowing down his cheeks, then he bent close to Luna and he put his magic palm on her forehead. And Luna opened her eyes, and she saw Superhuman, then she started to smile at him, and Superhuman smiled back at her with tears who were still flowing down his cheeks.

Then, Superhuman helped Luna to get up, and they were standing up looking each other in the eyes without saying a word, and after a few minutes Superhuman broke the silence by saying, "I am so sorry." Luna replied, "You do not have to be sorry." And she put her right palm on the cheek of Superhuman by looking in his eyes, then she said, "I love you." Superhuman put his right palm on her cheek, by looking in her eyes and he said, "I love you too." Then, Luna walked two steps in the arms of Superhuman, and they took each other in their arms.

And after a minute, Luna cried out by calling, "Alex." And she turned her head by looking at Superhuman. Superhuman looked at her by saying, "Do not worry, Alex is safe." Luna said, "I am glad to know that Alex is alright because I was worried for him." Then, she looked at Superhuman with a surprised face by asking, "What happened to you for that you have blood on your body?" Superhuman replied, "I fought with the lion when I was releasing Alex from the Jail in the forest." Luna cried out, "Alex was in jail in the forest?" Superhuman replied, "Yes." And he added, "It's a long story we will talk about later." Luna asked, "How did you find me here? because I know that your magic can not see me here like I am in a jail built with the stones." Superhuman replied, "I know the road of this jail because I was a prisoner here, and when my magic stopped to watch you, I knew that King had kept you imprisoned here." And he added, "My magic is working now because the door is opened, and my magic is in contact with the air coming from outside."

Then, Luna noticed that the light was shining on the magic hand of Superhuman, and she said, "The light is shining on your magic hand." And Superhuman looked at his magic palm, then he suddenly grabbed the hand of Luna by saying, "Follow me." Then, Luna and Superhuman ran to the jail of Maria, and Superhuman used his hand to open the jail door, and they released Maria, then they went and released Doctor Thomas and the parents of Superhuman. Then, Superhuman stole a big car in the parking of the palace, and he carried all of them inside that car he drove away. And all employees of the palace, security men, and the police of the palace had just watched how Superhuman was releasing all prisoners of Hector and King without saying a word, and they were just saying in their mind that King would become crazy, and they were hoping that King would not send the storm outside. King and Hector had started to get bored inside the basement, despite the fact that they were staring at the plan of the house by wondering who had built that house. King looked at Hector by saying, "It's been a while that we are waiting for Superhuman."

Hector said, "I am wondering where Superhuman is."

King said, "We have to go now." And he added, "What matters is that we know where Superhuman hides."

Cynthia looked at King who was getting up from his chair, and she said in her mind I have to prevent them to get outside of this house as Superhuman had told me, and she remembered about the magic book that Superhuman had told her, then she opened her mouth and she said, "We have to look for the magic book."

Hector looked at Cynthia with a surprised face, and he asked, "Where is that magic book?"

Cynthia replied, "It will be somewhere in this house."

King asked, "How do you know about the magic book?"

Cynthia looked at King by saying, "I know that there is a lot of secret inside that magic book."

Hector said, "We need that book."

Cynthia said, "We have to search it in this basement."

Hector turned his head through policemen by saying, "Search this basement, and find me that magic book."

A policeman said, "We do not know what that magic book looks like."

Hector replied, "Show me any book you will find."

Then, policemen started to search the basement, by moving stuff while Hector and King were still staring at the basement. Hector looked at Cynthia by asking, "How Superhuman goes upstairs because I am not seeing the stairs here?"

Cynthia asked, "Upstairs?" By looking at Hector with a surprised face.

Hector replied, "Yeah, upstairs." And he added, "We are in the basement now, so it means that there is upstairs."

Immediately, Cynthia remembered that when she came last night, she had seen the stairs, then she turned her head through the left side of the basement, where she had seen the stairs last night. Cynthia noticed that there was a wall that had been built there with plywood, then she suddenly understood that Superhuman had built a wall divided to hide those stairs and to divide the basement, and she understood too why the basement had become small. Then, Cynthia looked at Hector without knowing what to say, and she remembered that Superhuman had told her to not lie because King would check everything that she would say through his magic hand and that if she lied King would kill her, and although the fact that Cynthia knew that the magic of King was not working in that basement, she was afraid to lie. And at the same time, Cynthia knew that if Superhuman, Liza, and Philip had built that wall divided it was for a good reason, and she could not talk that the stairs were behind that wall divided, or that the basement had been divided, then she said in mind I have to find something who is true to talk to them. Then, Cynthia opened her mouth and she said, "I have never been upstairs."

Hector said, "There is no doubt that there is not the road, or the stairs here to reach upstairs, so the only explanation it's that Philip and Superhuman use the door of the basement and walk outside to go upstairs."

King looked at Hector by saying, "There is a way in this basement to reach upstairs." Cynthia looked at King with fear on her face, afraid that maybe King found out those stairs.

Hector looked at King by saying, "There is no way in this basement to reach upstairs, so how Superhuman and Philip reach upstairs, by using this basement."

King said, "The day I came here to visit Luna when she was living here, I was upstairs in the living room, sat in the chair, and I used my magic palm to find her, and my magic did not see her. And, after a few minutes, Luna walked into the living room coming from a corner, and I am sure that she was in this basement that day." And King added, "If there was not a way in this basement to reach upstairs, Luna should get inside the living room that day by using the front door, not by coming from a corner that is inside the house."

Hector lifted his head through the ceiling, then he took a deep breath and he bent his head by looking at King and he said, "It means that Luna was hidden in this basement by Philip when he removed her from the hospital."

King said, "Exactly." And he added, "That's the reason why I could not find her through my magic."

Hector said, "It means too that during all those times that we were looking for Superhuman and Philip without success it's because they were hidden here in this basement. And the rooms of Philip's house that were appearing on your magic palm were the rooms upstairs, and those rooms were empty because they were living here in this basement."

King said, "Yes, the rooms that we were seeing on my magic palm were the rooms upstairs." Hector said, "This house is very mysterious." Then he turned his head through policemen by asking, "Did you find that magic book?"

A policeman replied, "We searched all the rooms of this basement, and we did not find a book."

King said, "I am not surprised that they did not find a book."

Hector asked, "Where can be Superhuman at this time?"

King said, "That's a good question."

Suddenly, the heart of Cynthia started to beat faster than normal, and her face was full of fear. And King looked at Cynthia by asking, "Where is Superhuman?"

Cynthia replied, "I have no idea about where he is, just that we should meet here at this time." And she added, "I am wondering why he has not yet arrived."

King and Hector noticed that there was fear on the face of Cynthia and that she was shaking when she was talking. And Hector looked at King by saying, "I think that this is a good moment to catch Superhuman."

King asked, "What do you mean?"

Hector replied, "We have to go outside, and there you will use your magic to find Superhuman." And he added, "I am sure that Superhuman is outside now doing something."

King smiled at Hector by saying, "That's a good idea." And he added, "Superhuman wanted to trap us, but we are the ones who are going to trap him."

Then, they turned through the door, and they started to walk. Suddenly, they heard the doorbell rang, and all of them stopped by looking at each other, and only Cynthia who was understanding the meaning of that doorbell because Superhuman had told her that when she would hear the doorbell, she would get out alone.

Then, Cynthia said, "I am going to open the door." King looked at Cynthia by saying, "No, I am the one who is going to open the door." Cynthia said, "Superhuman knows that I am here waiting for him, so it should be him, or Philip and Liza." King said, "No matter who it's, I am going to open that door." Cynthia looked in the eyes of King by saying, "The only way to catch Superhuman it's to hide inside this basement, and when he will get inside, I will try to talk with him about all the secrets that you want to know like the magic book, the mysterious person, the way that is inside this basement to reach upstairs, and there you will hear all the answers of your questions." King asked, "Why are you doing this, knowing that I am the wizard boy, that I am here to destroy this planet." And he added, "All those policemen obey me because they do not have a choice because if they do not obey, I will kill them." Cynthia looked into King's eyes by saying, "My love for Alex is bigger than this planet and more important than anyone living on this planet." King looked at Hector by saying, "Let's go hide."

Then, King, Hector, and policemen ran into a bedroom that was close to the living room, and they got inside that bedroom and they closed the door. Cynthia ran to the front door, and she opened the door and she saw Superhuman who was waiting for her, with his heart beating with fear that maybe King should prevent her from getting out. Then, Superhuman grabbed her hand, and they ran through the left side of the house. And they opened another door that Superhuman, Liza, and Philip had made when they divided the basement into two for their plan, then they got inside. And Superhuman introduced Cynthia to Luna and other people, and Cynthia was making acquaintance with Luna when her eyes saw Alex lying on the sofa like a dead person, but with his eyes opened. Cynthia suddenly ran through Alex, and she bent close to him, and she started to shake him by screaming his name, and Alex was just staring at Cynthia without saying a word. Everyone in the room was just staring at Alex and Cynthia, and most of them had tears flowing down their cheeks.

Then, Cynthia turned her head by looking at Superhuman, and she noticed that almost everyone had tears in their eyes, then she asked, "Why are some of you crying? And why Alex is not responding to me when I am talking to him?" Everyone was just looking at her without saying a word, and she was still looking at them. After three minutes, Cynthia broke the silence, by asking, "What is going on here?" Liza took a deep breath and she said, "Cynthia, you have to be strong." Cynthia looked at Liza by asking, "What do you mean?"

Then Luna walked till where Cynthia was, and she bent face to Cynthia, then she looked in the eyes of Cynthia, and she held the hand of Cynthia too. Cynthia and Luna were looking eyes to eyes, and the tears were still flowing down the cheeks of Luna, then Cynthia asked, "What is going on with Alex? Because he does not make a move" Luna replied, "Alex is sick" Cynthia cried out, "Sick?" and the tears started to flow down her cheeks. Superhuman said, "Cynthia, do not worry Alex will recover soon." Liza said, "The torture is over, and we are all here, and we will look after Alex." Then, Cynthia turned through Alex and she stared at him with her face wet with tears, then she laid her head on Alex's belly by crying. Everyone was looking at Cynthia and Alex with a sad face, and the eyes of Philip were focused on the eyes of Alex.

Suddenly, Philip started to smile, and he opened his mouth by saying, "A miracle has just happened." Everyone turned and looked at Philip, and Philip said, "Alex is smiling at us." Then, everyone turned their head through Alex, and they noticed that he was smiling. Suddenly, there was joy on the face of everyone, then Cynthia moved her head through the mouth of Alex and she started to kiss him, and everyone started to clap their hands by smiling at them. King, Hector, and policemen were still in the room where they had hidden, and they were already tired to wait, and they started to understand that it was a trap that Superhuman had organized with Cynthia.

Then, they got outside of the room, and they noticed that Cynthia was not in the living room, and Hector started to call Cynthia but she was not responding, and he ordered the policemen to search all the rooms of the house. After a few minutes of searching without seeing Cynthia, they left the room and they walked outside. Then, King used his magic to find where Cynthia was, and the house of Philip appeared on his magic palm, and he showed his magic palm to Hector. Hector looked at the magic palm of King with a surprised face, and he said, "It means that Cynthia is still in that house" King replied, "That's what the magic is saying." Then, Hector and King turned, and they looked at the house of Philip with a tired face, without saying a word.

Then, Hector broke the silence by saying, "I am wondering what kind of house it's." King replied, "It's obvious that it's a magic house," Hector said, "Or a cursed house." And he added, "We have to find where Superhuman is," King said, "Good idea." And he added, "Hope we will catch him this time like he is outside." Then, King asked his magic to find Superhuman, and the house of Philip appeared on his magic palm, and he showed his magic palm to Hector, and Hector was looking at it without knowing what to say. After a few minutes of silence, Hector looked at King by saying, "It means that Superhuman is in that cursed house of Philip." King replied, "The magic can not lie or make a mistake." Hector asked, "What is the meaning of all this." King replied, "It's the same question that I am wondering because I do not understand why Superhuman, Cynthia, and other people organized that plan to show us their hiding place that is the basement of the house." Hector said, "There is a reason why they did that because they could not send us Cynthia just because they wanted us to see the basement of that cursed house." And he added, "It's obvious that there is another hiding place in that house." King said, "There is no doubt that there is another basement in that house." And he added, "Let's return to the palace and there we will think what to do." Then, they walked to their cars, and they got inside, and they drove through the palace.

CHAPTER 10

$\diamond$

Luna In the Coma with The Ghost

Although the fact that Alex was doing well, everyone in the basement was worried because they had watched the whole conversation between King and Hector through the magic palm of Superhuman, and they were all afraid about the plan that King and Hector were going to think about. Mostly, they knew that Philip's house was the only place where they could hide, and they knew that King had the doubts that the house had another basement.

After fifteen minutes, King and Hector were to the palace, in their office, then King used his magic hand to watch at Alex in the forest, and he noticed that Alex was not anymore in the forest, and he was completely surprised by wondering what was going on, then he tried to watch Luna in her jail, and he found out through his magic palm that the jail of Luna was empty, and he told Hector what was going on. Then, Both Hector and King got up from their chairs and got out of their office, and they started to walk in the corner, through the jail of Luna, and they saw a security man, and they demanded this security man who released Luna from her jail. Then, that security man explained to them that Superhuman came to the palace, and he released all prisoners, then King and Hector looked at each other with a surprised face, and they immediately understood the reasons for the plan of Superhuman, Cynthia, and other people, and they turned and walked through their office. Superhuman sat in the chair and the rest of the people had surrounded him watching through his magic palm, King and Hector who was planning a plan since their office. Everyone in the basement around Superhuman was watching the conversation of King and Hector through the magic palm of Superhuman, with their faces full of fear, and their hearts who were beating faster than the normal by hearing the words of Hector and King.

After ninety-nine minutes, Superhuman and other people watched King and Hector got up from their chairs and walked through the door, then suddenly they turned their head in the room, looking at each other without saying a word, and there were the worries on the face of everyone, and some people had their mouths opened but no word was coming out. After a few minutes of silence, Superhuman broke the silence by saying, "I am going to the palace to confront King." Then he got up from his chair, and Alex looked at Superhuman by saying, "I am going with you." Then Liza looked at Superhuman and Alex by saying, "No one will go to the palace." Then, Philip, and Maria agreed with the idea of Liza. Superhuman tried to convince Liza and Philip that the better solution now was that he goes to the palace, to give himself to King and Hector before the worst happens. Philip and Liza have opposed again Superhuman's idea by saying that they could not give up now and that they would keep fighting to protect the Planet and to prevent King from destroying the planet. And that if Superhuman gave himself like a prisoner to King and Hector, the whole planet was going to suffer more, and nothing at that moment would prevent King and Hector to realize their project that no one knew what it was. Although the fact that Philip and Liza had watched the whole conversation of King and Hector, and they knew that the whole planet was in danger, they were trying to convince Superhuman to forget about the idea to go give himself to King and Hector.

Then, Luna and Cynthia joined the idea of Liza and Philip by saying that the whole planet was going to live a tragedy forever if Superhuman gave himself like a prisoner to King and Hector. Then, Luna noticed that the light was shining on the magic hand of Superhuman, and she told him about it, then Superhuman lifted his magic palm through his face, and suddenly his face changed like he was looking at his magic palm, while Luna and the rest of people were looking at him by wondering in their mind what was going on. Then, Superhuman looked at them by saying, "King and Hector started with their plan." And he turned his magic palm by showing it to them, and there was the surprise on their faces like they were watching John who was arrested by the police of the palace through the magic palm of Superhuman.

Everyone in the room took a deep breath without saying a word, and they were very afraid of wondering what the next step of Hector and King would be? And they knew that King and Hector would not stop till they realized their project. Also, they knew that King and Hector had arrested John to make pressure on Superhuman and Luna, knowing that John was the best friend of Luna. King and Hector were in their office thinking about how to realize their project, and for that, they knew that they should get rid of Superhuman who an obstacle for them was and for their project first. And King had tried to find the solution to how to get rid of Superhuman through his magic, and by asking his magic and his magic answered him that the solution to get rid of Superhuman was inside the magic book.

Since, King and Hector had known that there was a secret on how Superhuman had another way to get the energy of his magic that was not coming directly from Luna, they were not really any more interested in Luna again. And King and Hector were now interested in the magic book because they knew that this secret on how Superhuman was getting the energy of his magic was inside the magic book. King and Hector knew that Superhuman and people who were with him were watching them through the magic palm of Superhuman, and they were thinking to make more pressure on Superhuman by torturing John who was in jail of the palace, or by torturing the inhabitants of the planet since inside their house, although the fact that no one was getting outside.

And after a couple of minutes of thinking, King told Hector that the torture was not a solution to put the pressure on Superhuman because all the tortures they had used had not worked and that if the torture was the solution Superhuman should show up when they had tortured Alex, or now like the whole planet was living like the prisoners inside their houses without getting outside. Then, Hector agreed with the idea of King that the torture was not the solution, and he demanded to King what to do to catch Superhuman. King looked in the eyes of Hector by saying, "The death." And Hector looked back at King by asking, "What do you mean?" King answered, "The death is the only solution now to make Superhuman give up the fight." Hector asked, "Who are we going to kill?" And he added, "Because Superhuman has his parents with him." King replied, "It's true that if we had the parents of Superhuman with us again in the jails of this palace, it should be a great pleasure for me to kill them, to make Superhuman suffer, and it should be my revenge for the heart of Luna that he stole from me. And Superhuman should watch the death of his parents through his magic palm, but lucky for him he released his parents on time before I got the idea to kill them." And he added, "We will start to kill the best friend of Luna for her betraying, also for my heart she broke by choosing Superhuman, and by fighting by his side."

Then, Hector agreed with the idea of King to kill John, and he told King that John was not even an innocent, that John had always fought on the side of Luna. And King replied to Hector that John was someone who should die since the day he made a mistake by starting to love Luna, the girl that he was in love with. Then, they were looking at each other without talking, and after three minutes King broke the silence by saying, "Let's go kill John now." Hector said, "I have another idea." King asked, "What is that idea?" Hector replied, "Give me a minute to think well."

Everyone in the basement had surrounded Superhuman watching at his magic palm, and some of them like Luna, Cynthia, Maria, Liza, and parents of Superhuman had started to cry the death of John. They were all listening to the conversation between King and Hector, and all of them were full of fear, till some people like Luna and Cynthia were shaking. They knew that King and Hector had the plan to kill John, and they were all afraid about that, and now they were watching the silence that was between King and Hector, with the only hope that the new idea of Hector was to prevent the death of John. Suddenly, they watched Hector lifted his head by looking in the eyes of King, and Hector broke the silence by talking about his new idea to King, and all of them in the room turned their head by looking at each other with the surprise on their faces, and by

215

breathing deeply but by looking at their faces we could see that there was a little hope inside them.

After fifteen minutes, they watched King and Hector get up from their chairs and walk through the door, and all of them took a deep breath. Then, Liza said, "At least those two monsters of King and Hector are not going to kill John." Superhuman said, "We can not scream victory now because when John will stay a prisoner in the jail of the palace the worst can happen at any time." Maria said, "I am wondering when this tragedy that the planet is living will end." Liza looked at Maria by saying, "I am afraid that it will never end." And she added, "It's been the months now that there is a question that is going on in the mind of each of us here, and that question is how to end this tragedy that the planet is living and no one of us has succeeded to answer that question or to find the solution of that question, and even the magic of Superhuman is unable to answer that question."

Suddenly, Luna started to see the images that were appearing in her mind, and those images that were coming into her head were the images of her last dream, she did when she was a prisoner in the palace, the dream where she was seeing her mom who was telling her about the solution how to end the tragedy that was happening on the planet. Then, Luna opened her mouth by saying, "I have the answer to that question." Suddenly, everyone turned their head through Luna by looking at her, then Liza asked, "Which question?" Luna answered, "The question that you were talking about." Superhuman looked into Luna's eyes asking, "You mean you have the solution of how to end this tragedy?" Luna answered, "Yeah, I have the solution of how to put an end to this tragedy that the planet is living." Then, the face of everyone changed, and there was the surprise on their faces, and they were wondering what was going on with Luna, no one was understanding her. Then, Philip broke the silence by asking, "What is that solution?" Luna opened her mouth to talk, but suddenly her mouth started to shake, and she was unable to say a word. And Cynthia asked, "Luna, are you all right?"

Then, they noticed that the whole body of Luna was shaking, and Superhuman screamed the name of Luna, and all of them immediately ran through Luna. Then, Superhuman held Luna, and she fainted in his arms, and everyone screamed in the room with fear on their faces by seeing Luna who had fainted in the arms of Superhuman, then Alex helped Superhuman to carry Luna and they took her to the long sofa that was close to them, then they lay Luna in that sofa.

Everyone had surrounded Luna, with fear on their face by wondering what was going on, and there were tears flowing down the cheeks of Cynthia, and Maria, like they were looking at Luna lying on the sofa with her eyes closed like a dead body. Then, Liza said, "We have to take Luna to the hospital." Philip said, "I do not think that the doctors can help Luna." Maria looked at Philip by asking, "What do you mean?" Philip replied, "What Luna has, it's not the sickness." Liza said, "Luna, will be tired and weak because it's been the months now that she is not sleeping, eating, and getting rest, mostly with the torture that she lived in the palace near to those two monsters named King and Hector." And she added, "I think it's the consequences of everything that Luna lived those last months who made her faint." Maria asked, "Where is the kitchen?" And she added, "I am going to make something to eat for Luna." Philip said, "It's true that the torture that Luna endured since the beginning of this tragedy till now, can have an impact on her health, but food will not help Luna." Superhuman looked at Philip by asking, "What to do now to save Luna?" Philip looked back at Superhuman by answering, "The answer is inside your magic palm." Then, Superhuman lifted his magic hand through his mouth and he demanded to his magic how to save Luna, then he looked at his magic palm and he read, "Put this magic palm on the forehead of Luna."

Then Superhuman walked three steps through Luna's head, and he put his magic palm on her forehead, and the eyes of everyone were focused on the magic palm of Superhuman who was put on Luna's forehead. And after thirty seconds, there were worries on the faces of Superhuman and Philip, they were wondering in their mind why the light was not shining between the magic palm of Superhuman and the forehead of Luna because they knew that it should have a light that should be shining. Suddenly, a white light started to shine between the magic palm of Superhuman and the forehead of Luna, and everyone was looking at that white light without understanding what was going on, but there was still the fear on the faces of Superhuman and Philip like they were watching that white light.

After ten seconds, that white light turned into red, and suddenly Superhuman screamed out the name of Luna like he saw that red light that had started to shine between his magic palm and Luna's forehead, and he removed his magic palm on the forehead of Luna, then he bent close to Luna, and he started to shake her by screaming her name, with tears who were flowing down his cheeks and by telling her to wake up to not let him alone. Except for Philip, no one else was understanding what was going on, or the behavior of Superhuman and they all rushed through the sofa where Luna was lying, then Philip held Superhuman. And Philip was trying to calm Superhuman, while the rest of the people were shaking Luna who was still lying like a dead body without making any move.

Except for Philip, all of them had tears who were flowing down their cheeks by looking at Luna. Maria was sat on the sofa where Luna was lying, and Maria had put Luna's head on her laps, and she was trying to talk to Luna, and Cynthia had put her palm on Luna's heart to make sure that Luna's heart was still beating, while Liza had held Luna's wrist to make sure that her pulse was still beating, but unfortunately, Luna's heart was not anymore beating, and her pulse was not anymore beating too. Liza looked at Cynthia by asking, "Luna's heart is still beating?" Cynthia answered, "No, Luna's heart has stopped to beat. And she asked, how about Luna's wrist?" Liza answered, "Luna's pulse has stopped beating too, and Luna's blood has stopped to circulate." Maria looked at Cynthia and Liza by saying, "Luna is not making any move, and since I am talking to her, she has not replied to me back or made a sign to me." Alex said, "It means Luna is gone."

Everyone turned the head through Alex, looking at him with the tears that were flowing down their cheeks, and Alex was looking back at them with a sad face full of tears, and there was silence in the room no one was talking, and everyone was breathing deeply. Then, Maria opened her mouth to talk but her mouth was shaking that she was unable to pronounce a word, then suddenly Maria burst into tears, and the rest of the people followed Maria by bursting into tears too, and all of them started to cry the death of Luna, except Philip who was not crying, but he was staring at Luna lying in the sofa, with his eyes wet of tears.

After fifteen minutes, there was the light that was shining on the magic hand of Superhuman, and Alex saw that light, and he told Superhuman about it, and Superhuman refused to pay attention to the message that the light that was shining on his magic palm was sending him. But Philip succeeded in changing the mind of Superhuman by convincing Superhuman to look at the message that the light that was shining on his magic hand was sending him. Then, Superhuman looked at his magic palm, and he turned that magic palm by showing it to everyone, and they all saw King and Hector who were talking in their office. Only Philip who was looking at the magic palm of Superhuman with a surprised face and Philip said, "It means it's not yet over." Superhuman replied, "Of course that it's over." And he added, "Luna is dead, and I can not keep fighting without the energy of my magic, and only Luna had that energy but now like she is gone it's impossible for me to keep fighting." Philip looked at Superhuman by asking, "How about the reserve of the energy of your magic that Luna had made?" Superhuman answered, "I finished that reserve of energy to go to the forest to save Alex." And he added, "Even if that reserve of energy was not over it should not work because Luna is dead."

Liza looked at Superhuman by saying, "It means that you can still use that reserve of energy that is inside your body for more than 48 hours again because you had explained to me that the energy of your magic expires after 72 hours in your body, and it's less than 24 hours that you took that energy to go save Alex." Superhuman said, "That energy I have inside my body come from the body of Luna, and for that that energy works Luna must be alive, and it does not matter how many hours of time that that energy is inside my body, even if it's been a second that I took that energy, once when Luna dies that energy inside my body die too because that energy is connected to Luna."

Suddenly, there was silence in the room, no one was talking, and they were all realizing that everything was over, and that King had won the fight, and that Hector and King were going to realize the project they had for the planet. After seventeen minutes, Philip broke the silence by saying, "There is a question who is going on in my mind." Liza asked, "Which question?" Philip replied, "I am wondering why King is not aware that Luna is dead because by seeing King and Hector in their office through the magic palm of Superhuman, they seemed to be happy thinking about their plan." Alex looked at Philip by asking, "What do you mean?" Philip answered, "Luna was linked to Superhuman and King, and her death should have an impact on the magic of Superhuman like on the magic of King." And he added, "When we all watched King and Hector in their office through the magic palm of Superhuman, we all noticed that King was communicating with his magic without a problem, and it seemed that king's magic was not affected by the death of Luna." Everyone looked at Philip with a surprised face without saying a word, then Cynthia broke the silence by saying, "It means that Luna is still alive." Suddenly, everyone turned the head by looking at Cynthia, and no one was talking, and their heart started to beat faster than normal, and some of them like Liza, Maria and Cynthia were breathing deeply.

Then, Philip looked at Superhuman by making the signs with his head, and Superhuman was understanding the message that Philip sent him. Then, Superhuman started to walk through the sofa where Luna was lying, and the eyes of everyone were focused on him, watching him walking, then he reached the sofa and he put his magic palm on the forehead of Luna. The eyes of everyone were focused on the magic palm of Superhuman that was on Luna's forehead, and their face was full of fear with their heart beating more and more faster like if someone was beating it, and their mind was full of hope that Luna was still alive. Then, they noticed a red light that had started to shine between the magic palm of Superhuman and Luna's forehead, and the hope who was on their face was gone, and the sadness had taken place of that hope. Then, Superhuman said, "Luna is gone forever, and there is nothing that we can do." Alex looked at Superhuman by asking, "What makes you think that Luna is dead?" Superhuman answered, "The red light that is shining between my magic palm, and Luna's forehead means death."

Suddenly, Cynthia screamed by handed her finger through the magic palm of Superhuman who was put on Luna's forehead, saying, "The light changed the color." And everyone turned the head through the magic palm of Superhuman and they noticed that there was a blue light that was shining between his magic palm and Luna's forehead. And everyone took a deep breath by smiling, and the hope who had disappeared on their face had come back, although the fact that except Superhuman and Philip, the rest of the people did not know the meaning of the blue light that was shining between the magic palm of superhuman and Luna's forehead, they were just happy because they knew that the red light that meant the death had changed to blue. Then, Superhuman removed his magic palm from Luna's forehead, then he looked at his magic palm and he started to read what was written on it, while the eyes of everyone was focused on him, waiting for him to say something. Then, Alex broke the silence by asking, "Luna is still alive?" Superhuman looked at everyone with a smile who was shining on his face by answering, "Luna is still between us." Maria asked, "It means my daughter is still alive?" Superhuman looked at Maria by answering, "Yeah, your daughter is still alive."

Suddenly, everyone screamed of joy in the room, and there was happiness on their faces. Superhuman said, "We have a big problem." Liza asked, "Which problem?" Superhuman replied, "I have no idea of how we will wake up Luna." Liza looked at Superhuman by asking, "Your magic can not tell us what to do to wake her up?" Superhuman replied, "No, even my magic can not help us to wake her up." Philip asked, "What does Luna have?" Superhuman answered, "I read on my magic palm that Luna is paralyzed by the link of the magic of King who is inside her." Philip asked, "What do you mean?" Superhuman answered, "Luna has the solution how to put an end to this tragedy that the planet is living, and the connection of the magic of King who is inside her is preventing her from talking, that's the reason why she fainted when she wanted to talk about that solution." Maria said, "Let's take Luna to the hospital, maybe the doctors can help us to wake her up." Superhuman looked at Maria by saying, "Sorry, nobody can help Luna, even the doctors." Philip said, "Except King." Superhuman replied, "Yeah, except King who can help Luna to wake up." Cynthia cried out, "Who?" By looking at them with a surprised face, she asked, "Why is there only that monster of King who can help Luna to wake up?" Superhuman answered, "Because Luna is linked to King and his magic, and there is only King who knows how to control his magic, and only him has the power on his magic, and like it's his magic who has paralyzed Luna, there is only him who can help Luna to wake up."

Everyone looked at each other without saying a word, and they were amazed by what Superhuman was telling. Then, Liza broke the silence by asking, "Does that mean that King won the fight?" Philip answered, "King has not yet won the fight because Luna is still alive; that means that Superhuman can keep fighting by using the energy of his magic." Superhuman replied, "It's true that I can still keep fighting by using the energy of my magic, but it will be only for some hours again like 59 hours because the reserve of the energy of my magic that Luna had made is finished." And he added, "The energy that is inside my body is going to expire in less than 60 hours because it's been almost twelve hours that I took that energy, and with Luna paralyzed I can not get the energy of my magic from her." Liza looked at Superhuman by saying, "You told me that the body of Luna can give you the energy."

Superhuman replied, "Yeah, it's true that right now I am getting the energy from the body of Luna like I am close to her, but that energy that I am getting from her body can not stay inside my body, and to fight I need the energy inside my body because I can not carry Luna to go everywhere when I will be fighting." Philip said, "It means that we have less than 60 hours to find a solution how to wake up Luna, and for that, we must use the feelings that King has for Luna, and we will find a strategy of how we will make King wake up Luna without arresting Superhuman." Suddenly, they heard dogs barking coming from outside. And Maria cried out, "Berly?" With a surprised face. Cynthia asked, "Who is Berly?" Maria answered, "Berly is a dog of the palace, a dog who loves Luna too much." And she added, "I am going outside." Then, the light started to shine on the magic hand of Superhuman, and he looked at his magic palm, then he looked at Maria by saying, "I am going outside to meet Berly." Maria said, "I am going with you." Superhuman looked in the eyes of Maria by saying, "Please, let me go alone, it's very important." And he started to walk through the door, while everyone was looking at him with a surprised face without understanding what was going on. Liza cried out, "Important?" And she added, "I do not understand why Superhuman did not want Maria to go outside with him." Cynthia said, "Me too, I do not understand why Superhuman refused that Maria goes with him outside to see the dog, mostly that it's Maria who knows that dog well like she was living in the palace with that dog." Philip said, "Only, Superhuman who can answer that question of why he refused Maria to come outside with him."

Superhuman opened the door and he did not see Berly, but he saw a small box front to the door, and he bent, and he took that small box and he looked at it with a surprised face, by wondering who had put that box. Then, Superhuman started to scream the name of Berly, and he noticed that there was the light that was shining on his magic hand, and he looked at his magic palm, and his face changed like he was reading what was written on his magic palm. Then, Superhuman turned, and he locked the door behind him and he started to walk inside by still looking at that box, then after a few seconds walking he reached the living room, and the eyes of everyone was focus on him, and Maria asked, "Where is Berly?" Superhuman answered, "I did not see Berly." Liza asked, "What do you mean by that?" Superhuman answered, "When I reached outside Berly was already gone."

Everyone turned and looked at each other with a surprised face without saying a word. After a minute, Maria broke the silence by saying, "I am going to search Berly." Superhuman looked at Maria by saying, "You will not find Berly." Liza looked at Superhuman by asking, "Please, can you explain to us what is going on? because we are completely lost." Superhuman replied, "Myself, I do not understand what is going on." Cynthia cried out, "What?" by looking at Superhuman with a surprised face." And Cynthia added, "You are the magician boy here between us, and the one who has the magic, so you are the one who is supposed to know what is going on." Superhuman replied, "Myself, I wish to understand what is going on." And he added, there are a lot of questions that are going on in my mind that I am trying to answer, but unfortunately I can not find the answers to those questions." Liza looked at Superhuman by asking, "What do you mean?"

Superhuman showed them the box he had in his hand without saying a word, and they all were looking at that box, and Philip asked, "What is that box." Superhuman answered, "I have no idea." Liza asked, "Where did you find it?" Superhuman answered, "I found it front to the door." Alex asked, "Who put it front to the door?" Superhuman answered, "I have no idea." Liza asked, "What are you going to do with that box?" Superhuman answered, "There is oil inside this box, and I am going to rub it on Luna." Liza asked, "Why rub it on Luna?" Superhuman answered, "Remember that I told you all here that there are questions who are going on in my mind, that I am unable to find the answers and the question you are asking me it's one of those questions that I can not answer."

And everyone was looking at him with a face full of fear and surprises without understanding what was going on, and by looking at them staring at Superhuman, it was like they were dreaming. Maria asked, "How are you going to rub the content of that box on Luna if you yourself do not know what it's, and who put it, and the reasons why you are going to rub it on her?" Superhuman answered, "It's my magic who demanded me to rub the oil that is inside this box on Luna." Cynthia asked, "Why not ask your magic all questions that we want to know the answers like who put that box in front of the door, why rub the content of that box on Luna, and where is Berly?" Superhuman answered, "I demanded all those questions to my magic, but unfortunately my magic did not answer me." Philip said, "We must trust the magic of Superhuman and rub the oil that is inside that box on Luna."

Then, everyone turned their head through Philip looking at him without saying a word, and Philip made the signs with his head to Superhuman, and Superhuman started to walk through the sofa where Luna was lying, and the eyes of everyone was focused on Superhuman like he was walking through Luna. Then, Superhuman reached the sofa and he knelt close to Luna, and he opened that box he had in his hand, then he threw the oil that was inside that box inside his magic palm, and he started to rub that oil on Luna's body with his magic palm. There was the light that was shining between the magic palm of Superhuman and the body of Luna, like Superhuman was rubbing that oil on her body. And the eyes of everyone was focused on the body of Luna, looking at the light that was shining on her body like Superhuman was passing his magic palm inside her clothes by rubbing her body with the oil. Luna had still the eyes closed, and she had not made any move, but the oil that Superhuman was rubbing on her body had started to have effects on her.

And Luna was seeing the images in her head, and those images were fuzzy, and she was not seeing very well what those images were, and she was fighting to talk but she was so weak to open her mouth or make a move and she was feeling suffocated. Then, Luna saw a face who appeared in her mind, and she did not know to who belongs that face, and she did not even know if it was the face of a woman or a man because that face was not clear, and she heard a voice who was telling her to stop fighting to talk because she was fighting against the link of the magic of King that was inside her and that she could not win that magic. That she was paralyzed by the magic of King, and that King's magic was preventing her to talk, but that the oil that Superhuman was rubbing on her body would help her to wake up, and that when she would wake up, she would not say a word about the solution how to end the tragedy that was happening on the planet.

Because if she tried to talk about that solution the link of the magic of King that was inside her would paralyze her again, and she would get into the coma, and if she got in a coma again, she would die, she would have no chance to get out of that coma alive. But that when she would wake up, she would walk till where she had hidden the magic book before going to the palace, and she would open that magic book to the last page and she would put her right palm on the writings of that last page, then a light would shine between the writings of that last page and her palm, then the writings of that last page would change, and nobody would be able to read the content of that last page even Superhuman and King. And that she already knew the content of that last page because she was only the one who had read that magic book till the end, and she would keep the writings of that last page secretly, and no one would never know about the content of that last page.

Because that last page talks about how she made the reserve of the energy of the magic of Superhuman, by using the energy of the magic Superhuman who was inside her body, and how she connected that reserve of energy to the magic of Superhuman. And that this secret of how to make the reserve of the energy of the magic of Superhuman would be one of her secrets that she would keep for a long time because she would use that secret in the future to give the energy to the magic of Superhuman for their next fight and that when someone would ask her how she was giving the energy to the magic of Superhuman to fight when she was not near to him or when she did not kiss him, the fuzzy images would appear in her mind, and she would answer that she did not remember.

And that it was her own magic that would help her to change the writings of that last page of the magic book, and that no one would know that she has the magic because she would use her own magic in the future to defend herself, to save Superhuman and to protect the planet in case of danger because the fight would not end here, and that she had to be careful because she could fall in love with the wrong person in the future and that if it happened she would not only put the whole planet in danger, but she would also put her own world called the wizarding world in danger because she, Superhuman and King had their own world called the wizarding world, that they would discover for the first time during their next fight.

Because she and Superhuman would travel in the wizarding world to find the solution to save the souls of children of the planet when the souls of children of the planet would be controlled by a devil. And she and Superhuman would even fight in the wizarding world to save their world, and the population of their world because there was a devil named Deo Caeli who was destroying their world and killing the inhabitants of their world. Because even if she, Superhuman, and King were born on this planet, they were not children of this planet because they all three have their world, and the inhabitants of the wizarding world are like them. And that there was a great secret that was hidden behind the reason why they were all three born on the planet of parents who were different from them. And that it was important that Superhuman and she win this fight to be able to save the wizarding world, their race, their identity, and their traditions and cultures.

And that she and Superhuman had no right to fail their mission because their world needed them because it's been more than three decades that Deo Caeli was destroying the wizarding world, that the inhabitants of their world were dying. And that although the fact that all the inhabitants of their world were born with powers and magic, no one had succeeded to kill that devil named Deo Caeli, only Superhuman could kill Deo Caeli because Superhuman was unique and Superhuman was born with something different from the rest of inhabitants of the wizarding world. Then, she would take that magic book and walk till Superhuman without saying a word, and she would hand that magic book to Superhuman by asking him to read because it was very important for him to read it.

There was silence in the room, and everyone was looking at Luna with the worries on their face, and their heart who was beating more and more, waiting for Luna to open her eyes. Suddenly, Cynthia broke the silence by screaming, "Luna moved her finger." All of them turned their head through Cynthia and they noticed that Cynthia had the finger handed on the hand of Luna, and everyone turned his head through Cynthia's finger who was handed on Luna, and they noticed that Luna was trying to move her hand. Then, Alex cried out, "Luna opened her eyes." And everyone turned their head through Luna's head and they noticed that Luna had the eyes opened, and they looked at each other in the room with the mouth opened without saying a word, it was like they were watching a miracle, then the smile appeared on their face, and they took a deep breath with their head lifted through the sky.

Then, Superhuman looked at Alex by saying, "Please, help me to lift Luna." And both Alex and Superhuman held Luna and helped her to get up. Luna sat on the sofa looking very tired and weak, and all of them were looking at Luna with a smile on their faces, they were so happy that Luna woke up from her coma. Cynthia looked at Luna by asking, "Are you alright?" Luna answered, "Yeah, just that I am tired, and I am feeling the headaches." Cynthia said, "We are glad that you are still among us because we were all afraid." Luna replied, "I am sorry if I scared you." Liza asked, "Did you remember what happened?" Luna answered, "Not really."

Then, they noticed that the light was shining on the magic hand of Superhuman, and Superhuman looked at his magic palm with a smile on his face, and everyone had the eyes focus on Superhuman even Luna, and after three seconds they noticed that the smile who was on the face of Superhuman was gone and that the fear had taken place of that smile. Luna asked, "Superhuman, what is going on?" Superhuman looked at Luna by answering, "Nothing." Luna asked, "Why are your eyes full of fear, if there is nothing who is going on?" Alex looked at Superhuman by saying, "You know well that there is nothing you can hide from us because sooner or later we will face or confront what is happening." Liza said, "Superhuman, we are already in the war, and we are ready to confront what is going on, no matter if it's good or bad." Superhuman looked at all of them without saying a word, then he turned his magic palm by showing it to them, and they all read on his magic palm, "You are all in danger, and a tragedy or a disaster is going to happen in three hours, and that tragedy will be the end of the fight and the victory of King, so the whole planet is in danger right now in the hands of King."

Suddenly, there was the fear on the face of everyone, and their heart was beating of fear, and some people like Maria, Cynthia, Luna, and Alex started to breathe deeply like they were going to have a heart attack, and they were all completely lost with the eyes still focus on the magic palm of Superhuman, none of them was understanding what was going on, or was realizing what was happening. And no one was talking, then Liza turned her head through the watch that was on the wall and she noticed that it was 9:00 p.m., so the tragedy was going to happen at midnight.

Then, Luna broke the silence by asking, "What is that tragedy?" Superhuman answered, "I have no idea about that tragedy that is going to happen." Luna asked, "Why not ask your magic about that tragedy?" Superhuman turned his magic palm through his face and he started to talk with his magic, by reading the answers on his magic palm, while all eyes were focused on him. After nine seconds, Superhuman looked at them by saying, "My magic is unable to tell me what is that tragedy." Liza cried out, "Are you serious?" By looking at Superhuman with the anger on her face, and she added, "We are going to live a tragedy in less than three hours, and your magic is unable to tell us what that tragedy will be?" Cynthia cried out, "Less than three hours?" Liza looked at Cynthia by saying, "The watch is to your left side on the wall." Everyone turned their head through the watch that was on the wall, and they noticed that it was 9:07 p.m.,

Then, Luna looked at Superhuman by saying, "In less than three hours this planet will be in the hands of two devils who are King and Hector, and we must prevent it to happen, but to prevent it to happen your magic must tell us what is that tragedy." Cynthia looked at Superhuman by saying, "It means that the whole planet is going to die in less than three hours if we do not do something now." Philip said, "It's not the fault of Superhuman if his magic is unable to tell us what is that tragedy." They all turned their head looking at Philip without saying a word.

Then, Alex looked at Superhuman by asking, "Why is your magic unable to tell us what is that tragedy?" Superhuman answered, "We missed a conversation between King and Hector, and it's in their conversation that they set a plan, and that plan is the tragedy that is going to happen in less than three hours." Cynthia asked, "Why not use your magic to watch that conversation that happened between King and Hector, and there we will find out what is that tragedy?" Superhuman answered, "It's impossible for me to watch that conversation by using my magic because my magic can not see things that have already happened." And he added, "My magic can only see things that are happening or warn me about things that are going to happen like my magic just warn me about that tragedy that is going to happen in less than three hours."

Liza looked at Superhuman by saying, "We watched through your magic how Alex had left the house to go to the palace when Alex was already gone, so I do not understand why your magic can not show us that conversation between King and Hector." Superhuman replied, "What happened with Alex is different because my magic can see the past or something that had already happened when it's related to someone natural or something natural, except something who is related to the wizard magic or wizard person, so my magic can not see something that already happened when it's related to King."

Luna asked, "Where are King and Hector?" Superhuman answered, "King and Hector are in their beds deeply asleep." Liza said, "King and Hector have had that conversation when we were all focused on taking care of Luna." And she added, "The magic of Superhuman warned us about that conversation because at that time we all saw King and Hector in their office talking but we did not pay attention to them because we were all worried about Luna."

Suddenly, Luna started to remember about the fuzzy images she had seen, and the conversation she had heard when she was in the coma, then Luna got up and she started to walk through the corner without saying a word, and everyone was looking at her by wondering what was going on with her. And Superhuman wanted to follow Luna but Philip demanded him to not follow her to let her. Luna got in her bedroom, and she took one of the pillows that were on the bed, then she opened the closure of that pillow, and she removed the magic book she had kept inside that pillow. Then she opened the last page of that book, and she put her right palm on the writings of that last page, and after three seconds, there was the light that was shining between that right palm and that last page, and the writings of that last page were changing, and the shape of the writings were changing too. After three minutes, that light stopped shining and all the writings of that last page had changed. Then, Luna lifted the book through her face and she looked at the writings of that last page with a surprised face and she was trying to read it, but unfortunately, she was unable to read it. Then, she opened other pages of the book and she noticed that only the writings of the last page were different from the rest of the pages of the book, but she was not quite surprised because in her coma that voice had told her what should happen.

Then, Luna turned, and she started to walk through the door with the magic book in her hand, and after a minute of walking, she reached the living room, and she walked to face Superhuman. Then, Luna handed the magic book she had in her hand to Superhuman by saying, "Read this magic book it's very important for you to read it." Superhuman took the magic book by looking at her. Philip looked at Superhuman by saying, "You must read that magic book in nine days, not more than nine days." Superhuman cried out, "Nine days?" by looking at Philip with a surprised face, and he added, "It's impossible to read this huge book in my hand in nine days." Luna looked at Superhuman by saying, "It's not impossible to read that magic book in nine days because I read it in nine days." And she added, "Make sure that you will finish that magic book in exactly nine days, and that you will not even exceed a second on those nine days." Alex looked at Superhuman by saying, "By seeing the huge magic book that you must read in nine days, the responsibilities you have, and the life full of dangers, the risks, the tortures, the fear, the sadness, the tears, and headaches that you are living without closing the eyes even for a second to sleep, I do not wish to be the magician boy."

Everyone looked at Alex by smiling, and Philip said, "Alex is not completely wrong because it's not easy to be the magician boy, but it's harder to be the witch girl." Liza said, "I have agreed with Philip that Luna is the one who has the most difficult life because she is linked between two enemies who are Superhuman and King." Cynthia looked at Luna by asking, "What is the solution to end this tragedy that the planet is living, that you wanted to talk about before you get inside the coma?" Luna looked back at Cynthia with silence, and she was remembering what had happened when she was in the coma, the voice who was telling her to not talk about that solution, and she opened her mouth by saying, "I am very hungry." Suddenly, everyone looked at each other with a surprised face by wondering what was going on with Luna. Then, Philip said, "Since this morning nobody has put something in the mouth." And he added, "We have to go to the kitchen to look for something to eat."

Then, all of them walked through the kitchen except Superhuman who sat on the sofa and started to read the magic book. After that they had done to eat, they were all tired and weak, and almost all of them went to bed, although the fact that they knew that there was a tragedy that was going to happen in an hour, and they told to Superhuman to wake up them at midnight at the time of the tragedy because Superhuman and Luna were still in the living room. Superhuman sat on the sofa and Luna lay in his arms and both were reading the magic book, and Luna was there not because she wanted to read the magic book, but because she wanted to stay with Superhuman, she did not want him to stay alone like everyone was asleep.

After a couple of minutes, Luna saw the light that was shining on the magic hand of Superhuman, and she told him about it, then both looked at the magic palm of Superhuman and they saw King who was taking his shower. And Luna was looking at that magic palm with a surprised face, wondering what was going on, and she was not understanding why King was taking shower at midnight, then she looked at Superhuman by asking, "What is going on?" Superhuman looked at her by saying, "Let's get up." Then both got up, and they were face to face looking at each other in the eyes, and the face of Luna was full of worries, while the face of Superhuman was full of sadness.

Then, Luna noticed that the tears were flowing down the cheeks of Superhuman, and she asked, "Why are you crying?" Superhuman answered, "Do not forget that it's midnight." Luna said, "The tragedy." And she walked in the arms of Superhuman with tears who were flowing down her cheeks, and Superhuman had taken her in his arms and he was trying to calm her by saying that everything will be fine. Luna lifted her head and she looked at him by asking, "What is going to happen." Superhuman answered, "I have no idea, but I must go." Luna cried out, "go?" by looking at him with fear in her eyes. And she added, "I am going with you." Superhuman said, "I can not take you with me because you must stay to avoid the danger to happen." Luna cried out, "Me?" by looking into his eyes. Superhuman replied, "Your presence will prevent the worst to happen." Luna said, "I do not understand."

Superhuman said, "We do not have enough time to talk." Luna asked, "Where are you going?" Suddenly, they noticed that the light was shining on the magic hand of Superhuman, and he looked into her eyes by saying, "It's time." Luna said, "Please, promise me that you will be back, that we will see again." Then, she asked, "Do you still love me?" Superhuman answered, "With all my heart." Luna said, "I love you too, so come back to me for that we live our love" Superhuman replied, "I promise you at the name of our love that I will be back." Then, they started to kiss, and after a few minutes of kissing, Superhuman took the magic book and he started to walk through the door with it in his hand, and with tears that were flowing down his cheeks, while Luna was watching at him walking away with tears that were flowing down her cheeks. Superhuman reached outside, and he used his magic hand to call the hawk, then he flew on his hawk through the palace.

After a few minutes of flying, he landed on the roof of the palace, then he saw King, and Hector and other men outside in the yard of the palace with the big cars and trucks, and he understood what King and Hector were going to do. Then, Superhuman opened the magic book to page three hundred-one and light got out from that page and went to shine in the middle of the roof, and he ran till that place where that light shone. Then, Superhuman put his magic palm on the middle of the roof where the light had shone, and the light shone between his magic palm and the roof, then the roof opened, and he saw a ladder and he started to climb down that ladder with the magic book in his hand.

Then, Superhuman saw a window and he put his magic palm on the window glass, and he opened the window. And he looked inside and noticed that it was an empty bedroom, then got inside that empty bedroom through the window. Superhuman looked at his magic palm and he saw the plan of the building of the palace, on his magic palm, and he got out of that room and he started to run inside the palace by looking at his magic palm, and everyone in the palace was deeply asleep, except King, Hector, the police of the palace and other men who were outside. Superhuman got inside the library of the palace, and he looked at his magic palm then he walked to face the shelf where the books were ranked. Then, he started to move the books away, and he saw a small board with the picture of Berly on it that was on the wall and removed that board, then he saw a keyboard on the wall that was hidden by that board that had the picture of Berly.

Then, Superhuman looked at his magic palm and he saw the numbers on his magic palm, and he dials those numbers who were on his magic palm on that keyboard that was on the wall. Then, a wall in the form of a door opened on another side of the room, and Superhuman put back the board he had removed on the keyboard, and he put back all books he had moved on their place. Then, Superhuman ran through the door that was opened, and he got inside that door, and he closed that door behind him, and he saw the stairs, and he started to climb down those stairs. Then, he reached a small basement, and he used his magic to turn the light on in that basement, and there was only a small sofa in that basement then he started to walk through that sofa with the magic book in his hand.

Luna was still in the living room alone, sat on the sofa with her face full of fear, and she was waiting for Superhuman, and she suddenly heard the noises of cars and trucks coming from outside, and she rushed through the small hole that Philip had made on the wall to watch outside in case of danger. Luna looked through that hole and she saw cars, and trucks to destroy the houses and men, and she immediately turned and ran till bedrooms, then she woke up everyone to get out of the house. Philip looked at Luna by asking, "What is going on?" Luna answered, "We will all get out of this house right now, or we will all die in this house because King and Hector are outside with men and trucks to destroy the house." Cynthia cried out, "What?" with fear on her face. And Philip said, "Let's get outside now." And he added, "They have started to destroy the house." Then, all of them ran through the door with their face full of fear, and after a couple of seconds, they were outside facing King and Hector.

King looked at them by saying, "It misses one person and it's the most important person." Liza, Cynthia, Philip, and other people looked around them looking for the person who was missing like they had not noticed that Superhuman was not there.

Then, Luna looked at King by saying, "Superhuman is not there."

King asked, "Where is he?"

Luna answered, "I have no idea."

Hector looked at Luna by saying, "Stop lying."

King looked on his magic palm, and he looked at Hector by saying, "She is telling the truth."

And Hector looked back at King by asking, "So where is Superhuman?"

King was looking at his magic palm with a surprised face, and he showed his magic palm to Hector, and Hector saw the picture of the palace on the magic palm of King, then he cried out, "Superhuman is in the palace?" looking at King with an amazed face.

King said, "Myself, I do not understand."

Hector asked, "We need to see him in person."

King replied, "That's the problem, my magic is not seeing where he is in the palace."

Hector said, "Search all the rooms of the palace through your magic, even under the beds, and washrooms."

King replied, "I searched the whole palace, even outside the palace but Superhuman is nowhere, I am not seeing him although the fact that my magic is telling me that he is inside the palace."

Hector looked at King by saying, "I do not understand why you are unable to see Superhuman through your magic if he is inside the palace."

King replied, "Myself, I am completely lost that Superhuman is not appearing on my magic palm because all the rooms of the palace are appearing on my magic palm."

Hector looked at Philip by asking, "Why did Superhuman go to the palace?"

Philip answered, "It's now that I find out that Superhuman is inside the palace, none of us was aware that he went to the palace."

King looked at Hector by saying, "Do not worry, we will find him in the palace, we will even use the hidden camera to catch him." Then, King smiled at Luna by saying, "Finally I found you, and you are mine now because your superhero named Superhuman abandoned you and ran away when he saw the danger." And he added, "Now you are going to tell me about how Superhuman was getting the energy of his magic when you were to the palace."

Suddenly, Luna started to see the fuzzy images that were coming into her mind, and those fuzzy images were making her forget about everything, she was also feeling the headaches, and she was shaking a little bit, and everyone noticed that Luna was not feeling good. Then, Maria and Cynthia held her by asking her if she was alright, and Luna told them that she was doing well. Then, Luna looked at King by saying, "I do not remember."

King looked back in her eyes by asking, "How did you give the energy to the magic of Superhuman when you were at the palace?"

Luna answered, "I do not remember." Suddenly, the face of King changed, and he stared in the eyes of Luna with his face full of anger by saying, "Do not make me use my magic hand on one of your friends, at least if you want to bury one of your friends now."

Luna said, "Why not use your magic palm to find out if I am telling the truth?" King lifted his magic palm through his face, and he was looking at it with a surprised face, then he showed his magic palm to Hector and Hector read on it, "True." Hector looked at King with a surprised face by saying, "I do not understand." King replied, "Myself, I am lost."

Hector looked at Luna by asking, "Who was giving the energy to the magic of Superhuman?"

Luna answered, "Me."

Hector asked, "How were you giving him that energy?"

Then, the fuzzy images started to appear in the mind of Luna, and she looked at Hector by saying, "I do not remember."

Everyone was looking at Luna with surprised faces without understanding what was going on with her, then King looked at her by asking, "Are you still giving the energy to the magic of Superhuman?"

Luna answered, "No."

King asked, "Why?"

Luna answered, "Because that energy is over."

King looked at his magic palm, then he looked at Luna by asking, "When was the last time you gave the energy to the magic of Superhuman?"

Luna answered, "I kissed Superhuman an hour ago."

King looked at his magic palm, then he looked at Hector by saying, "She is telling the truth." And he added, "It means that the last time that Superhuman got the energy of his magic it was at midnight." Hector looked back at King by saying, "You must destroy the energy of the magic of Superhuman she has inside her now."

King replied, "I will do it later."

Then, there was silence and they were looking at each other, and King looked at Alex, Cynthia, Philip, and Liza by saying, "Before I kill you all, I want you to tell me how you had succeeded to organize your plan, to prevent me from catching you."

Philip looked into the eyes of King by saying, "We were all living in the basement of my house and we were watching you through the magic palm of Superhuman, and we were aware of all your plans. Then, a couple of days ago, we found out that your plan was to destroy my house, and we were all worried about that because the basement was only our hiding place, and that it was the end because your plan was to destroy the house and to trigger the storm to arrest Superhuman.

Then, we all spent the whole night in the living room thinking and trying to find the solution to how to prevent you from destroying the house, and it was morning when we found out that Alex was at the palace, and we understood that Alex had run away during the night when we were to the living room thinking. And Alex had chosen to sacrifice himself by coming to see you in the palace because he wanted to distract you, Alex knew that you should pay attention to him and forget about your plan to come to destroy my house, and he was ready to die to save the planet and to prevent you to destroy the planet like all of us here. Then, when you kept Alex prisoner in the forest, we decided to plan to save Alex, and we involved Cynthia in our plan, and Superhuman told Cynthia exactly the words she should use when she should be in front of you, and she should not answer a question that Superhuman had not told her the answer. Then, we divided the basement into two, and when you were to one side of the basement, we were to another side watching you, and that's how Superhuman went and released all the prisoners."

King looked at Alex with his face full of anger by saying, "Without you, Superhuman should be in his special jail now, I should be already married to Luna and I should be realizing my project now, but you decided to make my plan fail and for that, you will have a special death."

Hector looked at King by saying, "Let's take Luna with us, and kill all the rest of them now."

King looked at Hector by saying, "We will not kill them now because we will use them to arrest their superhero who is Superhuman because he will be back for them." And he added, "The energy who is inside Luna's body will be destroyed in a couple of hours to prevent Superhuman to be able to fight again." Then, Hector and King ordered their men to destroy the house of Philip, and they took Luna and her friends at the palace where they were kept prisoners.

Superhuman was still in the basement of the palace, sat on the sofa reading the magic book, by communicating with his magic, and his magic was explaining to him what he was not understanding in the magic book. But there were still some questions that his magic was not answering him, by telling him that he would find the answers to those questions in the next magic book in his next fight in the future because the tragedy of the planet would not end now and that kids of the planet would be attacked in the future. And Superhuman so focused on reading the magic book that he was not aware that Luna and other people were kept prisoners in the palace.

Luna was in her jail alone lying on the bed, thinking about Superhuman wondering where he was hiding inside the palace, for that the magic of King was unable to see him, and her heart was beating with fear thinking about the energy of the magic of Superhuman that would be destroyed inside her. And she was thinking about how she could prevent King from destroying that energy, but she had no idea about how King was going to do it, so it was impossible for her to prevent it from happening. Suddenly, the shadow of her mom appeared face to her and Luna got up from the bed looking at the shadow of her mom, and cried out, "Mom, mom, mom." With tears who were flowing down her cheeks. The shadow of her mom said, "My daughter stops worrying everything will be over soon and do not swallow the saliva of King when he will kiss you, also stop worrying for Superhuman because he is safe, and you will see him in less than nine days." Luna said, "Mama, mama, please take me with you." The shadow of mom said, "No, my daughter I can not take you with me because the whole planet needs you, and Superhuman needs you too because without you it's impossible for him to fight, and if you are not there the whole planet will be destroyed." Luna said, "Mom, I want to see papa."

Then, the shadow of her dad appeared close to the shadow of her mom, and Luna was looking at the shadows of her parents by crying. Luna said, "Papa, papa, papa, I am alone on this planet." The shadow of her dad said, "My daughter, you are not alone, your mom and I are looking after you, and we are protecting you from where we are, and you will never be alone because your mom and I will always look after you." Luna said, "Dad, I want to live with mom and you like we were living before." The shadow of her dad said, "My daughter, we are all still living together even if you can not touch us, and we can not take you with us because you already have your destiny, you were born for a mission and you have not yet done your mission and you can not abandon your mission because you carry this planet and the life of all his inhabitants on your shoulders." Luna asked, "Why me?" The shadow of her mom answered, "My daughter, nobody can answer that question, just that it's your destiny." Luna looked at the shadows of her parents by saying, "Mama, Papa, I am so sorry because it's by my fault if you both died in that car's accident because I am the one that Hector and King were looking for to destroy the energy of the magic of Superhuman that is inside me."

The shadows of her parents replied, "My daughter, you are not responsible for our death, and we are proud that you survived in that accident because if you died or if the energy of the magic of Superhuman you have inside you, was destroyed in that accident, this Planet should be hell now." Luna said, "Mom, Dad, I miss you" The shadow of her mom replied, "My daughter, we miss you too, and do not believe in the death of Superhuman." The shadow of her dad said, "My daughter, do not forget to not swallow the saliva of King." Luna said, "Papa, mama, I love you." The shadows of her parents replied, "My daughter, we love too." Then, those shadows disappeared, and Luna cried out, "Papa, mama please come back, do not let me alone." Then, she burst into tears.

It was 6:00 a.m., King, Hector, and all the security men of the palace were very tired because they had spent their whole night looking for Superhuman, without succeeding, and they had even used the hidden cameras, but they did not see Superhuman. King and Hector were completely lost, they were not understanding what was going on because the magic of King was telling them that Superhuman was inside the palace, then when King asked Hector if there was a basement inside the palace, Hector answered him that no, that he had the plan of building of the palace. And that the only house that had the basement on the planet was the house of Philip, and that Queen mother had forbidden everyone to build the house on the planet with the basement, and that even Queen mother did not know that Philip had the house with the basement.

Then they had decided to find the magic book because inside that book they would find where Superhuman was. Luna was lying in her bed, and she heard the footsteps and she lifted her head and she saw King and Hector who were walking in her jail, and she got up off the bed. King looked at Luna by asking, "Where is the magic book?" Luna answered, "Superhuman took the magic book with him." King looked on his magic palm, and he noticed that Luna was telling the truth, then he lifted his head by looking at her and he said, "We are going to marry in nine days." Luna asked, "Why are we going to marry?" King answered, "It's been a while that we are fiancé, so it's time now to get married." Then, King walked till front to Luna, and he started to caress her hairs with his magic hand, by looking into her eyes by smiling, while Luna was looking back at him without any expression on her face, then he started to kiss her, and suddenly she started to remember her conversation with her parents. After a few minutes of kissing, King let Luna, and they were looking eyes to eyes, and Luna told him that she wanted to go to the toilet, and he allowed her to go to the toilet.

CHAPTER 11

◆

The Death of Hector and King prisoner

After more than 72 hours, Philip was in his jail lying in his bed, thinking about Superhuman, and wondering where he was, then he heard the noises on his jail's door, and he got up from his bed, and he saw Hector who was walking inside with a chair in his hand. Then, Hector smiled at Philip without saying a word and he put his chair face to the bed of Philip, and he sat on it, then Philip sat on his bed and they were looking at each other without saying a word. Then, Hector broke the silence by saying, "Superhuman is dead."

Philip replied, "That's impossible because King can not kill Superhuman."

Hector replied, "The energy of the magic of Superhuman that is inside the body of Luna has been destroyed by King, so Superhuman is not anymore linked to Luna." And he added, "We both know that without the energy of the magic of Superhuman, his magic is useless, so Superhuman is living the life of the dead person now waiting for the day we will throw him in his grave."

Philip looked into Hector's eyes by saying, "Now the fight is over, and you are the winner, but still, I have no idea of your reason to help King to destroy this planet."

Hector replied, "I have a dream."

Philip asked, "What is that dream?"

Hector answered, "I want to be the god of this planet."

Philip cried out, "What?" by looking at Hector with a surprised face.

Hector replied, "I am going to be the god of this planet, and King is going to be my assistant, and this planet we belong to me." And he added, "I was tired of being the assistant of Queen Mother, and I always wish to be the god-like Queen Mother."

Philip asked, "Where is Queen mother?"

Hector answered, "I have no idea."

Philip said, "You betrayed Queen Mother and the whole planet."

Hector replied, "I am not the only traitor of this planet because you betrayed Queen mother and the whole planet too."

Philip replied, "I have never betrayed Queen Mother and the planet, and I will never do it."

Hector said, "You know well that Queen Mother had banned everyone to build a house on this planet with the basement, but you built a house with a basement and you stole the magic book."

Philip replied, "I am not the one who had built my house, but it's Queen Mother who had built it, and she is the one who had told me to leave this palace and go live in that house." And he added, "Queen mother is also the one who had kept the magic book in the basement of that house, with all stuff you saw in that house, then she explained a little to me what should happen, and I swore to never betray her."

Hector said, "I do not trust you."

Philip replied, "You know well that I was a jobless old man, without any income, so you must know that I could not afford that big house with all those stuff that was inside." And he added, "The only thing I did in that house, it was to build a wall divider with a plywood in the basement, and created another door in the basement when Superhuman made the plan to trap King to release all prisoners."

Hector asked, "How were you living during all that time?"

Philip answered, "Like you noticed the house, Queen mother had prepared everything, she had given me a lot of money for living. And when King started to look for Luna and me, we went to the basement because Queen mother had told me that the basement was a secret place to hide when there will a danger."

Hector asked, "How did you save Luna to the hospital?"

Philip answered, "Queen Mother had told me that there is a young girl that you will try to kill or to destroy, and she asked me to follow you to prevent you from killing that girl, and I started to follow you by hiding till the day I saw you inside the hospital in the room of Luna. Then, I understood that Luna was the girl that Queen Mother was talking about, and when I saw Superhuman who was arrested by the police of the palace and security men of the hospital, I immediately ran into the hospital's room of Luna and I took her with me." Hector said, "You were a jobless man, living in the street and begging for food, and Queen Mother saw you in the street and brought you here in the palace where you were working like a messenger carrying the news, letters, and newspapers. Still, I do not understand why Queen Mother gave an important secret like that."

Philip replied, "Because she trusted me."

Hector said, "I was the right hand of Queen Mother, I was like the son of Queen Mother and the second god of this planet, so still I do not understand why Queen Mother did not choose me for that secret." Philip replied, "Because Queen Mother knew that you were a traitor, that's the reason why she did not tell you about that secret."

Hector said, "I searched that magic book during the years, to know who the magician boy was, and who the witch girl could be, also to know about the magic of the magician boy." Then, Hector looked in the eyes of Philip by saying, "If I knew that you were the one who had that magic book you would've been dead a long time ago."

Philip replied, "I know." And he added, "I know too that you wanted to prevent Luna from meeting with Superhuman because you knew well that you could not kill Superhuman, and the only solution was to destroy the energy that was inside Luna's body or prevent her from meeting Superhuman."

Then, they were looking at each other without talking, and after a minute Philip broke the silence by asking, "Why did you hide King for more than eleven years? knowing that he was a danger for this planet." Hector answered, "King is a blessing for this planet, not a danger."

Philip replied, "You know well that King is a wizard boy, who was born with bad magic and that's the reason why Queen Mother was looking for him to destroy the magic he has inside him before he is eleven years old because Queen Mother knew that that magic was dangerous for the planet."

Hector said, "The magic of King was very important for me, and without the magic of King I should never realize my dream to be the god of this planet. And that's the reason why I hid King for more than eleven years till the age where he should be able to use his magic."

Philip said, "I am wondering where you hid King during more than eleven years and how he grew up because I know that King is an orphan without parents and siblings because King's dad died at the eve of his birth, and his mom died three minutes after she gave birth to him."

Hector said, "There are a lot of mysteries about the birth of King."

Philip asked, "What do you mean?"

Hector answered, "I have doubts about the parents of King."

Philip said, "Still I do not understand."

Hector said, "The parents that we all think that they were the parents of King, were not his real parents, even the mom who carried him in her womb was not her mom."

Philip asked, "Who are the parents of King?

Hector answered, "It's a mystery that I will find out." And he added, "I will make my own investigation to know who the ancestors of King were."

Philip said, "But, we all know that King was born on this planet."

Hector answered, "Yeah, King really was born on this planet."

Philip asked, "How did he grow up? Because I know that the mom who carried him in her belly died after his birth."

Hector said, "I took King outside of this planet after the death of the mom who carried him in her belly, so he grew up abroad, then I took him back on the planet at the age that he could use his magic because his magic should help me to become the god of this planet that I am today."

Philip said, "I am wondering why King and Superhuman started to use their magic at the same time." Hector replied, "Superhuman and King could be twins because they were born the same day, at the same time with no difference of second, in the same hospital with their magic inside them. And both should only use their magic after their eleven years old, and they should use their magic at the same time and the same time."

Philip asked, "How do you know that?"

Hector answered, "I know who the wizard boy should be because Queen Mother knew the mom who was carrying the wizard boy in her womb, and she had told me that when the wizard boy should be born, we should destroy the magic he has inside him, that's why I was able to hide King." And he added, "But, Queen Mother did not tell me who was the magician boy that's why I was unable to know who was Superhuman, but I knew that a magician boy existed, and I did not know his weakness too, till the day I started to read the magic book. And I found out that Superhuman and King were born the same day in the same hospital by reading the magic book."

Philip said, "I want to know about your magic ring."

Hector said, "It's Queen Mother who had given it to me to protect the planet in case of danger."

Philip said, "It's impossible that Queen mother gave you a ring to torture people."

Hector said, "When Queen Mother gave me that ring it was a magic ring, but King turned it into a cursed ring by destroying the good magic that Queen mother had put on that ring, and by putting his bad magic on the ring. That's why I am able to torture people with that ring, to read the magic book and it's that ring who helped me to cause the accident of the car of parents of Luna, where her parents died. And I should use that ring too to destroy the energy of the magic of Superhuman who was inside Luna's body, but the only thing I can not do with that ring it's to kill someone."

Philip said, "King and Luna were in the same school together, and I am wondering why King did not destroy the energy of the magic of Superhuman that was inside Luna at that time. After that, Superhuman had been arrested and kept in his special jail."

Hector replied, "The first time that King saw Luna on his magic palm, he immediately fell in love with her, and he wanted to seduce her not to scare her, he wanted her to accept him as her husband. King did not want Luna to know that he is a wizard boy. That's the reason he asked me to use my magic ring to destroy the link of magic she had with Superhuman, and after that, he should go by himself to win the heart of Luna. But I did not succeed in destroying that link of magic that Luna had with Superhuman, then after that Luna and Superhuman met together and they knew that they were linked together.

King and I planned to kill Superhuman because I have already started to read the magic book, and we knew some weakness of the magic of Superhuman, and that how King came into the classroom of Superhuman and Luna, and he started to cause the disasters in that classroom. And King was always watching Superhuman and Luna even when he was not in a class, then when Superhuman and Luna got the troubles in their relationship, and they were not any more kissing, King found out that Superhuman did not have the energy of his magic inside him, and he told me about it and that's how I came to school with the police and I arrested Superhuman. Then, King was trying to seduce Luna to win her heart and to destroy to link she had with Superhuman, but things did not go well and Luna found out that King was the wizard boy and she confronted him and he admitted it, then King did a big mistake by showing his magic palm to Luna and that's how the link of the magic of King who is inside Luna's body got in connection with the magic of King, when Luna looked on the magic palm of King for the first time, and that's how Luna used that link of King's magic who is inside her to save Superhuman."

Philip asked, "Why King did not destroy that energy inside Luna when she was in the palace?"

Hector replied, "There was something very mysterious that was happening when King wanted to destroy that energy of Superhuman inside Luna when she was in the palace, and that mysterious thing was preventing King to do it because Luna was always in the coma."

Philip asked, "How are King and Luna linked?"

Hector replied, "I have no idea."

Then, Hector got up by saying, "All people who fought close to Superhuman will be hanged in five days, except Luna because she links to the magic of King and that she will be the wife of King."

Then, Hector turned, and he walked through the door, while Philip was watching at him with a sad face, feeling sorry for Superhuman and all the people who had helped Superhuman in his fight, and feeling sorry for the whole planet too. The death of Superhuman was announced to all his friends who had helped him to fight, and they were all in their jail with a sad face, and they were all crying his dead, and they were very sad for Luna by saying that she should kill herself in her jail mostly like she was alone, also they were feeling sorry for the planet that they were unable to save. Luna was in her jail crying the death of Superhuman because King had told her that Superhuman was living the life of a dead person now because he had destroyed the link of the magic of Superhuman who was inside her body.

Although Luna was crying about the death of Superhuman, she was very confused because she was remembering the message that her mom had told her to not believe in the death of Superhuman. And she was calling her parents to come to tell her how Superhuman was, and she was wishing that the mysterious person who sometimes comes into her mind to tell her about Superhuman. King and Hector were in the palace celebrating the death of Superhuman, and they were planning to call a meeting in five days with all inhabitants of the planet, where they should announce the death of Superhuman and the end of the tragedy of the planet, also where Hector should declare himself like the god of the Planet. Hector had used the national radio and television to announce the end of the tragedy on the planet, and he had ordered everyone to get out and to go to their jobs. The following day, most of the inhabitants of the planet started to get out, despite the fact that they were still living with the fear inside them. After four days, the situation on the planet was going more and more better, kids were going to school, and everyone was going to their occupation. And they had heard the news from the radio and television also in the newspapers coming from Hector, who was saying that everyone should be in front of their television at 8 pm because there would be important news that he would talk about.

It was evening, the whole planet sat in front of their television, with their heart who was beating of fear, by wondering what Hector was going to announce to them, and after an hour Hector appeared on the television, and there was silence in all the houses of the planet, and everyone had the eyes focus on television listening to Hector. Suddenly, the expression on the face of everyone changed, some people had the eyes widely opened, and others had the mouths widely opened like they all heard Hector announced the death of Superhuman to the whole planet, and that the curse of the planet was over, and that all people who had fought close to Superhuman were going to be hanging, and that Queen Mother would be not anymore on the planet. Then that the planet was going to the new direction with a new destiny, that he was the new god of the planet, and his new name was lord Hector, then that there would a meeting the following day in the sacred yard of the palace at 12:00 p.m., and that everyone must attend to that meeting.

And everyone on the planet was watching Hector on the television with a sad face and the tears flowing down their cheeks, and they were all crying the death of Superhuman and all his friends who were going to be hanging, and families of Alex, Cynthia, and John were crying for their kids. After an hour, Hector had done with his speech, and people were crying the death of their Superhero, and his friends, and no one was paying attention to Queen Mother, although the fact that Hector said that she would be not on the planet anymore, even inside the palace people were front to their television crying the death of Superhuman and his friends because everyone in the palace knew that King was the wizard boy. It was midnight, Luna was in her jail lying in her bed crying, and she had covered her face with the blanket, then she started to hear the footsteps in her jail, but she did not remove the blanket on her face to see who was walking. Then, she heard a voice who said, "Stop crying, I am here."

Suddenly, Luna cried out, "Superhuman?" by removing the blanket on her face. Then, she saw Superhuman who was staring at her by smiling and she jumped from her bed by screaming and she hugged him, and there were the joy tears flowing down the cheeks of both. Then, Luna looked in the eyes of Superhuman by saying "I can not believe that you are here because I thought that I should never see you again." Superhuman replied, "Do not forget that we are linked for life, and that you have my heart." Luna smiled by saying, "You have my heart too." Then she asked, "Where were you?" Superhuman answered, "I was in the basement of this palace reading the magic book." Luna cried out, "Basement?" By looking at him with a surprised face. Superhuman replied, "Yeah, basement." And he added, "I found out in the magic book that this palace has a basement, and I went to hide there to read the magic book." Luna said, "I understand now why King was unable to see you through his magic palm, the day he came to arrest us."

Then, she looked at him by saying, "You looked very tired." Superhuman said, "I spent nine days without sleeping, eating, and without drinking water just by reading the magic book." Luna said, "I imagine because I lived the same life when I was reading that magic book." Superhuman said, "There are a lot of mysteries in that magic book, that I did not understand like I did not succeed to read the last page of that magic book." Luna replied, "The last page of the magic book is a secret that no one will know." Superhuman said, "It's not only the last page of the magic book who is a secret." Luna asked, "What do you mean?" Superhuman answered, "I am talking about the mysterious ghost, the old man in the sky who has the long white beard and how you are linked to King, also about the tragedy that is going to happen on the planet in the future."

Luna looked at him with a surprised face by asking, "Do you know who is that mysterious ghost" Superhuman answered, "Berly." Luna cried out, "Dog?" by looking at him with a surprised face. Superhuman replied, "Berly, is not a dog." Luna asked, "What do you mean?" Superhuman replied, "Berly, can be a human being who has the shape of a dog." Luna said, "I still do not understand." Superhuman replied, "We will find out who is Berly, who is the old man in the sky with the white long beard who helped us and how you are linked to King, maybe in the next magic book." Luna cried out, "Next magic book?" Superhuman looked in her eyes by saying, "The tragedy of the planet will not end now because in the future kids of this planet will be attacked, and to fight we will need the next magic book, and in the next magic book we may find the answers of all our questions we have now."

Luna looked in the eyes of Superhuman without saying a word, and she started to remember all that time she got in the coma it was because Berly had given her the chocolates, and biscuits and she understood what Superhuman was talking about Berly. And Luna remembered about the old man in the sky with his long white beard who had told her to use her left palm to open the jail of the prison of Superhuman, the day that she went to release Superhuman when he was a prisoner in the forest. Then, Luna remembered an unknown person who was talking to her when she was in a coma about her secrets, and about the next fight and she understood why there was another magic book. Then, Superhuman noticed that Luna was quiet, and he asked, "Are you alright?" Luna looked in his eyes with tears that were flowing down her cheeks. Superhuman asked, "Why are you crying?" Luna looked at him without saying a word, and tears were still flowing down her cheeks. Then, Superhuman started to wipe her tears with his hand, by looking in her eyes, and by telling her to stop crying that she was not alone and that he was there with her.

After a few minutes, Superhuman succeeded to calm Luna with his beautiful words, and he looked into her eyes by saying, "Please, stop crying because I do not want your beautiful eyes to be wet of tears." And he added with a smile on his face by saying, "Although the fact that you are still beautiful when you cry." Luna smiled by saying, "You are more handsome when you smile." Then they were looking each other eyes to eyes by smiling, without saying a word, then Superhuman started to caress the long hairs of Luna with his magic hand, and Luna started to caress his cheek with her right palm. After eleven minutes, they noticed that the light was shining on the magic palm of Superhuman, then both looked at his palm and they read "The time has come." Luna looked at him by asking, "What it means?" Superhuman answered, "I am going to fight." Suddenly, the face of Luna changed and the smile that was on her face was gone. Superhuman asked, "Why is there sadness on your face?" Luna answered, "We can not save this planet, the fight is over, and we lost our mission because you can not keep fighting." Superhuman said, "I do not understand." Luna looked in his eyes with tears who were flowing down her cheeks, and she said, "I am so sorry." And she added, "I did not succeed to prevent King from destroying the energy of your magic inside me." Superhuman started to smile by wiping her tears.

Luna looked at how he was smiling with surprise, and asked, "Why are you smiling?" Superhuman replied, "You do not notice the wind that is blowing since I am in this room." Suddenly, the face of Luna changed, and her face was full of smiles and surprise, then she said, "It means this wind that is blowing is coming out from my body, and it's because you are here close to me that this wind is blowing." Superhuman replied, "Exactly." And he added, "This wind is blowing because the energy of my magic is still in your body." Luna said, "It means that King lied to me that he destroyed the energy of your magic that is inside me." Superhuman said, "King thinks that he destroyed the energy of my magic that is inside you, that's why he announced to the whole planet that I have died." Luna asked, "What do you mean by what he thinks?" Superhuman answered, "Remember that you did not swallow the saliva of King when he kissed you." Luna said, "Still I do not understand." Superhuman replied, "The saliva of King contains the poison for the energy of my magic, so when King kissed you, it was to destroy the energy of my magic that is inside you with his saliva." Luna cried out, "My parents?" by looking at him with an amazed face. Superhuman replied, "Yes, your parents saved us, and they saved this planet too." Luna said, "It means that King does not know that I still have the energy of your magic inside me." Superhuman smiled at her by saying, "Exactly."

Then the light started to shine on his magic hand, and both looked at his magic palm, and Luna looked at him by saying, "I am very afraid." Superhuman replied, "Do not worry everything will be fine." Luna said, "I have the feeling that the worst will happen." Superhuman said, "It's true that we can not end with this tragedy now, but I learned something that will help me in the next fight." Luna asked, "What do you mean?" Superhuman answered, "By reading the magic book, I found out that my magic would become stronger in the future, and that kids of this planet would be in danger in the future." Luna looked at Superhuman with a face full of sadness and said, "I am very worried for the future of this planet, mostly for children of this planet. Because in the future the souls of the children of this planet would be controlled by a devil."

Superhuman looked at Luna with a surprised face and asked, "How did you know that?" Luna answered, "We would talk about what would happen on the planet later, but I know that we would even travel out of the planet to find the solution to save and protect this planet." Superhuman cried out, "We would travel out of this planet? Luna looked into Superhuman's eyes and said, "We would not only fight to protect this planet, but we would also fight to protect and save our world called the wizarding world" Superhuman asked, "What do you mean?" Luna took a breath a breath, and she looked into Superhuman's eyes and said, "Although the fact that we were born on this planet, we are not children of this planet." And Luna added," We have our own world and our own people who are in danger because there is a devil who is destroying our world and killing our people, and we must stop that devil and protect and save our world." Superhuman said, "I am completely lost." Luna replied, "I have no idea how and why we were born on this planet, but the only thing I know it's that we belong to the wizarding world, and the inhabitants of the wizarding world are like us, they all born with the powers and magic." And she added, "The only thing that matters now is to save this planet."

Then, they were looking at each other with eyes full of love, and they started to kiss. After a minute of kissing Luna looked into his eyes by saying, "I am coming with you." Superhuman replied, "No, I can not take that risk to take you with me because things can go wrong, and you can get hurt or kill." Then there was silence and Luna looked into his eyes by saying, "I want you back." Superhuman replied, "I promise you." Then, he turned, and he started to walk through the door, while Luna was looking at him with her face full of fear. Hector was lying in his bed deeply asleep, and suddenly the light went on, and Hector turned on the bed, and he heard a voice who was asking him to wake up, then Hector opened his eyes and he jumped from his bed, and he rubbed his eyes with his hands, then he was staring at Superhuman who was face to him with his face full of surprise. And Superhuman was staring back at him, and

Superhuman asked, "Are you seeing me clearly now or you need to rub your eyes again?" Hector asked, "It's really you?" by looking at Superhuman with his eyes widely opened. Superhuman replied, "You know well that you lied to the whole planet that I died." Hector smiled by saying, "But, now you are going to die forever." Then, pointed his hand that his finger wore the magic ring through Superhuman, and Superhuman handed his magic hand through him, then both started to fight with the sparks of fire.

Everyone in the palace was deeply asleep, even King was deeply in his bed, except Luna who knew what was going on, and she was walking in her jail with worries on her face and her heart beating with fear. After an hour Hector and Superhuman were still fighting with their faces full of anger, and Hector was standing up in the corner of the bedroom, while Superhuman was in another corner of the bedroom.

Suddenly, Hector disappeared, and Superhuman lifted his head and he looked at the ceiling, then he lifted his magic hand through the ceiling and the sparks of fire that were getting outside from his magic palm turned into the net, and Hector appeared in that net, then Superhuman pulled him down and Hector fell on the bed. Then, Hector tore the net with his hands, and Superhuman looked at him by saying, "You can not run away." Hector said, "You will never save this planet because I am already the god of this planet." Superhuman replied, "You will be the god of this planet, only on my dead body." Then, both went on with the fight, and Hector got out of the net, and he was standing up on the bed, while Superhuman was at the door and the door was closed behind him. After an hour of fighting, Hector started to be tired, and he wanted to escape, but Superhuman caught him with the net, and Hector was standing up on his bed surrounded with the net on him, and he was trying to tear that net on him.

Then, Superhuman walked two steps through the bed, and he lifted his magic hand through the face of Hector, and the sparks of fire were getting out from his magic palm and going through Hector's face. Suddenly, Hector started to scream like the sparks of fire that were getting out from the magic palm of Superhuman were burning his face, and those sparks of fire got inside Hector's eyes, and Hector had the eyes closed because those sparks of fire had made him blind. Hector was fighting without seeing where Superhuman was, while Superhuman had stopped to fight, and Superhuman was walking through another side of the room through the left of Hector.

Then, Superhuman stood to Hector's left side and he lifted his magic hand through Hector's finger who has the magic ring, then Superhuman started to send the sparks of fire through Hector's finger who has the magic ring. While Hector was still sending his sparks of fire front at him, without seeing where those sparks of fire were going through, and Hector was trying to turn but it was impossible because the net that had surrounded him was preventing him from turning. After an hour there was the wound that started to appear on Hector's finger who has the magic ring, and Hector started to scream pains by calling the name of King to come save him, and Luna was understanding the screams of Hector, and the screams of Hector had started to wake up people in the palace.

Then, Hector's finger, which has the magic ring, fell on the bed, and suddenly a blue light shone on that magic ring, and that magic ring disappeared. Then, Superhuman walked till face to Hector and he said, "I know that you can not see me, but at least you can hear me." And he added, "I cut your finger who had the magic ring that was protecting you to die, and who was making you different from other human beings, so now you are going to die." Hector said, "Your magic can not kill a human being." Superhuman replied, "I thought the same thing, but in the magic book, I found out how to use my magic to kill people like you, so you are the first person that I am going to kill."

Then, Superhuman looked at his magic's hand and he said, "Red sparks of fire." Then, he handed his magic hand through Hector's face and red sparks of fire got out from his magic palm and going through Hector's face, and Hector fell dead on his bed. Then, Superhuman turned, and he started to run through the door, and people in the palace were wondering what was going on and some of them were getting out of their rooms. Superhuman was running in the hallway, and he suddenly met King who was running through him, then both started to fight. There were some people in the hallways with their nightdress on them, and they were all surprised to see Superhuman like they all thought that he died. People in the palace were screaming like they were seeing the sparks of fire that were going everywhere in the palace.

After three hours, King and Superhuman were still fighting. The whole planet was already up, and no one on the planet had closed the eyes during the whole, and they had spent the whole to cry the death of their superhero, their magician boy who was Superhuman, and they were wondering who was going to protect them again in case of danger, and who was going to prevent the tragedy from happening again. Then, everyone on the planet was very afraid about their life who was in the hands of Hector and King, knowing that Hector had no magic to protect them and to protect the planet and knowing that King was a wizard boy, everyone was very scared of his own life.

Although, the fact that the whole planet was sad, they were getting ready to go to that meeting that was called by their new god, named lord Hector, and no one wanted to go to that meeting, but they knew that they did not have a choice, that they must go. There was still the fight that was happening in the palace between Superhuman and King, and they were running everywhere inside the palace, and the sparks of fire were going in all directions, while people were still screaming by watching them fight. Suddenly, a housekeeper who was standing up at her bedroom door to watch the fight, fainted on the floor like the sparks of fire that were getting out from the magic palm of King had touched her, and people started to scream like they saw that housekeeper fainted. And Superhuman wanted to go save that housekeeper who had fainted, but it was impossible because King was not controlling the direction of sparks of fire that were getting out from his magic palm. Then Superhuman noticed that by going to save that housekeeper, the sparks of fire of King could hurt or kill other people who were running in the corner, and Superhuman started to scream to people to go back to their bedroom and lock the door, then he started to run through the corner of the library while King was running after him.

All friends of Superhuman who were in jail had heard the voice of Superhuman, and they were very happy to notice that he was still alive, but at the same time, they were very afraid because they were not very sure about what was going on like they thought that the energy of his magic had been destroyed. Superhuman was in the library, and the door that he had used to go to the basement was opened, and he ran through that door, and he started to climb down the stairs while King was still running after him, then both of them reached the basement. And Superhuman turned and he looked at King who had handed his magic hand through him, and Superhuman looked in the eyes of King by saying, "As you noticed by yourself it's over." And King lifted his head through the ceiling, and he looked around him, then he looked at his magic palm, and he understood that it was really over. Then, King looked at Superhuman by saying, "The reason I could not find you in the palace, it's because you were hidden here, reading the magic book." Superhuman replied, "You got it right." King asked, "Where did you get the energy of your magic?" Superhuman answered, "Luna did not swallow your saliva."

Then, King started to remember that day where he kissed Luna, and that after he had kissed her, she went to the toilet, and he understood that Luna had spat his saliva in the sink, and she had brushed her mouth to make sure to not swallow his saliva. Then King said, "It's useless what you are doing because this fight will never end because you can not kill me." Superhuman replied, "I know well that I can not kill you, but you will not anymore scare and torture this planet and its inhabitants because this will be your new house, and you are going to stay here forever." King said, "Luna, betrayed me again, but it's not yet ended because I will be back." Superhuman looked at him without saying a word, then he started to walk through the stairs and King turned to follow him, then Superhuman turned and he handed his magic hand through King by saying, "Do not forget that your magic is not working here to protect you, so if you do not want me to burn your body stay where you are." Then, Superhuman turned and he started to walk through the stairs, while King was watching at him with his face full of anger, then King turned and he saw the magic book on the sofa, and he started to smile then he walked to the sofa, and he took the magic book and he opened it, then he sat on the sofa and he started to read the magic book.

Superhuman had locked the door that was between the library and basement, to prevent King from getting out of the basement.

Luna was walking in her jail with her heart beating with fear, and she was wondering why there was silence, and why she was not hearing the noises of the fight, then she heard the noises of her jail's door, and she cried out, "Superhuman?" And no one responded, and she called the name of Superhuman three times again and still, no one responded, but she was still hearing the noises on her jail's door like someone was trying to open her door. Then, Luna started to walk through her jail's door, and after a few steps of walking, she stopped and there was a surprise on her face like she was looking at the door, and she cried out, "Queen Mother?" Then, the door of her jail opened, and Queen Mother walked inside till face of Luna and she looked at Luna by saying "It's me, my daughter." Luna was still looking at Queen Mother with a surprised face, and she had opened her mouth to talk but her mouth was shaking that a word could not get out. Queen Mother said, "I know that you have a lot of questions who are going on in your mind, like everybody on this planet, but know that I am very proud of you all, you were all brave and you succeeded to save this planet." And she added, "I was not there during the fight because I could not live on the same planet with King because the magic of King is a danger for me, that's why I disappeared." Luna was just looking at her without saying a word, then Queen Mother asked, "Can I take you in my arms? Luna made the gestures with her head to say yes, then Queen Mother walked two steps through Luna, and she took Luna in her arms.

Superhuman had succeeded to save that housekeeper who had fallen on the floor, like sparks of fire coming from King's magic had touched her, and Superhuman had released all his friends to the jail and they were all happy to see him. The sacred yard of the palace, was full of people, and they were all looking through the balcony that was front to them, and that place that they were looking was where their new god should stay to make his speech, and none of them had the smile of the face, and their heart was beating of fear. They used to be happy to be in the sacred yard because the sacred yard was the place to receive the blessing, but for the first time they were unhappy to be there, and they were wondering what kind of blessing they were going to receive, the blessing coming from their new god who had no power, or the blessing coming from the wizard boy. And all of them were already tired to wait, and they were wondering where that useless new god who had no power was, and some of them were wishing that this new god would never come. Suddenly, the face of everyone changed, and there was a surprise on their face like they were looking at Queen Mother walking through the balcony, and no one was understanding what was going on.

Then, Queen Mother stood up to the balcony and she looked at her citizens, while they were still looking at her with surprised faces. Then, Queen Mother started to make a speech by apologizing for all tragedies, tortures, and fear that the whole planet lived, and like she was not there to protect them, then she talked about Jack like a hero that King killed in a car accident. And Queen mother talked about the plans of Hector and King, also about the rosaries that King and Hector wanted them to wear, and that those rosaries were made through the magic of King and that those rosaries were to destroy their soul.

Then, Queen Mother thanked Superhuman, Luna, and all people who fought with them, while everyone was listening to Queen Mother with silence, and they were looking at each other by wondering if they were not dreaming if it was really Queen Mother, their god who was talking to them. Suddenly, there were the screams, everyone was screaming the name of Superhuman with joy on their face like they heard Queen Mother said that Superhuman was still alive. And it was impossible for Queen Mother to keep on with her speech because there were a lot of noises, and everyone was asking for Superhuman. Then, they started to jump, by screaming Superhero and most of them were crying like they were watching Superhuman who was walking through the balcony by holding the hand of Luna, by smiling at them, and there were Alex, Cynthia and other people who were walking behind Superhuman and Luna.

After an hour, the meeting was over, and they had received a blessing from their god Queen mother, and Superhuman and other people went back to their home, except Luna who stayed in the palace like she had lost her parents in the car's accident, and Maria had taken Luna like her daughter, and Philip had received another house coming from Queen mother. It was a great day for the whole planet. There was a feast on the planet, Superhuman and Luna keep living their life and relishing their love, like Alex and Cynthia. All of them were still going to the same school and they were spending their time together. Till a night that the magic of Superhuman told him that King had escaped from his jail, and Superhuman understood that the planet was in danger again and that the time of his next mission had come, mostly that he and Luna would go to the wizarding world to save the wizarding world.

To Be Continued in Superhuman 2.

CPSIA information can be obtained
at www.ICGtesting.com
Printed in the USA
BVHW070710300721
613191BV00002B/326